SLAY

SLAY

LAURELL K. HAMILTON

BERKLEY
NEW YORK

BERKLEY
An imprint of Penguin Random House LLC
penguinrandomhouse.com

Copyright © 2023 by Laurell K. Hamilton
Penguin Random House supports copyright. Copyright fuels creativity, encourages diverse
voices, promotes free speech, and creates a vibrant culture. Thank you for buying an authorized
edition of this book and for complying with copyright laws by not reproducing, scanning, or
distributing any part of it in any form without permission. You are supporting writers and
allowing Penguin Random House to continue to publish books for every reader.

BERKLEY and the BERKLEY & B colophon are registered trademarks of
Penguin Random House LLC.

Library of Congress Cataloging-in-Publication Data
Names: Hamilton, Laurell K., author.
Title: Slay / Laurell K. Hamilton.
Description: New York: Berkley, [2023] | Series: Anita Blake, Vampire Hunter
Identifiers: LCCN 2023013957 (print) | LCCN 2023013958 (ebook) |
ISBN 9780593637845 (hardcover) | ISBN 9780593637852 (ebook)
Subjects: LCGFT: Vampire fiction. | Thrillers (Fiction). |
Novels. Classification: LCC PS3558.A443357 S58 2023 (print) |
LCC PS3558.A443357 (ebook) | DDC 813/.54—dc23/eng/20220831
LC record available at https://lccn.loc.gov/2023013957
LC ebook record available at https://lccn.loc.gov/2023013958

Printed in the United States of America
1st Printing

This book is for all the readers who picked up the first Anita Blake novel, *Guilty Pleasures*, thirty years ago and for the readers who found Anita and her world with each new book. Your enjoyment and love of the books allowed me to keep writing exactly what I wanted to write, until my imaginary friends became your friends, too. I am grateful for every one of you who told me that Anita or one of the other characters in her world helped you be braver, stronger, wiser, happier in your own lives. Thank you for helping me make it possible for there to be thirty Anita Blake novels in thirty years. That's right—Happy Thirtieth Anniversary to the Anita Blake series! Thank you to all who came along for the journey, and to all who have just joined us, welcome aboard. I'll keep writing, you keep reading; so many more adventures ahead.

SLAY

1

I WAS STANDING AT the arrival area for the A gates at St. Louis Lambert International Airport trying to see through the continuing crowds of people that kept spilling out past the TSA agent sitting at the little lectern. Arriving passengers had been streaming past the roped-off lines of other passengers waiting to go through security and depart. None of them had been my family, either coming or going. I was nervous, which made me want to touch the nine-millimeter Springfield EMP at my waist, but since I was carrying concealed and people tend to panic if you flash in the airport these days, I resisted the urge. Flashing the gun would have flashed my U.S. Marshal badge, too, but I'd found that people who wanted to freak about the gun never seemed to see the badge clipped next to it. I really didn't want my dad's and stepmom's first glimpse of me in eight years to be kneeling on the floor with my fingers laced behind my head while some newbie from Metro police was yelling at me to comply. I was also really beginning to regret the high, spiked heels I wore. They took me from five-three to five-eight and made my legs look long and shapely, and looked amazing with my short swishy skirt, but the heels weren't made for standing around in the airport on hard tile floors. Walking in them was fine—I'd even been learning to dance in heels this high as we looked at possible footwear for the wedding—but standing was beginning to hurt.

"You're actually scared," Nicky said beside me. He stood like a friendly, blond mountain, so muscled that he'd had to get his leather jacket custom tailored to fit over his upper body. The jeans he had gotten from a bodybuilder site, but he'd wanted a jacket that could cover carrying concealed, and for that he'd had to special-order and even then he'd had to find an in-town tailor to alter it. He wasn't nervous and reaching for his gun like a dangerous comfort object. He was standing cool and calm, keeping an eye on the crowd and the customers who went into the little store against the opposite wall. I caught a glimpse of a slender figure picking up a magazine from the rack near the entrance to the store. They were wearing an oversized hoodie, nondescript jeans, and jogging shoes. They looked like a dozen teens to twenties that had passed by us, so I wondered why they had caught my attention. I tensed, trying to feel if it was a vampire or something else supernatural that wasn't on our side, and then Ru turned around so I could see his face and a bit of his short blond hair. His bored why-did-my-parents-make-me-come-here expression never changed, but his startling dark eyes looked into mine. He was part of my security tonight. He and his sister, Rodina. I hadn't even caught a glimpse of her yet, and then I realized that Ru had done something small on purpose so I'd look at him. He was still undercover, but he wanted me to see him so I'd feel better. It did help me feel better about Deimos, the ancient vampire that had come to town recently and attacked us. We'd almost canceled my family's visit, but Deimos had left us alone after the first attempt. We were hoping he'd found us too powerful and just gone back into hiding. We'd delayed my family's visit for weeks, but when we couldn't find Deimos, and he didn't try to find us again, we finally had to move forward with fitting my dad for his outfit if he was giving me away. Since he was very Catholic and I was marrying a vampire, that was still up for debate. Hell, my family was only now agreeing to meet Jean-Claude. They might not even be coming to our wedding.

Ru turned away, putting the magazine back and sighing so heavily his body language clearly said just how bored he was with the magazine, being in the airport, waiting for some stupid relative, or . . . I had no idea how he and all the Harlequin did it, they were some of the best covert operatives in the world, maybe the best, but I hadn't met enough covert ops people to judge.

I looked at Nicky. "I was going to say I am not scared-scared, maybe nervous enough that's a type of fear, but if Ru broke cover to try and reassure me, then he's picking up on more than just nerves."

"The three of us can feel it, Anita, it's more than just nerves."

I frowned up at him, and in the four-inch heels I was only a few inches shorter than him, so I didn't have to strain my neck. I almost said, *Aren't you scared of your family?* Most people say it as an offhand remark, a joke almost, but Nicky looked down at me with his one blue eye, and a eyepatch where the other eye should have been. I wouldn't joke with Nicky about scary families because his mom was still in jail for what she'd done to him and his siblings. My family had its problems, and some of them had screwed me up pretty bad, but compared to Nicky's childhood mine had been a cakewalk on Sesame Street.

"I don't think I'm afraid of my family," I said, shifting my weight again in the heels. Nicky gave me a look that said plainly he didn't believe me, but I believed me, so it was okay.

Was I really afraid of my very Catholic family meeting Jean-Claude for the first time? I ran my fingers down the pleats of my skirt. I was regretting it like the heels. I wasn't usually a pleats kind of girl, but they made the skirt swing as I moved, and it was the nicest skirt I had that wasn't skintight. Somehow skintight and short wasn't a meet-the-family outfit. So, pleats with a royal blue silk shell blouse that matched the blue in the plaid of the skirt. The short bolero jacket was black, which matched the rest of the color in the plaid. The jacket didn't quite hide the badge clipped to my waistband but did hide the gun that was in an inner "pants" holster just behind the badge, and the extra magazine/ammo holders on the other side of the skirt. I had a tailor who reinforced all the waistbands on my girlier clothes, otherwise the skirt would never have held up to this much equipment.

I was even in full makeup, which I almost never wore. I looked like I was ready for a hot date instead of seeing my family for the first time in years. I knew why I had dressed up, and thanks to being metaphysically connected to Nicky and other people in my life, they knew, too. I'd been prepared to see my dad and stepmother, Judith, to discuss if he was walking me down the aisle or if they were even coming to my wedding, but I hadn't expected that my stepsister Andria would be coming with them. She and I were both over thirty-two. She was a lawyer, and I was what I was; she was even engaged to another lawyer. Of course she'd get engaged if I was engaged. I couldn't beat Andria at anything that mattered to my family.

Andria was the girly one. The perfect blond, blue-eyed, straight-A student. She was even tall like her mother. I got good grades, but not as good. People told me I was pretty when I cleaned up or wore makeup or dressed nice. She was always dressed up, always perfect. She had a sense of style and what clothes matched and flattered her that only dating Jean-Claude had taught me. Fashion was neither natural nor a strength for me, and I found the fact that Jean-Claude didn't have any comfy clothes disturbing. What kind of person didn't have any sweats, or lounging jammies? He had pajamas, but they were all silk and he never slept in them. I wasn't complaining about sleeping in the nude, and silk looked great on him and felt even better next to my skin, but I had old jeans and sweatshirts I'd had since college. I had clothes to do yard work in, or paint something. He didn't. Centuries of being judged constantly by the other vampires so that any sign of weakness was used against him and using his beauty to survive had made him always be on, always aware like some wandering photographer would come by at any second. To me it would have been a terrible pressure; to Jean-Claude it was normal. Dressing up made him feel better. It had taken me a long time to realize that. I knew that now and accepted it, but it would never be my version of comfy. I wanted my clothes to cover me and to serve a purpose. Today's purpose was to be the beautiful swan instead of the ugly duckling. Sad but true that my family's opinion of me still mattered that much. I'd really hoped I'd grown past the need for their approval since I was almost certainly not going to get it. I was marrying a vampire, so to them I might as well be marrying a demon straight out of hell. If they'd ever met a real demon they'd understand the difference, but they hadn't seen real evil with a capital *E*. They lived in ignorant bliss while people like me risked everything to fight against the forces of evil, so they could come here and be self-righteous and tell me I was corrupt and going to hell.

I caught a glimpse through the crowd of people coming our way. Did I recognize that blond head? Was that them? My stomach clenched tight, my pulse racing into my throat so it was hard to breathe. Was Nicky right, was I actually afraid of my family? That was ridiculous; they'd never laid a hand on me in violence, well, no one who was coming on this visit. It wasn't like Nicky's past, or Nathaniel's. Nothing that violent or monstrous. The relief when I realized the people were strangers was huge. Damn it, my dad wasn't that bad.

There was a lull in the passengers going past us; I guess they were between planes or something. Only a handful of people were in line to go through security. Ru had vanished again, though I don't know how. I didn't look around for him because, like concealed carry, if you mess with undercover people you draw attention to them. The long hallway that my family would be coming down sometime soon stretched empty until you got to the bored TSA security person at the small podium. They were the one who would tell people they'd crossed the line and couldn't go back.

Nicky leaned over me and spoke low for just me as people rushed past to make their planes. "It's not a game of who had the suckiest childhood, Anita. It's okay to be afraid and to feel fucking traumatized if that's how you feel."

I stared up at him, his face so close to mine. "But I wasn't traumatized," I said.

"Your lips say that, but your pulse rate and the sweat on your palms and down your spine say different."

"Can't hide anything from a shapeshifter," I whispered.

He grinned and said, "Therianthrope, or didn't you get the new vocabulary memo about using a more inclusive term for lycanthropes and other shapeshifters?"

It made me smile like he knew it would. "You don't give a damn about politically correct vocabulary."

He smiled down at me, his face so close it filled my vision. "Not a damn bit."

"You're always telling me you can't bodyguard and kiss in public," I said.

"I think we're safe unless someone runs into us with a roller bag," he said, and moved in for a kiss and I helped him lay his lips against mine. I was wearing bright red lipstick and full-on base makeup, so we had to behave ourselves, because if we smeared it I didn't have the makeup with me to fix it. Usually I don't do base, so I just clean off the lipstick and then reapply, no muss, no fuss. But I didn't have the products or the skill to fix clown-makeup lipstick if we got carried away today. It was one of the most careful kisses Nicky and I had ever shared. He pulled back with a line of red down the middle of his lips. Some of the men in my life had coined the phrase *the go-faster stripe*. Couldn't really argue so I hadn't.

Nicky smiled and whispered, "Zoom, zoom."

I giggled, which I almost never did. "You read my thoughts."

"Part of my job," he said. He wasn't wrong. He whispered, "I'm your Bride, you're supposed to fuck us, throw us at your enemies so we delay them and allow you to escape. You're not supposed to keep us around this long, and you're definitely not supposed to fall in love with us."

"I guess if I'd been a vampire I'd have known the rules," I said.

"Necromancers, all the vampire powers, none of the downsides," he said, smiling.

"Not all the powers," I said, smiling up at him, and somehow we were holding hands while I gazed up at him far too romantically for public when my face had been plastered all over the place in connection to Jean-Claude. Not long ago the internet rumors had me dumping Jean-Claude and running away with Nicky. It had gotten so bad he'd had to stop being my main bodyguard, but then Deimos attacked and I'd wished for Nicky that night, so screw it, safety first. The public and the press knew we were all polyamorous and in a larger-than-normal poly group, but knowing Jean-Claude and I both had other lovers, some shared, some not, didn't stop outsiders from defaulting to monogamy rules and trying to apply them to us. One gossip site had posted pictures of Jean-Claude with Angel, one of our shared girlfriends, on his arm for a public event (I'd been serving a warrant of execution in a different state), and the rumor mill said he'd dumped me for her.

We broke the kiss and turned to see a group of younger women, either high school or early college age, texting busily on their phones. Shit. They'd post it to social media before I could collect my family from the plane and flee. It wasn't Deimos I was afraid of finding us but various hate groups, or media. The first vampire king of America was getting married to one of the U.S. Marshals with the Preternatural Branch, which meant he was marrying someone who hunted down and executed rogue vampires and shapeshifters, or any other supernatural citizen that started piling up a body count. That was news. And I wasn't any preternatural marshal, I was the Executioner, I was War. The first was a nickname the vampires had given me back when I still believed sincerely that I would never, ever date a vampire, but the second nickname the other marshals had given me. It was a play on the Four Horsemen of the Apocalypse; I was War because I had the highest legal kill count of any marshal. Well, my best man, Marshal Ted Forrester, aka Death, had a much higher count if all his kills were counted, but Edward wouldn't tell and neither would I. Marshals Bernardo Spotted-Horse and Otto Jeffries were Famine and Plague, respectively. They knew Edward's background, too, but since they had secrets of their own they weren't talking either.

Nicky took a Kleenex out of his pocket and started wiping at his mouth to get off the go-faster stripe. "Let's not confuse your family."

"They know I'm poly," I said.

"Knowing it and being able to deal with it aren't the same thing," he said.

He had a point, so I let him wipe my lipstick away and reassure me mine still looked perfect. Another big group of people started down the hallway's slight curve toward the TSA check desk. I caught a glimpse of very blond hair again, but this time when the crowd parted it was my dad. He hadn't seen me yet. His face was neutral. He was five-eight, still trim, and looked, well . . . like my father. He was wearing khaki slacks with a blue polo shirt, and some sort of jacket unzipped. Even his wardrobe was the same. He looked like he always did, always had, and part of me was relieved and part of me resented it. I don't know why that last part. He turned his head to speak with someone and I caught a flash of pink. The crowd thinned as people passed us with their bags. My stepmother, Judith, was with him: tall, slender, smiling. It wasn't unexpected. I knew she'd be here, but my stomach knotted anyway. What I could see of her bright blond hair was fastened back with a bright pink scarf or headband. The hair was smooth and styled and perfect. Her makeup would be the same. She was wearing a pink designer sweatshirt, I couldn't see what else, and then I realized she had a pink shadow with her. It was Andria in a matching outfit, with her own straight blond hair tied back with a pink band. They'd done matching outfits a lot when we were younger. Mother-daughter outfits in pastels, which I looked terrible in but made both of them look great. I'd protested the outfits until Judith stopped including me in the mix when I was about eleven. I hadn't wanted to be excluded since Judith was now the only chance for a mother that I had; I just hadn't wanted to wear pink.

Nicky moved me behind him automatically as some other passengers almost bumped me. It hadn't been on purpose, but he was officially my bodyguard, so I let him do his job. The hate groups had gotten worse as the wedding got closer. They didn't want us to have a happily-ever-after ending, monogamous or otherwise.

My father's face lit up when he saw me; he looked genuinely happy to see me, which was great, because that hadn't been a given. It made me smile back and wave. He waved and then they were there with us. He hugged me with enthusiasm, and I did the same, and then his hand found the gun at my belt and he tensed, unsure where to put his hands, so he pulled away awkwardly. He hadn't been a fan of his little girl working with the police, let alone becoming one; too dangerous.

Judith hugged me next, and it had enthusiasm to it, too, which caught me completely off guard since she stopped hugging me about the time I turned twelve. She kept her arms around my shoulders so there were no gun issues. "Anita, it's so good to see you again. You look great!"

Andria said, "Seriously perfect outfit." She didn't seem upset that I was better dressed than she was, which spoiled it for me a little. I'd wanted to be the best dressed for once, but I'd wanted her to feel bad about it even more. Yes, it was petty, but at least I acknowledged my motives instead of hiding from them now.

"Thanks, you both look cute and comfy for the plane."

They put their arms around each other, heads together like they were posing for a camera. "It's been so long since we did mother-daughter outfits, I couldn't resist," Judith said. They then both showed their white athletic shoes with bright white and pink sparkles on them like they'd been bedazzled, but I knew they'd come that way. I also knew they'd paid three to four hundred dollars for each pair. I'd seen them at one of the stores where I'd done emergency shopping for my outfit. I'd paid that much for shoes, or Jean-Claude had paid that much for shoes he wanted to see me in, but nothing quite like these.

Dad held his hand out to Nicky and said, "Are you Micah or Nathaniel?" Neither of them looks anything like Nicky, which meant my dad hadn't even bothered to google me.

"Fredrick," Judith said, "Micah Callahan is on the news all the time and he looks nothing like this gentleman." She offered her hand. After the slightest hesitation Nicky took the offered hand. Her hand was big enough to match his, and she'd always given firm handshakes.

"Then this must be Nathaniel Graison?" my father said, smiling and looking relieved, like he was getting his feet under him in the conversation.

Judith and Andria laughed together. It was a very we've-got-a-secret-you-don't-know laugh. It was usually a laugh that women make when they've just said something dirty about a man in the room, but they don't want to tell him, but somehow they want people to know they're bad girls. I'd never liked that attitude of "safe" naughtiness that so many American women seemed to adopt. I started adding the *American* when too many women I knew who weren't raised here pointed out that it wasn't the same in every country. Either way, I didn't like the laugh or the attitude that went with it, but maybe I'd spent too many years being on the outside of their girl secrets and I was projecting? I'd keep that as a backup thought. I'd try to be fair.

"Fredrick darling." She said his name like that a lot, his first name and then *darling* as if that was his real last name. Sometimes it was an endearment that I'd hoped to feel for someone myself someday, but sometimes it was that sly, condescending tone that seemed to say, *Poor men, they just don't understand.*

He looked at her, waiting for her to add to the sentence. If he didn't like the unpleasant look on her face, then he hid it, but again maybe I was projecting on the unpleasant part. My therapist and I had talked a lot about this visit and how it was going to be difficult for me to see Judith and Andria, but especially Judith, in a fair light. So fucking true.

"Didn't you look at any of the links Mom sent you about Anita's boyfriends?" Andria asked, in that condescending voice that only women and catty gay men seem to have—oh, and one other group: mean girls from junior high when they start practicing the attitude and going into their twenties, and to the grave for some women. I had a moment to realize that Judith and Andria were mean girls, and the revelation suddenly made my childhood make so much more sense.

Dad looked flustered and then he blushed, so that's where I got it from. "I . . . They weren't links I was comfortable with looking at."

"You sent him the link to Guilty Pleasures, where Brandon dances," I said, trying to keep my face blank as I pictured my incredibly conservative and very straight father looking at a website full of male strippers.

"Such a cute . . . stage name," Judith said with just enough hesitation to let me know she meant something else.

"Oh, Dad," Andria said, rolling her eyes.

My dad blushed harder and didn't make eye contact with anyone.

Judith laughed and hugged his arm to her and leaned her perfectly straight hairdo on his shoulder like they were still honeymooners. It made him smile and lean into her. He loved her still, and maybe she really loved him. I wanted Dad happy after Mom died, and he was once he fell in love with Judith. The fact that his happiness added to my sorrow never seemed to compute for him.

Nicky's hand found my right one and for once I didn't argue with him compromising my gun hand. I needed the hand-holding more than I needed my gun. If violence broke out around us we'd react, but right now the touch of his hand was the best protection I had against what was happening inside my head and my heart.

"I'm sorry," my dad said, "for assuming who you would bring to the airport to meet us, Anita. I understand that you are polyamorous as your lifestyle. I just . . . It's hard for me to think about my little girl living like that."

"Living like what, Dad?" I said, and realized that I sounded angry, mean. I didn't want to be like that to him or anyone else. I could be angry, but I didn't want to be a mean anything.

He looked up, giving me the full stare of his perfectly blue eyes. "I'm sorry, Anita."

I wanted to ask *sorry about what*, but I took a deep breath, squeezed Nicky's hand, and tried not to be childish and still stand up for myself. "Let's start over, Dad. I had planned on easing you into how big our poly group is, but it didn't occur to me that you wouldn't look online and google Micah, Nathaniel, and Jean-Claude. This is Nicky Murdock, he lives with me, and he is part of our poly group."

He offered his hand to Nicky again as he said, "I know what the vampire looks like. Judith made me watch some of his interviews online."

Nicky took the handshake and very carefully didn't look at me. He knew how I'd feel about Jean-Claude being called *the vampire*.

"His name is Jean-Claude, Dad, not 'the vampire.'"

My father shook his head. "He is a vampire, Anita."

"I'm aware of that," I said.

"I just don't understand how you can want . . . to be with . . . him."

Andria said, "Did you see what he looks like, Dad?"

"He's fabulous, Anita," Judith said, and seemed to mean it. She even wasted a smile on me like we were friends.

I nodded but had to fight to manage a smile, because Judith being friendly was just too weird. "He is fabulous," I said.

"Not that this one isn't a ruggedly handsome hunk," she said, wasting a smile on Nicky. He didn't smile back either. Let's all be sociopaths together; it was the only sane reaction to my family dynamics.

"I never thought you had it in you, Anita," Andria said.

"Had what?" I asked, finally looking at her again.

"Dating such hunky men; you were so terrible with boys when we were growing up."

"You mean I wasn't popular, and you were."

She shrugged her pink-clad shoulders. "You were always so gloomy when we were growing up. No man likes someone with that kind of attitude."

Nicky said, "Anita's bad attitude is what brought us together."

The women looked up at him like a choreographed movement. They had a lot of body movements that were mirrored; the matching outfits weren't necessary to let you know they were mother and daughter. "Really?" Andria said it like she didn't believe him.

Nicky smiled and it looked like a real smile; it even filled his one blue eye. "Really," he said, voice soft. I didn't need to read his mind to know he was already beginning to think of ways to at least hurt her for real. He was reacting to my dislike of her and that she was being snide to me. I played at being a sociopath, but he was the real deal. Only my having a conscience and sharing mine with him metaphysically had tamed some of his . . . issues.

I wanted to say *no killing my family on this visit*, but didn't think saying it out loud would help smooth things over. He knew it, because he could literally read at least my feelings and a lot of my thoughts, and then I realized that it caused all my Brides literal pain for me to be unhappy sometimes. Damn it, I shouldn't have brought Nicky today. He leaned over and whispered into my hair, "I'm supposed to keep you safe, I needed to be here."

I smiled up at him, then heard my name called in a happier tone. "Anita!"

I looked past my family to find a very tall, young blond man that it took me a second to realize was my baby brother. He was in college now and a foot taller than the last time I'd seen him. "Josh!" I said, and went to greet him through the crowd, leaving Nicky behind with the others. He wouldn't hurt them in front of this many witnesses. They couldn't hurt him emotionally because his emotions didn't work that way. Everyone was safe, or so I thought as Josh bent down so we could hug.

Then a voice with a thick accent said, "Anita Katerine, God has sent us to save your immortal soul from damnation."

Josh stiffened and whispered, "I'm sorry."

I turned from him to see an elderly woman who was even shorter than me walking up behind us. I said the only thing I could say. "Hi, Grandma."

2

"ANITA'S IMMORTAL SOUL is just fine, Grandma," Josh said.

"She is still raising the dead, which is only for God and his saints to do."

"She saw the video from Colorado on the news," Josh explained.

"I found more videos on the computer," she said.

"Grandma has her own computer now," Josh said.

I stared at the tiny woman, who seemed to be even tinier than the last time I'd seen her, as if she'd shrunk. She didn't look scary at all as she clutched her black purse and peered up at me with those bright blue eyes that matched the color of the button-up sweater she was wearing. The high-necked blouse underneath was as white as her hair there. There were still some streaks of faded blond, but not as many as the last time I'd seen her. She looked harmless, so why did my stomach clench and my throat feel like I was choking as if she was still huge and could tower over me? My voice sounded almost normal as I said, "I thought computers were the devil's work."

"Computers are tools, Anita; they can be used for good, by good people."

"Grandma is online more than Josh is now," Andria said as she joined us.

I glanced back to find Judith and my father having a very quiet but intense argument. They never yelled at each other, but the energy and the body language was them fighting. They fought that way at home, too, so controlled. One of my earliest clear memories was of my mom and dad having a screaming fight. It had scared me, which was probably one of the reasons I'd remembered it. When I was a little older they'd explained that sometimes when you loved each other the passion had to come out. I hadn't even understood the talk, but I'd liked that they tried to explain how they worked as a couple to me when I was so small. Dad with Mom had been like a completely different couple than Dad with Judith. It had taught me at a young age that the same person wasn't the same in every marriage.

Nicky was standing a little away from either of my family groups. He was closer to a group of men that seemed to match what he was wearing, almost. Women will ask why you're standing near them in a crowd, but men don't care as much. My grandmother wouldn't realize he was with me yet. He was giving me time before he got introduced to my grandmother, because she wouldn't like the multiple relationships any better than she liked the rest of my life. Wait until she found out I was dating men and women.

"What are they fighting about?" I asked.

"Who knows? She just sent me over here so they could talk in private like I'm still not a grown-up." Andria looked resentful under all the artful pink-toned makeup.

"We're both over thirty," I said.

"Don't remind me," she said.

I frowned. "I didn't mean it that way. I just meant that we're both adults and should be treated accordingly."

"Mom still treats me like I'm twelve," Andria said.

"I think I'm still about ten in her head," Josh said.

"You don't have to let her treat either of you like that, you know," I said.

"Andria and Josh are good children who honor their mother and father," Grandma said.

"Yeah, I'm the bad girl, the rebel. I remember, Grandma."

"You were always a disobedient child," she said, and the look out of those perfectly blue eyes made me fight not to shiver. She couldn't hurt me. I was all grown up and bigger, stronger, faster than she was, logically. Logically all that was true, but childhood issues aren't about logic, they're about bogeymen and the monster under your bed or at your grandparents' house.

"Yep, that's me, the black sheep."

"That is not a word, Anita. Reply with 'yes,' or don't reply at all."

"I'll reply any damn way I please."

Grandma looked scandalized; boy, she hadn't heard or seen nothin' yet. "A lady does not curse."

"I was never a lady by your definition, just a virgin, and that's so not the same thing."

Andria gasped. Grandma said, "Anita!" like I'd shocked her.

"Mom and Dad are coming this way," Josh said, and I didn't know if he was trying to short-circuit the talk between me and Grandma Blake or giving us a heads-up like he thought I wouldn't want the parents to hear what I'd said. Did he not remember that I didn't care if they heard what I said? Then he walked toward them to meet them partway. Was he going to tattle on me, or did he just want out of the conversation?

Nicky moved toward us as the men he'd been standing near moved away. Grandma gave him a disapproving look, though I wasn't sure why. He was usually in the background of the online pictures if he was included at all. We didn't normally kiss in public, but then come to think of it we weren't normally just the two of us in public.

"What do you want, young man?" she asked him as if he were trying to get her to put money in a dirty coffee cup, instead of just standing there.

"Grandma, this is Nicky."

She looked back at me, frowning, then at him, then at me, frowning harder. "Nicky what? Has he no last name?"

I tried to hide the smile as I said, "Nicky Murdock."

He offered her his hand, smiling and projecting that charm that he could turn on and off. You had to know what his real smile looked like to realize it was an act. It fooled most women, but not Grandma. She stared him up and down, not offering to shake hands. "If you are with my granddaughter, does that mean you are a supernatural citizen?"

His smile slipped closer to his real one, which was colder and far less pleasant. It left his one blue eye almost as cold as her own.

"Grandma, you can't just ask people that," Andria said.

"Why not?" she asked.

Nicky looked at me, and I shrugged.

"Yes, I'm a supernatural citizen," he said. He moved around her to stand with me.

"What kind of supernatural?"

"Grandma," Andria said at the same time that Judith said, "Mother Blake."

She looked at all of us as if she didn't see anything wrong with what she'd said. "He is not a vampire because he does not look like an animated corpse, so what is he?"

"You've been watching too many horror movies," I said.

"I have seen the real videos on the internet, not the ones where the vampires cloud people's minds and make themselves look alive."

"Grandma, we showed you videos of Jean-Claude and other vampires so you'd know that vampires can look just like us."

"I told you it is all lies, Joshua, just illusions and the devil clouding men's minds."

"Don't call me Joshua," he said automatically, like he'd been doing since he was old enough to care. She had always objected to his name being shortened for everyday. *Joshua* was in the Bible; *Josh* wasn't.

"Who's the devil in this scenario, Grandma?" I asked.

"Vampires are all in league with the devil, Anita, you know that."

"You and Dad certainly raised me to believe it."

"Then how did you end up in a demon's bed with his ring on your finger?"

"Mother, that is not polite, or necessary," Dad finally said.

"What were you and your wife arguing about so politely?" Grandma asked, pinning that cold blue gaze on him. He flinched under it just like I did. Interesting.

Judith answered, "That Fredrick didn't call ahead and tell Anita that you had invited yourself along on this visit."

"It is a family visit, and I am part of the family," she said.

"Dad," Andria said, "you didn't call and tell Anita that she was coming with us."

"Why should he?" Grandma Blake said.

"Yeah, Dad, why should you have given me a heads-up, instead of springing this on me," I said, looking at him, and for once I was with Andria and Judith on the attitude.

"Josh, Andria, can you please take your grandmother into the shop so we can talk in private with Anita?"

They tried, but Grandma said, "I will not be gotten out of the way as if I am the child. Whatever you have to say to Anita you can say in front of me, Fredrick."

He sighed, his shoulders rounding a little as if he were trying to lift a weight that was too heavy for him. "Fine, Momma, have it your way."

"Doesn't she always," Judith said quietly under her breath. Apparently Grandma didn't hear it because she absolutely would have commented on it.

"Well, speak up, Fredrick, we are all waiting to hear your secrets."

He stood up straight like he hadn't realized he was hunching forward. "I didn't call Anita and tell her that my mother was coming because I knew Anita would have said no."

"No to what?" Grandma Blake said.

"To you coming with us, Momma."

"She has no say in this; she is a child, you are her father."

"I'm over thirty, Grandma; I have a say in my own life."

"Both you girls over thirty and no great-grandchildren yet."

I glanced at Andria, who sighed and rolled her eyes like this was a long-standing complaint. I hadn't spoken to Grandma in so long I hadn't heard it before. Both Andria and I had still been on the why-aren't-you-married-yet list for Grandma back then.

"You don't want us to have children out of wedlock, do you, Grandma?" Andria said.

"Of course not!" She sounded outraged.

"Then you have to wait for Anita and me to actually get married before there's a chance for great-grandchildren."

Grandma glared at Andria, then turned to me. "Though there will be no children from your marriage. Your demon lover is too old to beget children."

"Mother Blake!" Judith said, then turned to me. "I'm so sorry, Anita, she had no right to say that about your fiancé."

"Don't apologize for me, Judith. I meant what I said, he is a demon lover. He's an incubus, it's all over the internet."

"You can't believe everything you read on the internet, Grandma," Josh said. "We've had this talk before."

I kept my face both blank and suitably outraged because she wasn't exactly wrong. Jean-Claude was a vampire, not a demon, but his bloodline could inherit the ability to feed on lust, which was the definition of an incubus or succubus. If my grandmother had called him an incubus to his face he wouldn't have denied it, just been shocked that she knew, like I was shocked. It was supposed to be a deep, dark secret even from most of the supernatural community. So how did my grandmother know it?

I heard Jean-Claude whisper through my mind, *How indeed?* My reaction to my grandmother's comment combined with thinking

about him too hard had opened me to him, but I didn't mind since
he needed to know if our real secrets were out on the internet.

"What was that?" Grandma Blake asked.

"What was what?" I asked, looking at her.

She shivered, then glared at Nicky. "You did something just now,
didn't you?"

"I didn't do anything," he said.

Had she felt Jean-Claude's power inside me? The thought was
enough; Jean-Claude breathed power through me again. She rubbed
her arms as if she was cold.

I stared at her and felt myself smile. It wasn't a happy smile. It was
the smile I got when bad things were happening and I was ready to
do something even worse to serve and protect.

"Ever seen a ghost, Grandma?" I asked.

"What are you babbling about, Anita?"

Jean-Claude was in my head thinking, *You didn't know?*

Grandma turned to Nicky. "You are doing something to me with
your unholy powers."

Nicky almost laughed. "It's not me."

I stepped closer to her, invading her personal space. "Are ghosts
all you can see, Grandma?"

"I do not see evil spirits."

"Swear to God," I said.

"What?" she asked, taking a step back from me.

"Swear before God and all his saints that you have never seen or
felt the presence of a ghost."

"Anita, why would you ask her that?" Dad said, coming to stand
by his mother.

I didn't use my ties to Jean-Claude; this time I called my own
power. The psychic ability that let me raise zombies, sense ghosts,
and be on the brink of becoming queen of the vampires, all while
still being alive.

I watched the hairs on my grandmother's arms stand to attention. I felt something inside her pulse like a faint, answering heartbeat, almost lost. She wasn't a necromancer, but she was something, had always been something. While she told me I was evil and a monster because of my gifts, she'd been hiding her own.

3

GRANDMOTHER BLAKE DIDN'T want to be close to Nicky and me after that, which was fine with me. I needed time to think about what the hell had just happened. In fact, she stayed silent for the short walk to the luggage carousels, though they never seemed very much like merry-go-rounds to me, more like flat metallic snakes. As a child on the last big vacation before Mom died, I remembered running ahead to see the carousel and being so disappointed that there weren't horses to ride. Now I looked through the crowd of strangers waiting for their luggage to find my grandmother talking low and urgently with my father. She was fingering something at her throat, and I knew the gesture from childhood. It was the gold cross that she wore constantly. It must have been hidden under the blue button-up sweater and high-necked blouse she was wearing. My cross was hanging on a long chain under my clothes for safety, always so awkward to spill out around the vampires I loved, but in case there were vampires around that weren't my friends I wore it anytime we weren't at home. How had I never realized that Grandma Blake had her own spark of death magic hiding behind all her Catholic self-righteousness? Nicky leaned over to whisper, "How would untrained-child you know it wasn't your magic?" He was right. It was such a small flash of power that even just ten years ago I wouldn't have realized it wasn't mine.

I smiled up at him and had to fight off the urge to hug him. God, I wanted the reassurance of touch from Nicky so badly.

"How about I take over bodyguard duty for a few minutes?" Ethan said as he came up to us to help with the luggage. I looked up into his perfectly gray eyes set into a handsome face with his white hair and its gray lowlights, that one dark red streak that went from the thick fall of hair near his eyes and all the way to where the back was so short it was partially shaved. The colors were all-natural, showing most of the different weretiger clans that ran through his genetics. The new haircut looked good on him, but it was his girlfriend's approval that mattered, not mine.

"Your opinion matters," he said, softly.

I shook my head. "Not as much as Nilda's opinion matters."

His face filled with the happiness of being in love with the werebear Nilda. It made me smile to see that look on his face and feel a wash of the emotions that went with it. I wanted to give him a hug, just because I was happy for him, but I couldn't compromise both of them and I needed Nicky's arms more in that moment.

I realized that it wasn't just Ethan who was here to help with luggage and security. I hadn't sensed them, and some of them were metaphysically connected to me. Shit, I had to do better than this in public.

Andria came to stand with us. "Is this another member of your poly group?"

I started to say no, then realized that Ethan and I did have sex occasionally and I was the only woman that Nilda was willing to share him with, so technically . . . "Yes," I said without trying to explain more.

She did a quick eye flick up and down on Ethan, then looked at me with a smile on her face that I couldn't quite read. "How do you find this many handsome, in-shape men to date when most women can't find one?"

"Just lucky, I guess," I said, because the real answer was too complicated for public, especially with someone who had never kept my secrets the few times I made the mistake of confiding in her. We'd been kids, but I'd learned my lesson.

Nicky took my hand in his and turned me into his body like the beginning of a dance. I wrapped my arms around him, hands tracing the curve of his body underneath the leather jacket, so I could put my hands in that pocket of warmth behind his back where the jacket trapped the heat. I had to be careful to go above the gun at his waist so I wouldn't raise the leather jacket and flash it to the general public. He looked scary enough without the gun. If his waist hadn't been proportionally smaller than his upper body, I wouldn't have been able to encircle him with my arms. I rested the side of my face against his chest, letting myself sink into the solid promise of him. His arms tightened around me with only a fraction of his strength pressing me closer. I knew how much tighter he could hold me, but now was not the time for that.

"Later," he murmured, and laid the gentlest of kisses against the top of my hair. When we had sex it was rough, bondage that scared a few of my shared lovers who had seen us together, but we were also this together. It was the combination that made it work for us. Without these moments we'd have been play partners but not in love. Now it was like we breathed each other in, melted against each other's bodies, and drew energy, love, hope from each other.

I drew back so I could gaze up at him, and he loosened his arms so I could do it comfortably. His face was open and shining with love, the smile too open for public, but I could feel that mine was the same. Love is great, but it's different from being *in* love, like the difference between gazing over the cliff edge at the great view and leaping off, trusting that the love you share will catch you before you hit the ground. *In love* was a leap of faith.

"If this is how you are with the man you're not going to marry, I can't wait to see you with Jean-Claude," Andria said. I think she was trying for teasing, but when I glanced at her face it didn't match the lightness she was trying for; she looked serious, her eyes full of unhappiness bordering on sorrow. She seemed to realize she'd shown me too much, because she blinked and turned away with "Your hunky security guards have all the luggage."

"Then let's head for the exit," I said.

She turned back with a smile plastered on her face, but her eyes still held an edge of that unhappiness. What was happening in her life to put that look in her eyes? "I better go help with Grandma, and make sure she rides with Josh and me. You'll have a hard enough time with Dad in the car with you, you don't need both of them."

"Thank you, Andria," I said.

She smiled a little more, so her eyes looked less haunted. "You're welcome, Anita." Then she walked away to help wrangle Grandma Blake.

"I know you don't know what that was all about," Nicky said, "but I still want to ask it."

"I have no idea," I said. We extracted ourselves from the hug. He went back to being my main bodyguard like a switch had been flipped from romantic to threatening physical presence. Ethan went to help with my family and their luggage. I'd expected Judith and Andria to overpack, but they hadn't been the only ones. We'd be lucky to fit it all in three SUVs.

4

NICKY HAD BARELY backed out of the parking space and headed for the short upward-sloping tunnel that was the exit from the parking garage when my father said, "I know you're upset that your grandmother is here, Anita."

I turned around in the passenger seat as far as the seat belt would allow, trying not to yell at my dad but to still protect my personal boundaries and honor my own trauma. Yes, that is therapy-speak for trying to keep your shit together when you feel betrayed all over again by your parent who is supposed to protect you but keeps failing. Judith sat beside him, and for once she was on my side.

"Fredrick, how could you not call ahead and ask Anita if it was okay to bring your mother with us?"

"Mother would not take no for an answer, you know how she's gotten." He wouldn't meet my eyes, or hers. He stared at a point on the back of the seat, and I finally realized that my father was at best far more passive than I'd ever realized, or at worst a fucking coward.

"Then you should have called me and told me she was coming," I said.

His eyes flicked up at me and then back to the car seat. "I knew you'd refuse."

"Damn right, I'd have refused!" I was yelling and I had to pause to take a few deep breaths before I could control my voice enough to say, "She was horrible to me as a child. How could you bring that woman near me?"

"She's my mother," he said, as if that explained anything.

"Fredrick, that is not a reason," Judith said.

"No, it's an excuse," I said.

His eyes flicked to me, then to Judith, then back to nothing. I wanted to scream again. If he'd tried this passive-aggressive shit on solid ground instead of in the car I might have pushed him, forced him to look at me. I was so angry with him. The rage that was always inside me was like lava waiting to erupt and spill all over something, because I couldn't be this angry with my father and still be a good person, a good kid, a good girl, well, fuck that shit. He'd made the mess, and he didn't get a pass this time, because it was his fault. I couldn't even blame Judith on this one, and God knows I'd spent most of my childhood blaming her for anything I could. The thought came that maybe I'd blamed her far more than she deserved because I couldn't hate my father as much as I let myself hate her. I pushed the thought away because I couldn't deal with the insight right now. One emotional crisis at a time.

Nicky was pretending he was deaf like a good bodyguard, though he was so much more than that to me. Either Dad agreed he was family, or we were both taking the only chance we might have tonight to talk without Grandmother Blake with us.

"She's my mother, Anita . . ."

"And I'm your daughter, so what?"

He looked at me then. "She's not well, Anita."

"If you mean she's crazy, then she's always been crazy, Dad."

His blue eyes darkened, which meant he was finally getting angry. Great, and I meant that. I wanted to fight with him about this. "She is not insane, Anita."

"Well . . ." Judith started to say, but he turned that gaze on her, and she stopped talking, seeing the anger. It was her turn to stare out the window and stay out of things as far as sitting in the middle of it would allow. Welcome to family life.

He looked back at me. "She is not well, and if she has never been well, then it was . . . quieter than this."

"Quieter? Quieter? Really? What you mean is she lost her victim of choice when I left the family and without a specific target she's spreading it around, or did she choose a new preferential victim?"

His eyes were still angry, but his voice didn't show it as he said, "I don't know the term 'preferential victim.'"

"Try 'preferential abuser,' have you heard that one?"

"What are you saying, Anita?" he asked.

"She told me I was ugly, clumsy, stupid, and you let her babysit me for years. After Mom died it just got worse. I was with someone who told me I was worthless, and she kept telling me all that anytime we were alone together, and worse."

He looked at me now, and there was sorrow in his eyes, that old pain of my mother's loss that had stopped me from pushing issues for so long. I wanted my dad happy, not sad, but fuck that. I wasn't a child anymore and neither was he—two adults finally dealing with so many things.

"I am sorrier than I have words to say, Anita, for what she did to you when you were a child. I am even sorrier that I didn't believe you when you tried to tell me what she was doing."

"'Sorry' doesn't fix it, Dad."

"I am ashamed that I didn't believe you, and more ashamed that I kept sending you back to her day after day, night after night if I had an emergency."

I stared at him then, ashamed. Ashamed that he was ashamed? How did I feel about that? I didn't even know. It was like I'd hit an empty spot, a great black silence that just floated between us because I had no box to put it in or react to.

"I don't know what to say to that," I said at last.

"I do," Nicky said softly.

I wasn't sure that Dad or Judith heard him, but I turned in my seat so I could see the side of his face. "What would you say?" I asked.

"That if someone says they're sorry, but keeps repeating the behavior, they aren't really sorry."

"He has no stake in this fight," my dad said.

"Fuck that, Dad."

"Anita, language," Judith said.

I laughed, but it sounded bitter even to me. "Really, the fact that I said 'fuck' is more shocking than that you brought my abuser to visit without warning me."

"She is not your abuser, she's your grandmother."

"She's both," Nicky said.

"Stay out of this, young man," Dad said.

"I want to hear what Nicky has to say," I said.

"He's not your fiancé, so he doesn't have a say in family arguments." My father sounded so sure of himself. I was happy to tell him he was wrong.

"I told you that Nicky lives with me, with us, right?"

"You did, but that doesn't make him family."

"He is family to me, Dad."

"He's not going to be your husband, and he's not your fiancé. How can he be family?"

"I'm poly, Dad, which means here in the United States I can't legally marry everyone that I love. Hell, I still have to pick just one like it's some romance novel and fucking soul mates."

Judith said, "Language."

I stared at her as I said, "Motherfucking son of a bitch, what's wrong with my language, Judith?"

"Anita," Dad said, "there's no call for saying things like that."

"The hell there isn't. Do you guys even listen to yourselves, really listen to yourselves? It's like as long as we're polite to each other it'll be okay. Nothing is wrong so long as we don't cuss, and we say please and thank you, and don't do anything that looks bad."

They looked at each other, and then Judith reached over and laid her hand on his on the seat. "She may have a point, Fredrick."

"There's still no reason to curse," he said.

"The hell there isn't," I said.

"Anita," he said in that voice that had made me behave when I was a teenager.

"What the fuck, Dad?"

He glared at me. I smiled back because it was all so ridiculous that I couldn't be angry about the language issue, not when there were other, better things to fight about.

Judith said, "Your father is having a little trouble understanding the whole poly situation. I did look it up online, but it seems so dependent on each couple that I'm not sure I really understand it either."

"*Poly* is just a fancy word for cheating," Dad said.

"No," I said, "it's the opposite of cheating."

"What does that even mean, Anita?"

"It means that if I wanted to sleep with someone new, our poly group would have to all agree to it. Either everyone is happy with an addition, or you don't add them to your group," I said.

Nicky added, "Unless someone has a long-standing relationship from before the poly group formed, and then it's more complicated."

I nodded. "True, some people have one relationship outside the group that can be continued even if the majority don't like the person, as long as it doesn't negatively impact the rest of the group."

"Do you have one of those in your . . . poly group?" Judith asked.

I nodded. "We do, but when you're dating vampires they can have a lot of very old relationships that you have to take into account."

My dad's face tightened, and the anger was just back. I remembered him as more controlled than this, or less easily angered, but maybe I just hadn't seen him clearly when I was younger? How do we ever see our parents as real people and not just parents? It was like the reverse of them seeing us as children forever.

"Are you even going to try and meet Jean-Claude with an open mind?" I asked.

He looked startled then, as if he hadn't realized that his thoughts were so clear on his face. "I don't understand what we did wrong that you would even have dated one of them, Anita. You were raised a good Catholic, and you know what the Pope says about vampires."

"They're either seen as suicides or as dead bodies animated by demons or other evil spirits, so either way vampires are damned in the eyes of the Church," I said, like I was quoting.

"If you know all that, then how did it happen? How did you date one of them, let alone be willing to marry one?"

"I want to marry Jean-Claude; the fact that he's a vampire isn't really the important part," I said.

"How can you say the fact that he's a vampire isn't the important part? That's the only important part here," he said.

"More important than my happiness?" I asked.

"No, don't do that, don't make this about happiness or unhappiness, this is your immortal soul at stake, Anita. If you marry this creature, then you will be damned to hell for all eternity. Don't you understand that, Anita? Love is important, but it's not more important than that."

"So why did you come, Dad? If that's your final word on the topic of my marriage, then why didn't you just stay home in Indiana?"

He leaned forward until the seat belt tightened and wouldn't let him move anymore. "It's not my last word on your wedding, Anita, just on you marrying one of these creatures."

"If you call Jean-Claude a creature one more time I . . . I don't know what I'll do, but it won't be good." There was a time in my teens when I would have made some extravagant threat, but I tried to never say anything I wouldn't really do, and right now I couldn't see hurting my dad for real.

"Fredrick, I showed you that article that Anita sent us about the fact that people who become vampires never lose brain function completely, so in effect they don't die. It was just so faint that no one could detect it without the technology we have now." She tried to touch his hand again, but he pulled away. She gave me a look like *I'm sorry.*

I gave her a thank-you nod and had to fight not to feel angry that it was my hated stepmother on my side against my dad. It just felt weird. It was like there was more to Judith than I'd remembered and less to my dad. It made my chest tight. Damn it, I would not cry about this.

Dad shook his head. "The Pope made his views known about the new medical evidence. The Church's stance is unchanged; vampires are damned and anyone who marries them is damned with them."

"Wait," I said, "do you mean the Pope actually added that last bit for real, that anyone who marries a vampire is damned?"

He nodded.

Judith widened her eyes and gave a much more nervous nod, like she didn't want to do it.

"Well, since I'm Episcopalian now it doesn't really make a difference to me."

"You only left the Church because of the ruling about raising the dead," he said.

"Yeah, I raise the dead, so I'm excommunicated from the Church. Trust me, Dad, I didn't forget why I became Episcopalian. All the salvation, half the guilt, it's great," I said.

He gave me a beseeching look. "You're a U.S. Marshal now, surely you could give up your side job as an animator."

"It's not a side job, Dad, it's my psychic gift."

"Fredrick, we discussed all this when Anita was fourteen and the dead animals started following her home. She must use her gift, or it finds other ways to . . . to be used."

"It's not a gift, it's a curse and a blasphemy in the eyes of the Church."

"You sent me to my grandmother Flores to learn to control my animating abilities, Dad. Thanks for not choosing the exorcism that our priest was recommending."

"I couldn't do that to you, you weren't evil, there was no demon inside you. You just inherited a family curse, and that's my fault, our fault, but your mother didn't have it. None of her sisters had it. We thought it had died out with her mother. We thought you were safe."

"Are you saying that if you had thought I could inherit the family magic that you and . . . Mom wouldn't have had children?"

"We would never have given you up, but I am so sorry that the curse is inside your blood. Your mother would have been so . . . We never meant to do this to you."

"The summer I spent with Mom's family everyone seemed to respect Grandma Flores. No one was afraid of her or treated her like she was cursed."

"You never heard the stories about your mom's childhood."

"I was eight when she died, Dad, so yeah, I was probably too young for zombie stories."

"We didn't mean to do this to you, Anita, please believe that."

I stared at him, trying to figure out what to say. "Do what, Dad, make me who I am? If I hadn't been able to raise the dead I wouldn't be a U.S. Marshal with the Preternatural Branch. I wouldn't have ever met Jean-Claude, or Nicky, or Micah, or Nathaniel, or anyone in my life."

"Jean-Claude is the only vampire on that list, correct?" he asked.

"Yeah, Dad, he's the only vampire in that list of names." I didn't add that Jean-Claude wasn't the only vampire I was dating. That was what he was really trying to get at, but one hurdle at a time.

"Nicky, are you a wereleopard like Micah and Nathaniel?" Judith asked. Jesus, she really was trying.

"No, I'm not a wereleopard."

There was that pause while they waited for him to say more, but I knew he wouldn't. I explained but didn't answer the question. "Shapeshifters are being encouraged not to share what their animal form is with people outside their community. There's been a rash of cases where people make false allegations against shapeshifters, trying to get them killed by the police."

"That's awful," Judith said.

"So he doesn't want to share his animal form with us, because we might use it against him?" Dad asked.

"We, I mean the police, are encouraging shapeshifters not to share their animal half with people they don't know, so that it can't be used to frame them."

"But we're your family, Anita, we would never do that," he said.

"Sorry, Mr. Blake, but the way you're talking about vampires doesn't make me feel very secure about how you might feel about the rest of us." Nicky's voice was neutral, and he kept his eyes on the road, not even a glance back at them.

"I'm a veterinarian. One, I know that it is a disease and that any human can catch it. Two, I find accounts of those in your . . . community who write articles explaining how their senses and thinking shift with their bodies fascinating. It's like a chance to know how my patients see the world."

"Your patients are animals, Dad, Nicky isn't an animal."

"I didn't mean . . ."

"No, that's okay, we are as close as you're going to get to pulling the Dr. Doolittle thing of talking to the animals."

"Thank you for understanding," Dad said, then he looked at me.

"You're a vampire executioner, Anita. How can you be about to marry one of them?"

"I'm aware of the irony, Dad, trust me."

"You told me once that it didn't bother you to kill them, because they weren't human."

I sighed and rolled my shoulders back because I was already hunched up. I hadn't been dealing with my family for an hour yet. Sweet Jesus. "I'm aware of the attitude I had back in the days when I first started as a legal executioner for the state."

"When did your attitude change?" he asked.

"Oh, I don't know, Dad, maybe when a morgue had a vampire tied down with chains and holy items and I let them bully me into driving a stake through his heart while the vampire was still awake and aware."

"The vampire had earned a warrant of execution by killing humans."

"Maybe. I'll be honest, Dad, I've killed so many that I don't remember the crimes attached to them all, but I remember their faces. I remember the ones who begged for their lives. The ones who cried as I had to pound a sharpened piece of wood up under their ribs with a mallet. It's not a quick death, and it's sure as hell not painless."

"That sounds awful," Judith said.

"It is. I use bullets and blades with high silver content anywhere the law allows. I try to execute, not butcher." I heard the tone in my voice that let me know that I was haunted by things beyond a screwed-up childhood.

"I'm sorry that you have to do things that are hard for you, Anita, but the Pope has declared that slaying vampires is a holy cause."

I turned in the seat so I could see him again. "I know, a get-out-of-hell-free card if you kill enough monsters. You know, that's part of what's set off this last round of hate crimes that's been sweeping the country, encouraging people to drag vampires out into the sunlight to fry during the daylight when they don't risk themselves at all."

"They aren't human, Anita."

"No vampire that has died in this last rash of murders has been guilty of any crime, Dad. They've all been innocent citizens."

"They aren't innocent, Anita."

"Fredrick, this last arson didn't just kill the vampire father; his wife and two young children were trapped and died with him. It was all over the news yesterday. It was horrible."

"I am sorry that the vampire's family was caught in the fire, but there was no arson involved, Judith."

I said, "Someone opened the drapes to the parents' bedroom while the vampire was helpless after dawn. The sunlight fried him, but at least he probably didn't know what was happening to him. His wife and kids knew what was happening to them."

"Let us pray that smoke inhalation got to them first," he said.

"Practical, but vampires burn almost pure, no smoke. They burned to death because the wife tried to save her husband."

"She should have gotten her children out instead of trying to save the creature."

"He wasn't a creature, Dad!"

"Anything that bursts into flame with the touch of sunlight is evil, Anita."

"Fredrick, that's a horrible thing to say to Anita."

"It's the truth, Judith."

I turned around to look at Nicky. "This is never going to work, is it?"

"If you mean is your father going to walk you down the aisle to marry Jean-Claude, no. That's not happening."

"You can't answer for me, young man."

"Your prejudice is answering loud and clear, old man."

"How dare you . . ."

"Don't bother, Dad, you are older than Nicky." Then I realized that he might not be. Shapeshifters aged a lot slower than normal humans. Rafael the rat king was over fifty and he looked like thirty, at most.

Nicky smiled. "No, I'm not that old. I still match my packaging."

"You're not how old?" Dad asked.

"Sorry, Nicky read my mind. Skip it, Dad, just skip it."

"I have not made up my mind, Anita. I will try and meet this . . . fiancé of yours with some hope that I will see in him what you see."

I laughed; I couldn't help it. Jean-Claude dressed in silk, leather, and lace. He owned more high-heeled boots than I did. He'd taught me how to walk in heels and how to do my curls so they lay just right. He owned several clubs around town, including a strip club, which he occasionally still danced at—he was quietly fabulous, and not so quietly scrumptious. My dad with his khaki pants, polo shirts, and practical shoes would never have liked someone like Jean-Claude: vampire, human, or whatever. I couldn't have picked anyone less like my father.

"I don't see the humor," Dad said.

"I don't either, Dad, except you've seen him on TV and online, Jean-Claude I mean?"

"I have."

"If he were human, you still wouldn't like him."

"He's not the type of man that I expected you to marry."

"Who knew you were going to catch the most beautiful man in the world," Judith said.

"It's just rumors that Jean-Claude is in the running for *People*'s Sexiest Man."

"I'd vote for him," she said, and I turned in time to see her smile. I smiled back because she was really trying. I guess one of them had to.

"Honestly, I kind of hope he doesn't get it. The publicity around the wedding is getting out of hand now. If he gets that high-profile I don't know how bad it will get."

"No such thing as bad publicity," she said.

"I'm useless for undercover work now, because of all the wedding stuff online."

"I hadn't thought about it affecting your job, Anita. I'm sorry," she said.

I shrugged and realized she'd never see it around the car seat. "I didn't do much undercover, but now there's no way."

"The engagement video was like a fairy tale," she said.

"Yeah, I didn't even know there were such things as proposal consultants complete with videographers."

"Kirk took Andria to the Bahamas and there was a video, but nothing like yours. I half expected you to refuse to get in the horse-drawn carriage. It was everything you thought was stupid and romantic when you were a teenager."

"Yeah, I was pretty disdainful of all that romance stuff." Truthfully, I still was, and if my family had really been my family to the point where I could trust them to keep a secret, I could have told them that the *big* proposal had been the public one. The real one had been weeks earlier in the shower after sex. Jean-Claude had spontaneously proposed, and I had said yes. I think we'd both been shocked with that yes. I just wasn't really the marrying kind. Can we say commitment issues?

"Isn't your young man here upset that you're marrying someone else?"

"No, old man, the young man isn't upset about her marrying someone else," Nicky said.

"There was a time that saying 'young man' wasn't an insult."

"His name is Nicky, Dad."

"Fine, Nick, aren't you upset that Anita will be with just her husband if this wedding goes ahead?"

"Nicky, not Nick."

"Nicky, I meant no offense."

"Sure, and no, Anita isn't planning on being monogamous after the wedding, so I'll still be one of her lovers. It's a win-win for me."

"Anita, you will be taking vows, real marriage vows if this happens, correct?"

"Yep, if we avoid the religious extremes there are plenty of clergy happy to marry us, but we're not exchanging traditional vows. No language about honoring each other above all others or being exclusive or obeying anyone."

"It's not about the vows, Anita, it's holy matrimony. I may not like that you have so many . . . people in your life, but once you marry it will be adultery."

"Are you serious?" I asked, turning in my seat to see his face.

"About the Ten Commandments and your immortal soul, yes, very."

I moved so I could see Judith. She gave me wide eyes and a little *I'm sorry* shrug. Jesus, when did Judith become so much less religious? Then I had to think about that for a second. Had she ever been as much a zealot as Dad, or had she gone along with him because she was a good Catholic and a good wife? I suddenly started reviewing my childhood again and realized that when Dad and Grandma Blake got extremely religious about dogma, Judith just stopped talking. I tried to think of a single time in my childhood where she'd talked about sin, or shit like that. I thought and thought and couldn't come up with anything. Damn it, I did not want to like my wicked step-mother better than my own father.

"So you're okay with Anita breaking some of the commandments, just not the adultery one?" Nicky asked.

"I take all the commandments very seriously."

"You're okay with her killing."

"Vampires do not count against the Fifth Commandment."

"Because the Pope said so," I said.

"Not just that, but yes."

"Hell, Anita kills enough of what the Catholic Church thinks are monsters, shouldn't that offset anything else she does?" Nicky said.

"What do you mean?" Dad asked.

"Killing my way out of hell," I said.

"As long as it is self-defense and the slaying of evil, then she is clean in the eyes of the Church."

"You sound like Grandma Blake," I said.

"Your father has become more zealous over the years," Judith said.

"My daughter is consorting with demons; how could I not be wondering how I've failed as a parent and as a Catholic?"

"Oh no, no, this is not my fault. You decided to get all holier-than-thou on your own, and I am not consorting with demons. If you'd ever seen one for real you wouldn't use the term so loosely."

"His mother is worse," Judith said.

"Judith," he said, sounding a little outraged.

"It's the truth, Fredrick. You are zealous, but she is fanatical."

"So you're both just going to ignore the fact that Anita just said she'd seen real demons; that's not important or interesting to either of you?" Nicky said.

"It's like coming home bloodied from getting jumped in junior high because some kids got scared when a dead bird started following me around. Dad did first aid, but once they had the facts all they talked about was the church bake sale that week."

"So they always did this?" he asked.

I nodded.

"That fight was one of the reasons I agreed to send you to your Grandmother Flores," he said.

"Nice of you to tell me that at the time, Dad."

"I didn't want you to think that it was somehow your fault you were being sent away, just because you couldn't defend yourself."

"There were five of them."

"I taught you how to box."

"I'm small and a girl, Dad. Boxing isn't the best self-defense for that combo."

"I taught you what I knew, Anita."

"You never said your dad boxed."

"He was on his college boxing team."

Judith said, "He still practices at home."

"It's how I stay fit," he said.

"Demons," Nicky said. "Anita has seen real demons and you're super religious, but you don't have any questions about that?"

"Do you want to talk about seeing real demons in your job?" Judith asked. Damn it, she was really trying. Sometimes family is like having a crush; the boy you like is never the one that wants to walk you home.

"No, thank you for asking, Judith. I'm depressed enough without talking about things that disturbing."

"Why are you depressed?" my dad asked.

I looked at Judith. She looked at me. I looked at my dad. He looked back at me; nothing on his face showed that he understood why his question had been ridiculous. I sort of hated that Judith got it and my dad didn't, but that wasn't her fault, that was his.

Nicky took one hand off the steering wheel and laid it on my thigh and the silky thigh-highs I was wearing. I put my hand over his, and just that much touch helped me let out a deep breath and come back to my center, to me. I wasn't the little girl who needed my dad's protection and didn't get it anymore. I was all grown up, with all the benefits that came with it. I turned around in the seat so I could just hold his hand and feel the warmth of his hand through my hose. If we had been alone his hand could have reached far enough to find out I was wearing silk panties. Date night would have been so much more fun than dealing with my family.

I hadn't expected to be ambushed with my grandmother, but I'd been talking for weeks in therapy about protecting my boundaries. Learning that protecting myself physically and emotionally was not being disrespectful or mean; it didn't make me a bad daughter, but was simply self-care and demanding to be treated like the grown-up I had become, not the child they remembered. My grandmother being here didn't change any of that; in fact, it made it easier, because my dad had played dirty first. I'd told him over a month ago on the phone that she could not come on this visit. It wasn't that he hadn't asked me first, he'd done it after telling me he wouldn't. I could not let that stand or he and she would bully me the entire visit. I said the next part without turning around, because seeing his face would have made it harder. I stared at the dashboard of the SUV like I was trying to memorize it, and said, "When we come to pick you up for dinner, if Grandma Blake is dressed up and coming we won't be going to dinner tonight."

"I can't leave her alone at the hotel tonight, Anita," he said.

"Then Josh and Andria can arm-wrestle over who gets to stay with Grandma, but if she's at dinner you know that there will be no way for you to meet Jean-Claude without her making it all about her and her prejudices."

"Fredrick, Anita has a point."

"She came all this way, Judith. She got on a plane; you know she's afraid to fly."

I hadn't thought about the fact that my grandmother and I shared that phobia. She'd just always been afraid of anything she considered too high-tech, like planes. Mine had been a near accident that scared the pilot and flight crew, but it was still a shared phobia. I hated that we shared anything and thought again about that spark of magic at the airport.

I let go of Nicky's hand and turned so I could see them. "Dad, I'm not saying Grandma won't get to meet Jean-Claude this trip, I'm just saying not tonight."

"She'll never agree to it."

"I don't need her agreement. I've said she can't come tonight, and I mean it, Dad. I don't want to overwhelm Jean-Claude with too many people who think he's the spawn of Satan. One will be plenty."

"I have never called him that." He sounded indignant.

"You said you agree with the Church's view that marrying him imperils my immortal soul."

"It does."

"If you believe that, then which Church-sanctioned theory do you support: that he's a corpse that's demonically possessed, or a suicide that's damned to hell once he stops being the walking dead?"

"I . . ." My dad opened and closed his mouth, then didn't seem to know what to say.

"Thanks for making my point, Dad. Your hatred for the undead will be enough at dinner; I won't subject my future husband to you and Grandma doubling up on him tonight. I won't do it, so you have to man up and tell her she has to stay at the hotel tonight, or you can all get a good night's sleep, and we'll try again tomorrow night, but that means that the lunch I had planned so you could meet Micah and Nathaniel gets postponed."

"I don't see why we can't meet them as planned tomorrow," my dad said.

"Because if you meet Jean-Claude and can't get past the fact that he's a vampire, then why should I introduce you to anyone else in my life? I mean, would you come to visit me in St. Louis after the wedding and just never meet my husband?"

"No, of course not, I realize that I need to meet Jean-Claude first, but I do want to meet more of your poly . . . group."

"Really?" I said.

"Yes, if this is truly your preference, then I want to try and understand it. I can't promise that I won't at some point throw my hands up and say I can't deal with more, but I will try, Anita."

I didn't know whether to cry or not trust it. It sounded too good to be true after the rest of the conversation. "That's great, Dad, it gives me hope that this visit won't . . . suck."

"Anita, please, ladies do not say 'suck.'"

I sighed and turned around so I wouldn't have to look at him anymore. Nicky offered his hand again and I clung to it like a lifeline.

5

I'D HAVE RIDDEN the rest of the way to the hotel in silence, maybe Dad would have, too, but Judith couldn't stand it. She started talking about her real estate business and how Josh was doing in college. I did learn that he was double majoring in business and biology, which sounded like Judith and Dad's influence. I wondered if that was really what Josh wanted to major in; I'd find out before they flew back home if I could. When I'd left the parts of my family that hurt me, I'd abandoned Josh, too, so maybe he didn't owe me insight that would put him at odds with our dad and his mom? Josh and I had done FaceTime calls for a while, but Dad and Grandma couldn't leave it alone; they'd kept interrupting the calls. Josh was too much the peacemaker to defend our privacy, and I couldn't do it without his help.

Judith's progressively more forced conversation finally ended as Nicky pulled in behind the first of our SUVs; the second one pulled in behind us. Dad reached for his door handle. "Don't open the door, Mr. Blake," Nicky said.

Dad started to click the handle anyway, but Nicky hit the child locks so he couldn't. "Why are you trapping us in here?"

"It's your daughter's safety I'm worried about."

"What are you talking about?" Dad sounded irritated, bordering on angry.

"No one opens their door until another bodyguard is there to open Anita's door."

"Is it really that serious?" Judith asked.

"Is what that serious?" Dad asked.

"There are rumors about threats against Jean-Claude," Judith said.

"What rumors?" Dad asked.

"Fredrick, I told you that there were possible threats against Jean-Claude from some of the vampire hate groups."

"That was just one of those gossip sites, Judith. It's never true."

"Unfortunately, Dad, this one's true."

"Marrying this vampire is endangering your physical safety, on top of your immortal soul!"

I shook my head. "No, Dad, I've gotten threats for years."

"Why?" he asked.

"I'm an executioner, Dad; some of the people I've killed had families, loved ones."

"Oh," he said, as if it had never occurred to him before.

"Some of the vampires don't want Jean-Claude marrying me because I'm a necromancer and I've killed a lot of them over the years."

"See, this wedding is endangering you."

I turned in my seat, unbuckling the seat belt so I could turn and see him better now that the car wasn't moving. "Jean-Claude has more death threats now, because he's marrying me."

"Why?"

Nicky answered, "Anita has the highest kill count of any preternatural marshal, Mr. Blake. She's like a bogeyman to the supernatural set, especially the vampires."

"They see their king marrying me as him betraying them," I said.

"And the human hate groups see Anita marrying Jean-Claude as her betraying humanity," Nicky said.

"You must love each other very much to go up against all that," Judith said.

I looked at her, and her face looked soft, genuine, like she meant it. "Yeah, only true love gets you through shit like this."

"Must you cuss constantly?" my father said.

I looked at his unfriendly face and had to resist saying a string of curse words he hadn't heard from me yet. "Must you constantly correct how I speak?"

"Anita's life is in danger, and you're more worried about her vocabulary," Nicky said.

"That is not true," Dad said.

"That's how it's coming across, Dad."

He blinked and looked at Judith. Apparently she could read his expression better than I could because she answered his silent question. "It does seem like we could forgive Anita's language just this once and concentrate on the threats against her and her husband-to-be."

He stared at her for a second, then put his hand over hers and turned to me. "If I have made it seem as if your safety is secondary to anything, then I apologize."

"Thanks, Dad, good to hear."

"I hadn't thought about how the vampires might view someone with your job, Anita. They must hate you the way that some of the human hate groups hate vampires."

"Pretty much."

Nicky patted my thigh and motioned with his head toward my window. Ethan was there waiting for me to notice; that I hadn't meant I was even more out of it than I thought. If the bad guys had attacked in that moment they could have shot me through the window without me even realizing it. Yes, I had a herd of security people just outside the car, helping unload the luggage. I'd notice the fight that would have broken out before they got that close to me, or Nicky throwing himself on top of me like a meat shield, but still, I was the only one with a badge in our group currently and I should have been paying better attention.

"Wait until Anita is safely out . . . please," Nicky said behind me. I was betting my father had reached for his door again. Ethan opened my door and offered me a hand. Normally I not only didn't need it but got pissed if it was offered; sometimes in really high heels I took the help, but it was more than that. The moment his hand touched mine I felt that hum of energy that was always there for the sharing with my animals to call. The warmth of it spilled over me like a blanket, so that by the time I was standing I leaned into his body so he could put one arm around me and keep the other free for weapons. I was armed, and normally I'd keep my hand free, but . . . I started to lean away, to be prepared, but Ethan tightened his arm slightly and leaned over me so he could whisper, "I've got this, Anita, just take the comfort for a second."

I hesitated, then let myself lean into him and share the energy between us: safe. *Safe* it said, *home* it said, because that had been Ethan's heart's desire when I met him, and the echo of that was still there between us. It was one of the gentlest connections I had, maybe because Ethan was gentle, or maybe because he was in true love with someone else so there was no pressure for more between us. Whatever caused it, in that moment it was exactly what I needed: comfort with no strings.

"Is this another of your . . . young men?" my dad asked.

I drew back from Ethan, but he kept his arm around me, so I stayed in the circle of his comfort. Before I could answer my dad, Andria came up to us and answered for me. "Yes, he's part of her poly group."

"Dad, this is Ethan Flynn," I said.

Ethan offered his hand to my father as Nicky walked around the front of the SUV and joined us. Dad took the hand and shook it. When that handshake was finished my dad turned to Nicky and offered his hand. "We didn't get to do this at the airport."

Nicky hesitated a second, then shook hands with him. "You take care of Anita the way Judith does for me. I noticed in the car, and if you're that important to my daughter, then I want to know you better." He looked at Ethan and said, "Both of you."

Ethan looked at me. I had no idea what to say, because Ethan was Nilda's love of her life, not mine, and Nicky's background was too tragic and too illegal to share with my dad. "I really appreciate that, Dad, seriously."

"You're welcome and I'm sorry you're having to thank me for common courtesy toward the men in your life, Anita. I should be able to do at least that."

I thought about hugging him, but I didn't really want to, and if you don't want to touch someone, even family, you shouldn't touch them. I stayed with one arm around Ethan. Nicky moved back from the handshake to be on my other side, so if anyone else had wanted to hug me they'd have to get between us. I didn't think Dad would do that, but he never got a chance because Magda started our way. She stalked toward us with that warrior swagger that she used sometimes when she wanted to provoke a fight so she could prove she could back it up, or when she was insecure about a situation, which wasn't often. She was five-ten, with thick blond hair that looked even more yellow brushing the shoulders of her all-over black outfit: lightweight jacket to hide weapons at her waist, tucked-in T-shirt, leather belt with a blackened buckle, tactical pants tucked into the tops of tac boots. I had outfits just like it. Nicky had dressed to look more normal in dress pants, shoes, and the leather jacket that was too warm for tonight, but he looked like he'd dressed for a "normal" person's date night. I hadn't realized until that second that he'd dressed to meet my family. Magda had not. She'd dressed to look like the badass she was, aggressive and unapologetically not feminine. I loved her in that moment, and wished I'd dressed to match instead of dressed up to impress my family.

I must have stared too long because my dad looked behind him, and then Judith did because he did. Magda offered her hand to my dad, and he took it automatically while he gazed up at her. He'd raised me to give good eye contact when you shake hands. Some people thought it was aggressive, I just thought it was normal, but Magda wasn't hooked into me metaphysically, so she took it as a power play.

She smiled at him, and I knew that smile. I could have stepped in and stopped whatever she was about to say, but I didn't. "I hope it's not just the men in Anita's life, but all of us," she said.

Andria stifled a laugh. Judith did a little gasp. Dad didn't get it as fast as they did. I didn't have to see his face to know he was frowning up at Magda. I could tell by the set of his shoulders that he was caught off guard and thinking about what she'd said. I think if the other two women hadn't reacted to it, he might have just not caught it at all. We were about to see whether my dad would hate me dating women more than me marrying a vampire.

6

HE LET GO of Magda's hand and turned to me. "Anita . . ."

"Yes, Dad."

"What did she mean by that?"

"By what?" I asked. I realized I didn't want to make this easy on him, which meant I was angry and doing it out of anger. That wasn't cool, because I wanted him to like Magda and the other women in our poly group, and being petty and bitchy wasn't going to accomplish that. It was just so tempting, and the smile on Magda's face said she would help me do it. Soooo tempting.

Nicky whispered, "I'll support whatever you do, but is this the right play before dinner tonight?"

Ethan leaned in and whispered, "What he said."

I sighed, closed my eyes for a second, then shook my head.

"Does that mean this woman is . . . teasing me about your . . . her." He stopped; he knew it wasn't a complete sentence but didn't seem to know how to finish it, so he just looked at me with an almost pleading look in his blue eyes.

Magda looked at me, the smile fading out of her gray-blue eyes first, then leaving her face. She'd let me pretend if that was what I decided to do, but she'd never forgive me. I wanted to make sure she understood that wasn't what I was thinking at all.

"Dad, this is Magda Sanderson," I said, and left the security blanket of Nicky and Ethan to go forward and hold out my hand to Magda. The smile was back on her face as she wrapped her bigger hand around mine.

He looked at our hands first, then at us together. He actually went a little pale, eyes blinking rapidly. "Are you . . . dating . . . her?"

Technically we didn't date, unless you counted gym time and sex; we did a lot of both of those. Since I couldn't figure out how to explain that *dating* wasn't quite the right term I just said, "Yes, we are."

Magda squeezed my hand, letting me know how happy she was that I'd just said it, no overexplaining. It made me feel better about myself and the visit. I could just tell them the truth about my life; it was up to them to deal with it. What a freeing thought.

"I think you're needed at the luggage," Nicky said, and if it had been almost anyone else I'd have thought he was jealous, but that wasn't it. He was pulling rank as leader, Rex of their lion pride. I didn't want to know what Magda had done to make him feel like he needed to do it, but I'd learned that if I interfered in the small things between the werelions, they turned into big things.

"As my—" She almost said *Rex*, but finished with "Of course." She didn't even smile at me before she went back to all business. I'd ask Nicky about it later.

"Fredrick, I did tell you that there were women in Anita's poly group," Judith said.

He turned to her. "But that was pictures of Jean-Claude with other women on his arm, or Anita and another woman with them. I don't remember seeing any pictures with Anita and a woman without at least Jean-Claude with them."

I fought the urge to ask why that mattered, but luckily the rest of our security rescued us from the awkward possibilities. "Hey, boss, the luggage is inside, along with your grandmother and brother."

"Well, hello," said Judith, offering her hand, "are you another of

Anita's poly group?" Her reaction and Andria gazing up at Custer made me do a double take at him. It wasn't that I didn't know he was tall, dark-haired, and traditionally handsome, but to me he was Custer, nicknamed Custard, or Pudding, or just Pud by his fellow former Navy SEALs that we'd hired when they popped hot for therianthropy. They'd become wereanimals in defense of our country, and then that same country had said, *Thank you for your service, but if you can't pass a basic blood test to prove you're still human, then you get a medical discharge.*

"No, ma'am, I just work here," Custer said to Judith's question.

"Does that mean you're single?" Andria asked.

"You're engaged," my dad said.

Custer looked pleasant but puzzled as he said, "Yes, but you're my boss's sister, so it doesn't matter."

"What's that mean?" Andria asked.

"It means that they won't risk their jobs to flirt with you," Nicky said.

"You're engaged to Kirk, you shouldn't be flirting with anyone," Judith said.

"Nothing wrong with feeling admired, Mom."

"Kirk should be making you feel admired," Dad said.

Did that mean that Andria's fiancé wasn't making her feel attractive? I hoped not, because if you were having trouble when you were only engaged, that didn't bode well for the marriage. "Do you have a date set for the wedding yet?" I asked.

"Not yet, do you?" she asked, and she sounded hostile. I didn't take it personally; I shouldn't have asked about wedding dates when she was already upset about the topic. Her reaction let me know that there was something seriously wrong with her and Kirk.

"December, though we're still trying to get everything lined up for the exact date," I said.

"A Christmas wedding!" Judith gushed, face alight with what

looked like genuine happiness about it. She actually grabbed me in a huge, spontaneous hug. I was so caught off guard I just stood there and let it happen, even giving her an awkward pat on the back.

"If it's not until December, then why do I have to come now for my suit fitting?" my dad said.

I extracted myself from Judith and said, "Because it's not a suit fitting, it's the tailor taking your measurements and he and the seamstress creating a bespoke outfit for the wedding."

"There will be at least two more fittings after this one," Nicky said.

"Two more!" Dad looked shocked, maybe even a little horrified.

"If it's too much trouble . . ." I started to say.

"No, I want to walk you down the aisle, Anita, I just . . . I don't think I've ever been to a wedding that was this . . . fancy."

"Me either," I said.

"If it's fancier than the engagement video," Andria said, "then short of royalty, no one has."

"Jean-Claude is royalty," Judith said, as if Andria should have remembered.

Andria rolled her eyes in an expression I'd endured throughout our teens. It always meant she wasn't impressed. It pissed me off even after all these years, and it was my only excuse for what I said next. "But don't worry, Andria, you won't have to address me as queen."

"What?" she asked.

Nicky touched my shoulder, but I was already sorry I'd said it. "Sorry, Andria, I'm a little weirded out by the whole marrying-a-king thing. I said yes to Jean-Claude, not to a king."

"He's just king of the vampires, that's not a real legal title." She had that edge of whine in her voice that went with the eye roll. Was she that upset that I'd asked about her wedding date? If so, then her wedding was a very touchy subject. I wondered if Judith knew what was going on. I knew Dad didn't. He'd be as oblivious of that as he was anything else he didn't want to see.

"You're right, it's an empty title as far as the U.S. government is concerned."

"Then why use it at all?" she asked.

"Ask Jean-Claude at dinner, he'll explain it better than I will."

Nicky put his arm around my shoulders as he said, "We need to go home and pick up Jean-Claude if we're going to make the reservation."

"Oh, look at the time," Judith said, "we better hurry if we're going to be ready by the time you come to pick us up." She grabbed Andria's arm to pull her toward the hotel.

Dad lingered and looked at me with Nicky's arm around me and Ethan standing close by. "Am I meeting anyone else tonight besides Jean-Claude?"

"Just Jean-Claude," I said.

Nicky said, "Ethan and I will be nearby at another table, as will other security for Jean-Claude."

"Are any of the other security guards part of the poly group?"

"Some," I said, "but they'll be at tables nearby and only Jean-Claude and I will be sitting with you."

"How many of your group will be here tonight, Anita?"

"We don't plan on springing them on you tonight, Dad, so you don't have to worry about meeting anyone else but Jean-Claude."

"But if they're there tonight, won't they think it's rude if I ignore them?"

I stared at him for a second, then said, "I really appreciate your concern, Dad, really, but anyone there tonight will be more concerned about our security than meeting my family."

"If you're sure, Anita, I don't want to be unintentionally rude to your . . . people." He looked so sincere standing there that I hugged him, and I meant it. I didn't know what would happen later tonight, but in this moment he was really trying.

7

THE HUGGING ENDED and Nicky said, "We really do need to go if we're going to make the reservation."

I glanced around and found that the rest of the family was inside the hotel. I saw Magda and the rest of our security through the glass front of the hotel; my family was hidden behind them except for Josh, who towered over half of them. It was going to take me a while to get used to him being that tall.

"I better join the rest of the family," Dad said.

"And I need to go pick up Jean-Claude so we can meet you at the restaurant."

"I thought we were all driving together to the restaurant," he said.

I smiled brightly the way I would at work if I wanted to be pleasant but didn't mean it, because I'd realized that there was no way on God's green earth that I wanted Jean-Claude and me to be trapped in a car on the drive to the restaurant with them. I had options, and that included telling security to drive my family to the restaurant and we'd meet them there. Jean-Claude and I could drive separately and only be subjected to the interrogation during the meal.

My father just agreed and walked toward the hotel doors. Ethan waited until we wouldn't be overheard, then said, "You already feel better."

"Taking more control always makes me feel better."

"We need to let everyone know the change of plans," Nicky said.

"You don't approve?" I asked.

"No, I think you're right that your family will be more polite in a public restaurant than in the limo driving over like the original plan."

"Yeah, though now Jean-Claude rented a limo to impress my family and they won't be riding in it."

"If the dinner goes well, maybe they can ride back in the limo with you," Ethan said.

"Maybe," I said.

"I think Milligan and Custer should drive your family to the restaurant," Nicky said.

"Because I'm not dating either of them," I said.

"That and they both look more like your father expects security guards to look."

"He'll like that they're ex-military," I said.

"He doesn't seem like he was ever in the military," Nicky said.

"He wasn't, but he's just very guy-guy, so he likes people who don't make him think too hard about what's traditionally female and traditionally male."

"Wait, I thought your dad raised you to be a tomboy?" Ethan asked.

"He did, he just assumed I'd grow out of it and turn into a girl at some point."

Nicky put his arm around my shoulders and said, "You look like a girl to me." He kissed the top of my head and drew in a deep breath, gathering the scent of me the way other men would look at you. I'd thought it was kind of creepy when wereanimals did it at first, but now, years later, it was comforting. I'd even started doing it myself. I wanted to do it now but wasn't sure how much my makeup would stand up to rubbing against his shirt. I compromised and reached up for his hand on my shoulder and breathed in the scent of his skin, though hands smell more of everything you've touched. If I really wanted to huff him I'd go for the back of the neck or bury my face against his bare chest. I pressed my mouth against the back of his hand and left a very careful lip print against his skin. It made me happy to see my mark on him.

He made a sound that was halfway between a growl and a purr. If someone had been close enough to hear they'd have looked around for an animal, a very big cat. I hugged him tighter to me. "I'll have to wash it off before dinner."

"Why?" I asked, loosening my arms so I could look up at him.

"If people see it they'll ask questions."

"I don't care about strangers, and my family knows we're dating."

"It's usually you that wears my marks," he said, leaning down.

"Your marks are a lot more fun than lipstick," I said, and shivered a little as I thought about his teeth marks decorating my body. I leaned up, still shivering, to meet his lips in another careful kiss.

He drew back and said, "When all this is over I want to kiss you like normal and spread that damn lipstick all over your face."

"You'll ruin the makeup."

"That's the idea," he said, and the look on his face made me want to say *let's do it now and to hell with the dinner*, but that wasn't just me wanting to be with Nicky, that was me being afraid of dinner with my family and Jean-Claude. I couldn't chicken out.

"Later," I said.

"You'll be with Jean-Claude later."

"I'll have them do full makeup on me one night just for you," I said.

He gave me a fierce grin. "No waterproof mascara, I want to see you cry black tears for me."

I just smiled and nodded. Ethan had to keep us on track to get back in the SUV and head for home to pick up Jean-Claude. I wanted to see my main squeeze, but delay meant delaying the dinner where I introduced my family to him. I loved him and I loved them, and I was about to be put in the middle of all of them.

8

THE BRIGHT LIGHTS of the Circus of the Damned looked like a flashing neon dawn in the distance; from here we couldn't see the giant vampire clowns twirling slowly on top and its garish posters advertising the acts inside. *See vampires fly!* It was our trapeze act under the permanent big top. *See the Lamia half snake half woman! Professor Wolf trapped as half man and half wolf reads his latest poetry live for this week only! See the skinless horror of the Nuckelavee!* We wouldn't get to see the front of the building tonight. We didn't have the time to get caught in the traffic jam that started after dark and continued until the Circus closed for the night.

The first time I'd gone to the Circus it had been helping the police with a vampire-related case, but the first time I saw the underground part of the Circus, where no customers were allowed to go, that was because the old Master of the City, Nikolaos, wanted to see me. I'd tried to say no, but you don't refuse the Master of the City and live. Jean-Claude had shared the first vampire mark with me to save my life, and the second to save his. The rest, as they say, was history.

Ethan drove us around to the back where the bright lights and eager crowds out front weren't allowed. The employee parking lot was off-limits to customers, but the most off-limits part was what lay at the bottom of a set of stone steps so old that they'd been here before the building over it was built. The vampires said that the stairs were here when the city of St. Louis was outfitting people for the California gold rush and the Oregon Trail. The steps had always led down to the cave system that ran under more of the city than most people realized. Hell, most didn't even know the caves were there, but I knew. First because I almost died in them and second because now I lived in them half the time. I'd tried living in them full time, but I needed sunlight. All of us who weren't vampires needed more sunlight, so we rotated between the underground and houses/apartments elsewhere. Jean-Claude owned safe houses that were just for his nonvampire employees to rack out at, so they didn't grow depressed and ill from lack of natural light.

The three of us stood in the little storage room staring through the open door at the stairs that fell away in front of us until they were lost to sight—and that was before the bend in the stairs; literally they were so long that when you stared from the top they vanished from sight. The outer door that led from the parking lot into here was to our left, and behind us was a door that led to the midway of the carnival with smaller, more intimate shows that didn't work in the huge Circus tent just off the main entrance. There was a full-size Ferris wheel and other rides, plus food booths and games like a traveling carnival that had settled down permanently. Out there it was so loud that it was hard to have a conversation unless you wanted to yell loud enough for strangers to hear, but in here it was utterly quiet. The soundproofing had originally been put in place by Nikolaos, the last Master of the City, so that the happy families buying cotton candy wouldn't hear the victims screaming for help.

"The first time I saw the back of the Circus I thought I'd never get out of here alive, and now I'm the boss."

"Queen," Ethan said.

I glanced back at him, then turned back to stare down the stairs. "Yeah, queen, or about to be." Sometimes I wondered how things had ended up this way. The me that had been threatened and nearly killed before I even got to the stairs had believed sincerely just like my dad. Vampires were inhuman monsters, trapped outside of God's love and mercy. The me standing here now knew beyond doubt that not only were vampires not all monsters without Grace, but that human beings could be lost souls beyond any redemption. The only difference from the Church's perspective was that vampires were dead, so they couldn't repent, but the bloodiest serial killer could still be saved if they were truly repentant. I'd met serial killers both undead and alive, and they weren't savable. What they had done to their victims put them outside of God's Grace or the salvation of Jesus Christ. I believed that sincerely now. I was suddenly peaceful. I wasn't the same girl who came here ten years ago, because I'd seen too much, endured too much, killed too many people, to be the same person. It's not just years that age you, it's events.

A figure rounded the bend in the stairs all that way down, and before my eyes told me who, the energy we shared danced over my skin as if he'd brushed his fingertips over parts of my body that were hidden under my clothes. I shivered as I watched him lift off the steps and start floating toward me. It made me laugh and say, "Now there's a solution to all these damned steps."

He rose toward the ceiling, his long black hair spilling out around him like a dark aura. His hair wasn't streaming out around him because he was flying toward me but moving in the wind of his own power, so that his black curls writhed and boiled like a dozen hands were playing with it, but it was his magic, just his magic.

He needed one of his usual lace, leather, and sexy-boots outfits for all that hair to frame, but he was dressed in one of only two modern suits I'd ever seen him in; the first time it had been to save the feelings of a grieving family, and this time we were trying not to give my father any other reason to hate him. In that moment I knew I didn't care if my dad liked him or not. I loved Jean-Claude and nothing my dad did would change that.

He landed lightly on first one foot, then the other, until he stood beside me at the top of the stairs. I wrapped my arms around him, but the traditionally long suit jacket felt wrong on him. He either did no jacket or some version of a bolero so that it hit him somewhere between his lower ribs and just below his natural waist. He had a fabulous ass, and it seemed a shame to cover it up.

He wrapped his arms around me and laughed. "*Ma petite*, we chose this suit precisely so it would cover more of my body, so I did not shock your family."

I stared up into that beautiful face with the darkest blue eyes I'd ever seen, set in thick black lashes with a perfect curve of eyebrows that were all natural; he didn't even need mascara. So unfair to the rest of us. His face was almost feminine in its beauty, but there was something about the line of his chin that turned all that gorgeousness a little more masculine. He was still androgynous, but it leaned a little more to the male side. The long black curls framed his face and trailed down his shoulders almost to his waist. My family thought long hair was only for girls. Putting him in a traditional men's suit really didn't make him look more like the type of man my family would approve of, but hey, at least we were trying.

"I won't ever look into your face without thinking how beautiful you are, and why are you marrying me?"

"I believe that is the man's line, *ma petite*."

I grinned and said, "Traditionally it is, but most men don't look like you."

"That you compare yourself to me and think yourself the lesser beauty means you do not see truth when you look into the mirror, *ma petite*."

"I second that," Nicky said.

I glanced at him and couldn't help but smile at the look on his face. "I know I don't always see the truth in the mirror. Nicky and Ethan have met who messed me up." I turned back to Jean-Claude. "That delight is still ahead of you."

"I am looking forward to it, *ma petite*, and before you complain I

would give much if my mother and sister were alive for me to introduce you to them. That I can meet your family, however broken, is
a gift to me."

"Please tell me you're not saying that I should be grateful for
them regardless?"

"Don't answer until you think about it, Jean-Claude," Nicky said.
"I know you heard or felt some of it. You're too connected to Anita
metaphysically to have missed it all."

Jean-Claude went quiet in my arms as if he was starting to pull
away, but I shook him a little. "Don't do the whole statue thing
where your body doesn't feel human anymore. You know I hate that."

"I do not want you to read what I am thinking, *ma petite*, because
it might make you angry with me, and we need a united front at
dinner."

I hugged him tighter, feeling the suit jacket and hating it because
it didn't feel like him; even the high-collared mandarin shirt that
was a royal blue to match the blue in my own outfit wasn't enough
to set it apart and make it his style. "You're right, but promise me
this is the last meeting with my family where you dress like this. It
feels like I'm hugging you in someone else's clothes."

He smiled. "Very well, I will dress as I please except for tonight's
dinner."

"Good, now let's get this disaster over with," I said.

"Of course, but first a kiss, *ma petite*."

"I'm sorry," I said.

"For what?" he asked.

"That I didn't kiss you already; nothing should make me forget
that, not even my family."

He gave me that smile that wasn't for the stage, or publicity, or
all the hundreds of photos where he was always smiling perfectly,
posing. This smile wasn't for the camera, it was for me. It was a smile
that said he loved me, trusted me, and it wasn't perfect, but to me it
was the most perfect of all.

9

ETHAN HAD TO change from tactical to a suit before he accompanied us to the restaurant; all Nicky needed was to replace the leather jacket with the jacket that matched the pants. We started down the steps, but Jean-Claude caught me around the waist and lifted me to the step he was standing on. "I know the shoes are not as comfortable as some," he said, leaning over me so that he could whisper, "but I would very much like to undress you until those shoes are all that remain." He pressed his mouth against my hair and breathed the last few words. "And we make love with them wrapped around my waist, and over my shoulders, and . . ."

"Sorry to interrupt," Ethan said, "but if Anita isn't coming downstairs to change the shoes we have to stay up here to guard her and you."

Jean-Claude raised his face enough to gaze down at them. "We are in our inner sanctuary; surely here we are safe."

Nicky and Ethan shook their heads in unison. Ethan said, "We're already breaking the rules by having just Nicky and me on guard duty for both of you. It's supposed to be a minimum of two guards per protectee."

"And our inner sanctum is down the stairs behind the big door," Nicky said, "not here, where we have two doors that are easily accessible from the public areas. I'm honestly surprised that the Wicked Truth let you out of their sight this close to the exits."

"We had little choice when he ordered us to wait out of sight," Wicked said, as he turned the bend in the stairs to start walking up toward us. I thought he was wearing a black suit with a deep blue shirt until the light showed that it was navy. It reminded me of Jean-Claude's eyes, though it was an even darker shade of blue. The colors made his shoulder-length blond hair look more yellow than usual, as the blue shirt brought out the blue in his blue-gray eyes, so that his eyes were the most vibrant blue I'd ever seen him have. It must have been the shirt color. Wicked was always beautiful with a face formed of very masculine angles, but there was a deep dimple in his chin, a line here and there that made his face beautiful but almost painfully masculine. It matched the wide shoulders and the athletic way he moved up the steps. He was so male, not at all the androgynous beauty that I preferred in my men, but just because it wasn't my preferred look didn't mean I couldn't admire the view.

"Why would you order them out of sight when you're this close to the exits?" Nicky asked.

"I wanted to make an entrance," Jean-Claude said in that neutral voice he used when he wasn't lying but he wasn't telling the whole truth either.

There was a knock on the door that led out into the public area of the Circus. It got Ethan and Nicky up the stairs in double time. Wicked called out, "It's Truth; we refused to both hide on the stairs. It was too far away in case something went wrong."

Nicky and Ethan kept coming until they stood beside us as the door opened and Truth stepped through. His suit looked almost identical to his brother's—hell, it might have been his brother's suit, because left to his own devices Truth was a jeans-and-T-shirt kind of guy. Truth had suits of his own for when he needed to dress up for work, but since they were the same size in every way, they could trade clothes. They were brothers; they'd been sharing clothes and life in general for centuries.

Truth's shirt was a soft gray with a silver tie; as he got closer to us the suit stayed black, no play of color, so his eyes looked solid gray with all the blue drained out of them. His face was almost a mirror of his brother's: a little narrower through the cheeks, a shade less square through the jaw, but you had to know their faces intimately to see it. Truth's hair was brown, not blond, and it had a little bit of wave to it, unlike Wicked's board-straight hair. It was also maybe a couple of inches longer.

They were so handsome that men and some women didn't like standing next to them, because they took too much attention away. That Jean-Claude stood between them as his bodyguards almost nightly said just how secure he was in his own beauty. The only reason you'd look at anyone else with Jean-Claude standing there was if you wanted your men utterly masculine with not a drop of androgyny; then you might prefer the brothers.

They were my security with benefits, but my plate was overflowing with emotional dating relationships. I didn't have time or energy to devote to them and they deserved that from someone, so I'd been low-key trying to fix them up with other people. Wicked had taken up the chance to date—read "sleep with"—more women, but Truth had refused. He was like some knight of old, devoted to my service. For all I knew he'd been a knight for real at some point, but whatever the reason, he had asked me to stop matchmaking, so I had. The women that Wicked had dated had gotten the word around that if you just wanted good sex, he was great, but if you wanted more, date someone else. So to save the women's feelings, I'd stopped matchmaking for Wicked, too.

"Looking snazzy there, Truth," I said, and got the expected frown when he wasn't in jeans.

"Don't tease him, Anita, I had a hard enough time getting him to wear the new suit," Wicked said as he came up into the storeroom with us.

"Sorry, Wicked," I said, turning to look at his brother again. "You look very handsome tonight, Truth."

"No offense to Jean-Claude's preference for dressing up, but when is the next casual date going to be so I can wear my jeans while I'm on duty?" Truth looked so uncomfortable that we all laughed, except for Nicky.

Nicky said, "You can always pair up with me on Anita's detail if you want more casual clothes on the job."

Truth shook his head. "Wicked and I are a team, always."

"You just offered that to irritate me," Wicked said.

Nicky grinned. "A little bit, but Truth's style is closer to Anita's, just like your designer suits match Jean-Claude's vibe more."

"Did you just say 'vibe'?" Ethan asked.

Nicky said, "Yeah, what about it?" He gave Ethan a look.

Ethan held up his hands like he'd meant no offense. "Perfectly good word."

I smiled at them both. Jean-Claude turned me in his arms, so I was looking up into his face. "Damn, you are gorgeous," I said, still smiling, but it was a different smile. Until the last few years, I hadn't understood that I had different kinds of smiles. Jean-Claude hugged me. I tried to put my face against his chest like normal, but the suit just didn't feel like him. I had to pull away and look up at his face, as if I was double-checking.

"If you were any other woman I would return the compliment, but I will do as you requested while your family is visiting and not tell you that you are beautiful."

"Thank you, I know it's weird, but my therapist said it would help me not to dwell on those issues and free me up to concentrate on the issues that have to be addressed while they're here."

"Like the fact that they hate vampires and you're marrying one," Nicky said.

"Yeah, that one," I said, looking at him.

"I can feel you delaying because you don't want to go, but it's my job to make sure you do, so Ethan and I will go downstairs and change. I know you're not going to change shoes now."

"We will guard them until you return," Truth said.

Nicky nodded at him and started down the stairs. Ethan followed without a word like he so often did. I'd asked him about it once, and he said, "I can feel what you're feeling, hear your thoughts, so why should I say all that out loud?" I'd asked why the rest of my animals to call talked more, then. His reply was, "You'll have to ask them." A perfect Ethan answer.

Truth moved closer to the door to the parking lot, so he was between us and the potentially scary outdoors. Wicked got a tie out of his jacket pocket and started putting it on. The tie was the same dark navy as the suit with a tiny pattern of brighter blue fleur-de-lis running through it.

"Seeing you without your tie already in place is almost like seeing you nude in public," I said, smiling.

He grinned. "I had trouble deciding on the tie, and you can see me nude anytime you want, just extend the invitation."

The far door to the public part of the Circus opened again. Wicked put himself more squarely between the door and us, but it was a crowd of the security guards in their Halloween-orange shirts that read *Circus of the Damned* in big letters on the front with tiny letters saying *Security* underneath. *Security* in big letters was on the back. Three of them came through the door like an orange wall; they and the four guards behind them were all five-ten or taller with imposing physiques so they almost hid the equally tall figure between them, but the bright red cloak that covered him top to bottom was too eye-catching not to see. That was one reason Asher wore it for the opening of his part as ringmaster, but he didn't exit his performance for the night still wearing it, surrounded by guards.

The last man through the door closed it and stood guard beside it. The moment he did that I knew there'd be someone else on the other side in the same stance. I also knew that something had gone very wrong.

"What has happened?" Jean-Claude asked.

Asher pulled his hood down, spilling all that wavy golden hair around his face, but the cloak kept the hair from falling free so that it mounded up, hiding most of his face except for glimpses of his pale blue eyes and the face that had made people paint him as Cupid and other Greek Gods centuries before I was born.

Jamie, one of the security guards who was so clean-cut All-American college kid that even I wanted to card him every time I saw him, said, "One of the people in the meet and greet hit him."

Asher turned on him, snarling and showing fangs; for a second he was frightening, the beast showing through the beauty. "And is it not your job to keep that from happening?"

Jamie backed up, holding his hands up as if to show he was unarmed or meant no offense. "Yes, it is our job."

The vampire's power just folded away, and he was all beauty again, the beast gone so fast it was like a switch had been thrown—on monster, off leading man. "Then how did a human hit me hard enough to break the custom-made mask I was wearing?"

Jean-Claude grabbed Asher's arm. "Are you hurt?"

He finally turned to face us and there was a cut on his cheek about two inches long; it wasn't bleeding much yet, but it was there. An angry red line above where the holy water scars started. The Church fathers had tried to burn the devil out of Asher one drop of holy water at a time, but even those long-dead priests hadn't been willing to damage his ice-blue eyes, the perfect line of nose to that kissable mouth. I had been wondering if one of the reasons they took him for torture and not immediate execution as they usually did with vampires back then was because one or more of the Church fathers involved had been attracted to his beauty. Attracted to it, so they had to destroy it, but too enamored of his face to be willing to ruin it completely.

Jean-Claude reached up to touch the small wound, but Asher grabbed his hand, saying, "I was cut where his fist broke the porcelain against my skin. What kind of master vampire am I that porcelain and human strength could slice my flesh?"

"The guy was huge," Jamie said, "superstrong for a human."

"Tell me about it," one of the newer security said, turning his face to show off the swelling on his face right next to his eye. His name was Kirby, and I still wasn't sure if it was his first or last name. "If I'd been human he'd have broken my orbital bone, or maybe worse."

I almost asked what was worse than breaking the bone around your eye, but I already knew that you could pierce the eye itself and squish it like a grape. I'd done it once to save myself from being the unwilling star of a rape/snuff film. I was glad I'd been willing to do it and save myself, but it wasn't a sensation I wanted to dwell on, and I hoped to never, ever do it again.

"Are you hurt anywhere else?" Jean-Claude asked.

"I am fine." Asher sounded bitter when he said it, but it was more anger than physical pain.

I went to stand in front of him and look up into that amazing face. He moved his head just enough so I couldn't see the scars on the right side. I hated that he was hiding from me again; he'd almost stopped. "Something else is wrong," I said.

I asked, "I know you wouldn't all be here if he'd escaped, but who's holding him for the cops?"

"Claudia was walking the floor tonight to check on some of the new security additions," Jamie said.

"Our would-be Hercules wasn't expecting a six-foot-six Hispanic Amazon to show up. The look on his face was almost worth getting hit." Kirby grinned, then winced.

"He called himself a Spartoi," Lelio said. He was the darkest-skinned of this group of security, but whatever people guessed about his heritage they were always wrong. They weren't being racist, or stupid, it was just that no one was ever going to guess that he belonged to an extinct branch of the species tree that *Homo sapiens* now thought it was the only survivor of, except for truly ancient vampires and equally ancient wereanimals that called the ancient vampires *master*, as far as I knew. I'd stopped speaking in absolutes about some things, and this was one of them. I was still wrapping my head around the fact that among the oldest vampires were some of our original humanoid ancestors, direct or not so direct. I could answer the question now about whether our ancient relatives could speak like we do. They could be and often were more articulate than most of the *Homo sapiens* I ran into daily. I was still trying to persuade one of them to talk to someone in ancient anthropology, archaeology, or one of the many specialties that would lose their shit at the opportunity, but so far they'd all refused on the grounds that they didn't want the humans to know they were still alive.

"I thought he said 'Spartan,'" Kirby said.

"No, he said 'Spartoi,'" Lelio said.

"I don't know the word," I said.

"It's Greek; beyond that I do not know. I will ask those of my brethren who spent more time in ancient Greece than I did if they are familiar with it."

Jean-Claude brushed Asher's hair aside until he could see his face more clearly. Asher jerked away at first, then apologized. "It is just that until tonight I was the mysterious and beautiful ringmaster of the Circus of the Damned, but now . . . the video of my deformity is already on the internet."

"There were people with their phones ready," Jamie said.

Kirby said, "There were some women and maybe a man with the attacker. They had their cameras ready."

"They were the only ones in the crowd that showed no surprise at the attack," Lelio said, "but they seemed surprised or even disappointed that Asher wasn't more inhuman under his mask."

"They expected me to be like the Norse Goddess Hel, with half my face skeletal or rotting," Asher said.

"They said that, out loud?" I asked.

"Not the Goddess Hel, but it was the only metaphor I could think of, once my attacker yelled at me, angry that I was not a rotting corpse under the mask. One of the women with him said something about where are the bones."

I went for the door, but Wicked blocked my way. "Anyone who would attack Asher could see you as a target, Anita."

Lelio said, "The attacker and the entire group are detained, awaiting the police."

"Claudia and the rest of us have it handled, Anita, I swear," Jamie said.

"I believe you, Jamie, I do. It feels weird to stay away from the emergency."

"It's not an emergency anymore, it has been dealt with," Lelio said.

I stared into his dark, serious face and nodded. In the front of my head, I knew he was right, but in the back where all the messy stuff lives I felt like I wasn't doing my part. "I know you're right, but I have a gun and a badge; we don't have to wait for the cops, I am a cop."

"*Ma petite*, remember the homework the therapist gave you?"

"I'm supposed to give myself more downtime and not take responsibility for everything. I am not the only cop in the world, and I'm not the only competent person in my life."

"Thank you, *ma petite*."

"You're welcome, though honestly, knowing how pissed off Claudia would be if I intruded when she's got things handled is an incentive to stay out of it."

"I thought you were friends with our tall, dark, dangerous beauty,"

Asher said. He came closer to me, smiling but still holding the red cloak very tightly closed. The new outfit he wore as ringmaster was sexy and hot, and showed off his body. He'd been flirting with all of his lovers in it since he started wearing it, so why wasn't he doing that now?

"Are you hurt somewhere besides the small cut on your face?" I asked.

He huddled the cloak tighter around him and said, "No," but he wouldn't look at me. I was suddenly looking at a thick spill of his hair hiding all of his face from me.

"Show us where you are hurt, *mon chardonneret*," Jean-Claude said.

Asher bowed his head lower. "I cannot show you my heart, or mind, or ego, and that is where it hurts."

We came in from both sides to touch his hair at the same time, sweeping it back so we could see his face. The pain in his eyes was so raw it hurt to see it, but I didn't look away, because we were in love with him. When someone you love hurts like this, you stay in the pain with them; even if you don't know how to help, you stay with them.

"Asher, what is it? What's wrong?" I asked.

The cloak opened a little as he reached his hands up to unfasten the neck of the cloak. He let the scarlet cloth slide down his body, revealing his bare chest and the torn remnants of his costume barely clinging at his waist. It was designed to leave the left side of his body as bare as possible and hide his right side behind glittering gold cloth. It was so skintight it was hidden under black satin slacks, a blue-and-gold vest, and a blue tailcoat like the traditional ringmasters wore. There was a blue top hat that went with it. The red cloak was to help him do the magic trick where the magician act would vanish the lovely female assistant and Asher would appear again in an outfit that was almost identical to hers, though it was like the her/his version.

The audience loved it because he looked gold and almost nude and perfect. They never saw beyond the illusion. The long-ago priests that had wanted to spare some of that gorgeous face hadn't felt the same about his chest and stomach. The scars on his chest and upper stomach were the worst; it was like the skin was just scars with only his nipple and some of his stomach left bare and as originally made. The rest looked like flesh that had melted and cooled like a candle, except rough to the touch.

"There are video and pictures of me on the internet now like this; no illusion will hide the horror of it now."

"Never say that about yourself again," I said.

"I have eyes and mirrors, Anita. I know what I look like."

I wrapped my arms around his waist, making sure to press my body against the scarred side, my hands encircling all of him from smooth to rough. "You can't see what I see if you use words like *horror* to describe yourself."

He put his arm around me because it would have been awkward not to. "You love me because you see me through Jean-Claude's eyes before the Church ruined me."

Jean-Claude came to stand in front of us, but it was Asher's eyes he gazed into. I hugged Asher tighter, resting my head on the spot between his shoulder and neck. The skin was rough against my cheek, but it just felt like Asher.

"I loved you when you were the envy of all who saw you. I loved you when you thought yourself lost. I loved you even after you hated me. I loved you when vengeance was all that filled your heart for me and Anita. I love you now, not out of nostalgia for what was lost, but for you standing before me as you are."

I hugged Asher and took Jean-Claude's hands and cried happy tears. I could feel what Jean-Claude was feeling and it was wonderful. I watched them kiss above me and it was the same thrill it always was, one of my favorite things.

I heard a sniffle, and Jamie said, "Sorry to ruin the mood, but damn. I thought nobody talked like that outside of rom-coms."

"And that is why I do not date," Truth said. "If I cannot feel that for someone, then it is not worth trying."

We all turned and looked at him where he was still on guard by the door leading to the parking lot. His face showed nothing as emotional or romantic as his words had sounded. It was as if he hadn't spoken at all or hadn't meant to speak out loud.

"He has always been the romantic of the two of us," Wicked said.

"I'm sorry about trying to fix you up with other women, Truth; I didn't realize how uncomfortable it made you at first."

Truth just nodded his acknowledgment.

"You can keep fixing *me* up," Wicked said.

I shook my head, arms still around Jean-Claude and Asher. "The women are the ones who called that off. You're a great first date and lover, but not a good boyfriend, apparently."

"He won't say it, but he seeks that one all-consuming love just as I do. He's just given up on finding it," Truth said.

"Don't speak for me on this, brother." And something about the way Wicked said it made me believe his brother was right about him.

Jamie touched his earpiece. "Claudia says the police are here and want to get our statements." Each club's security had their own frequency for the communication. Our security for tonight would be on their own comms so there wouldn't be any confusing cross-chatter.

"I don't like taking him into the open again," Kirby said.

"Do you think the police would let me ask them why they expected me to be a skeleton or rotting under my mask?" Asher asked.

"You won't get to question them," I said.

He looked down at me. "Can you find out later from your fellow police?"

"If you would show your true self more and talk about the cruelty and persecution of the Church to our kind, you would settle the rumors with truth," Truth said.

"When your face is something that makes women scream before they control themselves, then you may lecture me about such things."

"There are videos on the internet about the rotting vampires," Wicked said, "for people who don't know that's a completely different kind of vampire from what we are. They might think that's why you hide yourself."

"Again, when it is your face, your body, you can decide what you show to the public, but until that time you can keep your perfect beauty out of my business," Asher said.

"Perfect beauty is overrated," Nicky said from the door.

Asher started to say something harsh, but staring into Nicky's face with its own scars and knowing why he wore the eyepatch stopped the vampire. "Perhaps," Asher said.

"Anita is in love with you and with me, Asher, and that's not because we're perfect."

Asher looked thoughtful.

"I don't mean to rush things with what's happening, but if we're going to make the restaurant in time to see Anita's family, we have to go," Ethan said.

"If you need us to stay, we will," I said.

Asher smiled but shook his head. "I am a grown-up vampire. I will have security with me, and I will not be your excuse to miss introducing Jean-Claude to your father."

"You can't feel my feelings, or hear my thoughts, so how did you get to be so smart?"

He grinned wider, flashing a little fang and making the scars on his face stretch. It was his smile when he was comfortable and feeling loved. It made me happy to see it. "I do not need to read your mind, only your face and the way you hold your body. That told me everything I needed to know."

I went up on tiptoe and gave him a careful kiss good-bye. "I wish I could kiss you more thoroughly, but I'm wearing too much makeup to smear my lipstick."

"We will have other nights to smear your lipstick on more interesting parts of my body than my mouth," he said with a look in his eyes that made me shiver against him and Jean-Claude.

"Come, *ma petite*, before we both forget ourselves and stay here."

We left to make the restaurant reservation and introduce Jean-Claude to my dad. I'd rather have stayed and talked to the cops, or at least held Asher's hand while he talked to them. I didn't wish for a fresh crime scene to get me out of dinner, though I used to do that, but too many times my phone would ring right after, and someone would be dead. It got me out of the awkward social situation, but I'd started to feel almost like I was cursing the victims, causing it somehow. My therapist said that was magical thinking and not true, but I could raise the dead from their graves. If I could do that, what's a little magical manifestation? So I very carefully did not think I'd prefer a serious crime scene to dinner with my family. I was a grown-up; I could do this. Jean-Claude took my hand in his and said, "We can do this, *ma petite*." Funny, I believed it more when he said it.

10

JEAN-CLAUDE HAD RENTED a stretch limo for tonight since we'd planned on bringing my family to the restaurant in style; with just us Nicky, Ethan, and the Wicked Truth it had seemed a little empty, but I was still happy with my decision. My dad would behave himself more in public than in the privacy of a car. He'd proven that on the drive to the hotel. The first time Jean-Claude met my dad, a fancy restaurant sounded like a much better bet to keep Dad under control. I'd given orders to the security duo that was driving my family to the restaurant that my grandmother couldn't come. If my family tried to bring her, security should call me, and I'd tell them over the phone that the dinner was off. I trusted Milligan and Custer to do their jobs and to call me, but my stomach was still tight with anxiety as I walked on Jean-Claude's arm toward the table. The hostess had left her station at the front of the restaurant to escort us; that was part of her job, but she was enjoying it a little too much. She was tall and slender, with just enough curve to fill out the shining, curve-hugging dress in the appropriate places. She acknowledged my existence but saved her smiles for Jean-Claude. I didn't mind her flirting with him; I mean who wouldn't. It wasn't even that she was doing it with me on his arm. What bothered me was she was so damned blatant about it. One touch to the shoulder or back to direct us, I'd give her that, but adding two touches to the arm that didn't have me hanging on it was a bit much. The last straw was her touching the small of his back to direct him to his chair when I was still standing right there. If her hand went one inch lower I was going to have to defend his honor.

I settled for moving him around like you would on the dance floor, so I was suddenly closer to her. She looked almost startled as if she'd forgotten I was there. I smiled up at her with my best business smile, bright and empty of real emotion. "Thank you for walking us to our table, we're good now."

She blinked at me, her glance sliding to Jean-Claude and then back to me as I stepped forward ever so slightly to invade her personal space. She took two steps back, almost stumbling on her high heels. They were too high for standing all night; maybe she'd worn them just for Jean-Claude. I smiled brighter.

"Of course," she said, "my pleasure." She did one quick glance at Jean-Claude as she said it. "Your waiter, Paul, will be with you momentarily. If there's anything else you want, don't hesitate to ask." She finished the sentence gazing into Jean-Claude's eyes and even did the girl eye flutter like she should have a fan to wave in front of her face.

Ethan stepped up and said, "Could you direct us to our table? It should be very close to theirs." He even wasted a smile on her. It took her a second to smile back, and then smile more. Ethan wasn't Jean-Claude, but he also didn't have a fiancée glaring at her. I realized that Ethan had redirected her away from us; not all bodyguarding is about violence. I hoped she didn't take his flirting too seriously, because his girlfriend Nilda was a lot less tolerant than I was, and she was a werebear. The thought of what Nilda might do to the hostess put a real smile back on my face as Jean-Claude turned me toward the table and my chair.

It was only then that I let myself look at my family seated around the table. I realized that the flirty hostess had helped calm my nerves, and that I had been convinced that Dad wouldn't stand up to his mother, and even though our security hadn't called to warn us, I was still expecting Grandma Blake to be sitting at the table scowling at me. The relief when I saw everyone but her and Josh at the table was so immense I felt weak at the knees. That was when I acknowledged that Nicky had been right at the airport; I was afraid of my family. My grandmother because she abused me, and the rest of my family because they didn't protect me from her.

11

"Thanks for leaving Grandmother at the hotel," I said.

"What choice did we have? You made yourself very clear that if we brought her you would refuse to sit down and talk with us about your upcoming marriage or anything else," Dad said. Great, he was going to start out angry. Worked for me.

"I still can't believe you brought her after I told you not to."

"She's my mother, and she is worried about your immortal soul."

"I'm your daughter and my immortal soul is just fine."

He pushed his chair back and stood up, facing me across the table. "That remains to be seen, but Josh will miss tonight because you insisted on your grandmother staying at the hotel."

"Fredrick!" Judith said. "Sit down." She touched his arm.

He turned his glare from me to her. "I cannot allow her to disrespect her family this way."

"You're making a scene, Fredrick," Judith said; her voice was low but angry. Maybe we could all have a fight before we even sat down and then it would all be over. They'd fly home, and Jean-Claude and I would marry without any of them. I could walk my own damn self down the aisle.

"*Ma petite*, introduce me to your family."

I turned to glare at him, but the moment I looked into his face I felt petty and unreasonable, and damn it, I would not be the unreasonable one tonight.

I started speaking while I was still looking at Jean-Claude. I would not make a mess of tonight. I would not disappoint the man that I loved by behaving badly. I was better than that. "Dad, this is Jean-Claude; Jean-Claude, this is my father, Fredrick Blake."

"Doctor Fredrick Blake," my father said.

"Really, Dad," I said as I turned and looked at my dad.

Judith was tugging on his arm trying to get him to sit down. "Fredrick, please."

"As you wish, Dr. Blake." Jean-Claude bowed from the shoulders and neck with one hand coming to his chest as if he still owned a hat with a plume on it to finish the gesture. It was elegant and old-fashioned and gracious, and in that moment my husband-to-be was being the bigger man than my father. That helped me gain control of myself better than anything else could have, I think. I realized I didn't want to fight with Dad; I wanted to be right, I wanted to be the grown-up to his child, I wanted to be the logical, reasonable, open-minded one to his illogical, superstitious, prejudiced bastard.

Judith saved the awkward moment as she continued to tug on Dad's arm. Her voice was even showing no strain as she said, "We're so glad to finally meet you, Jean-Claude."

"It is lovely to meet you, as well," Jean-Claude said, with a nod that looked closer to a bow.

Judith smiled and it was a good smile; charming, as if she felt completely comfortable in the moment. I'd always envied her ability to be at home and even in charge of a party, or a dinner, or almost any social gathering. She would take over from a friend who was floundering at their own party, and she'd do it in such a way that they welcomed her help instead of resenting it. There was a reason she'd done so well in real estate for decades. It was how she and Dad met; she sold him a house. He'd felt overwhelmed by memories of my mom and needed a fresh start to heal. I'd found the memories of my mom comforting, and at age ten it was the only home I'd ever known, but in that moment I saw a woman who had no idea that she'd fall in love with the Indiana veterinarian or try to be a mother to his little girl or help them grieve as she was still grieving her dead husband and trying to raise her little girl on her own. Our family home had just been one more sale to her, a commission. Even if she had known she would fall in love with him, she had to sell the house. They couldn't start a new life surrounded by the old one.

Tonight, she was wearing her favorite shade of dusty blue that always made her eyes look even bluer. I didn't need to see her standing up to know the dress would be at the appropriate length: neither too short nor too long, but just right.

I had the weirdest urge to hug her.

"Dad, you're embarrassing yourself in front of the whole restaurant," Andria said.

I glanced around and she was right. The people nearest us were looking, including Ethan and Nicky at their table. Then I realized that biggest table near us, a four-topper, was also full of security. The Wicked Truth in suits and ties with Echo in a formfitting navy blue dress with a short matching jacket that would hide the weapons she was wearing, and Fortune in a suit of her own, with her white men's shirt flared out so the wide collar framed the strong lines of her face. She'd used layers of purple and blue eye makeup to bring out the natural blue in her hair. I couldn't see if she was wearing a skirt or pants under the table. Wicked wore more suits than his brother, so that Truth was already pulling at his tie to loosen it. They were pretending to be on a double date. Echo looked delicate touching Wicked's arm, a very convincing smile on her oval face, her dark blue eyes gazing up into his as if hanging on his every word. Since she had been a couple with Fortune for over a thousand years, they had recently had a very quiet ceremony and become wife and wife. They were also part of our poly group.

I fought the urge to look around for more of our security. I forced myself to pay attention to our table and the almost disaster that had already happened.

"Andria's right, Dad, you don't want everyone near us to be tweeting about Anita Blake's dad yelling at her and Jean-Claude, do you?"

He glanced around at the restaurant, and I realized that most of the people were looking at us; some were even using their phones, but the waitstaff was urging them to stop. Nicky and Ethan were looking, but they weren't undercover. The foursome at the table should have been looking; instead they were playing like they were two couples so into each other that they weren't noticing anything else, not even standing customers having a borderline fight. I'd talk to them about it later, after I'd made it through dinner with my dad.

He sat down with Judith's hand still on his arm. Jean-Claude pulled out my chair for me, but he allowed me to scoot my own chair in, though he did hover beside me until I was finished with the awkward scooting. I was even more awkward when someone else tried to do it, so this was our compromise. Once I was settled at the table, he sat down gracefully, as he did almost everything. If you were too insecure you couldn't date Jean-Claude, because after six hundred–plus years he was almost perfect through sheer repetition. Actually, the fact that I'd grown up thinking I wasn't beautiful, not blond enough, blue-eyed enough, tall enough, white enough to my family meant that I hadn't even thought to compete with Jean-Claude in the way that some of the beautiful women he'd tried to date had, like Envy. Yes, that really was her name. Jean-Claude was gorgeous, that was just a fact; he was also an extrovert, an exhibitionist, and I was none of these things, so the fact that all eyes went first to him when we entered a room just made sense to me. I didn't try to outcompete him for attention from strangers because I didn't care. My family trauma had helped make me the woman who could marry Jean-Claude. I wondered if they'd get the irony.

"Well, we're all sitting down, so it's a start," Andria said.

"Andria," Judith said, and I wasn't sure what she meant by it.

"She's right, sitting down at the table for the meal is a start," I said.

Andria smiled at me, and I smiled back.

"It is a pleasure to meet you all," Jean-Claude said, and ended with a smile in Andria's direction, because she was on the end of the table.

She smiled back at him in her pink dress with the shiny jacket over it, which probably meant it had spaghetti straps. Judith and Dad had never liked us to show too much skin. She'd themed her makeup in pinks and metallics to match her clothes, like she was going to prom or going to be in a music video. It was definitely not the conservative makeup Judith was wearing. Hell, it was more out there by far than mine, but weirdly it worked for her.

"You look great," I said, "but you should have saved it for Danse Macabre. The makeup will really pop in the lighting there."

She smiled and it filled her whole face with how much she'd enjoyed the comment. Usually, people only react that much to compliments from family when they haven't been getting them anywhere else. It made me happy I'd said it, and more convinced that her fiancé was falling down on his game.

"Well, I think it's too much for dinner tonight," Dad said.

Andria and I exchanged a look that only siblings can share. "Well, I like it," I said.

"Me, too," she said.

The waiter appeared beside us, offering us menus, making sure the water glasses were filled or refilled. Jean-Claude put his arm across my shoulders so we could hold the menu together, his free hand on one side and my two hands holding one side and the bottom of the menu, so it was easier to turn the one page. You always know how fancy the restaurant is by how small the menu is. I leaned into the curve of his arm and the back of the chair while we picked my meal together. He couldn't eat solid food, but he could taste what I ate.

"I never thought I'd see you let any man pick your meal for you, you were always so disdainful of anything like that," Andria said.

"Jean-Claude isn't picking my food; we're negotiating what I'm getting."

"Why are you negotiating with him?" Dad asked.

It wasn't common knowledge that I was Jean-Claude's human servant, and it definitely wasn't common knowledge that a human servant could eat for their vampire master on long voyages, or when traveling through hostile territory. Vampires had been in the coffin, or closet, for most of human history, so hiding the fang marks or not having to take blood at all helped master vampires hide.

"Though I cannot consume food, I can enjoy the scent, and other things, as *ma petite* eats her meal."

"I can't believe you are okay with that nickname," Andria said. "You hated anything that implied you were small when we were in junior high and high school."

"Well, I love the nickname," Judith said. "It sounds so romantic when he says it."

"Everything sounds more romantic in French," I said, with a smile.

"I don't think it's just that it's French," Andria said, raising her water glass and half pointing, half toasting at Jean-Claude.

I smiled and knew it was one of those half-dopey smiles you get when you're talking about the person you're in love with.

"I'm so happy that you found someone to love, Anita," Judith said.

"I know I should be happy if you're happy," my dad said.

I looked at him across the table, though technically he was across from Jean-Claude, and I was sitting across from Judith, but it wasn't hard to glare across the table at his unhappy face. "I know you'd rather see me alone and miserable for the rest of my life than happily married to Jean-Claude."

"I do not want you miserable, Anita."

"I don't believe you, Dad."

He looked startled, though I didn't know why. "Of course I want you happy, I want all my children happy."

"But only if it's a type of happiness you approve of," I said.

"That's not true," he said. His blue eyes looked so sincere.

"I believe that you believe that, Dad."

"What does that mean?"

"Fredrick, let's pick our food so the waiter can do his job," Judith said.

The waiter was beside our table again, attentive, face pleasant, as if there was no problem at our table at all. He had probably seen a lot worse than our little squabble. We told him we needed a minute, and could he come back. Of course he could, but would we like to hear the specials first? Yes, we would.

The waiter recited the specials, two mains and one dessert. The mains included fish, sustainable of course, and a beef tenderloin dish on a bed of pasta. The fish was being served on a bed of couscous. Judith said yes to the fish special; the rest of us passed until they got to the dessert special.

"In honor of you gracing us with your presence tonight, our pastry chef has prepared a trio of traditional French desserts with a presumptuous modern spin."

"How could we resist such an offering," Jean-Claude said. "*Ma petite* and I will share the trio."

"We'll share one as well," Judith said.

Paul the waiter turned to Andria. "And you, mademoiselle?"

"Thank you, but I don't have anyone to split it with," she said.

"Take it back for Josh," I said.

She smiled at me, then said to the waiter, "Yes, please."

"The pastry chef will be most pleased."

We all smiled and nodded, and then he left us to our menus and picking the rest of our meal. "Does that happen often?" Dad asked.

"What?" I asked.

"Chefs making special menu items for you?"

"Occasionally," I said.

"Why would they do that for a vampire, when they know that he cannot eat any of it?"

"I cannot eat food, that is true, but if Anita finds something truly delectable, then I am able to taste it without consuming."

Andria giggled.

"What are you laughing at?" Dad asked.

She shook her head, but her shoulders were shaking with silent laughter.

"What is so funny?" he demanded.

Her voice came out gasping as she said, "Don't ask."

"I did ask, twice, and I expect an answer."

Andria shook her head and turned so her parents couldn't see her face, but even silent laughter is hard to ignore when your whole body is shaking with it. I had no idea what had amused her this much, but I also knew better than to ask if she didn't want to tell us.

Of course, Dad had never known when to stop asking us questions. Growing up it had usually been me that got in trouble for answering questions when I tried to avoid them, but tonight it looked like Andria's turn.

Dad kept pushing and finally Andria answered him. She was so out of breath from laughing that they didn't understand her at first, but finally she gasped out, "He doesn't swallow."

"He's a vampire, of course he can't swallow solid food," Dad said.

Andria's shoulders started to shake again, and then she got up and fled to the bathroom. I moved as if to get up to follow her, but Jean-Claude's arm tightened around me. The vampire king of America didn't want to be left alone with my parents. Andria would have to fix her makeup and her control on her own.

12

THE REST OF us managed to finish ordering our meal by the time Andria returned to the table. Her makeup was perfect and she was back to her usual sober and controlled self. She even managed to finish ordering her meal before Paul the waiter walked away. At least the food would come out at about the same time; that was something to look forward to as my dad started interrogating Jean-Claude.

"Have you ever been married before?"

"Once," Jean-Claude said, settling his arm more comfortably around me. I put my hand on his thigh. We could do this.

"Did you divorce?" My very Catholic father asking a very Catholic question.

"No, she died."

"Did you kill her?"

"Dad!" I said it with Andria duetting me.

Judith said, "Fredrick!"

"I meant your bloodlust getting out of control, not deliberate murder."

"Oh, that makes the question so much better, Dad," I said.

"It's just when they first wake, the bloodlust is all-consuming, so it was a natural assumption."

"Jean-Claude does not lose control of his bloodlust every night, Dad. That's just antivampire propaganda."

He looked uncomfortable. "They sleep in a coffin away from their loved ones for a reason, Anita."

"We sleep in a bed together, Dad, just like you and Judith."

"My wife died in childbirth," Jean-Claude said.

"Oh," Judith said, "I'm so sorry."

Dad looked uncomfortable, like he didn't know what to say, and then he jumped in his chair. I think Judith had kicked him under the table; good for her. "I'm very sorry for your loss, of course."

"We both know what it's like to lose a spouse," Judith said.

"Thank you for your kind words. My condolences on your own losses, as well."

"So you have a child?" Dad asked.

"She lived only a few hours after birth."

I stroked his thigh because it comforted us both. He'd told me the story in much more detail, and I knew he'd held his baby in his arms at the end when the doctor and the local midwife could do nothing for his tiny daughter.

"How terrible to lose both of them together," Judith said.

"I can't imagine," Andria said.

"Were you still human then?" Dad asked. He'd expressed sympathy, but I don't think he meant it.

"I was not a vampire yet, if that is what you mean."

"Dad, Jean-Claude is still human."

"You didn't believe that of any vampire when you graduated college."

"You're right, but I saw enough human beings who were more evil than the supposed monsters that I had to reevaluate my definitions."

"If you'd stayed away from police work like I asked you to, you wouldn't have seen the worst of humanity."

"What am I supposed to say to that, Dad?"

"Admit I was right."

"Fine, if I'd never joined the police I wouldn't have seen how vile my fellow human beings could be. Happy?"

"Why would that make me happy?" he asked.

"I don't know, Dad, I thought me getting married would make you happy, but I was wrong about that."

"How can you expect me to be happy about you marrying a vampire?"

"I'm not marrying a vampire, I'm marrying Jean-Claude," I said.

He looked across the table at my soon-to-be husband, then looked down at the table. "I don't know how to do this."

"You're afraid to look him in the eyes, aren't you?" I asked.

Dad glared at me. "Of course I am, he can bespell me with his gaze."

"Dad, he's not going to do that."

"It would be an easy way for him to win me over."

"*Non*, no, Doctor Blake, that would not be winning you over, that would be taking you over. That would not be a victory for me, it would be a loss."

"I'd give you my blessing for the wedding because you'd force me to do it."

"A forced blessing is no blessing at all," Jean-Claude said.

"You're treating Jean-Claude like he's dangerous . . ."

"He *is* dangerous!" He shouted that and got people at the other tables looking our way again.

"Lower your voice, Dad."

"I'm sorry, Anita, it's just that I do not understand how this happened. You hated vampires and saw them for the monsters they are, and then suddenly Judith is showing me images of you online dating one."

Judith said, "I thought he'd just like to see you all dressed up on Jean-Claude's arm, but that's not how he took it."

"I know."

"I'm sorry that he started calling you about Jean-Claude. I swear to you that wasn't my intent," she said.

"I know that, Judith. It hadn't occurred to me that Jean-Claude would be a big enough celebrity to interest your magazines and gossip sites."

"Are you kidding? Vampires and other supernatural celebrities are the hottest thing out there." She flashed a truly dazzling smile at Jean-Claude. It reminded me that when I was butting heads with Judith as a kid, I had resented her for being beautiful in a way that I could never be—tall, blond, blue-eyed, Nordic. The only thing I'd inherited from my father was the pale skin, so I had the dark hair and eyes but still couldn't tan at all. At least growing up we'd all had to slather on sunscreen.

I looked at her now talking animatedly to Jean-Claude about some of the rumors about other supernatural celebrities. Andria joined in some and it became small talk mostly about other people. Some we knew, some we didn't, but that was okay; it was small talk about other people you could speculate on without hurting the feelings of anyone at the table.

My dad didn't take part in the conversation, and mostly neither did I. He and I sort of stared at each other in matching brooding looks. Then my phone rang, and the dial tone meant it was Sergeant Zerbrowski of the Regional Preternatural Investigation Team.

"*Ma petite*, you promised no work tonight."

"I know." I hit the button to cut the phone call off. "I'll text Zerbrowski back and tell him to call another marshal." I was already typing on my phone. **What's up? I'm at dinner with family introducing them to Jean-Claude.**

I watched the little bubbles letting me know that he was typing back. The table had gone quiet, and everyone was watching me stare at my phone. "Sorry," I said, "this will just take a few minutes."

Zerbrowski texted back. **Sorry, forgot it was tonight. How's it going?**

I thought for a second, then texted, **Dad accused Jean-Claude of murder and damning my soul to hell by marrying me.**

He texted, **Jesus.**

"Is your ringtone from *A Charlie Brown Christmas*?" Andria asked.

"Yes," I said, still looking at my phone.

I'm so sorry, Anita. Hang in there. I'll call Kirkland tonight.

I texted back. **Let him put all that new FBI training to work.**

I don't think they teach this at Quantico.

I wanted so badly to text back and ask what he meant by that, but I'd promised Jean-Claude that I wouldn't abandon him for work tonight, no matter what the crime. I meant that, I really did, but still . . . I used the new mantra I was trying to work out with my therapist. I thought it loud in my head: *I am not the only cop in the world. I'm allowed to have a life outside the job. If I try to save everyone all the time, I end up losing myself.* I was still working at editing it down to something less wordy and easier to think or say quickly, but it was a start. I'd ask Zerbrowski for crime details tomorrow, after Jean-Claude and I had made it through tonight.

"What happened to you, Anita?" Andria asked.

I glanced at her, away from my phone and Zerbrowski's bubbles that let me know he was still typing. "What do you mean?"

"You wouldn't even admit to liking any of the Charlie Brown Christmas specials when you were a teenager. Now it's your ringtone. You vowed never to marry because it was stupid. You hated that I was pretend-planning my wedding when we were kids. You were disdainful of the whole idea. Now here you are planning the biggest wedding of the year, maybe the decade. How are you the same girl I grew up with? That's what I mean."

"It's not my ringtone, it's Sergeant Zerbrowski's ringtone."

"Why would you use it for a police sergeant?" Dad asked.

Zerbrowski texted back. **We got this tonight. You take care of you and Jean-Claude. Tell me all the juicy parts tomorrow.** That last made me smile as I looked back up at my family. The truth was that though his wife, Katie, was one of the neatest people I knew from clothes to house, Zerbrowski would leave the house just as neat and within seconds he just seemed to attract dirt, and his clothes wrinkled like magic. His car was one of the messiest I'd ever driven in, and that included boys I knew in college. The fast-food wrappers that piled up like an archaeological dig had disappeared when his doctor told him he needed to lower his cholesterol, but he'd just found other things to throw into his backseat. He'd once had a suspect claim that having to sit in the backseat of Zerbrowski's car was cruel and un-usual punishment. It reminded me of the character Pig-Pen from Charlie Brown, but I meant it like a cute idiosyncrasy, like you do with friends; my family would think I was insulting him, so I just said, "Zerbrowski and I work together a lot, unofficial partners, so it's the Linus and Lucy theme."

"That's still way too cutesy for you to choose for another police officer," Andria said.

"It's not just your attitude toward vampires that's changed, Anita, it's everything," Dad said.

"She grew up, Fredrick."

He shook his head. "No, she's not the same girl we raised. He's taken her over and turned her into someone I don't know."

Our appetizers came and saved us all from having to reply. Though call it a hunch, my dad wouldn't forget the thread of the conversation.

13

"HE HAS ALREADY bespelled you, Anita, don't you see that?" Dad said over his appetizer, which he hadn't bothered to taste yet.

Andria came to the rescue, saying, "That is not at all what I meant, Dad. I do not believe, nor have I ever believed, that Jean-Claude bespelled Anita into loving him."

"You said she's like a different person; what other explanation is there?" he demanded.

"If I had tried any vampire wiles on Anita, she would have known. Her necromancy meant I had to approach her honestly or not at all," Jean-Claude said.

"Fredrick, I showed you the videos from Colorado where Anita raised a zombie army. She is powerful in her own right," Judith said.

He shook his head like he was shaking the thought away, then glared at Jean-Claude for a second, looked down, then glared at me. "Those videos didn't prove to me that you were too powerful for him to possess you. They confirmed that he had corrupted you with his undead powers."

"Fredrick, please."

"I cannot raise the dead, Dr. Blake. It has never been a power granted to me either living or dead," Jean-Claude said.

"You would say that, wouldn't you?"

"I emptied the graveyards around Boulder, Colorado, Dad. I raised an army of every zombie that our bad guy hadn't already raised to be on his side. I sent them out to defend the people in the area. I may be the only necromancer alive today that could have done it."

Dad shook his head again like an adult version of putting your fingers in your ears and going *la, la, la*. "If he hasn't corrupted you, then I failed you, Anita."

"Failed me how?"

"I sent you to your Grandmother Flores's that summer to learn to control your powers, but maybe my mother was right. We should have exorcised this evil out of you instead of sending you to a voodoo priestess to learn more of it."

"Fredrick, stop this," Judith said.

"Anita uses her gifts to help people, not harm them," Jean-Claude said.

"Her zombies fought, you mean," Dad said.

Nicky came over to put a hand on my shoulder. "No, Anita doesn't stay behind the lines with her magic, she puts on her body armor, grabs her guns, and charges into the worst of it."

"Anita leads from the front like the generals of old," Jean-Claude said.

"She's a U.S. Marshal, Dad."

I touched Jean-Claude and Nicky and looked at my dad. He was a stranger to me; I hadn't seen him any clearer than he'd seen me. He was my dad, and I was his daughter; we weren't people to each other, we were family roles.

"You want to know why I changed, Dad?" I looked at Andria. "You want to know why I'm softer and more comfortable with the cuter stuff and willing to dress like a girl more?"

"I didn't mean to start all this," Andria said.

"I know, but here's what I learned in therapy. I found people who loved me and made me feel comfortable enough to be more feminine and softer, because I didn't have to spend all my time defending who

I was. They accepted me all dark and cranky and morose, so I could be softer with them because they didn't tell me there was something wrong with me constantly. They didn't see me not being all girly and pastel as a fucking crime. It freed me up to explore the parts of being a woman that I actually liked or was willing to try."

Nicky said, "You'll never be a fucking girl, all pastel and pink, that's not you. That's not someone I could ever love." I think he was glaring at my family, or maybe it was the words. Whatever, dinner was over.

"I'm sorry you didn't get to taste everything, but . . ."

"I will settle the bill, *ma petite*, go."

"Anita, please don't go," Judith said.

Nicky helped me get out of my chair. "I need some air. I'll see you for lunch tomorrow, but I'm done for tonight."

"I'm your father, don't you dare walk out on me." Dad pushed his chair back and stood on his side of the table.

"Please feel free to finish your meal," Jean-Claude said as he gestured and the waiter came over to the table.

Ethan came over to Nicky and said, "I'll get the bill for both tables; get her and Jean-Claude out of here."

Jean-Claude took my arm, thanking Ethan, saying something to my family, but I was done. My dad was still telling me not to walk out on him, that it was disrespectful or something. I needed air, I needed away from . . . I was so done. Wicked and Truth were suddenly on the other side of Jean-Claude. Wicked took the side, and Truth dropped back to take rear guard. Not that I thought my father would attack us from behind, but maybe there was another crazed vampire hater in the restaurant to guard against. Nicky got the door for us, and we were out in the fresh night air. I could feel the growing anxiety start to ease.

A vampire with short brown hair and a face still pale and too thin from not having taken blood yet tonight approached us. Most people wouldn't have realized he was a vampire. He looked so normal: just your average man, average height, average build, so nondescript he looked like he should have been in the dictionary next to *human male*, *white*, except he wasn't human anymore. "Jean-Claude, could I get a selfie with you? Please?"

Wicked tried to step between them, saying, "Sorry, not tonight."

"Come on, just one selfie?" He raised his phone up, standing in our way to block us, and I realized he was wearing black gloves. It was summer in St. Louis; you didn't wear gloves even if you were a vampire. Jean-Claude was apologizing graciously about an appointment we had.

Nicky loomed up behind us. "You heard him, move." He was angry because I was so upset. He started to come around the group of us. I wasn't the only one who thought he might hurt the selfie vampire, because Truth caught his arm and spoke low to him.

Wicked tried to move the selfie vampire out of our way without hurting him. "Come on, just one selfie with our king, come on."

I heard my father's voice shouting at me. "Anita, wait!" He'd followed us out. Damn it.

Jean-Claude said, "It will be quicker to let him have his selfie."

I heard Nicky say, "Get back inside the restaurant, old man."

The vampire stepped closer to Jean-Claude and started to position his camera in his gloved hands, and I saw the clear vial hidden inside his sleeve. I knew exactly what it was because I carried them in my vampire hunting kit. I didn't even have time to think, I just shoved my body into Jean-Claude's with everything I had, sending him stumbling backward. Wicked threw himself forward, Truth grabbed me to try to pull me back, and the vampire threw holy water all over us.

14

IF SOMETHING IS thrown in your face, especially liquid, there's always a split second of eye-blinking hesitation. Even a human attacker can use that to their advantage; a vampire is faster, a second is forever to them. I'd made the rookie mistake of turning away, throwing my left arm up as if holy water could hurt me. I saw Wicked's face boiling, screaming. Truth grabbed his brother and pulled him back with one arm; his other hand was bubbling with the holy water. I didn't look around for Jean-Claude; I'd have felt it if he was hurt that badly. He was safe, that was enough. The world had slowed down as if I had all the time in the world to turn back to our attacker. Everything was crystal edged, sharp and detailed with the rush of adrenaline, the rush of battle.

The vampire was standing right in my face, as if he wanted to see the damage he'd done or was waiting to cause more. You hit with your elbows, so you don't break your hand, but they're also better if someone is too close for anything else. I hit him in the face with my elbow, then hit him with my other elbow, a forehand-backhand combo. It staggered him, and I put a knee into his gut, which folded him. I grabbed him, planning to bring his face down into my knee as many times as I could, but the high heels threw my balance off, and I was left holding the back of the vampire's neck while I readjusted my footing. If he'd been trained to fight he could have hurt me, but like most vampires he thought just being a vampire would be enough.

He came for me mouth wide, fangs straining, trusting to his superior strength and speed to push me back. His eyes glowed like dark fire, his skin thinning down, until when he took me to the ground it was like looking into a skull with glowing eyes, like some Halloween decoration, except this decoration had weight and strength and was snapping at my face, spit landing on my cheek as he fought the arm I'd shoved against his throat to keep him from tearing out mine. I couldn't reach my gun, and my cross was trapped under my clothes; if I had to I'd give the vampire my left arm to gnaw on. What was one more scar, if it kept me from dying seconds away from help?

Then something started to glow, and it took me a second to realize it was me; the holy water that he'd thrown on me was making my face and hair glow, and the arm I had shoved against his throat. One minute he was a snarling, snapping animal determined to tear my throat out, and the next his humanity started to fill his face back up. I could feel the skin of his throat moving against my arm, blistering so fast it felt like his skin was moving on its own. I had to swallow hard against the sudden bile in my throat from the sensation. He blinked at me and whispered, "What is that?" That the pain hadn't hit him yet meant he was very new to vampiric powers. He was like a toddler that hadn't learned stoves were hot. I looked at him through the holy shimmer of light that he'd given me to harm, not to help. I watched his eyes slide back to human, face filling back out so his skull was invisible under his skin again. I couldn't see past the glow, and I didn't dare look away from the vampire on top of me to see if the wereanimals on our guard detail were close enough to help me. I didn't want him to escape; I wanted to know what hate group he belonged to, who sent him to hurt us. So, I wrapped my legs around him like in Brazilian jujitsu so that I was in guard. I wrapped my right hand in the rough cloth of his jacket and kept my glowing left arm against his throat. If he wasn't going to move, neither was I. Then the pain hit him. He shrieked, jerking his upper body back from my arm, but my legs and one hand kept him from raising himself too far from the glowing parts of me. I had a second to see the burned flesh of his neck, and then he was jerking and bucking for me to "Let me go!" There were no BJJ rules to how he fought to escape, there wasn't even any thought, just him wildly thrashing trying to get to all fours, but I kept flexing my legs at the small of his spine, flattening him back so he could only get his arms up. If he hadn't been so thin I'd have never been able to control him that well, but my guard was firm around him. He felt almost fragile as he screamed to be free, and screamed at the cold, holy fire so bright in his face.

Fortune was there above us both, saying, "Call Nicky over to help me."

I stared at her through the soft light, so much softer than a cross in full starlike glory. I wondered why Nicky couldn't just come to help, but I yelled, "Nicky, to me." He was just suddenly there with Fortune, and they tried to pull the vampire off me.

"Let him out of your guard, Anita," Nicky said.

I'd forgotten, not good in a fight. I unwrapped my legs and let go of the jacket as Fortune and Nicky lifted him off me. Ethan was there to take my right hand and get me on my feet. I had a moment of unsteadiness on the high heels and maybe a little bit of shock. Ethan caught me and started to hug me, but I pulled back, staring at my still-shining skin.

"It should be fading now that the vampire isn't attacking me with vamp powers, but it's not." I looked around the crowd of gawkers, but the vampire that was keeping the holy water glowing wasn't that close. If he'd been there all vampy, Ethan wouldn't have been this calm. But there was something unholy nearby that was activating the holy water. I drew my cross out of my blouse by its chain, and it glowed softly like an echo of the holy water; did that mean the vampire wasn't that close to us? I'd never had holy water glow on my skin before, or a cross glow so softly.

There was a vampire nearby with evil intent, but I didn't think it was actively using vampiric powers on me. It was as if the holy items were already activated so they reacted to the more distant threat. I was guessing, because even for me this was new. Was the vampire hiding from me? Watching? What? I opened my necromancy like unfolding a hand inside me. It was always there inside me waiting to be used. I didn't need ritual to call it up or get me in the right mindset; it was just there always. I searched for the vampire and . . . there, there it was, out of visual range, but it was trying to use power on us, on me, us, me. I wasn't sure, but that's why I was still shining with holy light, because the stranger was trying to use long-distance vampire powers.

"Tell the Harlequin on overwatch that there's an enemy vamp south of us. He, I think it's a he, is trying to use vampire powers on me, us."

"How far away is he?" Ethan asked.

"Not sure, but he's watching us, so close enough to see some of what's happening here."

"I'll let the others know," Fortune said. I didn't know how she'd do it, because it wasn't going to be by phone, but I knew if she said she could, she could.

I could hear sirens speeding closer. I'd probably been hearing them for a while, but they just hadn't registered.

"Anita, are you hurt?" And it was my dad.

I turned to him still glowing with holy fire. He reached out as if to touch me, then said, "Your eyes, they're glowing like a vampire's."

I let go of Ethan's hand and took a step toward my dad. He backed up. I spoke loud enough that he'd hear me over the sirens that were screaming closer. "If God is for me, who can be against me?"

"Anita . . ."

I didn't wait for him to find words. I turned and started walking toward the police car that screeched to a halt, lights twirling and sirens blaring. Ethan stayed at my side. I asked him, "Are my eyes still glowing?"

"Yes," he said.

I had him help me take off the high heels while I unhooked my badge from my waistband. I left Ethan holding the shoes so I could hold the badge high for the cops to see. I was yelling, "U.S. Marshal," before they got out with guns drawn like I knew they would. Maybe they didn't hear me identifying myself as a fellow officer, or maybe they didn't believe me, but it didn't matter. I could have been covered in badges and all they would have seen was someone glowing with pale phosphorous fire, their eyes shining like cognac diamonds held up to a flame. I was the scariest thing they could see, and they were going to treat me accordingly.

I didn't argue when they yelled for me to get down on the ground. I just did it; hell, it was why I'd taken my high heels off.

15

I WAS STILL ON the ground in handcuffs when the ambulance arrived. I was trying to lie still on the ground; if the skirt had been skintight it would have stayed in place, but I hadn't wanted to shock my family, so I'd chosen pleated to be more family friendly and now the ladylike skirt was not staying in place. At least I hadn't worn a thong tonight, and the panties were black. I was really glad I hadn't worn the royal blue one. I wasn't sure why, but bright color would have bothered me more. I also knew I was thinking about all the minutiae so I wouldn't be freaking out about how hurt Wicked and Truth might be, or lose my shit at the uniformed officers who wouldn't believe I was a U.S. Marshal. I understood them thinking I was a preternatural bad guy when they first arrived on the scene. I understood them disarming me, but they'd had time to call in and get my credentials verified a dozen times by now. So why the fuck was I still on the concrete with my hands behind my back and my lingerie complete with thigh-high hose bare to everyone? I needed to see Jean-Claude in person, though I could feel he was okay. I needed to find out what hate group our attacker belonged to; I needed to do a lot of things, none of which was lying here helpless, unable to do my job, or comfort my injured people, or . . . The one uniform was standing by me while his partner was at their car or doing something out of my sight line.

"Officer Linley," I said, through gritted teeth.

"I'm really sorry about this, Marshal."

I tried to crane my head up to look at him but could only get as far as his lower pants leg because of where he was standing. "So, you know I'm Marshal Anita Blake?"

"Yes, ma'am."

"Then why am I still handcuffed and flashing my ass to the world, because I can't use my hands!" I yelled a little bit and had to do some deep breathing to calm down. Yelling at people never gets you uncuffed faster.

"New protocol says we keep any supernatural on site in restraints until we get one of the preternatural marshals down here to verify that it's safe to uncuff or otherwise free the before-mentioned supernatural citizen."

"I *am* a preternatural marshal!"

"The new rule doesn't really cover the preternatural marshal being the supernatural citizen that we're detaining, so we're waiting on someone to tell us if we can uncuff you and have you be the marshal that says it's okay to uncuff you."

I struggled to be able to look at his face, and all I managed to do was make my skirt fall even further up my body. "Are you fucking kidding me?"

"I'm really sorry, Marshal Blake, we're both really sorry about this."

"So you're just going to let me lie here on the fucking ground flashing everyone, including my father? Until someone with some common sense calls you back?" I was yelling, fuck it.

"Oh, geez, I . . . maybe I can I help." He knelt down beside me, but it wasn't until I felt his fingers brush my ass that I realized he was trying to pull my skirt down.

"Get your motherfucking hands off me!"

Linley fell, landing on his ass beside me. "I'm sorry, I'm sorry."

I felt the warm rush of werelion energy dancing over my skin. I knew the feel of that heat; in other circumstances I might have even enjoyed knowing Nicky was behind me while I was lying helpless at his feet, but this was not those circumstances.

"Did you touch her ass?" Nicky asked, his voice so deep it was more growl than human words.

Officer Linley stuttered, "I . . . I didn't. I mean . . . I didn't mean to. I . . ." He actually crab-walked away from Nicky so that he ended up on the ground near my head. I could finally see Linley better but still had to strain my neck to see his face. I put my cheek back on the rough coolness of the sidewalk.

Another pair of cheap but serviceable shoes came over to stand near Linley. I assumed it was his partner, Maric. "Is there a problem?" he asked, like he wasn't nervous about someone with Nicky's size looming over us, or maybe he was taller than I remembered. Maybe Nicky didn't loom over him at all.

"Yeah, there's a problem," Nicky growled. "Your partner here just touched the ass of a U.S. Marshal while she was handcuffed."

"That's a lie," the partner said.

"I'm sorry, Maric, but I didn't mean to, I was trying to help her skirt get back in place. I mean it's undignified and . . ."

"Stop talking, Linley." Just the tone in his voice, full of world-weary exasperation, let me know he'd been on the job for at least two years, and I was betting more than five.

"I'm sorry—"

"Shut the fuck up, Linley, I mean it."

"I'm sorry—"

"Get off the ground and go sit in the car."

Linley got to his feet, still trying to explain. "I didn't mean to touch her, I swear."

"Go to the car and dust your pants off before you sit in it."

"Marshal Blake, I'm really sorry, I would never—"

"Go sit in the fucking car, right the fuck now, and stop fucking digging yourself into a deeper fucking hole." And yes, he was yelling.

Officer Linley walked away, toward the car I assumed, but I couldn't see past Maric's legs. He muttered a few words in a language I didn't understand, then in totally unaccented English said, "I can't apologize for him enough, let's get you on your feet at least."

"Can you uncuff me?"

"I'm sorry, truly, but until someone okays it, or I get permission for you to okay it yourself as a preternatural marshal, I can't take off the restraints, but I can get you up off the ground."

He leaned down to take my arm, and Nicky started to take my other arm, so they'd get me standing together. Maric stopped with his hand on my arm but no upward movement. "Who are you?"

"Her boyfriend."

"I thought you were her bodyguard."

"He's both," I said. I could feel the two men staring at each other over my back.

"As her security I can't let her be manhandled, as her boyfriend I want to start punching people in the face," Nicky said, voice a little less growly.

"I can understand all that," Maric said. "Let's get Marshal Blake up off the ground and you can help her with her skirt."

They lifted me together so there was as little strain on my shoulders as possible. I appreciated the effort. My skirt swung into place almost; Nicky gently pulled the pleats down and even fluffed the edges so that it lay nicely. I wanted to kiss him, but I was still trying to persuade the nice officer that I was the marshal they needed, and kissing on my lovers wouldn't up my credibility with the other cops. I had to settle for "Thanks, Nicky."

"You're welcome. Do you want Ethan to bring your shoes?"

I stood there feeling the cooler concrete under my stocking feet but shook my head. "No, my balance isn't good enough in them for handcuffs."

"The hose are slippery; do you want to take them off?" he asked.

I shook my head again. "They'll be fine until I get on a man-made floor, but you're welcome to keep a hand on my arm just in case."

"My pleasure," he said, then leaned in and whispered, "Maybe we can play with handcuffs at home sometime?"

My first instinct was no, and then I remembered the feel of him looming behind me as I lay on the ground, and . . . whispered back, "I love it when we play together."

He smiled, and so did I, and then Ethan whispered through my mind, "The Wicked Truth won't go into the ambulance until they see you."

Our smiles vanished, and I spoke over my shoulder to Maric. "I have to check how badly hurt my men are, so either take the cuffs off or I'm going to walk out of your custody wearing them."

"I'll come with you," he said.

I wondered if Officer Linley was safe to leave on his own, but it wasn't my job to keep track of him, so I just kept walking toward the restaurant. Nicky's hand was a reassuring presence on my left arm. "I appreciate you leaving my right arm free like normal, but since I can't use my hands and they still have my gun, maybe switch arms in case you need your gun hand free."

Officer Maric must have heard, because he said, "This is ridiculous, I know who you are and you're the victim here, not the perp."

Nicky turned us both toward him, guiding me with his hand on my arm. Maric had the handcuff key ready to go. I should have asked if he was going to get in trouble, but he was a grown-up cop and could make his own decisions; besides, I wanted my hands free. I wanted to touch Jean-Claude to see for myself that he wasn't hurt. Sometimes seeing isn't enough; I needed to touch something to believe it was real. Maybe that was the fear talking, because underneath all the bravery was the thought over and over that they'd tried to throw holy water on Jean-Claude. I had the memory of Wicked's face, him screaming. I wasn't afraid of my family anymore. If Jean-Claude was all right, then it didn't matter. I had to face the Wicked Truth injured protecting us, their beauty scarred maybe forever. They wanted to see me before they'd go to the hospital. What comfort could I give them? Ethan whispered through my head, *Hurry*. The cuffs came off and I fought the urge to rub them; never let them see they'd hurt you. That was the rule, right?

16

ETHAN MET US at the door with my shoes, which I let him help me put on now that my hands were free to catch me in case I fell. I put my hand on his shoulder as he knelt down and slipped the shoes on. I was staring at the wreck of the restaurant. Tables were overturned. Paramedics were clustered around two different areas; there were more uniformed cops inside, and a lot more of our black-shirted security guards. They must have come in while my view had been limited to Linley's shoes. A little bit more tension eased as I recognized familiar and trusted faces.

"It's like the prince in *Cinderella*," a woman's voice said. I turned to find Judith standing nearby.

"What?" I asked, as Ethan stood up from helping me with my shoes, which gave me a clue what she was talking about.

I wanted to yell at her, that this wasn't a fairy tale, and why would she say that, but I saw the fear in her eyes, the tightness around the smile, the way she was hugging herself. She was trying to lighten the mood to make me feel better. It wasn't the right way to soothe me, but she was trying. She'd left my dad wherever he was in the crowd to come and try to make me feel better. It wasn't her fault that she didn't understand she was doing it all wrong, and I wasn't a child to yell at her for not being the mother I wanted.

"They told me that Wicked and Truth won't go to the hospital until they've talked to me."

The tightness around her eyes and mouth deepened. She looked her age for a second even under all the great makeup. Her eyes were shiny not with power, but with tears. She nodded a little too rapidly, then pointed toward the cluster in the middle of the room. Andria came to stand beside her, putting an arm around her shoulders.

"They're asking for you," Andria said, and her makeup was smeared as if she'd been rubbing at it. Her dress looked . . . wet. What had been happening while I was trapped outside?

"We poured water over the wounds, tried to rinse the holy water out. Dad said treat it like any other caustic substance that wasn't water reactive, but be prepared, Anita," Andria said.

"Dad helped do first aid on them?"

She nodded.

"Your father wouldn't stand there and let them suffer if he could help," Judith said.

I didn't believe that, in fact I thought he'd use the holy water burning their flesh as more proof that vampires were demonic monsters. I didn't say it out loud, because maybe it wasn't true, and I would not be the one who made things worse again tonight. So I nodded at her, and Ethan and Nicky moved me forward through the crowd, but our security started to collect around us like particles attracted to us, so we moved in a cluster of black-clothed people by the time we got to Jean-Claude.

He'd lost his jacket somewhere, so that all I could see was the royal blue shirt with its round collar that seemed to frame his face so that his eyes were even bluer. I stared at his face, as perfect and impossibly beautiful as ever. My chest and throat were suddenly tight, my eyes burning. I knew as soon as he held me the tears would flow and there wasn't anything I could do about it, and for once I didn't care if I cried with other cops around.

Ethan stopped me with a hand on my shoulder. "You can't touch him until you've showered the holy water off."

That stopped me dead in my tracks. I stared across the room at Jean-Claude; my face must have shown the horror I felt at the thought of accidentally doing to him what I'd done to the vampire that attacked us, except I wouldn't have put my arm into his throat, I'd have kissed him. Jesus.

"It's okay, Anita," Ethan said, "you'll shower and be fine."

Jean-Claude was walking toward us. I hadn't realized I was backing up away from him until I smacked into Nicky. He held me and whispered, "We won't let you accidentally hurt anyone."

I had to crane my neck straight up to see his face. He kissed my forehead because that was the most he could reach at that angle. He meant it to be reassuring but now all I could think of . . . "You and Ethan will both need to shower because you've touched me."

Nicky grinned down at me. "Showering together isn't a hardship." For once I didn't smile back, because I felt like Typhoid Mary; everything I touched was contaminated for any vampire.

"*Ma petite.*"

I looked to his voice and there he was, standing just out of reach of me. Kaazim and Jake stepped between us, as if they were afraid we'd forget and touch each other. They didn't have to worry about me; I was afraid to touch Jean-Claude or any other vampire until I'd cleaned off the remnants of the holy water.

"This is unnecessary," Jean-Claude said.

Jake turned his white, brown-haired, average-looking self toward Jean-Claude. Kaazim turned his dark, black-haired, only-average-in-the-Middle-East self toward me. "We know how drawn you are to each other," Kaazim said, and his voice held more of his original accent than normal, which meant he was more emotionally overwrought than his calm demeanor was showing.

"I think we can resist until I know I'm not a danger to Jean-Claude."

"I'm sure you can," Jake said, peering over Kaazim's head at me.

They both had brown eyes, but Jake's eyes were a medium brown like most things about him. He was the perfect spy anywhere white was the main physical appearance. Kaazim's eyes were a brown so dark they looked black unless the light was a lot stronger than the restaurant lights. I thought of him as exotic, and Jake as bland, but that was my preconceived idea of what normal was; in other parts of the world Jake would have been the exotic standout and Kaazim the norm.

"But we will be more cautious than we have been with safety for both of you," Kaazim said, and something about the way he said it made me ask, "What does that mean exactly?"

Jake answered, "It means that there will be at least four bodyguards apiece for our king and queen from now on."

Normally I would have argued, but not tonight.

Jean-Claude and I looked at each other. I wanted to ask why I couldn't feel him in my head like normal. I realized that was part of my almost frantic desire to touch him. I was missing the constant low-level hum of his power running through me.

Ethan leaned over and whispered, "He's afraid his energy will reignite the holy water."

"It won't," I said.

"You cannot know that for certain," Kaazim said.

"I used power outside, and it didn't ignite my flesh if that's what you're worried about."

"Come see our Wicked Truth and then tell me that I am too worried for your safety, my bride-to-be." He'd never called me that as a nickname, it was always *ma petite*, Anita when he was upset. For some reason him calling me something new was unnerving.

"Fine, take me to Wicked and Truth so they can go to the hospital, and I won't touch them. If you're still worried about that."

"No," Kaazim said, "once you see them you will remember why you should not touch them."

That scared me, I didn't say it out loud, but it did. Of course, I might as well have said it out loud.

17

WICKED LAY ON the stretcher face up. He looked like his usual gorgeous self, and then he turned his head. The right side of his face was a red ruin. It looked like the upper layer of skin was gone and it looked like raw wounded meat. I know my emotions showed on my face for a second, before I got control of myself. He closed his eyes, and I gave a moment of thankfulness that his eyes hadn't been damaged.

He spoke with his eyes still closed. "You do not have to look at me, Anita, it is all right."

"I will always want to look at you."

He opened his eyes then and stared at me, searching my face. "Why are you crying?"

I wiped at my eyes; I hadn't even realized I was crying. I'd learned in therapy that if I felt like crying I should do it. I just hadn't meant to be doing it right now. I wiped at my eyes, but it didn't stop. I finally said, "You being hurt is worth crying about."

"I have not had a woman shed tears over me in a very long time," he said.

Truth came to stand on the other side of the stretcher. His face was clean, normal, unhurt. I wanted to touch his face to make sure my eyes weren't lying. I fought not to glance down at his brother and compare their nearly identical faces. Truth's eyes were very gray, the blue swallowed by anxiety and pain.

"Where are you hurt?" I asked, and my voice was already hoarse as if thick with tears yet to come.

He raised his left hand up. It wasn't just burned and raw, I could see bone through some of the reddened flesh. The tears dried up as I thought about one of our best warriors being down a hand. I wasn't a doctor but there had to be muscle, ligament, tendons, and things I didn't even know the name for damaged. The brothers were some of the most smoothly ambidextrous people I'd ever seen in or out of weapons practice.

"Oh my God, Truth." I glanced down at Wicked's face and then back at Truth. They were so calm. I wouldn't have been calm. I think I might have been hysterical. "Did they get new painkillers for vampires?" I asked.

A paramedic appeared around Truth. "No, we got nothing for most preternatural patients."

I looked at the brothers and said what I was thinking, without that pause to decide if I should say it out loud. "Why aren't you guys screaming?"

"Because I am taking their pain, *ma petite*," Jean-Claude said. He came closer to us, with Jake standing as if poised to stop us from touching, but he didn't have to worry about that. Kaazim was right that looking at the damage to Wicked's face and Truth's hand meant I was afraid to touch any of the vampires.

"Then why aren't you screaming?" I asked.

"I am not taking on their pain, *ma petite*. I am soothing them, so they do not feel it."

I started to say, *I didn't know you could do that*, but there were too many strangers around to share secrets. I tried to think it at him, clearly and carefully, but it was like there was nothing on the other end. It wasn't that I couldn't get through to Jean-Claude because he was shielding too hard, but as if he wasn't there at all. I was looking right at him, but the tie that made me his human servant was . . . blank.

Fear rushed through me so hard that it left my arms and fingertips tingling with adrenaline. I whispered his name, "Jean-Claude, I can't . . ."

He tried to move close enough to whisper back, because my hearing wasn't as good as his, but Jake stepped in the way. "We will not risk you until she has cleansed herself of the holy water."

"I can't feel . . . I . . ."

"Are you all right, Marshal Blake?" Officer Maric asked.

I motioned at Wicked and Truth. "How can you ask that?"

"You seem to be having an issue yourself, are you hurt? Did Linley miss something?"

Only a very few other police knew how close my psychic connection to Jean-Claude was, and if it became general knowledge I'd probably lose my badge. In that moment I wasn't sure I cared. The metaphysical connection was more than just master and servant, it was part of who we were as a couple, and as potential king and queen. I wasn't sure how much of my ties to everyone else was part of my sharing power with Jean-Claude, or vice versa, and I didn't want to find out.

"You look pale. Do you need to sit down?" Maric asked.

"No, I'm fine."

Jean-Claude whispered something in Jake's ear. He in turn leaned into Kaazim and whispered, and then finally Kaazim leaned in, pushing my hair aside so he could whisper directly into my ear. He made it less than a whisper, more like his breath became sound. "If Jean-Claude contacts you mind-to-mind he fears you will go up in flames. He has shielded you from all vampires until you clean yourself of the taint of the holy water."

I didn't have to move Kaazim's short hair out of the way to breathe back my own message into his ear. "I don't think that's necessary."

Kaazim leaned back, gave me a look, then moved just his eyes toward the Wicked Truth. He leaned in to whisper again, his breath hot against my skin, so that I fought not to shiver. "That is not a chance he is willing to take with you; are you willing to risk the holy fire traveling from you to Jean-Claude?"

I'd used holy items, even holy water, since I'd been his human servant. My cross had blazed until it blinded me, and it had never harmed Jean-Claude or me, but with visions of Wicked's face and Truth's hand dancing in my head . . . I drew back and just said, "Fine."

"You should let one of the paramedics look you over, Marshal Blake," Maric said.

"That won't be necessary," I said.

"But you could shower at the hospital, *ma petite*."

"I can shower at home." I was fighting not to be angry. I wasn't even sure what I was angry about, but it was my go-to when I wasn't sure what else to feel. I was working on other choices, but it was a work in progress.

"*Ma petite*, if you shower at the hospital then you can speak with the doctors about the Wicked Truth. They will not have a necromancer or anyone there who knows vampire biology as you do."

I couldn't argue that. "Okay."

He smiled at me; it wasn't quite our private smile, but it was a good one. "Thank you, *ma petite*, for taking care of them when I cannot."

"We're a couple, that means we're a team," I said. "You head back with Jake. I've got the Wicked Truth covered, as long as they let me shower first before I interact with them, or any vampires."

"I will make certain of it," Kaazim said.

"We will make certain of it," Nicky said, emphasizing the *we*.

"Of course," Kaazim said, almost bowing toward Nicky, to show he meant no offense. Kaazim was like that, very placating to others, but then he'd have to be to have survived as his master Queenie's animal to call for thousands of years. She looked for things to take offense at. She was one of the first Harlequin I'd met who specialized not in weapons but in magic, like real old-school spell-casting shit. Things I hadn't believed in until I saw it. I could use my "magic" to help out when I was working with other police, but I had nothing that was as good at general offense as Queenie. If only she wasn't so unstable and epically cranky about losing her old life as an agent of darkness doing her evil queen's bidding across the world she might actually have been useful. As it was, we were trying to get her into therapy, but so far she didn't want to go, and therapists who would work with supernaturals were too few and far between to risk getting one killed. She wasn't on security rotation, or in an act at one of the clubs; she was hiding in the underground of the Circus away from anyone that she could hurt either accidentally or otherwise. If her abilities hadn't been so rare, or if we hadn't liked Kaazim so much, we might have executed her for the safety of everyone, but if Queenie died she would reach out to him to use up his life force to save herself. She didn't have to do it, but that was the purpose of a beast half, or even a human servant—to keep the master vampire alive. Jean-Claude was in love with me, he'd proven he wouldn't trade my life for his, but Queenie loved no one more than herself.

I looked across the room at the vampire that loved me enough he'd been willing to let himself die more than once, so his death didn't drag me down into the grave with him. I wanted to try our metaphysical connection so badly.

The paramedics rolled the Wicked Truth past us, or rather rolled Wicked and helped Truth walk. Nicky hugged me from behind and said, "We need to follow the ambulance." I let myself lean back into the shelter of his arms for a second, then straightened up and moved away. I could be comforted later, when I deserved it.

"Is there anything else we can do to help?" my dad said.

I shook my head. "I let my temper get the best of me tonight and stormed off early before all our security could get in place. If I had handled tonight better Wicked and Truth wouldn't be hurt, because we'd have enough shapeshifters to put between this bastard and all the vampires, not just Jean-Claude, but I let our history together get to me, and other people paid the price."

"And if I had any part in what has happened here tonight, I am sorry, Anita."

"Your idea of treating the holy water as a caustic chemical prevented the injures from being far worse," Jean-Claude said.

Dad looked at him, nodded, and said, "Thank you; after what Anita said I am even sorrier for what I said and did at dinner." He looked at me. "I am sorry to both of you."

"That is most appreciated, Dr. Blake," Jean-Claude said.

"Call me Fredrick."

"Thank you, Fredrick."

"Yes, Dad, thank you for helping Wicked and Truth."

"I know that look on your face, Anita. I couldn't let anyone hurt like that if I could help them."

"I'm glad to know that, Dad."

"We have to go," Nicky said.

My dad looked at him. "Do I owe you an apology, too, Mr. Murdock?"

"Nothing you can do will ever hurt me, old man," Nicky said.

"Well, young man, I guess I deserve that."

"I don't know what you deserve, old man, but if you keep hurting Anita, I'll figure it out."

"Are you threatening me?" my dad asked.

"If Nicky ever threatens you, Dad, you won't have to ask," I said, then turned to Nicky and said, "Don't threaten my dad."

"Thank you, Anita," Judith said, with Andria standing beside her.

I shook my head and said, "If it comes time for threats, I'll do it myself."

"Anita!" Judith said, properly outraged.

"Sorry, that was childish; I'm angry with myself more than Dad. I knew better than to leave the table early without giving our security time to pay their bills and get into place. I'm the one who's had therapy, not you. I'm pissed at myself, and I'd love to take it out on you and the whole family thing, but I'm a damn grown-up and that's not how grown-ups deal with their problems."

"I am sorry, Anita," he said.

I nodded. "I know."

"We're all sorry," Judith said.

I managed a smile. "You did good tonight, Judith, thank you."

She didn't seem to know what to do with the compliment, but she seemed pleased and surprised. I guess I couldn't blame her. "Thank you, Anita," she finally said.

"Are they going to be able to help the Wicked Truth?" Andria asked. I wasn't surprised she knew their real nickname, as they were Jean-Claude's main bodyguards, so they were in a lot of the videos and pictures of Jean-Claude. No matter how we tried to keep our security out of the limelight, they were just too photogenic for people to leave them alone.

"I don't know, I hope so."

Andria looked like she was going to cry. I didn't understand why she was crying, but I didn't have enough emotional spoons left to deal with her angst; I wasn't sure I had enough to deal with my own.

"We'll pray for them," Judith said.

That was a surprise, but what else could I say except, "Thank you, Judith."

"Will it hurt them for us to pray for them?" Dad asked. The look on my face must have been a good one, because he hurriedly added, "If crosses and holy water harm them, are prayers safe?"

"Yes, Fredrick," Jean-Claude said, "I can say *mon Dieu*, my God, and no lighting strikes me, nor do I burst into flames."

"But that is you making an exclamation; prayers from us would be the faith of true believers. We've—I've contributed to what happened to them; I do not want to cause more harm to them when we are trying to help."

"He is sincere," Jean-Claude said, sounding surprised.

"He usually is," I said.

"So that's where you get it," Ethan said. He was smiling when I looked at him.

"We need to get going," Nicky said. He wasn't smiling. Of course, Ethan hadn't been in the car listening to my dad's tirade and Nicky had. I had, and maybe that explained why we were crankier, or maybe we were always crankier than Ethan. Yeah, that.

"We will take Jean-Claude back in the limo," Jake said. "You may take the SUV that Kaazim and I arrived in; it has your preternatural marshal kit in it."

"Thank you, Jake," I said, and I meant it.

"Most appreciated, but we cannot take credit for it," Kaazim said. "Your Nathaniel was most irate that he could not come with the rest of us, so he gathered your go bag, though it should be go bags with the arsenal your government insists all you marshals carry."

It made me smile to think of Nathaniel, and just like that I felt his anxiety miles away. He was afraid for us. I started to reach down our metaphysical link, wanting to reassure him, but he pushed back gently, which he'd never done before. It was like a second slap in the face after Jean-Claude cutting his energy from me. I realized that the metaphysics was like a constant touch, constant reassurance, and now it was gone from so many of my most loved people. What the fuck?

"*Ma petite*, please, just until you shower, then we will bathe you in our energy again."

"You felt what just happened, right?"

He just nodded.

"I didn't start to glow again, nothing bad happened."

"In an hour or less you will shower, is that short space of time worth taking such a risk early?" We looked at each other with Jake and Kaazim standing ready to intervene if we tried to get closer to each other. It seemed ridiculous. I caught a glimpse of my father in the crowd and realized that was one reason that this temporary ban on full metaphysical energy was bothering me so much. I needed reassurance badly, and I wasn't getting it. Damn it.

Nicky took my hand in his; it made me look up at him and smile, but I could feel my eyes burning as if tears weren't far behind. Damn it, damn it, damn it. I would not give my father more tears. I would not. My therapist could say tears were okay, natural, even necessary, but that wasn't what I really believed. I believed that anyone or anything that could make you cry had power over you. I wouldn't give this terrible night any more power over me. I would not.

One of the black figures from our security stepped closer to Jean-Claude. She was wearing a full burka that left only her dark eyes bare; the rest of her face was completely lost behind the black veils. Heavy eyeliner made her eyes even more exotic, but in or out of her burka Queenie was exotic to my Midwestern eyes.

"I have seen such things happen before, Anita," she said in a voice so low and rich it felt like she was always on the verge of singing a torch song in a deep contralto voice. Her voice made me think of words like *smoky* or smooth whiskey.

"The stories were most convincing, *ma petite*, be patient for a little bit longer and all will be well."

I looked from him to Queenie. It was rare for her to be included on a public security scene like this. She was one of the Harlequin who had not been willing to give up her mask, which they had all worn in public for centuries even among themselves. Only Kaazim had been allowed to see her full face, and Jean-Claude had insisted on us seeing everyone's face, no exceptions. The now-dead Mother of All Darkness had been the only one who knew all their faces. It had been a precaution to make certain the best spies and assassins in the world couldn't use their skills on her, or that had been the idea.

In the end some of them had used their skills at subterfuge to start her downfall, but it was still a precaution that Jean-Claude had demanded. They'd done it, all of them. We knew that Queenie was delicate and dark, and lovely with eyes that occasionally flashed a little crazy. She was a very old vampire, so old that her line didn't go as pale as the modern ones, so she'd gotten to keep her natural skin tone. You could have dropped her into the Middle East, and she'd have blended in perfectly just like Kaazim. Until I'd seen Queenie unmasked I hadn't even known that there was a vampire bloodline that didn't look corpse pale. She was one of the most alive-looking vampires I'd ever seen, even when she hadn't fed for the night. The Mother of All Darkness had brought her over personally; all of the vamps that could claim that looked more alive.

"Do you doubt my word?" she asked, and I realized I'd been staring at her for too long.

"No, it's just been a weird night."

"As you say," she said, and gave that half bow that Kaazim did with the one arm coming out almost in a flourish.

I took it as a sign of respect but always felt like I should do something back rather than just stand there. Jean-Claude knew what to do, or at least say: "Thank you for sharing your knowledge with us, Queenie."

"It is my duty," she said.

"*Ma petite*, we will choose security to take your family to the hotel. Go to the hospital and take care of our Wicked Truth for me." It was his very polite way of telling me to get a move on.

"Divide and conquer," I said.

"Always and forever, *ma petite*."

"Always and forever," I said.

I got my gun back from Officer Linley. The powers that be had cleared me to be the preternatural marshal on site who could decide that I wasn't a danger to anyone. It was an all-time, nonsensical low for the rules and regulations covering the Preternatural Service when interacting with regular law enforcement. I'd find time and energy to write up an official complaint about the ridiculousness of it, but first I needed a shower to get every last drop of holy water off me, and second I had to help Wicked and Truth navigate a human hospital where vampire medicine was still more experimental than practical. I prayed silently that I would be able to help them, really help them. I prayed for a miracle as Ethan drove the SUV, Kaazim rode shotgun, and Nicky and I sat in the backseat. My family wasn't here to disapprove, so we could finally cuddle.

18

I TURNED IN HIS arms so that I could press my face against his neck and breathe in the scent of his skin. Just that, and I could feel myself start to relax. His neck vibrated against my lips as he said, "Your makeup is already smeared. We could kiss the way I've been wanting to kiss you since the airport."

I moved back just enough to see his face. I was on the wrong side for his good eye, so he had to turn more to look back at me. I smiled as I looked into his one blue eye. It was always blue, no hint of gray, or green, but a clear, pure blue like my father's. I realized I'd been wrong earlier. I had fallen in love with someone who was blond-haired and blue-eyed like my dad.

Nicky studied my face. "Do I say, other than the hair and eye color I look nothing like your dad?"

Ethan chimed in from the front. "Nicky really doesn't look anything like your family."

Kaazim asked, "Are you all hearing her in your head as normal?"

Nicky and Ethan said "Yes" together.

Kaazim turned in the seat so he could look at Nicky and me, and then I realized he was looking at me. He wasn't a vampire, and were-jackals didn't have any special gaze abilities that I was aware of, but there was weight to his eyes in that moment. They looked as black as I'd ever seen them as the SUV drove through the night. When a streetlight spilled across us, his eyes glittered in the light in a way that human eyes never did. It made me wonder if he was one of a handful of shapeshifters that kept some of their animal form no matter how human they looked.

"According to my master, that should make any stray holy water on you react."

"You didn't see the holy water catch on fire from the human servant using vampire powers?" I asked.

"No, it happened years before she found me." He always said it like that: not *met me*, but *found me*, like he'd been lost, except something about his interaction with Queenie made it seem less benign than being found and restored to home. The vampires of the Harlequin seemed divided into two camps. The first was like Echo and Fortune, if not couples then at least friends and companions; the second was more servant and master and sometimes involved the vampire master abusing the shapeshifter. We'd stopped the domestic abuse, or thought we had until it flared up again. Domestic violence is always a hard cycle to break, but these cycles had lasted hundreds to thousands of years. It wasn't going to be fixed overnight. Kaazim and Queenie were not friends.

My phone rang and it was the theme to *Hawaii Five-O*, which meant it was some police officer that I knew well enough to have the special ringtone. I had to fish for it, since I made sure my gun and badge were more easily accessible than my phone; priorities and all.

I answered without checking the number. "Marshal Blake here."

"Anita, thanks for picking up, I know you weren't officially on call tonight." It was fellow preternatural marshal Arlen Brice. I could picture him on the other end: five-nine, in shape, with short brown hair and traditional good looks that had made all the single ladies on the police force try to date him, or at least hook up with him. Too bad for them, because he was gay, not bisexual, no middle ground, he was just not attracted to women. Nothing wrong with that, except that he was still in the closet and didn't want to come out, which meant he'd actually dated some of the women. They thought he was a perfect gentleman, so romantic, and none of them wanted to admit that they hadn't had sex with him, so when one lady lied, the others started to lie, too. Which meant that Brice had a reputation as a ladies' man without having done a damn thing to earn it. It was kind of hilarious and the best cover ever for him trying to hide that he was homosexual. It did mean that he wasn't able to date any men; the straight guys weren't interested in anything but dating tips or juicy stories of conquest, which he was too much a gentleman to give, and the not-so-straight guys thought he had no interest in them. Since I had come out of the closet as dating both men and women, I encouraged him to join me as at least bisexual to ease the rest of the cops into his true sexual identity, but so far he had kept his secret, and it was his to keep until he was ready.

"You're welcome, but it better be good, because I'm on the way to the hospital."

"Jesus, did introducing your family to Jean-Claude go that badly?" He sounded serious, but then when coming out to your family could end in them attacking you I guess he might worry that introducing family to a vampire lover might go the same way.

"No, it wasn't that, we got attacked by another vampire."

"What kind of idiot would try to go after you and Jean-Claude, let alone your security people?"

I explained briefly.

"The Wicked Truth, I . . . don't know what to say." In private he would have said something about how hunky they were, or how the fact that they had no interest in men was a heartbreaker for him, but there were other cops around to hear so he couldn't say anything he actually wanted to say. It was a hard way to live, but it was his choice and I had to respect it until he was ready.

"Yeah, there's a lot more to say, but I'll tell you why I feel guilty and responsible about it later. You called for a reason."

"I do want to hear the whole story," he said.

"I know, but you have until we get to the hospital to take advantage of my expertise, I'm assuming that's why you called."

"Yes, I'm still the newest marshal in town, even Kirkland knows more about this stuff than I do."

"Larry is only four years behind me, and you've been on the Preternatural side less than that. Give yourself a break, Brice. Now what's up?" I asked, settling back in the circle of Nicky's arm; might as well get some touch reassurance before we got to the hospital.

"We found footprints at the crime scene, but they're not like anything I've ever seen."

"Can you text me the images?" I asked.

"I'd feel better if you come and see them in person. You might see more clues to whatever the hell this thing is if you come to the crime scene."

"Zerbrowski is there, right?"

"He is."

"Then you're in good hands and so is the crime scene."

"Let me text you the footprints, then tell me that we don't need you here," he said.

"Fine, send them."

Kaazim said, "Anita, you do not have time to do this, we must get you to the Wicked Truth."

I muted the phone and said, "That's why I asked him to send me the footprints instead of agreeing to join him."

"My apologies for assuming you would allow yourself to be distracted."

My phone jingled, letting me know I had a new text. I unmuted my phone. "The first picture came through, let me look at it."

"Put me on speaker. I want to hear your reaction to the prints."

"Okay, you're on speaker, but I'm not alone just in case you want to talk about secret cop stuff."

He chuckled. "When are you ever alone? And I wish I had secrets to share about this scene."

"Okay, well, let's see if I can help shed some light on it." I looked at the picture he'd sent. It had only three toes and a rounded, oddly shortened foot. "What size is this?"

The second image he sent had a numbered bracket framing it. "Jesus, that's big. There's no native reptile in this area that could leave that footprint."

"Is it a reptile?" he asked.

"I'm not sure, I want to say some kind of lizard, but it's not alligator and that's not native to here anyway. I don't know what the tracks of a monitor lizard look like really, but maybe someone's pet got out?"

"That kind of lizard gets this big?" Brice asked.

"Komodo dragons are a type of monitor, so yeah."

"Aren't they endangered or something? No one would let someone bring one into this country, right?"

"Well, not legally, but you were a cop before you joined the preternatural service; you know that what's legal and what people do aren't the same thing."

"Well, that's for sure," he said.

I stared at the print on my phone, making it bigger. "I don't think this a monitor lizard of any kind, but google it and see. It's just the only natural animal I can think of that might have a similar track."

"Could a monitor lizard bite a person in half?"

I thought of what I knew about Komodo dragons and some of the wildlife films I'd seen of them feeding or fighting each other. "How big a person?"

"Are you serious?"

"Males can weigh two hundred or even three hundred pounds, though that's rare, and get eight to ten feet long; again, the larger length isn't typical, so I ask again, how big a person did this thing bite in half?" I said.

"How do you know this much about Komodo dragons?"

"Preternatural biology degree means I ended up studying animals that could be mistaken for one of the supernatural ones. When someone says they saw a dragon, you want to be sure they didn't see an alligator or a big lizard before you call out the big guns."

"I thought you were the big guns," he said.

"I didn't plan on being the big guns, or any guns. I planned on being a field biologist specializing in preternatural biology. I was going to be the scientist on the ground trying to decide if the police needed to be involved, or just the park rangers. There was no such thing as the Preternatural Marshal program back then; hell, police weren't even trained to handle supernatural crime."

"I remember," Brice said. "It was irritating as hell that we had to call in bounty hunters to help us with the monster attacks, but they had the experience and a license to kill without being brought up on charges, and we regular cops didn't."

"I was one of the first vampire hunters that didn't start out as a bounty hunter of humans," I said.

"No, you came out of the animator program. They hoped that the ability to raise the dead would translate to an ability with all the undead."

"Nice to know the government isn't wrong about everything," I said.

"Are you the only biologist in the preternatural program?" he asked.

"So far as I know; now how big was the person that got bitten in half?"

"Male, the legs look long, if the rest of the body matched he'd have been well over six feet tall, but if he was one of those people who have long legs but a short waist, he might be five-ten, or even as short as five-nine."

"I take it you just have the lower half of the body."

"Bitten off just above the belt, he has one of those really big metal buckles that only rodeo stars are supposed to wear, but his cowboy boots are the fancy kind that never fit into a stirrup."

"So is there any ID on the wannabe cowboy?"

"None that we've found."

"How thick is the waist you have left?" I asked.

"Thicker than mine, the legs are muscular like he lifts seriously, or lifted."

"Half again as thick as your waist, twice as thick as your waist, give me a ballpark here, Brice."

"Twice, or not much smaller."

"I don't believe a Komodo dragon could bite someone that big in half."

Kaazim motioned at me to mute the phone. "Give me a second, Brice," I said, and made sure no one could overhear us. "We're clear, what's up?"

He asked, "Is the other marshal certain that it was one bite that cleaved the man in two, or could it have been multiple bites?"

"Excellent point," I said, and unmuted the phone so I could ask Kaazim's question worded a little differently.

"The medical examiner is going to answer that one. To all of us standing here looking at what's left, it looks like something huge just bit the body in half, but none of us are experts on animal attacks, and I have never seen anything like this in any of my supernatural training."

"I'd ask you to send me pictures of the bite marks, but I've never seen anyone bitten in half; torn in half, but not bitten."

Kaazim motioned at me, so I looked at him. He mouthed, *I have.* Huh? "Brice, I've got a security person in the car who says he's seen injuries like this. Are you cool with me showing him the pictures?"

"If you trust him, that's good enough for me, and if he knows anything that can help us on this I'll share everything we got."

"Dolph wouldn't agree with that."

"The lieutenant isn't here, Sergeant Zerbrowski is."

I smiled. "True, send us the pictures of the bite marks, I'll let him look at the prints now."

"I'll hang up, see if any of the looky-loos are actual witnesses. You'll have the other photos in a minute."

"Good luck, though if they saw anything this big and this inhuman they'd be babbling and having hysterics by now."

"You'd think, but you never know." I heard his voice distant like he was talking to someone else, and then he hung up. I handed my phone to Kaazim so he could look at the footprints. He made them larger and smaller, studying them, and then the phone bingled again.

Kaazim asked, "Do you wish to look at the new photos first?"

"No, help yourself." In my head I thought I'd seen enough torn-up bodies for one lifetime. I'd delay it as long as I could since I didn't think I had a clue what kind of beastie had done this. I cuddled closer to Nicky and was content to wait for a new nightmare to be added to all the others in my head.

"Your fellow marshal is right about one thing," Kaazim said.

"What?" I asked. Nicky hugged me a little tighter as if he felt some nervousness that I wasn't even aware of. I didn't protest; closer was good.

"It is a single bite."

I started to sit up straighter, but Nicky pressed me closer, and I realized he was right, there were no other cops to complain about me cuddling while I discussed the crime. I let myself put one hand on his thigh and make slow circles on his slacks.

"Do you know anything that could do this?"

"Bite a man in half, yes, but the tracks don't match any of the beasts I know."

"Yeah, there are like Greater Trolls in Europe still that could do it, but the tracks would be totally different," I said.

"Some ogres were even larger than the Greater Trolls," Kaazim said, "and there were ogres in every country in the world that I have visited. Some would be considered giants, they could do this, but all such things in most countries are long dead, extinct you call it now."

"If they can do that kind of damage, I'm glad they're gone," Ethan said; apparently he'd gotten enough glances at the pictures to spook him. He didn't spook easy. Now I really wanted to skip the pictures. If I couldn't help, then I didn't need to see them, right? I started stroking my hand back and forth on Nicky's thigh.

"Would Edward know more monsters?" Nicky asked.

I stopped petting him and said, "Wow, I am slow tonight. Edward has seen more creepy-crawlies in more countries than I have, so yeah, he might have a clue."

I took the phone back from Kaazim so I could call my fellow U.S. Marshal Ted Forrester, aka Edward, former military, former secret squirrel, assassin to monsters because humans got to be too easy. We'd started out as enemies, but I'd been best man at his wedding and now he was returning the favor. He'd mostly given up the assassin gig for being a full-time preternatural marshal now, but I'd learned to never say never where Edward was concerned.

Of course, if I was going to ask my BFF to look at the pictures, then I had to look at them first. I couldn't have Edward think I was losing my nerve. I sighed and sat up a little straighter beside Nicky. He didn't try to snuggle harder this time, he just let me sit up and look at the pictures of the body, or what was left of the body. Nicky held me while I looked at them; he even looked with me. I appreciated both his arm around me and that he didn't flinch at what he saw; I didn't either, not visibly, but Ethan and Nicky could read my emotions and they knew exactly how I felt about seeing the bloody remains. Nightmare fuel, and out there in our city, or our suburbs, was the thing that had turned a large, adult man into bloody meat with his spine showing like the stick in a lollipop.

19

EDWARD ANSWERED ON the second ring; neither of us were big on just calling to chat, so if it was our ringtone we picked up. "Anita, how's it going?" he said. His voice was upbeat and thick with an accent that was somewhere in the Southwest, maybe Texas. It was Marshal Ted Forrester's voice when he was with people where he had to pretend to just be a good ol' boy, or at least just one of the guys.

"Hey, Ted, need some of your monster expertise on some crime scene photos." I matched my upbeat voice to his and was careful to use what I'd learned was his birth name. Theodore Forrester had joined the military at eighteen, and somewhere between then and when we met he'd become Edward. I didn't know much about what had happened in between, just that he'd been chosen for some sort of supersecret soldier program. No, don't think Captain America, think Batman. Human soldiers trained to the absolute limits with weapons, hand-to-hand, all forms of combat, and may I say that I was guessing on some of that. Edward kept secrets better than any other human I knew.

"I've got an armful of daughter, how bad are the pictures?"

A high happy voice said, "Hi, Aunt Anita!"

Yep, I was Aunt Anita to his kids. "Hey, Becca," I said, and I couldn't help but smile.

"I'm dancing the young version of Clara in *The Nutcracker* this year!"

"That's amazing, kiddo! Who's the most amazing ballerina ever?"

"I am!" she said in a high, happy voice. It reminded me of the voice she had at six when I met her. The fact that at twelve she still had that same happy voice in her with everything that she'd survived was a testament to great parenting, good therapy, and just the person that Becca was at her center.

We chatted for a few minutes about other happy, normal things. I learned that her brother, Peter, who had just turned twenty, was at the dojo teaching a class tonight, but that he had a new girlfriend.

"Becca"—it was Donna's voice—"Peter told you that she is not his girlfriend, and even if she was he doesn't want you talking about his personal life to Anita, or anyone else."

"But, Mom, they make such a cute couple."

Edward said, "That doesn't mean they're a couple, Becca."

"But, Ted . . ."

"Would you want Peter telling everyone about your boyfriend?"

"Don't be silly, I don't have a boyfriend. I'm a ballerina, I don't have time for distractions." That serious tone, that was all Becca. Donna had tried to encourage more play and less devotion to her art, but Becca had other ideas. Donna actually regretted starting her on dance lessons when she was five, but Becca had asked like almost every little girl asks; it just turned out that this little girl had been serious about it. I loved that about Becca.

I wondered what girl she was trying to fix Peter up with; it was unusual for her to play matchmaker. I felt like I needed more information, but if I asked her questions that would encourage her to keep shipping Peter and whoever. Until I talked to Peter about it, I didn't want to add fuel to the little-sister fire.

There were a few minutes more of family noise, which grew more

distant until Edward said, "Send the pictures." There was still a
trace of his Ted accent, but the short sentence was more Edward.

I texted the pictures. It's not always as instantaneous as you think,
so we had a few seconds of silence that once we'd have left empty, but
now it was Edward who filled it. "Did you get to introduce Jean-
Claude to your family before you went to the crime scene?"

"Dinner's over, but I turned down the crime scene, told them to
call another marshal. They did and Marshal Arlen Brice called me
for feedback on the tracks and body."

"I know it was hard for you to turn down the request," he said.

Nicky hugged me a little because he literally knew how hard it
had been for me. "Yeah, but like you said, if we save the day every
time they call, how will the other marshals get enough practice?"

He chuckled and it was a real laugh from him, not the ones he
could turn on and off for undercover work. I valued the sound of it.
"I haven't met Brice yet, he any good?"

"Good enough that I was okay with Zerbrowski calling him when
I couldn't leave the dinner."

"Ouch, turning down your in-town partner in crime busting must
have been even harder."

"Yeah, but they're not ass-deep in alligators." Then I thought
about the tracks and added, "Bullets aren't flying and there's no ac-
tive danger, just a dead body and tracks. Brice or Kirkland can handle that."

"We're allowed to have a life, Anita."

"Weird that we both have one now."

"Yeah, putting you on speaker, so I can look at the pictures."

I didn't have to ask if we could be overheard; if he thought speaker
was a good idea, we had privacy. "Full disclosure, I'm in one of our
SUVs with Nicky, Ethan, and Kaazim."

"Anyone who went to Ireland with us can hear us talk shop."
They all three had, but it was still high praise from Edward about
non-cops, or anyone.

"Is this near water?"

"I thought the same thing, that maybe some idiot had gotten an alligator as a pet, then let it go once it got too big."

"People have done that with things even more dangerous than alligators," Edward said.

"I know, but if it is an alligator, Edward, then it's huge. That might go unremarked in Florida, but not here in Missouri. People would have video on their phones before it got big enough to do this."

"I won't suggest crocodile; they would be less robust to your colder weather than alligators."

"I thought maybe a Komodo dragon on the list of illegal pets released into the wild, but they don't have the bite radius to do this," I said.

"No, they don't," he said.

I realized suddenly, "You don't know what this is either, do you?"

"All the things I can think of that could bite a large adult male in half are even less likely than what we've already mentioned."

"Yeah, if people haven't noticed a super alligator, they sure as hell wouldn't miss a fully grown hippopotamus."

"Your local zoo would have reported it missing," he said.

"So it's something preternatural," I said.

"When you have eliminated the impossible, whatever remains, however improbable, must be the truth."

"Did you just quote Sherlock Holmes to me?"

I could hear the smile in his voice when he said, "We're reading them as a family."

"Like reading them aloud to each other, or book club?" I asked. "Aloud."

"We're between books to read to each other; I hadn't thought about trying Sherlock Holmes."

"We got the idea from Nathaniel telling Peter and Becca that you read out loud to each other," he said.

"And here I thought we'd only ever share shooting tips with each other," I said.

"Becca overhead some of the dance moms complaining that men don't really have best friends the way women do, but she set them straight that her dad had a BFF. She came home indignant that the dance moms were so sexist."

"That's our girl," I said.

"I think you can take credit for the fact that she calls out sexism wherever she finds it and whoever it's aimed out."

"The sexual double standard hurts all of us," I said.

"As Becca reminds us all."

"Think how much worse an influence I'd be if you didn't live all the way in New Mexico."

He laughed again.

Ethan said, "We're going to be at the hospital soon."

"I've just been reminded we need to focus on business," I said.

"I want to reach out to Bernardo and Olaf, see if they know what preternatural beastie this could be," Edward said.

"Bernardo, okay, but I don't want to give Olaf an excuse to come to St. Louis."

"I'm just reaching out to them for information gathering, Anita."

"Olaf will use any excuse to work a case with me, Edward, you know that."

"He and I have an agreement, Anita. He's not allowed to come to St. Louis unless I'm going to be there first."

Nicky held me close and said, "You don't need to be afraid of Olaf with me and everyone else we have here in St. Louis."

"Put me on speaker on your end," Edward said.

I didn't argue, just did it. "Hey, Edward," Nicky said.

"Hey, Olaf is well aware that you have a small army of vampires and wereanimals at your beck and call in St. Louis."

"You've made sure he knows that we've beefed up our security since his last visit here," I said.

"We agreed that I would."

Nicky said, "Olaf is good at researching a target. If you didn't tell him, he'd find out."

"I keep forgetting that you and he used to run in the same business circles," Ethan said.

"If you mean that my old lion pride used to work for some of the same people that Olaf freelanced for, then sure."

"It is interesting that Anita keeps attracting such dangerous men," Kaazim said.

"You make it sound like she dates us," Nicky said, "but it's not like that."

Edward said, "When people try to hire others to assassinate Anita, they have to find the most dangerous and capable people they can afford."

"And our new queen seems able to win them to her side, every time," Kaazim said.

"Not every time, sometimes I have to kill them before they kill me and mine."

"If Jean-Claude had not found you first, you would have made a wonderful devotee to the bloodlines that feed on violence or killing," Kaazim said.

"Vampires that feed on violence feed on the deaths that violence causes," Edward said.

"You fought the Master of Death and his minions along with Anita, did they feed on violence?"

"No," Edward said, "the violence was incidental to what he fed on—fear—and making more vampires of his bloodline and raising zombies empowered him."

"Think if he had found Anita and she had been amenable to joining him. They could have drowned the world in zombies."

"I would never have joined with him."

"The Dragon would have been a better match for you, but she is far too removed from the world."

"I've never met her."

"But Primo, a descendant of the Dragon, visited you."

I didn't ask how he knew the Dragon had sent Primo to test the waters. The Harlequin knew a lot of shit about a lot of people, spies and all. "Yeah, Primo visited a few years back."

"What gained him power?"

"I'm beginning to feel like you're quizzing me, but Primo gained power through violence. The more the security at Guilty Pleasures fought him, the more powerful he became, like he fed on violence and harm but not death. A dead body can't fight back."

"If the Dragon could have turned you, think of the power you could have raised fighting the world at her side," Kaazim said.

"Is there a point to all this?" I asked.

"Only this: I know that you suffer damage to your reputation among your fellow police and your family from being polyamorous and having many lovers, but think of the damage you could have caused if the Dragon, or the Lover of Death, or the original head of the bloodline that Wicked and Truth are now the only descendants of were your master. Logically you would have made a better warrior or necromancer in their army than a lover for Jean-Claude."

Edward said, "I don't remember you babbling like this in Ireland."

"Anita will be having lunch with her family tomorrow to introduce them to Micah and Nathaniel, and her father will not like them either, but I wanted Anita to think how much better this is than all the other bloodlines that could have found her, only Jean-Claude, not even Belle Morte herself, would have helped Anita create a life full of love and friendship. Let that stand firm against all slings and arrows from wherever they are flung."

"If you weren't sitting in the front seat I'd hug you," I said.

He smiled. "You may hug me later if you wish, but I for one am very happy that Jean-Claude and no one else found you first."

20

ETHAN HAD TROUBLE finding a parking space at the hospital, so Edward and I had time to finish debating on adding Olaf to our information pool. "Bernardo has done more work in Central and South America than I have, and Olaf has done more of Asia than I have."

"I told you, I'm fine with Bernardo, but I don't like asking Olaf for help," I said.

"He's just looking at pictures, that's it."

"What could Olaf know that you and Bernardo combined don't?"

"Olaf has traveled in countries that Bernardo and I haven't. He's hunted things we haven't."

"Show them to Bernardo; if he doesn't know what it could be, then contact Olaf."

"And if this thing eats someone else, when Olaf could have helped prevent it?"

"Damn it, Edward, I do not want him here."

"I don't want him anywhere near you."

"Then why consult him?"

"Because I've never hunted monsters in China, and he's seen most or all of what used to be the old Soviet Union, and I've barely hunted in that area of the world."

"My family is in town to meet Jean-Claude for the first time. I do not need my serial killer boyfriend lurking around on top of that."

"Olaf has no interest in your family, Anita."

"Yeah, he doesn't like blonds. And fine, show the pictures to Olaf, he won't come to town without you and you'll warn me first." I was suddenly tired in a way that a nap wasn't going to fix. "I have to check on Wicked and Truth at the hospital, I don't have the spoons for dealing with this right now."

"Back up, the Wicked Truth are Jean-Claude's main bodyguards. I know he's not hurt, or you would have started with that, but what could possibly send both of them to the hospital?"

"Holy water, meant for Jean-Claude."

He was quiet for a second on the phone, then said, "Tell me."

I gave him the thumbnail version. "I'll fill in more details later, but I'm supposed to help Wicked and Truth by talking to the doctors, and telling you everything will just exhaust me more."

"Telling me can wait, I really hope the doctors can help them."

"Me, too," I said.

"I'll tell Donna to light a candle for them."

"I'll take all the help I can get."

My phone beeped, letting me know someone else was trying to get through; I checked, and it was Echo. "It's Echo, she went ahead to the hospital."

"Go, take care of your people." He hung up.

I hit the button and was talking to Echo. "The doctors are wanting to do things that will injure Truth further."

"Tell them no, and that I'm almost there."

"You are not family; they will try to kick you out as they have us."

"I'm the vampire expert."

"They might listen to that," she said.

Nicky said, "Tell them you're their girlfriend."

I glanced up at him and nodded. "Do girlfriends count as family?"

"I don't know."

"Technically you live in the same house with them," Ethan said from the front seat.

"How about live-in girlfriends?" I asked.

"Excellent idea," she said. "I'll tell the doctor, that should help, but you must all clean off the holy water before you touch the Wicked Truth."

"Ask the doctor if they have a shower we can borrow, and maybe some scrubs, we can't risk the clothes touching them either."

Fortune's voice was on the phone. "We're on it." I heard a man's voice I didn't know, and Fortune whispered, "It's the doctor, get here ASAP."

"Is something else wrong with Truth and Wicked?" I asked; my pulse filled my throat and let me know I still had enough adrenaline to push past the tiredness.

"No," she whispered, "just a doctor that thinks he knows vampires better than the vampire talking to him."

"We're almost there," Ethan said.

I started to repeat it, but Fortune said, "I heard. We're still in the ER, come find us before my beautiful wife starts yelling or worse." She hung up, and Ethan drove a little faster as we saw the sign that glowed *Emergency Entrance*.

21

ETHAN WAS STILL struggling to find a parking spot. Big surprise that the emergency room was packed on the weekend. "No, you can't get out until we've parked and can all go into the hospital together."

"Was I thinking it that hard?" I asked.

"No, but I know you," he said as he looked in his rearview mirror at a car behind us.

My phone rang again. Fortune started talking as soon as I picked up. "They tried a painkiller for vampires. It worked; Wicked and Truth are unconscious."

"Great that they have a painkiller that works on vampires."

"Of course, but now the doctor has a new treatment that he's wanting to try out."

"What kind of treatment?" I asked.

"He's wanting to cut off all the damaged flesh so he can try this new experimental thing where he can make vampire flesh regrow."

"Are you serious?"

"It's worked in the lab, but this is his first chance to try it on a subject outside of the study." She sounded disgusted and angry.

"Put the doctor on the phone," I said.

"Can't you just come inside? I can feel your energy and Ethan just outside."

"Can't find parking and after the debacle at the restaurant I'm not allowed to run off without security in place."

She was quiet for a second, then said, "Can't argue that."

"So put the doctor on the phone," I said.

"As you order," she said.

"Don't be pissy, I'm cranky enough without your attitude rubbing up against mine."

She sighed. "I'm sorry, genuinely sorry, it's been a cranky night for all of us."

"Apology accepted, now put the doctor on the phone."

"I'd like to put him on the ground," she said, her voice suddenly sweet and sounding far more girlish than Fortune ever sounded. "Dr. Boden, Truth and Wicked's live-in girlfriend is on the phone. She would like to speak with you."

The doctor came on with that rich, male tone in his voice that was very pleased with itself. I didn't have to see him to know he'd be good-looking, maybe even handsome, that he'd always been smarter than, better than, in a lot of ways and now he had this new theory he wanted to try out. I had taken enough pre-med to keep my dad happy and to have met a lot of classmates just like Dr. Christopher Boden.

He tried to dazzle me with science, but since I had a science background and no patience left I cut him off. "Dr. Boden, when you say you've had success in the lab, define 'success' for me."

"Vampire grew new flesh to replace old flesh that had been excised."

"So it was flesh cut away from a vampire, not a burn injury."

"Well, yes, but not a vampire. We didn't cut pieces off vampires. They're citizens in good standing just like the rest of us now."

"So, what vampire flesh did you cut away and regrow?"

He started to try to drown me in scientific mumbo jumbo, but I'd had just enough of my own science-speak to translate the important parts. "You grew vampire flesh in the lab, in a petri dish, right?" He hadn't said that last part, but when the headlines say things like *liver grown in lab*, they usually mean a few liver cells grown in a petri dish. It's a breakthrough, but it's not what the headline actually implies, nor is it ready for human testing, or vampire testing.

"Well, yes, and it worked every time. It's one of the reasons I'm here in St. Louis, so we can find subjects to test it out on."

"My lovers are not your test subjects."

"But they could be. Think of how it would help the entire vampire community."

I hadn't given him my name, nor had he asked. Now I said, "You'll need to write this up so I can read it before any vampire in St. Louis will let you experiment on them."

"You can deny me access to your boyfriends, but you don't speak for all the vampires in St. Louis."

"You keep thinking that, Dr. Boden," I said.

Ethan had finally found a parking space. It was going to be a tight fit for the SUV, but there was no way we were waiting for another spot to open up. "I'll be right up, Doctor, so we can talk in person."

"I look forward to explaining the science behind this new treatment to you." He still hadn't asked for my name, and I was going to wait until I could flash my badge to tell him.

22

Dr. Christopher Boden didn't disappoint. He was white, though if Echo and I were white, then it seemed the wrong word for his skin tone. He had an olive complexion like he'd tan darkly if he tried. But whatever I thought, he had that white male arrogance of someone who had been tall, in shape, all his life. Plus good at getting great grades, so he also thought he was brilliant, and maybe he was, but he relied on his charm, too. His short brown hair was cut and styled so that it flattered but did not distract from his square, manly jaw or the clear blue gaze of his twinkling eyes. They twinkled because he was smiling at me. The smile managed to be both boyishly good-looking and slightly condescending, as if once he'd aimed the smile at someone they would agree to his every wish and be happy to do so, but I wasn't his usual audience.

"So let me test my understanding, Doctor. You want to use an experimental substance that you created in a lab so recently that there have been no human trials at all."

"Vampire trials," he corrected me. We were having the conversation in the little curtained area around Wicked and Truth's beds on wheels. Our vampire attacker was only a few spaces down with a uniformed officer standing outside the curtained area. He was out cold just like Wicked and Truth. Echo and Fortune had let the doctor give our attacker the new medicine first to see how it worked; only then did they let the doctor use it on our guys.

"Vampires are humans suffering from a disease, or didn't you read the new paper about vampire brain activity mirroring that of coma patients? Proving that vampires don't actually die, we just didn't have the technology to detect the super-low brain activity."

"Of course I read the paper."

"Then you know the conclusions drawn from it."

The smile drooped. "Yes, it supported, even vindicated my own theories. I believe that vampire biology will be the answer to ending aging in humans."

"So you're not trying to heal vampires."

"That wasn't the main aim of my study, but if we can help vampires heal wounds that they couldn't normally heal and help humans age more like vampires, it's a win-win." He smiled, very pleased with himself.

"But you've only healed vampire skin in a petri dish in the lab, right?"

"Well, yes, but the results were very promising. I can offer your boyfriends a chance to be back to normal, to heal burn damage, which is impossible for them, or for shapeshifters."

"What happens if you put the new ointment or whatever you're calling it onto their wounds and it doesn't work?"

"Then they're no worse off then they were before," he said.

"You have no idea what your invention will do to Wicked and Truth," Fortune said.

"That is not entirely accurate," he said, "but what are your other choices? You either allow me to try and heal them or they are forced to stay disfigured and crippled."

"We have more options," Kaazim said as he stepped closer to me.

"There are no other options," the doctor said.

"We are graced with powers that you cannot comprehend."

"What does that even mean?" Dr. Boden asked.

"It means no, Doctor," I said.

"We are not going to give them over to you for experiments that are meant to benefit humans instead of us," Echo said.

"What do you mean, 'us'?"

Echo stood there slender and pale; her eyes were always big and beautiful, but with the eyeliner and makeup they were impossibly large. They dominated her face so that it was hard to notice its delicate oval shape, but once you did she was breathtaking. Literally I stood there and stared at her for a second, her beauty and her nearness freezing me in place so I could just stare.

She was the first woman I'd fallen in love with, or started to fall in love with, but she had asked for space. She had been fine with Fortune and her being part of our poly group, when it was just sex and a bid to be closer to the inner circle of power, that is, Jean-Claude and me. What she hadn't expected was love. It hadn't been Fortune who started to return my feelings, it had been Echo, and for whatever reason that had frightened her. So she'd asked for space in the poly group, and we'd all honored her request, because that's what you're supposed to do. I'd complied mainly by staying away from her, because if I wasn't careful I stared at her like a lovestruck teenager.

She was head of security at Danse Macabre, so as long as I didn't visit the dance club I didn't run into her much. Tonight, Claudia and the other heads of security had chosen Echo and Fortune to help guard us, and I figured I could cope for one night.

Echo turned to Dr. Boden and smiled wider than she had, so that the delicate tips of her fangs showed. The doctor stumbled back as if she'd done a lot more than just smile at him.

"I . . . I didn't realize you were one of them."

One of them, calling vampires not human; he was afraid of his "test" subjects, so why had he chosen to study them?

Ethan came to stand beside me, saying, "The person who can give eternal youth to the world will be famous and rich."

"Of course, he can hate and fear vampires and still work with them if it prevents old age. The fountain of youth and all that jazz," I said.

Ethan put his hand on my shoulder, and I patted his hand. I was happy for the comfort, because as much as I tried to be a grown-up about it, Echo asking for space still hurt. It was like she'd gone back to being monogamous with Fortune, except that Fortune liked men a lot. She liked being with the love of many lifetimes and getting to have extra lovers. Only Echo had retreated.

Dr. Boden was still staring at Echo. "If you could help make everyone in the world ageless and immortal, wouldn't you want to try?"

"If I thought it could be done without damaging their souls, yes, but unless you do to every human's brain what is done to a vampire's brain, how will they survive and stay sane as the years pass?" Echo asked.

"If we use vampire DNA, then the brain-storage-versus-brain-health issue may resolve on its own," Boden said.

"A young ageless body with advanced Alzheimer's doesn't sound good," I said.

"We are in the very beginnings of this brave new world. First we must heal the vampires, then use the vampires to heal the rest of us."

"Go back to your lab, Doctor; I won't let you experiment on them," I said.

"There will be other vampires whose families are more far-sighted. This will happen."

"Not in St. Louis, at least not until I've read your notes over."

"I don't have to show you my work; you've already refused, but you can't keep me away from every vampire. Eventually one is going to come into the hospital that will say yes. You're only postponing my work, not stopping it."

"You never asked my name, Doctor."

He looked startled. "I'm sorry; I was so excited to be able to offer hope to your boyfriend and his brother, I forgot."

"I'm Anita Blake."

"I'm sorry, what did you say your name was?"

I got my badge off my belt and held it up near my face. "Marshal Anita Blake."

"You're Jean-Claude's fiancé," he said. I was holding up a federal badge and I was still just someone's girlfriend instead of a cop.

"Yeah," I said, "and this badge combined with me about to marry the vampire king means I can tell all the vampires not to take part in your experiment."

"Why would you deny them a chance to be healed?"

"I wouldn't. Show me your data, explain it to me so I understand what you're trying to accomplish and how it works. Convince me you're as brilliant as you think you are, and I'll find you test subjects, but until then leave the vampires alone."

"What if they choose to get my treatment?"

In my head I thought, *If they go against express orders they won't need to be healed*; they were undead but that didn't mean they couldn't die for real.

"Ms. Blake, please, this is important work."

"It's Marshal Blake to you, and if it worked it would be a medical miracle, but you don't know what it will do to a real vampire, not just tissue in a lab experiment, but a whole living being—you don't know if it will work or have some horrible side effect. Until you have your safety protocols in order, you touch none of our people."

"I'll speak to Jean-Claude, he's their king, not you."

Fortune, Nicky, and Ethan laughed. Echo and Kaazim just stared at the doctor. "Wow, you are new in town," I said.

"He can't be the only doctor in the hospital," Nicky said.

"True. Let's find a new one."

"No one has my expertise on vampires."

"Right now, we need someone with expertise in treating burns," I said.

"We need the burn debrided," Kaazim said.

"I am more than capable of doing that," Dr. Boden said, indignant.

"Then do it; doc," Nicky said. He stood up straighter and moved a little closer to the doctor. Boden didn't like that. I realized that Nicky had already sized up the doctor as one of those men who would be easily intimidated by someone his size and build, so he'd hung back until he could use the reaction for us instead of against us. Or until it amused him; sometimes he, like me, couldn't resist poking at arrogant men who thought they were God's gift to everything.

I heard the familiar voice of Lieutenant Rudolph—Dolph—Storr through the curtain. Dr. Boden opened the curtain to call for a nurse to help him, but Dolph standing there made him startle enough he stopped in midspeech. Dolph was six-eight with his dark hair cut close so that it didn't dare touch his ears; anytime it got that long he'd head to his barber. He matched the term *white* closer than Boden did, but Dolph didn't suffer from white man arrogance; he was just Dolph, a quiet force of nature that had taken a task force that was meant to fail and turned it into the first and best preternatural unit in the country. He'd been invited to lecture all over the country on how he did it. It's not arrogance if you really are that good. His tie was knotted tight and perfect over his crisp white shirt. The whole suit looked freshly pressed like his workday had just started, but six hours from now he'd still look neat. It was like a magic power; nothing dared muss his clothes, and if something did, the rest of us would be covered in gore while he barely had a spot of blood on him.

I smiled and said, "Dolph."

"Anita." He gave me a nod and the edge of a smile. He'd have smiled more if the doctor hadn't been there. He knew most of the others with me, but he'd assume they were working as my bodyguards, and one thing you try to avoid is naming your guards publicly. If strangers know their names, they can shout out and distract them. Dolph knew the rules, so he just nodded at Nicky, who nodded back. He hadn't been formally introduced to anyone else.

Boden turned back to me and demanded, "Who is this? We can't allow you to bring more people to clog the ER."

"Lieutenant Dolph Storr, meet Dr. Christopher Boden."

"Dr. Boden," Dolph said, looking down at him with a pair of brown eyes that showed no emotion, everything hidden behind his blank cop face. Normally he would have smiled or tried to win Boden over, but he'd wait for me to guide him in since I'd been on site longer. We'd worked together eleven years now.

"I'm so sorry, Anita," Dolph said, and his face showed the sympathy in his voice.

I nodded. "Thanks, Dolph, it's, well, you can see for yourself." He was tall enough to see everything; for once I was glad I was too short to see any of it. All I could see was the untouched side of Wicked's face, and Truth's hand was hidden behind the rise of his brother's body.

"Dr. Boden was just going to get a nurse to help him debride Wicked's and Truth's burns."

"If you need to be with them while that happens, questions can wait."

"As long as they stay unconscious, Echo and Fortune can stay with them."

"I thought they were your live-in boyfriends," Dr. Boden said, instantly suspicious.

Kaazim said, "We had holy water thrown on us in the same attack that injured our comrades. If you will be caring for any other vampire patients tonight, you do not want to touch any of us."

"We're holy water free," Fortune said.

"The four of us are not," Kaazim said, motioning at Nicky, Ethan, and me.

"Ms. Fortunada and Ms. Constantine told me that Marshal Blake was here to help the injured vampires. If she can't touch them, how can she help?" Boden asked.

I had a second of wondering if it was Echo Constantine on her legal ID, or something else, because I knew that Fortune's passport name was Sofi Fortunada.

"We need to shower off and change into clean clothes before we can do anything," I said.

"We have showers here and scrubs that should fit most of you." His gaze flicked past me to Nicky. "You may end up in a hospital gown."

"I'll deal," Nicky said.

"Thank you, Doctor," I said.

"I'll have someone take you to the showers while I treat your boyfriends," he said. He glanced up at Dolph. "Unless the Lieutenant says he needs to talk to you before you clean up?"

I asked Dolph, "Can it wait?"

"We can walk and talk on the way, if that works for you, Anita?" Dolph said.

"Works for me," I said.

23

ONCE THE DOCTOR walked away to find someone to help us, Dolph said, "There have been more attacks on vampires than we have personnel to send to each crime scene tonight."

"Sunshine murders?"

"We won't know until dawn."

"Sorry, of course, but are you saying there were more holy water attacks?"

"No, this is the only one of those, but the attack at the Circus of the Damned is one of five where a human tried to physically overpower a vampire or other preternatural."

"Where, and who were the other victims?"

"Hold that question, because that's just the tip of the iceberg for crimes against vampires tonight."

My pulse started to speed, because not all my sweeties were safe inside the Circus or with me right now. Nathaniel was dancing at Guilty Pleasures tonight. I didn't even wait to ask Dolph; I reached out through the marks that bound us, I had to know if he was okay. I was just suddenly in his head; I had a dizzying moment of dancing onstage, body moving, muscles, fierce grace, and then he shoved me out enough for him to fall to his knees, the front of his body bowing flat to the stage, his hair long enough to spill in an auburn pool across the floor. His amazing ass was left looking bare and inviting up in the air, the thin line of his thong lost to the audience's view. He began to use his fingertips to crawl his upper body backward until he was on all fours, but with his head hanging low so that he looked out at the audience through the long, thick fall of his hair like a red-brown jungle for his lavender eyes to gaze at all the screaming women as he crawled slowly, sensuously around the edge of the stage using muscles that we mere humans just didn't have. Hands held money out toward him, hoping he'd choose them to pause in front of, upping the ante hoping for a touch, a taste, a moment.

He was enjoying it all, my voyeuristic boy. He loved knowing that I was just above him watching it all. He'd end the night in half-leopard form, and he'd come home to the Circus that way. He would come home to me if we timed it right and use all that built-up lust with me. He wanted me to stay and watch and had totally forgotten pushing me away earlier from Jean-Claude's caution. I was so happy to be this close to him and nothing bad happening that I forgot myself for a minute.

A hand touched my shoulder in the room I was standing in, and I was gone from Guilty Pleasures and back in the ER. Ethan squeezed my shoulder, then drew me into a one-armed hug. He could feel that I was a little shaky from the metaphysics, the abrupt end to them, and the relief that Nathaniel didn't know anything about the other attacks.

Dolph was still standing there patiently waiting; he was one of the few cops who knew just how tight I was with the preternatural set. He waited for my eyes to look like they focused on him and said, "Guilty Pleasures didn't get hit. I won't ask why you tripled the security there in the last two months, but it was enough to keep the club off this list tonight."

"Worth all the complaints from the new guards saying they're bored there," I said. I clung to Ethan a little. I wasn't sure why I still felt shaky; I could usually go in and out of connection without this much residual effect.

Kaazim said, "That was deep and prolonged contact."

I just nodded, still resting in the steadying circle of Ethan's body.

Dr. Boden came back with a nurse and more protective gear over their clothes. He had a doctor that he introduced as an intern. They would take us to the showers. I looked at Dolph. "How much of this is things we're okay with civilians overhearing?"

"I don't want to feed any of the rumors that are already out."

"Give us directions," I said to the intern.

"It's not that easy to find, and you need one of us with you to get inside, in case someone asks who you are," Boden said.

"I'll go ahead," Ethan said, and kissed the top of my head. He thought at me, *I'll bring you to me.*

I turned and offered a kiss, which he took, soft and tender. Definitely not a friend kiss, because from the moment we'd met we had been more than that. "Always more than friends," he whispered, and handed me to Nicky like it was a dance and I was changing partners. Once I was settled into the curve of Nicky's body with his left arm around my shoulders, Ethan followed our guide toward the elevators.

We started after them, leaving Fortune and Echo behind to watch over the brothers. "If they wake during all this, call me," I said.

Echo came a little toward us, so we stopped in a small space that probably put us in the way of a wheeled bed, which we moved so it could go past. "I have a question for the Lieutenant."

We moved closer to the elevators, where Ethan and the intern were already waiting for the doors to open. When we were more out of the way of the people who were trying to help people or be helped, but still had some privacy, Echo asked her question.

"Lieutenant Storr, were there issues at Danse Macabre tonight?" She was normally head security there, and would be tomorrow, but tonight she'd been moved to protect me. The rest of her team were excellent, but they weren't her.

"A customer started a fight with one of your dancers; minor injuries and your security handled it very calmly from the initial witness statements."

"Which dancer?" she asked.

I didn't bother asking; I reached out to Damian, but I was more careful this time so that I didn't put myself inside him, instead I hovered a little in front of and above him. He looked up with the greenest eyes I'd ever seen, set in the whitest skin of any vampire I'd ever met, with long, straight bloodred hair, but that's what happens to a Danish Viking when he's locked away from the sun for a thousand-plus years. He was still dressed for his job as manager and entertainer at Danse Macabre, which meant he was shirtless with only a pair of black leather pants tucked into boots that covered his lower legs. It was part of an outfit that Jean-Claude designed for him; left to his own devices Damian was much more casual.

He thought at me, *I thought we weren't supposed to contact each other until Jean-Claude said so.*

"Screw that, what happened?" I said it out loud because someone with me asked but was quickly hushed.

Damian didn't have to use words, he just let me have the memory. I'd been weirded out by being able to do that once, but now it just saved so much time. I knew Damian was worried; he knew about the attack on us at the restaurant, and he was so happy to see me well, but he now knew what had happened to Wicked and Truth. That scared him for them and for all of us. Since it scared me, too, I couldn't protest. We exchanged memories of the evening, because I'd asked first, and while he gave me what I wanted, he took what he wanted from my mind. He was my vampire servant, but of the three of us Nathaniel was the one in the driver's seat of our triumvirate-of-power bus, because Damian and I had been conflicted about what we wanted out of it. Nathaniel had been the only one who knew exactly what he wanted, and he eventually helped us both figure out what we wanted, too.

Nicky hugged me a little tighter, and I blinked back to the hospital. I'd missed some of what Dolph had said, but I already knew that one of the male vampires had been hit in the face by a human customer who claimed that him feeding off his girlfriend had ruined her for any human. He'd actually accused the vampire of doing more than taking a willing and very public blood donation from the girlfriend at Danse Macabre. She'd been one of the many people who signed up nightly for a chance to be fed on by one of the vamp employees. They had to sign a waiver to even have a chance at being chosen. Then the donors lined up and the vampire flirted with everyone in line, and then picked someone, or Damian chose for them, or sometimes he chose for himself. I was okay with him eating at work; he came home to me and Nathaniel, though recently we'd added Pierette. She was my official girlfriend. Unlike Echo, she liked the title and happily introduced me as her girlfriend. Being wanted is its own aphrodisiac, and Pierette and I wanted each other and our shared men.

"Anita, are you listening?" Dolph asked.

I shook my head, trying to clear it. "I'm sorry, Dolph, I'm not . . . I know about what happened at Danse Macabre, but if you said anything else, then I missed it."

"Doctor checked you over, right?" he asked.

I shook my head. "I didn't get hurt."

"Did you hit your head, or get hit?"

"No."

"It's not physical," Nicky said.

"I should have been there," Echo said.

"If it was just Danse Macabre that got hit, I'd say maybe they knew you wouldn't be in charge of security tonight, but they hit too many other places. I think it would have happened tonight regardless," Dolph said.

The elevator doors opened to an empty car. Echo said, "I need to know what else happened so I can do my job."

"You can't get in the elevator with us until after we cleanse ourselves," Kaazim said.

It was like she'd forgotten for a second. She nodded and stepped back. "I will need a report later."

"You'll get one," Nicky said. He led me into the elevator.

"I'd like Anita to tell me that."

The others got on and for a second I couldn't see her past Dolph. Once he cleared the way, I said, "You heard Nicky. Now, go help Fortune watch over Wicked and Truth. If they wake up, call me. If you need more backup, call us."

"As you command," she said, and there was just a touch of temper to her words, unusual for Echo. She was usually cool, calm, and collected.

We weren't dating anymore; that meant I didn't have to hold her emotional hand, so I didn't ask what was wrong. She wanted to just be one of our guards, so she could be that, but if I wasn't getting sex, and she didn't want me to love her, then I didn't have to do the rest of the relationship. She wanted space, she didn't want to date me, and she didn't want to be my girlfriend. She'd said it was too much that Fortune had been her girlfriend for centuries, and that was the only person who got the title. I'd respected that, too. I'd done everything she asked, but if she wasn't my girlfriend, or my lover, then I could let the elevator doors close without asking her why she was angry. It wasn't my business anymore.

24

I TOLD KAAZIM WHAT button to push, because thanks to Ethan having gone ahead I knew exactly where we were going. I held on to Nicky while the elevator went up. Dolph read down the list from one of the small notebooks that he'd been carrying since we met. "The same group that hit Asher at the Circus took responsibility for punching a waiter at Burnt Offerings, and two vampires in the Riverfront district getting punched in the face. They call themselves the Brotherhood of Samson."

"Are they as Christian and alt-right as that sounds?" I asked.

"Religious, yes, and they only take followers of 'the religions of the Book,' their words, not mine. They believe that the devil has made the Christians, Muslims, and Jews fight among themselves so that the forces of Satan—read 'preternatural'—can infiltrate our society and turn all humans into second-class citizens."

"I decry what they are doing," Kaazim said, "but I find anything that gets all three faiths to work together promising."

"It's mostly Christian and Muslim at this point, though one man arrested today claimed to be Jewish."

"Why do you say 'claimed'?" I asked.

"Because I'm not as familiar with Jewish extremism as I am with the other two, so I want to do more research before I say publicly that all three faiths were involved."

"Never assume," I said.

"You helped me learn that," he said.

I just smiled at him, holding a little tighter to Nicky. I realized I'd let him have his right hand free in an admission that I wasn't doing well. I wasn't sure if it was my family, or the attack, or what, but I wasn't tracking well. I trusted Nicky to shoot the bad guys and give me time to untangle my arm and join the fight.

"The worst injury is the waiter from Burnt Offerings; they hit one of the waiters that was human, just wearing fangs for work. He's still unconscious with a concussion."

The elevator doors opened and we walked out into a dimmer hallway, like they saved all the bright and pretty stuff for the patients but needed more lightbulbs up here for the staff. I said, "Burnt Offerings is mostly pretend for families that don't want to take the kiddies to see the real thing at Circus of the Damned. Most of the vampire waiters wear those big fake fangs that kids used to wear for Halloween."

"Witness statements from coworkers say this waiter wore realistic fangs that fit over his real teeth. He'd gotten them fitted at a dentist that specializes in it."

"It makes no sense for them to hit Burnt Offerings. It's got horror movie posters up all over, and some staff wrap themselves up as mummies, or wear big rubber monster masks; they're all camp, no reality. The adult bar has more real vampires behind the bar, but during the day they dress up as zombies or vampire victims. It's Halloween every day there," I said.

"The Brotherhood of Samson believe that Halloween is a sort of gateway drug for children, desensitizing them to the real monsters."

"Are you quoting?" I asked.

"It's part of their manifesto that they posted to the internet.

They claim to have chapters in major cities around the world, and that St. Louis is just the beginning."

"Do you believe them?"

He gave me a look.

I nodded. "Sorry, I forgot Cop 101—everyone lies."

He nodded. "Exactly. I'll want to do more investigation into their claims before I believe anything they said, except that they punched people in the face that they thought were vampires."

The intern came over in their white coat. "Your friend is getting dressed; if one of you could please get in the shower next, so I can finish this errand and get back to my patients."

"As soon as Ethan is back at your side, I will shower," Kaazim said.

Dolph glanced at him, then at Nicky, then back to me. He stared at me. "Is there some other attack by the vampire hate groups that the rest of the police don't know about yet?"

"I swear, Dolph, I'm not keeping anything from you."

"You seem too upset for small things like this."

I stepped away from Nicky and faced him, the anger just there instantly. "Jean-Claude was the target for the holy water throwing. What it did to Wicked and Truth was meant for him. If someone tried to do that to Lucille, wouldn't you be shaken up? Afraid for her?"

He nodded. "I'd do whatever it took to keep her safe."

"It's not one of the Brotherhood of Samson, Dolph, this nut job was a one-off."

"The uniform on scene said that one of your security team claimed the vampire that threw the holy water wasn't trying to kill Jean-Claude, just disfigure him."

"Yes," I said.

"That the motive was—" He turned some pages in his notebook, then read, "The perp is terrified that he might be gay, but he blamed Jean-Claude for all his unnatural urgings. He believed that if he could disfigure Jean-Claude's face, then he wouldn't be beautiful anymore and the perp's homosexual attraction to Jean-Claude would go away and he would magically be straight again."

"Yeah, that was the bastard's motive."

"How did your security person get all that out of the perp?"

I blinked and fought to keep as empty an expression as possible, because Echo had used vampire powers to make him talk and that was illegal. The confession would never be able to be used in court. Shit. I would have said *Ask Echo*, but I wasn't positive she understood she'd need to lie and say he just started babbling, no idea why. Fuck.

"She vamped him, coerced the confession from him, didn't she?"

"Honestly, I don't know. I was either outside handcuffed by the first cops that arrived on the scene, or across the restaurant trying to make sure Jean-Claude wasn't hurt."

Ethan whispered through my head, *Called Echo, she knows what to tell him.*

Nicky wrapped his arm around me from behind, drawing me in against the front of his body. It took me a second to realize the timing meant when my body relaxed minutely from Ethan's message that Dolph would think it was because Nicky hugged me. It made me stroke his arm where it encircled me and relax even more against his body.

"I don't know how you manage to love this many people at once; Lucille and I are all each other can handle."

"We're polyamorous, you and Lucille aren't," I said.

"I accept that, and I'm happy for you"—he looked over my head at Nicky—"all of you."

"Thank you, Lieutenant," Nicky said.

Ethan came to stand with us. He was dressed in green scrubs, that odd shade that seems so popular in hospitals. "Hello, Lieutenant, did something else happen? And who's next in the shower?"

"I will go," Kaazim said. He walked back toward where the intern was starting to bounce with impatience.

"There are two shower stalls," the intern said.

Ethan said, "I've got Anita, and the lieutenant is here, though Nicky's shoulders may not fit in the shower stall."

"They're that tiny?" I asked.

He nodded and smiled.

"Drat, shower sex will have to wait until later," Nicky said, and kissed the top of my head.

I laughed and turned in his arms to trail my fingers down his arm as he walked toward the showers.

"I'm glad to see you in good spirits, Anita. With everything that's happening I was worried."

"I may start gibbering at any minute, but right now I'm okay."

"Zerbrowski is out in St. Peters handling two arson attacks on houses."

"Wait, are you saying that these crackpots set fire to two houses with vampires in them at night?" I asked. Ethan took my hand and I held on, because nothing good was coming out of any of this.

"Three fires set at homes either owned by or with a vampire living inside them," Dolph said.

"No one attacks vampires at night, not if they can help it. It's suicide," I said.

"Well, one perp poured gas on the porch of a house while the vampire and his family were out. Luckily, neighbors saw it and called the fire department. Damage was restricted to the porch and front entrance of the house. Perp didn't wait around, so no suspects yet."

"Yay for nosy neighbors," I said.

"Two trees in two different yards were set on fire at two different residences. One was another family with a vampire member, but the other was in front of one of the group homes where the newer vampires from the Church of Eternal Life bunk until they get their lives together enough to live on their own."

"Damn, I bet that's what Zerbrowski called me about."

"He said he called you first, but then he called Kirkland, and he called the Church, so they sent some of their new deacons out to help with handling the new vampires," Dolph said.

"Yeah, I helped his wife set up a program between the Christian witches that she's a part of and the Church of Eternal Life, since the Catholic Church is talking about disbanding their mystics, including their witches," I said.

"Zerbrowski says Kirkland handled it just fine."

"Which hate group claimed the fires?" I asked.

"The porch fire is unknown, but the two where trees in the yard were set aflame are being claimed by a new group called the Holy Flame. They seem to be made up of radicals from both Humans Against Vampires and Humans First."

"How radical?" I asked.

"They want to use fire to cleanse the world of evil. They wear red hoods that look like they copied KKK hoods."

"Funny how one hate group feeds into another," I said.

"Funny that," he said.

"I hear that the deacon program at the Eternal Life was your and Jean-Claude's idea."

"The church was firebombed once before all this new round of hate started. Training up some of the members to do basic security issues just made sense," I said.

"Zerbrowski says they were pros about it all."

"I'm really glad to hear that; we had our people train them up, but training isn't the same as a real emergency."

"Well, they helped calm all the newest vampires down; not a single one of them attacked a human. In fact, I've been talking to police all across the country and there are almost no regular vampire attacks on unwilling humans. It's almost a zero-crime stat since Jean-Claude took over, not just here but all over the country."

"I'll tell Jean-Claude that we're making progress."

"We all are, but as the violence committed by vampires goes down, the violence committed against them seems to be getting worse."

"You think it's because the hate groups aren't as afraid the vampires will fight back?" I asked.

"That's one theory."

Ethan said, "I hate that vampires being nicer paints a bigger target on their backs."

"Me, too," I said.

"The thought that they could target Darren and Erica's house like this, just because she's a vampire, scares the hell out of me."

"I don't have any comfort on that point, Dolph. The main vamp in my life was already attacked and two of my people are hurt."

"I'm not looking for comfort, Anita, I know better."

I realized that everything he'd told me could have been done over the phone, so why on a night when his unit would be spread the thinnest of all was he here in person? Then I realized he was here to check on me. If we'd had that kind of friendship I'd have hugged him, but since we didn't I smiled and asked, "How is the second surrogate working out for Darren and Erica?"

He smiled then, the cop weariness fading. "So far so good, they keep telling us not to get excited this early in the pregnancy, but Lucille is already shopping for baby clothes and talking about putting a car seat in one of our cars." They were hopefully going to be the first grandparents with a vampire daughter-in-law, thanks to a surrogate who thought it was awesome to give vampires a chance to have their own children. We'd managed to keep it out of the news so far, but eventually it would get out. The hate groups would hate it lots. Dolph had never been a member of any group, but a few years back he'd certainly been one of the haters.

"That's great, I can't wait to get to call you Grandpa."

He grinned, but said, "You don't get to call me Grandpa, but I'm looking forward to being one."

"You know it's all that Zerbrowski's going to call you once it happens," I said.

He just smiled. He wouldn't care. "How did the dinner with your family go?"

"You remember how you felt about vampires a few years back?"

The smile vanished. "I do."

"My dad is that bad, but with less hands-on violence and way more religious zealotry."

He looked grim. "You promised me that if anyone else ever laid hands on you like that again, you'd report them, get their asses arrested for assault and battery no matter who it is."

If I'd followed that advice when he was at his most unstable from hating the monsters, he'd have lost his badge and maybe seen jail time. He'd been put on unpaid leave and forced anger management, and had been encouraged to get more therapy and basically get his shit together or else. He and I had finally talked it out with Lucille's urging. Dolph had never hit me, but when a man his size grabs you in anger you know you've been grabbed. I could have ruined his career and I even had witnesses, so why didn't I? Because only a few years earlier I'd believed what he believed, that vampires were just evil walking corpses. I understood that to Dolph, his son's vampire girlfriend was going to kill his son by turning him into a vampire. She was about to murder his son. Who wouldn't want to destroy the world to stop that?

"My dad never laid hands on me, he left that to his mother."

"She doesn't get to lay hands on you either," Dolph said.

"No, no, she doesn't," I said.

If he'd been a different sort of person we might have hugged at that point, but we were who we were. He offered me his hand. We shook. He left to handle the antivampire crime wave. I stayed to try and help two of the victims.

25

THE WICKED TRUTH had slept through the debridement, which was for the best; now they were in a private room on the floor reserved for vampires and other preternatural patients. I sat beside their bed dressed in green scrubs, my wet hair sticking to the back of the chair anytime I didn't flip it out of the way. There were more uniforms in the hallway by the door to our attacker's room, because of course he had to be on this floor, too. Dolph had left to help coordinate the aftermath of tonight's crime spree. I was waiting for Wicked and Truth to wake up; the idea was that I'd use my healing abilities to fix their open wounds now that the burned flesh was gone. Honestly I was exhausted and just wanted to go home and wrap my loves around me and sleep. Also, fresh burns hurt like fuck; how could either vampire be in the mood for literal sexual healing? You'd have to be more of a pain slut than Nathaniel, who was the biggest masochist in our poly group; the only person I knew who was a bigger masochist was Narcissus, and burns would be beyond his hard limit since it was one thing even the Oba of the werehyena clan couldn't heal.

Neither Wicked nor Truth was into pain, so I wasn't sure why I was still sitting here. I wanted to go home, and the idea of having sex in the hospital room, even for a good cause, was not a happy thought.

There were cops just down the hall, I really didn't want to tarnish my reputation even more, but it wasn't just that. After everything that had happened tonight I just wasn't in the mood, or maybe I just wasn't in the mood for anyone but Jean-Claude. Whatever he'd done to diminish the marks between us made it feel like a piece of my heart was missing.

Nicky and Ethan had gone to try and find food worth eating. They thought my low mood was partially from lack of fuel. Echo and Kaazim stood outside the closed door keeping watch; Fortune leaned against the wall near my chair. The dark blue suit looked black in the dim lights of the hospital room. She looked taller and more slender as she leaned against the wall like a female version of a mob enforcer, or the bad guy's pet assassin in a James Bond movie. Then she looked down at me with her dark curls like a short halo around her head and grinned at me. All movie illusions were spoiled, but the truth was that I was sitting beside one of the best spies and assassins alive regardless of how cheerful she looked. I knew her vampire master was over two thousand years old, which meant she could be near the same age.

"There's another chair," I said.

"You know why I'm standing," she said.

"Because sitting down it's harder to draw weapons."

"See, I knew you'd know why I was standing."

I wiggled the gun in my hand. "Until I get something with a heavier waistband I'm going to be brandishing my gun."

"There are pockets on the pants and top," she said.

"I know, my phone fits just fine in them," I said, patting the right-hand pocket.

"The gun doesn't fit at all?" she asked.

I put the Springfield EMP in the pocket of the top. The top of the gun stuck out and the bulk of it pulled and pressed against the material so that it looked like I had a gun in my pocket, like this was all it could be. "If I walk with it in here I have to keep a hand on it because otherwise it bounces oddly against me every time I take a step."

"Looks like it might catch on the material if you tried to pull it out in a hurry," Fortune said.

"I can fit my hand in with it, sort of, so I'd probably just shoot through the cloth."

"If you only wanted to hit someone low in the body," she said.

"True, I have smaller guns at home that would fit in this pocket. Hell, I have a two-shot Derringer that I used to take when I jogged outside more that I shoved in the pocket of my shorts."

"There are sports bands that you can reengineer for carrying that are a lot more comfortable than a Derringer in your shorts pocket."

"Yes, but I didn't know there were specialty places that would modify clothes for weapons back then, and awkward was better than not having a gun when I needed one."

"A Derringer," Fortune said, shaking her head. "They have to be right up on you for you to be certain of your shot."

"If the bad guys weren't close enough for the Derringer to be useful, then I had enough space to run like hell and get away."

"At least you had a lanyard for your badge and tactical boots and socks in the marshal gear," she said.

"Yeah, the high heels didn't really go with the scrubs," I said.

She grinned wider, her eyes shining with it even in the dim light. It made me think of Jason, one of my best friends and Nathaniel's BFF.

"Your face went from happy to serious within seconds, what happened?" Fortune asked, her face sobering.

"Sorry, you're beautiful, but your grin reminded me of Jason, and I'm beginning to have second thoughts about his visit crossing with my family's visit."

"I've still never met your Jason Schuyler," she said.

"He moved to New York to be a ballet dancer before you moved here."

"I remember the timeline," she said. "You, Nathaniel, and Jean-Claude have been looking forward to his visit for weeks. Why would you cancel it?"

"Not sure I have enough spoons to deal with my family and Jason. I want to really visit with him and I'm not sure that will happen with everything else."

"Doesn't he have to get his first fitting for the wedding clothes?"

I smiled. "Yes, Jason is going to be standing on my side of the aisle."

"That's the most relaxed I've seen you all night; you need your friend to come visit."

"I'm happy for Jason and his great new dancing career, but we all miss him lots," I said.

"Then don't cancel."

I nodded. "Okay." I went back to staring at Wicked's perfect profile. I wasn't tall enough to see much of Truth in the other bed, so they looked like they always did except that they were totally asleep from a drug. "What are we supposed to do, just sit here while they sleep off the drug, or until dawn comes?"

"That's your choice," Fortune said. "Honestly I thought the showers were going to take longer. Fastest shower I've ever seen you take when Nicky was there to share."

I couldn't help it, I smiled. "The shower stalls were too small for two people, especially if one of them was Nicky."

"You've had sex in the locker room outside the showers before," she said.

I shook my head. "One, that was at home at the Circus of the Damned. It's our stuff to do what we want on, not other people's stuff. It's just rude to leave body fluids in public." I made a face to go with how icky I thought that was. "Besides, we're all shapeshifters and they're still debating if it's just our blood that's contagious or all body fluids."

"That's a fair point," she said.

"Two, I don't dare have sex with anyone until after we are all holy water free; it would put any vampire we touched at potential risk."

"Another excellent point."

"Thanks," I said, and sat there wanting to reach out to Jean-Claude so badly. This psychic separation was making me feel depressed, or maybe it was dealing with my family. I shook my head, the wet strands of hair clinging to my cheeks until I pulled them free.

"What's wrong now?"

"I'm missing Jean-Claude. It's like this dead zone every time I think about him."

"Jean-Claude shouldn't have dimmed the tie between the two of you."

"Queenie said that if I drew on his vampire powers, I might set one or both of us on fire."

"Queenie is full of shit; most of the time just because she's one of the few true mystics left in the Harlequin, everyone listens to her."

"Do you think she's wrong?"

"Yes," Fortune said, kneeling beside me so she could look up into my face.

"Why would she lie about it?" I asked.

"I didn't say she lied, I said she was wrong. Your ties to Jean-Claude and your triumvirates were formed by new magic that she doesn't really understand. I think it makes her feel insecure, like she doesn't contribute enough, so she's started proclaiming more knowledge when it's really just a guess."

"Well, it feels awful. It's like something's been cut away that I didn't even know was there, or hell, I don't know how to explain it, but it's like I'm missing that part of me that is Jean-Claude's power running just below the surface like the electricity that runs a house. You don't think about how much of it is there until it doesn't work, and then the house is dark and cold."

"That's a good description of what it feels like," she said.

"When has Echo pulled back from you like that?"

She shook her head. "The old queen damaged our marks to punish us once."

"Why would she do that?"

"Because she could; one of her names was the breaker of bonds."

"I know, I inherited the ability, but I've only used it to save my life and the lives of others, or to free people from masters that were abusing them."

Fortune kissed my hand and smiled again. "You are like a bright opposite to her darkness, Anita. Thank you for that."

Again, she made me smile, which was probably one of the things that made her remind me of Jason. He could always make me smile.

"Did you agree to wait for the others to return before you called Jean-Claude?" she asked.

I shook my head, freed an errant strand of hair, then thought about what she'd said. "Shit, I'm holy water free, I can call him and tell him to stop blocking our power exchange."

"You can."

"I'm not thinking clearly tonight."

"Call Jean-Claude, then you'll think better." She patted my hand, then stood up, back to her casual wall stance. It was her usual guard stance unless someone forced her to stand straight. She said it was from too many years undercover. It just looked more comfortable to me.

I realized I was nervous about calling Jean-Claude, as if I was afraid he wouldn't answer. I knew he'd pick up, but the anxiety was still bubbling around inside me like unhappy butterflies in my gut. It reminded me how I used to feel when I dated, or when someone had started to pull back and I didn't know how to stop it.

I'd almost forgotten how nervous I had been when I dated. It made me wonder if my security in matters of the heart and libido had come through the marks with Jean-Claude. I'd thought I'd matured and gotten better at it, but maybe I had just been borrowing

his suave and debonair skills? I'd ask him later, but right now I just
wanted to hear his voice.

His number was at the top of my favorites list, so I just hit his
name and listened to it ring through. Someone picked up, but there
was no *hello, ma petite*, no cheerful greeting from any of the people
who usually answered if he was indisposed—just silence. My heart
fell to my stomach, because my first thought was that someone had
his phone and maybe him, which was stupid with all the security we
had, but that was my first thought.

"What's wrong?" Fortune asked; she'd noticed the change in my
pulse, probably smelled the fear on my skin.

I shook my head and spoke into the phone. "Whoever is on here,
say something."

"Anita," said a woman's voice. I didn't recognize it, which did
nothing to calm me down.

"Who the fuck is this?" I asked, and I was happy that I sounded
angry instead of afraid.

"Why must you resort to foul language at the drop of your proverbial hat?" she asked.

I still didn't recognize the voice, though the accent narrowed the
world down to Middle Eastern somewhere. I put the phone on mute
and told Fortune, "Call the security at the Circus and get security
to Jean-Claude now. Find out why he's not answering his phone and
why I'm talking to a strange woman with a Middle Eastern accent."

I unmuted my phone, and the woman was in the middle of talking. "Anita, why are you ignoring me?"

"Why won't you tell me your name?" I asked, and my voice was
even, unfriendly. I realized I'd had my gun sitting across my lap, and
that all the anxiety was gone. I was utterly calm; I felt nothing,
thought nothing, I was just here in this moment trying to get information from this woman. I couldn't afford to think about anything else but this moment. Fortune was standing across the room

talking on her phone. She was doing what I'd told her to do; my job was this.

"You are our queen; you should be able to sense who we are without a word."

At least I knew it was one of the Harlequin; they were supposed to be on our side, right, but the negative voice in my head that was never far away said, *Are they, though, all of them?* The ones like this that kept reminding me that I wasn't good enough, or evil enough, to take the place of their dead queen—they kept pushing me, pointing out my weaknesses, trying to get Jean-Claude and me to let them be the bogeymen of the supernatural set again. It was like holding the leash on a pet tiger; it was great until the day the big cat decided it didn't want to stay on your leash, or anyone's leash.

"Fine, as your queen I order you to give the fucking phone to Jean-Claude, now!" I didn't yell; my voice went low, almost a growl, because I knew if I lost control of my voice I would lose control of myself, and control is everything when you've got something bigger and scarier than you are on a leash.

"No need to curse," she said, and then there was a moment of silence, and then, "*Ma petite*, what has happened now?"

"I could ask you the same thing," I said, and still sounded angry, as if it wasn't him on the phone.

"Who was on the phone just now?"

"Queenie, she said there was something wrong."

"What was wrong is that she let me think you'd been captured or hurt and couldn't come to the phone." I still sounded pissed and couldn't seem to stop, when what I'd wanted to do seconds ago was damn near sob with relief that he was okay. Now I sounded angry when what I really wanted to do was be there to hold and be held. I wouldn't feel like we'd won tonight until we could hold each other.

"I am sorry, *ma petite*, Queenie made it sound as if there was something she was attending to on your end of the phone."

"I'll deal with her for scaring the shit out of me later."

"I will deal with her myself," he said, no sweet French nothings, just a tone to his voice that boded ill for Queenie. I was good with that.

"Okay," I said, and sounded calmer. "I really need to wrap myself around you soon."

"And I, you, *ma petite*."

"I'm all cleaned up, no more holy water to interfere with anything."

"Are you certain, *ma petite*?"

"I'm sitting here in borrowed scrubs in a shade of green that you would hate with my hair soaking wet from the shower. I didn't have any hair products, so I didn't bother to do anything but wash it. I'll have to start over at home."

"If you get home before dawn I will happily help you redo your hair in the bathtub in our room." He'd started calling it *our room* just recently. I couldn't actually argue with him since we almost always slept in there now, and when I say *we*, it was the poly *we*. When we spent time at the Jefferson County house, if Jean-Claude stayed with the rest of us who needed more sunlight he slept in the main bedroom with us.

"I could come home now," I said.

"What of our Wicked Truth?" he asked.

I explained about the doctor and his new drug that worked on vampires. "I don't know when they're going to wake up."

"This new drug sounds very promising."

"It does, though we'll need to keep an eye on Dr. Boden, as he's a little too eager to get a chance to test his stuff on real vampires instead of just tissue samples."

"We will bear that in mind, *ma petite*."

"We'll need to leave security with them until they can take care of themselves," I said.

"Do you think that Dr. Boden would use them as his subjects without our permission?"

"He already did, Jean-Claude. This medication took their pain, but the doctor didn't know it would put them out, or he used too large a dose."

"Will you report him for it?"

"I hadn't planned on it; they'd shut down his entire program and this is the first drug I've seen that can put a vampire out when the pain is terrible. If we keep an eye on the doctor and look into the program more, I think we can let it ride."

"How would you keep an eye on him?"

"We're supposed to have the greatest spies on the planet; let them figure out how to keep an eye on the doctor and his program."

"A wise use of resources, *ma petite*."

"I'm trying."

"I hear recrimination in your voice, but I do not know why," he said.

"If I hadn't blown up at my dad and stormed out before all our security was in place, the Wicked Truth wouldn't be lying here like this. God, Jean-Claude, you were the one that crazy bastard was after tonight. If they hadn't jumped in the way, it could have been you, it would have been you, and it would have been my fault."

"No, *ma petite*, it would have been the fault of the person who threw the holy water on us. It is always the fault of the person who does the evil, never those who are the victims of the evil."

"I'm not a victim, I wasn't hurt," I said.

"You do not have to bleed to be the victim of a crime, *ma petite*, you of all people should know that."

I took a deep breath and tried to hear what he was saying. Logically I knew he was right. I'd worked around violence long enough to know that I was reacting like a victim. All police hate when they react just like everybody else. To do our jobs well, we have to believe we're tougher, more indestructible than humanly possible; finding out that none of that is true is always disappointing and infuriating.

"I do know that, but thanks for the reminder."

"It is one of the many things we do for each other, remind ourselves of the truths we already know."

I laughed a little. "I never knew that about being in love until you."

"What, *ma petite?*"

"Part of true love is telling each other the truth even when we don't want to hear it and reminding us again when we forget what we've already told each other."

"Some would call that nagging," he said.

"Then those people don't need reminding as often as I do. Thank you, and I love you to pieces."

He laughed then. "It is only with you that I learned that even true love needs actual truth to survive and grow, *ma petite. Je t'aime pour toujours.*" I knew enough French now to know it meant *I love you forever.* Since he was a vampire, he could really mean it.

"Then open the vampire marks between us again, Jean-Claude. It's been like a part of me is missing ever since you cut the power between us."

"For me as well, *ma petite*, and after Queenie's misbehavior tonight I wonder if the precaution was needed."

"Or if it was a power play on her part," I said.

"Something like that, *ma petite*, something like that." I felt the first whispers of his power trail over my skin.

"Stop teasing, Jean-Claude, just do it."

"Ah, but I love to tease you, *ma petite*, you know that."

"This isn't happy teasing anymore, Jean-Claude. It's been like wandering through a house after the power goes out and I can't find the candles. Without you running through my heart the world is cold and dark."

"Forgive me, my most beloved, I did not mean for it to be cruel.

The marks run both ways; you could have reached out to me once you had showered."

"Queenie spooked you with her cautions and you spooked me repeating them, and I had Wicked and Truth to remind me what could happen to you if she was right."

"Then allow me to do the honors, *ma petite*, though perhaps sitting down would be wise."

"I'm sitting down."

"Promise."

"Yes." A few years ago he'd have been right to ask, but I'd grown up some since then, or maybe just grown wiser. His power spilled across my skin, spilled my hair back like a cold wind, and then there was an edge of warmth like a promise of spring dancing over the snow. Then spring turned to summer and all the lights came back on in my cold, dark house. Not just lights and warmth, but Christmas with the smell of fresh-baked sugar cookies, vanilla, and it was Nathaniel and Damian, then hot chocolate, but not just regular hot chocolate, my mother's Mexican hot chocolate rich with cinnamon and something spicier, and it was Micah and all the wereleopards, my first animal to call, pine, evergreen from the tree, and it was Richard and all the wolves, Jean-Claude's first animal to call, then honey spilled over everything so sweet, and it was Dev, Mephistopheles, and all the weretigers, blue, red, white, black, gold like Christmas lights, shiny tinsel, ribbons of garland. I could taste candy on my tongue, and then I smelled herbs in stuffing spilling out of the turkey. It was a feast of power. It felt so good, so perfect, and then it was like I was missing something. The meal wasn't finished, but what was I missing?

Beef, we were missing beef. A big, tender, rare roast beef, and Nicky was there and all the werelions. It still wasn't enough. Dessert, we needed dessert. Chocolate, chocolate cake, tender, just firm enough for me to think *soft* when I bit into it. Not cake, cupcakes, so that I could lick the rich, dark frosting off the swirl on top until I had just enough frosting left so that the balance between cake and frosting was just right. Rafael was there and all his wererats. I thought I was done, we were done, but it was like when you were craving something, but you couldn't quite figure out what. What did I need? Ice cream, vanilla, with caramel sauce and hot fudge swirled through every bite, and peanuts sprinkled on top, so you get the saltiness along with the sweet. Werehyena, it was werehyenas, but I didn't have a hyena tied to me, and neither did Jean-Claude, so the meal was complete and amazing, but we were missing a guest.

Jean-Claude's voice in my head. *"Ma petite."*

I blinked back to my body, or my consciousness, or some state of awareness that I didn't have a word for, and said out loud, "I'm here."

"Your hyena grows restive."

"Restive." In the darkness where the beasts hid inside me, a figure stepped out all golden with black spots, not leopard, but hyena. She turned her brown eyes toward me, their color with a tinge of red in them, so I wanted a new word to describe their color.

"Something is still wrong, *ma petite.* I have reenergized our shared marks, but we are still withheld from each other in some way I do not understand."

There was a knock at the door; Kaazim stuck his head in and said, "Ethan and Nicky are back with food, and there are more of our security here as reinforcements. Echo is ordering them to posts around the hospital in case the hate groups decide to storm the hospitals that have floors dedicated to the supernatural."

"Good thinking, I'm embarrassed I didn't think of it. It's an obvious target for these nut jobs."

"It is why we are here for you, my queen."

I said, "Thank you," because I didn't know what else to say. My hyena sniffed the air. There was something on the other side of the door that she liked.

"No thanks is needed; it is our duty to serve you." Then he was back with the door opening wide so Ethan and Nicky could come through with their arms full of food. Fortune went forward to help them with the food, but my hyena didn't care about that. The door closed and I stood up, because my hyena smelled another hyena on the other side of the door. It was weird, because I couldn't smell it yet, but she could, like her senses were more separate from mine than was possible.

"*Ma petite*, you did not eat dinner tonight. You must feed."

Nicky was standing between me and the door. They'd found dark blue scrubs for him that fit him only a little tight through the chest. He looked great in the color, but we wanted hyena, not lion. "Who's outside?" I asked.

"Jane and Seamus are on the door with Kaazim while Echo decides where everyone else will go," Ethan said.

"I know this is going to sound weird, but I need to smell Seamus. My hyena is kind of insisting."

"She doesn't smell that strongly on you," Nicky said.

"She's not like the other beasts, when she insists it's quieter, but she wants to smell the hyena on the other side of the door."

"Take a bite of something, and we'll open the door," he said.

She made a low evil sound in her throat that trickled from between my lips. "She won't take orders from a lion."

"That's new," Ethan said.

There was a knock on the door, and Kaazim opened it enough to say, "Jane says that you need her and Seamus inside the room."

"She's right," I said.

Jane was dressed in the black tactical clothing that all the guards wore, but she still looked like a petite blonde with more curves than was fashionable now and a pair of big blue eyes. I knew she wasn't just strong for a vampire, but strong because she trained hard; regardless, nothing took away her curves, which hid the muscle, so she looked like she was playing dress-up. A pale, porcelain doll-like Barbie dressed up in combat Ken's clothes; even though the clothes fit her perfectly, they didn't suit her.

Seamus, on the other hand, looked like he was made to wear tactical gear. He was all tall, lean muscle with skin almost dark enough to be called black and mean it. His eyes were the same reddish brown of my hyena, though you had to get up close to realize the pupils were slit instead of round, so most people never noticed that he had hyena eyes in his human face. He'd been kept too long in animal form a few centuries back and never been able to change back, like Micah's eyes stuck in leopard form.

There was no emotion on Jane's face as she looked at me. Whatever she felt was locked away so that she had no affect; no emotions played across her face ever, really. It was another reason she seemed doll-like. It stole something from her face, so that instead of beautiful she was just slightly unnerving. Her nickname among her fellow security people was Ice, because she was so damn cold.

Seamus's face showed more, but he'd learned to be careful around the vampire he served. Jane had been the one who kept him in animal form as punishment for some misdeed. She had stolen his ability to come fully back to human, but where she fought and trained cold, cool and collected, he flowed like dark water, always faster than you thought such a big man should be. The other guards had nicknamed him Water because of how well he moved. Water and Ice, they fought well together, but more than any other vampire and *moitié bête* pair we had, they seemed the most disconnected. They weren't friends like Magda and her master, or lovers like Fortune and Echo; they weren't an abusive couple like Mischa and Goran or Nilda and her master. It was like they were frozen—not friend, not foe, but still together forever or until one of them died.

Jane unnerved me and because she didn't like him working without her, I didn't have Seamus on my guard detail much either, but tonight I was glad to see them. I sniffed the air, drawing in the scent of hyena. I'd never been attracted to Seamus before. He was handsome enough, but he belonged to Jane, so he couldn't be the hyena that my female finally chose. My face was inches above his dark skin, breathing in the clean scent of him, the slight sweetness of something he'd used in his hair, but underneath all that was his hyena. That was what we wanted.

I went to Jane and sniffed along her skin, and found that she smelled like hyena and Seamus, too. They weren't lovers to my knowledge, my hyena didn't smell sex on them, but they'd shared a bed, or a coffin. Did he sleep curled around her smaller body? If they weren't lovers, or even friends, why would that be the sleeping arrangement?

Jean-Claude was in my head whispering, *Because the only constant in their lives for centuries has been each other.* That made sense, I guess.

My hyena sat down inside me puzzling over the two of them. She had no trouble with the idea of stealing Seamus from Jane, if the vampire wasn't strong enough to keep him from us, but just as the pair unsettled me, my hyena couldn't figure them out either. It was like whatever had made them master and servant was broken somehow, but the break didn't tear them apart, it just broke them both. Someday when I had time to poke at it I'd ask them more questions, but tonight my hyena needed something less complicated than these two.

"Go back to the door," I said.

"Your power is seeking a hyena to be your *moitié bête*," Jane said.

"I know, but Seamus is already spoken for, so go back to guarding."

"You must pick someone soon, my queen, or the beast inside you will choose for you. Trust me when I say that you do not want to be trapped for all eternity with someone you chose in extremis."

"As you chose Seamus," I said.

She nodded.

I had so many questions.

Ethan held out a grilled cheese sandwich for me. I looked at it, then at him. "Trust me, it was the best sandwich left in the cafeteria."

I made a face at him.

"You wouldn't have touched the burgers," Nicky said.

Ethan held out a Coke for me; that cheered me up. I was way

behind on caffeine, and coffee did not work with grilled cheese. "I'll feed this hunger and hope it helps the others," I said.

"Of course," Jane said, and then they both went back toward the door. I realized Seamus hadn't said a word. It made me want to call him back, but Ethan opened the Coke for me, and it smelled way better than it should have. I was dehydrated and hungry, and neither was helpful for controlling my metaphysical abilities.

I started eating the sandwich and washing it down with Coke. Ethan's shoulder rig was flapping around his shoulders with no belt to attach the bottom to, but at least he had his gun. I realized I didn't have mine and I didn't know where it was; I looked behind me, and it was sitting in the chair.

I swallowed, though my throat suddenly felt tight. I choked a little on the Coke and when I could speak I asked, "Did I just get up and walk toward them without checking where my gun was?"

"I kept track of it for you," Fortune said.

"That's not the point and you know it."

"Finish your sandwich and the Coke, then see how you feel," Ethan said.

I nodded and did it because I didn't have a better idea. The hyena faded into the dark inside me by the time I was finished with the food. That was good. I looked at Nicky standing to one side of Ethan, and I wanted him again, or at least wasn't angry with him.

"My hyena doesn't like lions," I said.

"They're natural enemies," he said.

"I know, but that's never impacted how I feel about you before."

"Jane's right about you needing a hyena to call," he said.

"But not tonight," Fortune said.

I shook my head. "No, not tonight, I'm too tired to make good choices."

My phone rang; the ringtone was "Leader of the Pack" by the Shangri-Las. It was Richard Zeeman, and Jean-Claude had picked the ringtone that we both used for the Ulfric, the Wolf King of St.

Louis. "Hey, Richard," I said, and it was just a phone call, no metaphysics. Normally I would have seen it as a politeness, but now it scared me.

"Our rule is that we check in with each other before we go mystical. Has that changed?" he asked. Yes, he and I were the only ones in the poly group who had that rule. We had a lot of history together, not all of it good; the fact that we were a threesome again with Jean-Claude didn't change that.

Relief flooded through me; I shook my head as if he could see it and said, "No, it's just I thought you couldn't reach me, because of the damage to the marks."

"No, Anita, no, if you want me to use the marks I can."

"I know we both wanted a warning before we entered each other's consciousness, but today I just want the mystic stuff to work," I said.

"Okay, but be aware that I'm at the Lunatic Café and someone threw a Molotov cocktail through the window."

"God, was anyone hurt?"

"No, they closed early because of all the other fires and vandalism. It's just property damage."

"How bad?"

"If you still want me to use the marks you can see for yourself."

"Do it," I said.

I felt his energy and I reached for it, for him. I started to get lost in that long wavy brown hair, the dark brown eyes, the high sculpted cheekbones, and all the rest that made him almost painfully handsome, but the room around him distracted me. The front half of the Lunatic Café was charred black; the old-fashioned cash register that they didn't use anymore but kept because it had been there since the place opened was a melted lump, as if the explosion had landed directly on it.

"Oh, Richard, what the hell?"

"It's not as bad as it looks," he said.

"Great, because it looks awful."

"I'm just glad that I'm finally out as a werewolf so I can handle emergencies like this instead of Micah having to handle it. It hasn't been fair that he handled issues that my wolves were having when he's the king of the wereleopards."

"Micah is head of the Coalition for Better Understanding between the Human and Therianthrope Communities; it's his job to take care of issues regardless of what animal group is involved," I said.

"Still, I'm glad that I could do this tonight. Our pack owns this place, it should be my job." I felt his guilt at letting Micah do so much for the local werewolves for so many years, and other guilt. He'd been Clark Kent while the rest of us ran around trying to be Superman for the werewolves.

"Jean-Claude wanted me to see if I could help raise the *ardeur* so you could heal Wicked and Truth, but neither of us is in the right head space for it."

I shook my head and this time he could see it. "No, not really."

"I wish I could help you more tonight," he said.

"You take care of the Lunatic Café. I've got help here; come to think of it you should have bodyguards with you."

"I do, I swear, I just wanted some privacy in case we did manage to raise the *ardeur*. Sometimes it spreads and I just don't feel that way about Jamil and Shang-Da."

That made me laugh, which was an improvement.

Then there was a sigh, and the rustle of sheets. A man's voice cried out in pain. The Wicked Truth were awake.

"They're awake," I said. "I've got to go."

"Go," he said, and I went.

26

THEY BOTH SAT up in bed at the same time, like it was planned, looking wildly around the room. They went for weapons they didn't have. Truth doubled over with pain, cradling his injured hand because he'd tried to reach with it. Wicked turned to look at his brother and it was his turn to bend at the shoulders, hand rising toward his face and stopping as he remembered. The pain in his eyes was replaced with fear.

"I'm here, you're okay," I said, as if that was helpful, or true. They were so not okay.

"Where are our weapons?" Truth asked, still holding his arm against his body and trying his best not to touch anything with his hand.

"We have them," Fortune said.

"Where?" he asked.

She walked between their beds and knelt down to draw a large white drawstring bag out from under Truth's bed. She cradled it in her arms like there was something longer and harder than you'd expect in the bags that they gave us for personal effects. She laid it across his lap and he tried to undo the strings so he could reach into the bag, but he couldn't manage it one-handed.

Fortune untied it for him, her voice cheerful and teasing as she said, "We double-knotted it so nothing would fall out and scare the nurses."

Truth didn't smile back as she opened the bag for him, just reached in and wrapped his hand around the hilt of his sword. I'd known that was what he'd grab first. He was great with a gun, but his heart belonged to sharp things meant to cut and slice. I'd only recently realized that I preferred blades to guns, too, but not like Truth did. I'd never lived in a century where being good with a sword or axe was the difference between life or death.

Some tension lifted from his shoulders and face as he pulled the hilt out, so he gripped the sword across his thighs, the tip still inside the bag. "I can never carry anything that big concealed, I'm just not tall enough," I said. I was trying for light and ordinary, too.

"I . . ." Wicked said, and stopped, pain showing on his face again, and then he took in a breath and let it out slowly between barely opened lips. He swallowed carefully and then said, "Weapons, please." It hurt to talk, no big surprise, but it was still hard to see Wicked struggle with something so simple.

Ethan went to kneel on the other side of his bed so he wouldn't bump Fortune. He lifted the bag out and laid it beside Wicked's legs. He was able to open his own bag. He lifted out his FN 509, popped the magazine out to check that it was full, then pulled the slide back to eject the bullet in the chamber. He put the bullet back in the magazine, then put that back into the gun, slapping it home against the palm of his other hand. He pulled the slide back and the round went back in the chamber where it had started, and then he laid the gun beside his thigh, hand still touching it. It helped him feel more like himself; I knew that because I felt the same way about my guns. I loved blades, but if I had to choose in that moment I'd have gone for the gun.

He turned his head slowly and more carefully this time to look at his brother. Fortune was still in that direction, but we all knew who he was looking for; they were the Wicked Truth. "Truth's hand, less flesh . . . on it."

"The doctor cleaned all the burned flesh away while you were both unconscious," Fortune said.

"I'm grateful we slept through that," Truth said.

"Mirror," Wicked said.

"Let's get the doctor," Fortune said.

Wicked looked past her to me. "Mirror."

I nodded and got my phone out of the pocket of my borrowed scrubs. I brought the camera up and turned it, so he'd be able to see himself.

"The doctor asked us to get him when they woke up," Fortune said.

"Then go get him," I said, and went to stand beside Wicked's bed.

"Brother, don't."

"Need . . . to see."

Truth held up his hand; it looked like something from a medical textbook where they'd dissected a hand down to ligaments so the student could see how things attach and work. Wicked's cheek looked just as dissected except there were glimpses inside his mouth. If he'd thought to explore with his tongue he'd have felt the holes.

Wicked reached toward me, and I held the phone up for him. He wrapped his hand around my wrist, bringing the phone where he needed it. I watched his eyes as he looked at himself. They were so determined at first, and then he saw and the horror of it filled his eyes, drained the blue away to leave only gray behind like rain swallowing a summer sky until you forget that there will ever be another sunny day.

27

Fortune left to get the doctor and Kaazim came into the room before the door closed, which meant that I was back to three body-guards, with everything that was happening in St. Louis right now. But even three bodyguards couldn't save me from the emotional shit.

I was left with Wicked's hand around my wrist while he took a very thorough look at what the holy water had done to his face. I wanted to just give him my phone, but his hand around my wrist moved it where he wanted it, so I couldn't get any distance, not physically or emotionally. I had to stand there and see the first tear trail down his face.

"Wicked," I said.

He looked at me. The tears were leaving faint pinkish trails on his skin because of the touch of blood in all vampire tears. My throat was tight, my eyes burned, but I didn't blink. I held my eyes as wide open as possible. I would not add my tears to this moment; it was his moment, not mine.

He let go of my wrist. "You can't heal this."

"Jean-Claude thinks I can," I said, and talking must have moved my eyes, because the tears started down my face.

"How can the *ardeur* heal us?" Truth asked.

I glanced over at him, and I'll admit it was easier facing him than his brother, as long as I didn't look down at his hand where he was holding it up so it didn't touch anything for long. If I couldn't heal him, they'd need to do something to keep the hand elevated.

"I have never heard of the *ardeur* being able to heal before you, Anita," Kaazim said.

"It's not just the *ardeur*," I said, putting my phone back in my pocket. I pressed the back of my hand against my cheeks to wipe the tears without looking like I was wiping at tears. It was stupid because everyone in the room knew I'd been crying.

"If it was just the *ardeur* on its own, you're right, but I had already inherited the ability to heal with sex from Raina, the late lupa of the local werewolves. The *ardeur* sort of combined with it and made it more powerful."

There was a knock on the door. I expected it to be the doctor and Fortune, but though Echo opened the door it was two blonds who stepped through. Ru was still wearing the oversized sweatshirt and jeans from the airport, but he was standing up straight, going from maybe my height to every inch of his five foot seven. He was also smiling, the sulky teenager persona gone like magic.

Rodina came at his shoulder, almost the same height, her blond hair long enough to curl around her head as opposed to his short hair cut too close to know if it would curl or not. It actually didn't curl, but I only knew that because he'd grown it out once. She'd taken time to change since the airport because the black-on-black tactical gear would have been noticed. The new black windbreakers that we'd gotten for our security hid the weapons, but she still would have made airport security call the cops.

"Funny how you just keep collecting sex magic," Rodina said, her voice holding that unpleasant whining tease she did so well.

"If all I could do was sex magic, I'd have been dead years ago."

"Sister, we talked about this," Ru said.

She stalked past him into the room. "He wants me to be nicer to you. He enjoys being here in St. Louis with you, our new queen."

"I offered to let you travel internationally to check on some of the other vampire groups to see what they're doing now that they don't have the Mother of All Darkness and the old vampire council to keep them in line."

"My brother and I work together," she said.

"So because he won't go, you stay here and blame me that you're bored."

"Ru followed Rodrigo and me for over a thousand years with no complaints until he met you. You haven't even fucked him and he's already pussy-whipped." She sounded disgusted.

"Ru followed you because even he was afraid of Rodrigo. He was afraid of what his own brother would do to him if he tried to have a life of his own."

"I never knew what a coward Ru was until Rodrigo died," she said.

"Dina," Ru said, and he sounded shocked.

"If you wanted to go off on your own, you should have stood up to us and demanded it," she said.

"He would have killed me."

"He loved you."

"You love me, I'm not sure Roddy was capable of loving anyone."

"He loved us."

"I didn't feel loved, Rodina, I felt tolerated and bullied."

She didn't know what to say to him, so she turned on me. "You got Rodrigo killed and now look at us, babysitters at a hospital when we should be taking the battle to zealots who are targeting the supernatural."

"Rodrigo decided to kidnap me. I wasn't hunting him, or any of you. I had no quarrel with you. He made it personal when he killed Domino, when he forced me to watch Domino die. Even then you'd have been safe from my magic, except he shoved his fingers down my throat covered in my lover's blood. Tiger clan blood."

She was silent, not looking at me. "Tiger clan blood has always been powerful and was the only weakness of our Evil Queen that you slew."

"She was trying to possess my body and take over the world when I killed her, Rodina."

"Yes, you're always the victim, aren't you?"

"No, I'm not the victim. People keep treating me like I'm the princess in this story, someone you kidnap, or bespell to overcome your enemies, or use to make your kingdom bigger. But I am not the motherfucking princess, I am the knight that rescues her. It was your mistake, yours, and Rodrigo's mistake to treat me like a pawn when I am the queen!"

"But you are not my queen!" Rodina screamed.

"But she is my queen," Ru said, and his quiet voice filled the space between his sister and me. He stepped between us before anyone else could.

Kaazim was in the room with the door shut behind him. "Fortune and Echo are keeping the doctor distracted, but it will not last and we need him to help us with our injured."

"I request a different assignment for tonight," Rodina said.

"There are many entrances to the hospital, I'm sure Echo can find a use for you."

"Micah requested we stay with Anita so she could have leopard near her," Ru said.

"One leopard will be enough until she gets back to the Circus, then she has Nathaniel and Micah, and Pierette. She'll be fine."

"He is our Nimir-raj, and he gave us express orders."

"Yes, he's our leopard king, but until we came to this Gods-forsaken corner of the world we were a pard of three and that was enough for all of us. I don't want to make friends with other were-leopards. I don't want to have to obey two kings and a queen. I want my brother back and only one voice ordering me around."

"I like being part of the leopards here," Ru said.

"Of course you do." She looked at Kaazim. "May I go be reassigned?"

"It is not my pardon you must ask before leaving this room."

Her head slumped and took her shoulders with it as if she would fold in half, but she straightened and turned to me. "Anita, our white queen, may I find a new assignment for tonight?"

"Yes," I said.

"Thank you," she said, managing to make it sound like she wanted to say *fuck you*, but we didn't punish people for what they were thinking. Kaazim opened the door for her to leave and mentioned something soft to Echo, who was still on the door.

I heard Dr. Boden's voice. "I need to see my patients."

"We need to let the doctor see them," I said.

"What can he do for us?" Wicked asked.

"I don't know, honestly, but the new drug took your pain and let you sleep."

"Sleep doesn't help us heal like it does for humans and wereanimals," Truth said.

"Dead flesh does not heal," Wicked added.

"A trade-off with the whole not-aging thing, I guess," I said.

"Tonight, the trade-off seems less than ideal," Wicked replied.

I looked at him. "Yeah," I said.

"Maybe the doctor will have some ideas," Ethan said.

"Anita," Nicky asked, "why did Micah want you to have leopards with you?"

"I'm not sure."

Nicky looked at Ru. "Did Micah give you a reason for Anita needing leopards?"

"He just told us to go to Anita and stay with her."

"Did Rodina ask why?" I asked.

"He called me."

"And you didn't ask," I said.

He shook his head.

"I need to call Micah and find out what's going on."

"He wouldn't have sent them to you without a good reason," Nicky said.

"Yeah, and thanks for asking the question for me. I wouldn't have caught it."

"Part of my job."

"Ethan, stay with them while the doctor is in here; don't let him put anything on their injuries until you check with me."

"Nicky, Ru, with me." I went for the door and some privacy for the phone call. I didn't look back at the Wicked Truth. It wouldn't have helped, and right now it hurt to see them like that, because it was my fault. We'd have had more wereanimals around the vampires. They might have been hit by the water, but not this badly. They sacrificed themselves to save Jean-Claude. They'd done their job at great cost. I just hoped we could figure out a way to pay that cost, or the guilt was going to gnaw on me forever.

28

I WALKED TO THE far end of the hallway by the restrooms to call Micah. I was trying to get out of supernatural earshot. I leaned in the corner by the ladies' room, which made me realize that using it before I went back to the room wasn't a bad idea. Funny how you don't think of necessities during emergencies until something reminds you.

I called Micah, and he answered like he'd been waiting for it. "Anita, it's good to hear your voice." He sounded so relieved.

"Jesus, Micah, I'm sorry I didn't think that you aren't hooked into me the way everyone else is; I should have called you from the car on the way to the hospital."

"'Should' isn't a useful word, but yes, I'd like more phone calls in the future."

"Want to FaceTime?" I asked.

"Actually, yes."

"I'll hang up and call you back."

"I love you," he said.

"I love you more." Then I hung up so I could call him back with visuals.

Nicky and Ru were already standing facing outward so they could see anyone coming down either hallway, so there was no way to peek over my shoulder. I wouldn't have minded for Nicky, but he'd already picked up on my guilt about not thinking about calling Micah.

He answered the phone smiling, and something heavy and tight in my chest eased at seeing his face. He'd already started getting a tan from running outside, which he preferred to the air-conditioned track in the gym at the Circus. The darker his skin got, the more exotic his green-gold leopard eyes looked in the delicate beauty of his face. He was my height, short for a woman, shorter for a man, but I loved it. I'd met him the night the *ardeur* had first risen in me, and its magic had thrown us together, created love at first sight that had given us both our heart's desire in that moment.

"Hey, handsome, I wish I was there in person."

"You call everyone handsome, but I wish you were here, too."

I frowned. "Do I really call everyone handsome?"

He shook his head. "No, but it is your default."

"I'm sorry," I said.

"You don't have to apologize."

"You're upset with me."

"I was worried and upset that you didn't call me, but I'm not upset now. I'm just relieved to see you and hear your voice." He smiled and I knew he meant it.

"I feel better just seeing and hearing you, too."

He reached back and took the ponytail holder out of his hair, then shook all those dark brown curls around his face. "Come home and we can do more than just look at each other."

"Why, Mr. Callahan, are you trying to seduce me?"

He grinned, playing his fingers around the tight curls. His mother had sent him some new hair-care products that had turned his loose curls into a lot more tighter, smaller ones. It had turned his hair into a brand-new texture; even the scent of it had changed. I wasn't sure why, but it affected me like brand-new lingerie. Neither Jean-Claude's curls nor mine ever looked like that or could, because neither of us had any African genetics. He, like me, was a mix of genetics, though

I hadn't realized just how mixed until I'd met his mother just a few years ago. She'd now started giving us hair-care advice over the phone. Jean-Claude was loving it, even though most of it didn't work for his hair. He was always willing to learn new ways to pamper himself, or the rest of us.

"If I'd known it was such a turn-on for you, I'd have changed my hair more often."

Nicky said, "Anita, you're getting distracted."

"Wow, you're right."

"What's wrong?" Micah asked; the smile and flirting was gone, and he was back to his usual serious self.

"Why did you send Ru and Rodina to me?"

"So you'd have wereleopards with you."

I had to smile. "Don't be so literal. Why was it important for me to have wereleopards with me tonight?"

"I got distracted and flirted with you when this is serious. Jean-Claude says that there's something wrong with the vampire marks."

"Yeah, I know."

"We thought with the marks not working like they should, that you having some of every beast you carry would be a good idea."

"Smart," I said.

"Also, Nathaniel said that your connection to him and to Damian seems fine, like normal, so there's a chance that your connection to your leopard is stronger than the rest of your beasts right now."

"Why would that be?" I asked.

"Leopard was your first beast to call."

"Wolf was first."

He shook his head. "No, that was you sharing energy with Jean-Claude and his beast. Leopard was just yours and still is; even when he was choosing a second one, it was gold tiger, lion, hyena, or rat from what you all told me. I'm sorry I missed all the excitement, by the way."

"I'm sorry you missed it, too, but your negotiations on the West

Coast stopped the hostilities between two shapeshifter groups before it erupted into all-out war. You saved a lot of lives."

"I know that the work I do with the coalition is important, but you're important, my life in St. Louis is important, and I feel like I'm missing too much of it lately."

"You have been gone a lot," I said.

"I am trying to delegate more."

"But so far none of your delegates have your gift at negotiations."

"Socrates can do it," he said.

"But you gave him time off to help his wife with the newest baby," I said.

"They've got a six-year-old, a toddler, and the baby; if I went out of town on you with all that plus your job you'd never forgive me."

"You're going to be lucky to get one kid out of me, three is not happening."

"You know I believe that it's your body, your choice," he said.

"I do, and it's just one of the things that I love about you."

"Some of the men in our lives say that I can afford to be generous since I can't have children of my own."

"The fact that you had a vasectomy years before we met just makes me feel safer with you," I said.

"Tell me and I'll get one for you," Nicky said.

"You have but to give the order," Ru said.

I looked at them and knew they meant it. "I don't know what to say to that. It hadn't even occurred to me."

"You can think about it later, Anita," Micah said.

"He's right," Nicky said, "you still need to heal the Wicked Truth."

"How badly are they hurt?" Micah asked.

"Bad enough that I don't know if I can heal it."

Nicky said, "She's healed life-threatening injuries before. These aren't that bad."

"It's not like you to be this doubtful about your abilities, Anita," Micah said.

"I healed knife wounds once on one vampire, all the rest have been wereanimals. I've never healed anything this serious on a vampire before."

"Jean-Claude described the injuries to me, would you leave them like that without even trying?"

"No, of course not, but . . . I just. I don't know, I just don't feel like myself tonight."

"Is it seeing your family?" he asked.

I said, "Maybe."

Nicky said, "Yes."

I frowned at him.

"Don't let them make you doubt yourself, Anita," Micah said.

"I don't think it's just that, I think it's not having Jean-Claude's marks fully functioning."

"Why would that make you doubt yourself?"

"It's like all my game for dating and romance is gone and I'm back to being my old awkward self."

"You're doing really well with me," Micah said.

"I seem to be okay with people I love, but if it's less than that, not so much."

Ethan breathed through my mind, *Doctor's trying to convince the Wicked Truth that only his experimental skin will heal them.*

"Who's talking through you?" Micah asked.

"Ethan; the doctor is trying to convince Wicked and Truth to use his experimental treatment." I thought back to Ethan, *Don't let them do it.*

Ethan said, *That's what the rest of us told them, but Wicked is scared. Tell them I'm coming to try and heal them.*

"Go take care of the Wicked Truth," Micah said. "I love you."

"I love you, too." I didn't sound very convincing. "I'm sorry, Micah, I love you so much."

"I know that, now go do what you need to do to help Wicked and Truth."

"I'll do my best."

"Your best is always more than enough, Anita. Stop doubting yourself."

"I'm missing Jean-Claude's suave and debonair in my head, I think."

"Then go be charmingly awkward, I know you can do that without Jean-Claude's help." He was almost laughing.

"Charmingly awkward, really?"

"Really," Micah and Nicky said together.

I hung up and used the ladies' room, while Ru guarded the door and Nicky stood outside the stall. I tried to convince him that was a little too much bodyguarding, but unless I was going to order them to be less cautious of my safety it was faster to just go along with it, so I did.

29

I'D BARELY WALKED into the room when Jean-Claude called me. "*Ma petite*, Nathaniel and Damian say that you were able to visit them mind-to-mind, and it worked as it always has; let us try and see if we can repair the damage that Queenie's interference caused."

"You think she damaged our marks on purpose?"

"She is under guard as a precaution."

"She can do magic like out of legend or myth, Jean-Claude. Who do we have that can handle that?"

"We have reached out to our allies among the wererats. They have agreed to use their magic to aid us."

"I thought their magic only worked inside their inner sanctum."

"It is most powerful there, but their brujas are not helpless in the world at large."

"Good to know," I said.

"If coming to you in vision does not repair the damage, then come home. Allow me to seduce you as of old, *ma petite*, I think that will work."

"That sounds like a great way to end the night," I said.

"The best way to end every night, *ma petite*."

"Now I half want to fail so I can just come home to you."

"We must heal our Wicked Truth before we think of our own pleasure, *ma petite*."

"Of course," I said.

We hung up and then I felt him like a cool wind making me shiver in the cold, but it was missing that edge of warmth that sparked so much between us. Then I could see him in the big bed. The sheets this week were a royal blue that framed his long black hair and his pale upper body. The cross-shaped burn scar on his chest was shinier than the skin around it, but it wasn't an imperfection. It was just part of his body, a different texture to run my fingers and mouth over. The shine of the blue silk turned his eyes from midnight blue to almost as blue as the sheets. I loved when his eyes changed from the sheets, or his shirt, anything that was a lighter blue than his eyes.

"God, you're so beautiful," I said.

He gave that smile that let me know he knew exactly how beautiful he was and the effect he had on me. In the beginning I'd resented how attracted I was to him; I thought it stole my control. I hadn't realized that love always steals our control, it's just part of how it works.

"*Ma petite, ma petite*, come to bed."

I shivered so hard it almost made me stumble. "How can anyone resist you?"

"I do not want you to resist me, *ma petite*."

"I gave up trying to resist temptation where you're concerned," I said.

"Then give in to the temptation that is our Wicked Truth and bring them home." He closed the link down and I was left standing in the hospital room with my skin still covered in goose bumps. One minute I was basking in the afterglow, the next it was like the lights had been turned off again.

"I felt you reconnect with him, and then it was just gone again," Ethan said.

"Damn it," I said.

"Jean-Claude told you to give in to the temptation that is us, but unless the *ardeur* is inside you to take away our pain, I don't think we will be very tempting," Truth said.

"I'm so not in the mood to have sex in a hospital room," I said.

"Even to have a chance to heal the Wicked Truth?" Ethan said.

"Of course I want to heal them, that's why I came to the hospital and didn't go home with Jean-Claude."

"Jean-Claude wants you to give in to temptation and do what he can't, heal them," he said.

"So if I happen to find myself in the mood you want me to just go for it, in case it fixes the *ardeur*?"

They all said yes in unison. It made me shake my head. "Fine, if the mood hits me I won't fight it, but until that happens let's concentrate on a different problem."

"Did Jean-Claude say that Queenie damaged his connection to you on purpose?" Ru asked.

"He's not sure, but either she did it on purpose or she did it by accident," I said.

"If she did it by accident, we can't trust her abilities," Ethan said.

"And if she did it on purpose, we can't trust her," Nicky said.

"Would Kaazim know which is more likely?" I asked.

"He's her animal to call, Anita, he may not be able to answer us," Ru said.

"Why not?"

"Because she is his master."

"Well, Jean-Claude is mine, but I would still be able to tell someone if he was a traitor."

"You and Jean-Claude are more a partnership like Fortune and Echo; Queenie has never treated Kaazim as her partner."

"They don't like each other much," I said.

"He hates her, and she considers him less than . . ." Ru seemed to search for a word and then just said, "She considers him less than."

I wanted to trust Kaazim because I did trust him.

Ethan spoke mind-to-mind. *If Kaazim and Queenie are both traitors we need to get you away from both of them.*

I'd seen Kaazim in knife practice; he was amazing with a blade, but he was equally good with a handgun. Long gun was his weakest weapon skill, but that was like saying a Formula 500 driver wasn't quite as good driving his everyday car. Hand-to-hand he was wicked fast, and the only thing that kept him from damaging his training partners was that training wasn't supposed to hurt that much.

"I really like having him on our side," I said.

"The alternative would be bad," Ethan said.

"This is ridiculous, he's our friend. He's been on more missions out of country with Bobby Lee and the wererats than any of the Harlequin."

"We are the best spies that have ever lived, Anita," Ru said.

"So everyone keeps telling me."

"It means that we are the best professional liars that have ever lived," Ru said.

Truth said, "If there are traitors in our midst, we must take Anita back to the Circus now."

"Take her now, do not delay," Wicked said.

"I can't leave you like this," I said.

"You can and you will," Truth said.

"We can take more of the doctor's medicine and sleep pain free until you can come and heal us," Wicked said. It was the longest sentence he'd said since he hurt his face.

"If there are traitors among the Harlequin, then we can't leave you here unconscious and helpless," I said.

"She's right," Nicky said.

"Then let's get them some clothes and get the hell out of here," I said.

"Kaazim will want to ride back with us," Ethan said.

"Shit, you're right," I said.

"Can't Anita just order him to stay here?" Ru asked.

We looked at him.

"She's our queen now, her word is law."

"He'll ask why I'm changing Jake's orders," I said.

"A queen doesn't have to explain herself," Ru said, "that's part of what it means to be queen."

"Would we rather keep an eye on him?" I asked.

"No," Truth said, "if he is a traitor then farther away from you is where we want him."

"Agreed," Wicked said, "and I hope he's not in league with his master, because wounded we are not a match for him."

"I never thought I'd hear the two of you admit to any weakness," Nicky said.

"That is how high we hold him in esteem," Truth said.

"You mean that he's scary good," I said.

"Scary good," Truth said, "yes, Kaazim is scary good and I am down a hand."

"I have both my hands, but the pain is enough that I will not be at my best," Wicked said.

"And we all need to be at our best if we're going to fight Kaazim," Ethan said.

"Before you tamed me and gave me a conscience I'd have just shot him as soon as I saw him, no muss, no fuss," Nicky said.

"You mean you'd just kill him?"

Nicky nodded.

"What if we found out afterward that he wasn't a traitor?"

"Oops."

I stared at him. "I thought you liked Kaazim."

"I do."

I didn't know what to say to that, so I didn't try. Nicky could feel what I was feeling; that was comment enough.

"Because I can feel how unhappy you are with what I just said, and that causes me real pain that I have to say something I would never have said out loud."

"No," I said, "I don't want to force you . . ."

He put his hand over my mouth, gently. "It's not force like you think of it. If you had not made me your Bride I would have been one of those men who don't communicate enough to have a good relationship with a woman. She would never have understood me like you do."

He took his hand away from my mouth. "Say it."

"You have my thoughts and feelings in your head; of course we understand each other better than an ordinary couple."

He shook his head. "That's not what I mean, Anita."

"Okay, what do you mean?"

"I mean that I like Kaazim, and up to this point he'd have been on my short list to take into a fight, but I don't like anyone as much as I love you. I would destroy anyone and anything that endangered you, not because I'm your Bride and you force me to care for your safety, but because I am in love with you and you're in love with me. You're in love with all of me. You don't like all of the things I've done in my life, but as long as I don't go back to doing them, you accept my past. You love that I'm ruthless in a fight. You love that I'm violent when it's needed. You even let me take some of that violence into the bedroom with you and you enjoy it with me. You love all of me, because you have your own ruthlessness, your own violence. You taught me the only true gentleness I've ever known. You taught me that kindness isn't weakness. I've learned that I'm just as manly helping Nathaniel cook dinner as I am taking him to the shooting range. You tore my life apart, then showed me I could rebuild it into something better for myself. You wanted me to be happy, even if that made you uncomfortable or unhappy yourself. If you asked me to change, you were willing to change with me and find a better way of being together; for all that and more I would put a bullet through anyone's head. I would burn the world down if it would keep you safe and meant that we could go on loving each other one more day."

What do you say to a declaration like that? "God, I love you so much." And then I wrapped myself around him and kissed him like I meant it. We even tried a little heavy petting to see if the *ardeur* would rise, but there was no hint of it. I wanted and loved Nicky, but the sex magic that might let me heal the Wicked Truth eluded me. So we focused on business. We had other disasters besides the *ardeur* being gone.

30

I TEXTED OUR SUSPICIONS about Kaazim to Fortune since Echo had started ignoring my texts since we broke up, but to tell one was to tell both. Kaazim opened the door after Echo told him to, but Nicky blocked the way into the hospital room. "What has happened?" Kaazim asked.

Echo shoved a gun into his back, with Fortune being tall enough to block the view from the hallway. Kaazim didn't protest or act surprised, which could have meant he wasn't surprised and he was a traitor, or he didn't know what the hell was going on and was trying to be neutral and not provoke anyone.

I said, "Queenie has fucked up."

"What has she done now?" he asked; again there was no surprise, only a sort of weariness.

Fortune took Kaazim's bag of clothes and weapons from his un-resisting hand. Echo was patting him down from the back, even though the scrubs made it almost impossible to hide anything. I answered his question, telling him what Queenie had done from across the room where I'd been told to stand. Kaazim said, "I will allow Nicky to search and take any weapons he finds from the front."

"Nice to be allowed," Nicky said with a slice of sarcasm, but he searched Kaazim and managed to find a knife, though I wasn't sure where the hell Kaazim had been hiding it. Once we were sure he was weapons free and as safe as it was possible for him to be, then Echo followed him into the room, closing the door behind them. Fortune stayed at the door to keep any nursing staff from interrupting us.

Kaazim clasped his hands on top of his head without being asked, and said, "If Queenie has truly used her magic to damage the vampire marks between you and Jean-Claude, then you must kill her before she does more harm."

"That will probably kill you, too," I said.

"If she has done this evil thing, then it is a cost I am willing to pay. You do not know her as I do, Anita. She craves power and will survive at all costs. She grew so powerful once that the Queen of All Darkness stripped her of her territory, much of her magic, and offered her the choice of becoming a member of the Harlequin or to be executed. Queenie chose to live, and her choice forced me to become Harlequin with her."

"Wait," I said, "how did Mommy Darkest take Queenie's power?"

"I am not certain, but I know that for any vampires that possessed magic of their own, once they became Harlequin their magic was lessened. Physical and what you refer to as psychic gifts were strengthened, but magic she seemed to . . . consume."

"Did she gain their magic?" I asked.

"Not always, and she certainly did not use any of Queenie's magic once she had taken it."

Echo said, "When we became Harlequin we lost our territory, but I did not lose power; as promised I gained power by becoming Harlequin. Most of us were much diminished after her death."

"Until you became lovers with our new queen," Kaazim said.

"Yes, but Magda and her master, and others, have proven that it is only necessary for the beast half of the couple to be a lover of our new king or queen in order for the vampire half to regain their old strength."

She hadn't even said our names, just *the new king and queen*, as if she wanted to distance herself from us even with her choice of words. It surprised me how much it hurt.

"You gained power from the old queen, as did many, but she could only empower through death, violence, horror, and fear. Anita and Jean-Claude build us up through life, love, happiness, and lust. They are the antithesis of the nightmare that ruled us for so long."

"I am aware of the differences, jackal," Echo said, and sounded angry.

"Then how can you separate yourself from those sweetest of differences?" he asked.

I stared at him, because never by word or deed had he ever hinted that he wanted to be a part of those sweet differences. Kaazim and Jake both hit the dad or uncle space for me. It wasn't that Kaazim wasn't handsome, because I guess he was, it was just that I'd never thought to consider him like that before.

It must have shown on my face, because he said, "Do not worry, my queen, I am not putting myself forward as a new romantic possibility, for I did not lose power when the old queen died. I thought Queenie's magic returning was the reason, and it likely was, but I did not understand that instead of rejoicing at our new freedom as I did, my master was plotting against the very power that freed us of our nightmare slavery."

"If you had said that you had not lost power, then we might have guessed Queenie was growing in power," Echo said.

"I thought she would use the returned power to help Jean-Claude, not to hurt him."

"How can we trust you at our side again, Kaazim?" Echo asked.

"You will never be certain of me again, not if my master is truly a traitor."

"What do you propose we do about that?" Truth asked from the bed. His sword lay bare on the bed beside him, but his one usable hand was out of sight holding the gun he'd gotten out of his bag of weapons. He'd decided that if he was fighting Kaazim one-handed and in pain the gun was better. Wicked had his gun bare and show-ing in his hand. The rest of us decided we'd talk first.

"If you kill me, then it will likely kill my master, as well. It is the safest way to execute her, though if she has recovered more of her magic than she allowed me to know, I would contact whoever is guarding her and be ready to shoot her in case my death only disori-ents her, because once she feels my death she will know that you are trying to kill her."

"How can you sound calm about offering yourself up like this?" Ethan asked.

"Queenie stole me away from my family so long ago that I cannot even find their graves. They are all covered in buildings in a strange city I do not know. I lived to help find a vampire that could slay our queen of nightmares and rule us more kindly than she. I have helped bring that about, and now I have no purpose, no goal. A man with-out that is nothing, so I offer my life because it means very little to me. Perhaps if the Gods are kind I will see my wife and son again, though I fear I have been trapped too long in this body. They have had many lifetimes while I served my master. They will be full of experiences I did not have with them in the many lives they have had since they were taken from me, and I stolen from them."

I wanted to ask what faith he'd believed that still thought reincar-nation was a given, but it seemed too personal a question in that moment. It was idle curiosity and he'd just shared more of his past than I'd ever known. He'd offered to die to keep us safe. I couldn't cheapen it with questions that might cause him more pain.

"I don't want to kill you unless we have no choice," I said.

"If we can trust him, it would be a shame to lose him," Ru said.

"Especially over the treachery of the vampire that stole his fam-ily and his life from him," Truth said.

"If we have to kill Queenie, we'll kill her and hope that you survive her death, but I won't start with your death and hope she dies. You deserve a chance to live without either evil queen possessing you."

"If she dies and I have no second vampire master, then I will begin to age."

"Like age from where you are in what, your thirties, or do you mean age all at once like centuries?" I asked.

"I will age from where I am now, but as a human."

"Okay, plenty of time to hunt up a vampire that does jackals again," I said.

"Or a chance for me to finish living an ordinary life," he said.

"If that's what you want."

"If I survive her death, then I think yes, I would like a chance to see if there is any ordinary left for me in this world."

"A discussion for another night," Echo said. "We must decide, and then we must get Anita back to the Circus to be with Jean-Claude before dawn."

I decided that if Queenie could go under guard, so could Kaazim until we figured out if she was a traitor or just out of practice with her magic. Either way, I wanted him to have a chance. No one else argued with me, so Echo called in the security that she trusted to watch him and told them to find a storage room to put him in until they were relieved of the duty. We waited until Kaazim was gone with his new watchdogs. Then Fortune went to find the doctor so we could get the hell out of here. I wanted to see Jean-Claude as soon as possible, because accident or plot, we needed the vampire marks healed between us before dawn.

31

DR. BODEN TRIED one more time to convince us to let him use his experimental treatment on Wicked and Truth, and then they told him they were leaving the hospital today. Boden was not happy. He started bandaging and doing standard stuff for their injuries while he tried to persuade them to reconsider. Because they were still saying they were leaving as soon as he got the bandaging done, he offered for them to put the clothes they wore to the ER back on, but they had to refuse, not because the hospital staff had cut them off, but because if there was even the slightest chance that there was holy water still on the clothes, they couldn't even come near touching Wicked's and Truth's skin. So they got to keep the hospital gowns on for shirts. Dr. Boden said they'd loaned us quite enough scrubs for one night. When he'd bandaged Wicked's face and put Truth's arm in a sling with more wrapping to keep it close to his body and they still wanted to leave early, he got the paperwork for them to sign. The legalese was more involved, but it basically said, signing this meant you couldn't sue the doctor or the hospital no matter what happened later. He also conceded that maybe they could find them some scrub pants once the nurse damn near ran into a wall when she saw Wicked from behind. Happily, I knew they were both equally distracting from behind.

In fact, I was suddenly finding them more distracting in general. I wasn't sure if I'd worked through my guilt feelings super fast, or maybe the grilled cheese and Coke had been used up so I was looking for other food. Had the *ardeur* finally come back? Were the vampire marks up and running again?

The layers of gauze and tape and the sling on Truth, it wasn't that they hid the injuries, it was that without my sight to distract me I could feel their bodies, their injuries, almost in the same way I could feel putting a zombie back together in the grave.

"I think I could try and heal you now," I said.

They looked at me. "They are fearsome wounds, it would turn any lady's heart to stone," Truth said.

"If I have to cover my face for you to heal it, then so be it," Wicked said.

I shook my head. "No, that's not what I mean."

"Then please explain," Truth said, but the words were cold and not happy.

"When I've healed knife or gunshot wounds, the part deep in the body that I can't see with my eyes heals almost without me thinking about it. Same with zombies putting themselves back together in the grave. Your wounds were right there on the surface, and I had no idea how to put them back together. I stared at Truth's hand and thought, I have no idea how the ligaments attach to the bones or muscle. Wicked, your face was . . . Looking at the pieces I didn't know how to fix them, but now that I can't see them it's like my necromancy, or whatever I use to heal, can sense how to put everything back together again."

"You can call the *ardeur* again?" Truth asked.

"I'm not sure, but I can feel how to fix your injuries now."

They looked hopeful, but Echo said, "If you know how to heal them now, you will know how to heal them tomorrow night, but this night the priority must be to heal the vampire marks between you and Jean-Claude."

"She is right, brother," Truth said.

"Thank you, Echo, for reminding me of my duty," Wicked said.

"So we're not doing this right now," I said.

"We need to get you to Jean-Claude," Nicky said.

"Before sunrise," Ethan said.

"That must be our priority tonight," Truth said.

"My vanity will wait until tomorrow," Wicked said.

"Okay, then, let's go."

"I must stay here in charge of the security for the hospital," Echo said.

"Won't you need to be underground in the Circus before dawn?" I said.

"I'll stay with her," Fortune said. "I brought the travel bag with me in case it turned into a long night." The travel bag was a body-size duffel bag that I'd seen Fortune use on our trip to Ireland. Even Nathaniel had a bag for Damian; he'd copied the ones that the Harlequin used for their vampire masters. The bags were lightproof and the human or wereanimal could transport the vampire and keep them safe until night fell.

"That puts Anita down to three able-bodied guards," Nicky said.

"That's why I'm here," Pierette said from the door. I turned toward her, one of those big, stupid grins on my face that you get at the beginning of a relationship and, if you're lucky, forever. So far I was lucky in my other relationships with men; I was hoping Pierette would prove that I could have the same luck with women.

I went to her to get a hello kiss, but Echo stopped me with her arm in front of me. "There is no time for distractions, the night is waning."

The welcoming smile faded on both our faces, but I was tired and wanted something to go right tonight, and maybe I was still stinging from Echo's rejection. I realized that the two of them looked alike, both short, though Pierette was taller than both of us, but not by that much. Echo's hair was black and to her shoulders, Pierette's brunette and cut so short it left her earlobes bare. Black diamond studs decorated them; they'd been a gift from me, because the white diamonds that Jean-Claude got caught the light too much for security work. The black ones weren't as flashy, but she could wear them at work and that was the point.

Echo was the more classically beautiful, and I'd realized that her coloring was almost identical to Jean-Claude's, which may have been part of her appeal at first. Pierette's eyes were brown like mine, but more almond shaped. Her face was thinner, her chin just a touch pointed, her face more delicate than either Echo's or mine, because we had more curves everywhere. Seeing them side by side I definitely had a preferred type for women; my men were all over the place, but the women I was most attracted to fell into a very narrow physical type with one or two exceptions.

"Love is worth a distraction or two; now I'm going to kiss my girlfriend hello." I walked around Echo and took Pierette's hand in mine, drawing her into my arms. She came with a smile, wrapping her arms around my shoulders while I wrapped mine around her waist. Our bodies came together like they were made to fit as much as her body armor and weapons allowed. It covered her breasts so that I couldn't rub myself against them; it wasn't until I'd started dating her that I realized how much fun my own body armor stole from the people in my life. We kissed and it was like a surprise every time, how small her mouth was compared to the men. I drew a hand from around her waist so I could play my fingers down the side of her face. Tracing the delicate bones of her cheeks, and how the softness of her skin clung to them. No one was more delicate in my hands when we kissed than she was, and I loved it.

I drew back to stare into her brown eyes from inches away. We both gave each other those big, silly happy smiles. Echo had asked for distance, and Pierette had stepped into that space with no regrets and no holding back. Eagerness can be its own aphrodisiac. I finally understood what the men in my life had been telling me for years, that the fact that I loved sex with them so much with no games, no pretense, was rare and utterly attractive.

"I have a bag full of body armor and tactical clothing for you," she said, touching her own tactical boot to a bag at her feet.

"I love you," I said.

She grinned and said, "I know."

We'd introduced her to *Star Wars* last weekend, and yes, I kissed her again.

32

PIERETTE HAD ALSO brought one of the larger SUVs. Wicked and Truth got settled in the back with pillows and blankets so they could be as comfortable as possible on the drive. My big equipment bag full of even more weapons and vampire-hunting gear from the other SUV fit beside them. Ethan drove, and Nicky started to get in the backseat with me, but Pierette said, "Micah asked that Anita have wereleopards on either side of her on the drive home."

Nicky gave her a look that I could feel through the car where I was sitting. Ru was already sitting on my left between me and the door. Bodyguards always sat by the door with the body they were guarding in the middle. Pierette was new love and that's always intoxicating, but I was in love with Nicky in a way that I wasn't with her yet. "I know that I am not one of your lovers, and I would normally offer to move for them," Ru said, "but Micah was very clear. He thinks it's important for you to have wereleopards with you tonight."

"I know, he told me."

"You want me to move," he said. He looked so sad. He'd stood up to Rodina, his last remaining sibling, for me. He opened the door and I suddenly felt guilty. I reached out to grab his hand, and the moment my bare skin touched his, my inner leopard didn't just step out of the darkness, the yellow eyes were behind mine like my human face was the mask. The leopard's energy spilled upward like black ink that spilled down my hand and into Ru's.

I looked into Ru's black-on-black eyes; they were like mirrors of the inky darkness of my panther. Rich yellow-gold spilled into his eyes like gold paint pouring slowly into the black until his eyes were all leopard in his human face.

The seat moved behind me, but I didn't have to guess who it was because a hand touched the side of my neck, and it was a second leopard. Pierette spooned in behind me on her knees. I leaned back against her and suddenly felt both tired and better. I just wanted to curl up between them and sleep. That was when I realized that I was hurt, or tired enough that I needed to sleep between two of my inner beasts the way an injured wereanimal heals.

Nicky spoke from behind us through Pierette's open door. "I'll sit up front with Ethan, you sleep between the leopards."

I turned around enough to see him, but he'd already moved to the front seat. I'd lost a few seconds between when he spoke and when I turned to see him. I was suddenly exhausted, as if the entire night had just caught up with me all at once.

"Sleep, Anita," Wicked said.

"Why do I feel like this? You're the ones that got hurt, not me."

"Emotional wounds are still wounds, Anita," Ethan said from the driver's seat.

"Buckle up, and sleep," Nicky said, "we'll keep you safe."

He knew that I was afraid to sleep in cars, because of my mother dying in a car crash. "Thank you," I said.

I put on my seat belt and Ru did, too, because he knew how I felt about it. I rested my hand on his thigh and he put his hand over mine. I settled down lower so I could put my head on his shoulder. Pierette settled in on my other side, putting her arm across my shoulders, and because my head was on Ru's shoulder she touched us both, but that felt even better. I thought I would have trouble sleeping, but it was like all of us touching had completed a circuit of energy and comfort and it was exactly what I needed, what we all needed.

33

I DREAMED ABOUT IRELAND. I was chained up by my wrists and could hear the sea below the slitted windows. Nathaniel was chained in front of me by his wrists, and I knew that wasn't right. They'd wrapped him around with chains and hung him upside down with his ankle-length hair spilling to the floor. Then she had cut his hair and left it like an auburn pile on the floor. She'd promised when they came back they'd cut other things off him that wouldn't grow back. They'd ruin his beauty in front of me and feed off my terror and despair. In this dream he was standing in front of me with his man-acled wrists attached to long dangling chains like mine. That wasn't true, this was wrong. His hair was still long and uncut, not the shoul-der length of now, but a thick auburn sheet of hair that fell around his nude body like a modesty curtain to tangle around his legs. This wasn't right, it hadn't happened this way, and the thought was so clear, so strong it should have broken the dream, but it didn't. Fuck.

Nathaniel had tears shining in his lavender eyes. He was so much the victim in that moment, like when I'd first met him. He looked younger, less muscled; this was him at nineteen when he was every-one's meat. His hair fell across one eye and suddenly the hair was brown and so was the eye. The skin was tanned, the body taller, muscled, and beautiful and covered in bite marks. White scars, pink scars, like he'd been attacked by vampires for days, weeks, months, forever. I whispered his name: "Phillip."

He raised his face up and looked at me, tears shining in his brown eyes, fresh blood dripping down his body from new bite marks. He'd been addicted to vampires and their power; most of the bites that decorated his body he'd wanted, enjoyed, but not the ones bleeding now. He was chained against a wall and that had been true. I'd gone up and pushed his hair out of his eyes, as if that had mattered in that moment. He said, "A few months back, I'd have paid money for this."

I stared at him, then realized he was trying to make a joke. God. My throat felt tight.

Burchard, the vampire's human servant, had stood at the top of the stairs behind us. "It is time to go," he said.

I stared into Phillip's eyes, perfect brown, torchlight dancing in them like black mirrors. "I won't leave you here, Phillip."

His eyes flickered to the man on the stairs and back to me. Fear turned his face young, helpless. "See you later," he said.

I stepped back from him. "You can count on it."

"It is not wise to keep her waiting," Burchard said.

He was probably right. Phillip and I stared at each other for a handful of moments. The pulse in his throat jumped under his skin like it was trying to escape. My throat ached; my chest was tight. The torchlight flickered in my vision for just a second. I turned away and walked to the steps. We tough-as-nails vampire slayers don't cry. At least, never in public. At least, never when we can help it.

In reality, I'd walked up the steps and left him, because I thought I could negotiate for his safety, because I still hoped I could save him. I'd been wrong, I'd been so wrong. I didn't want to see the next part of this memory, I wanted to change it, I wanted . . .

I ran back down the steps and pressed the front of my body against his, my hands touching the blood on his skin, but that didn't matter. I went up on tiptoe and leaned up toward him. His brown eyes went wide, startled, because we'd only kissed once before and that had mostly been a trick on his part. I'd been so mad about it. Now, I of-fered him a kiss and he leaned down toward me. I touched his face, ran one hand through the warm thickness of his hair. Our lips touched and I gave myself to the kiss as I never had in real life. I kissed Phil-lip the way he needed to be kissed, like I loved him, and just like that I realized had he lived I might have. Physically he was so close to Richard, except prettier, more delicate of face like Micah, and he was addicted to vampires. He'd been trying to get clean to leave the freak parties and the abuse behind, but I'd forced him to go back to help me find the serial killer that had been killing vampires. I'd forced him back into his addiction and gotten him killed. He'd tried to protect me, to stand up to a master vampire, and she'd killed him for his insolence.

I kissed him in the dream as I never had in real life and let myself realize that he was like Nathaniel—submissive, everyone's victim, except he'd been trying to break free before I met him. He'd been trying, starting to succeed, and he'd gone back to help me. I kissed him for all the lost dreams, for what might have been, for the fact that I had never let myself understand why his death haunted me so hard. He was the first person I lost that I'd known, so I'd thought that was it, I'd been attracted to him, so that was why his death scarred me so much, but that wasn't all of it. This was all of it.

We kissed long and deep and it was so good. It felt so right, and then his arms held me back, and that felt right, too. We kissed wrapped in each other's arms, and then he drew back to stare down into my face with his eyes shining and happy. I'd never seen him that full of joy and wonder in real life. That one look was worth so much, so much.

"I love you," I said, when the truth was *I think I could have loved you*, but I knew he would die, was going to die, so I said the words that might have happened if only, if only . . .

"No one's ever loved me before," he said, and I was so happy that I'd said the words. The person I'd been when I knew him could never have said them to him. He was too broken, too many issues, and I didn't understand that I was broken and had too many damn issues. I thought I was fine, and I'd judged him too damaged, scary damaged, to ever date. I'd been a judgmental asshole.

"I love you, Phillip."

"Anita, Anita, I love you, I can't believe you love me." He touched my hair, put his hand against the side of my face, and I leaned into the warmth and weight of his hand. He smiled, eyes sparkling with happiness, and then the fear was back. His eyes wide and staring. He stumbled back from me, and his throat was a red ruin, blood fell like rain. I saw his spine glistening through all the blood, so much blood.

I screamed, "Nooo!" I would not live through this twice, and the dream changed. I was back in Ireland in the stone room, but this time the chains dangled empty. Nathaniel wasn't there, not even his cut hair.

"I'm sorry, I'm new at dreams." A man's voice that I couldn't quite place. Phillip's death was still too much in my head, I couldn't follow the voice. Ru was suddenly there, grabbing my hand. "We have to run." I started to ask why, but we were running through a night-dark forest full of short, twisted trees. The moon was huge and turning the world silver and black as we ran. A branch snagged my arm, and I stumbled hard enough that I nearly dragged Ru down.

He caught me in his arms, and then his hand came away from me with blood glistening black in the moonlight. "You're hurt," he said, and it was Ru's softer voice, and then he raised his hand up and licked my blood off his skin.

I tried to pull away from him, because I knew when he looked down at me it wouldn't be Ru anymore. His arms were suddenly tight around my waist, pinning my arms at my sides. It was the same face physically, but the cruelty in his eyes, the sneer on his lips, the force of his personality was someone else entirely.

I said his name. "Rodrigo."

He smiled and it filled his eyes with joyous evil. "Anita."

"You're dead," I said.

"I am."

"Then why are you in my dreams?"

"It's your dream, isn't it, shouldn't you know why I'm here?"

"Ru is sleeping with us."

"My brother is touching you in your sleep." He startled and looked behind us like he'd seen something. "He's coming."

"Who's coming?"

"He's erasing me, Anita." The fear in his eyes looked real.

"Who?" I asked.

"He calls me Phobos."

"Phobos." I repeated the name. "It means panic. Shit, you mean Deimos, terror."

He looked behind us again, panic rolling off him, but it left me untouched, and I wasn't afraid anymore. This wasn't my fear, it was his. "Be War for me, Anita, be Ares, be my god and save me."

"You killed Domino." And the minute I said it we were back in the hotel room in Ireland. Domino was bleeding out on the floor. He wasn't moving at all now. He just lay there on his side, but he'd fallen at an odd angle, unable to cushion or direct it. His neck was hyper-extended, which would make breathing even harder, or maybe easier. I didn't know anymore. But I could see his face, see his eyes too wide as he struggled to breathe, that awful wet sound coming from his chest, or his throat. Blood coated his chin and mouth. I could still taste his kiss on my lips. He shook, shivered; a gout of blood spilled out of his mouth and the horrible wet rattling breathing stopped. I saw his eyes start to go; the most alien of all the were tigers, flame colored orange, yellow, and red, and I had to watch the life fade from them. I watched him dying inches from me.

I screamed. I screamed for help. I screamed because there was nothing else I could do. The man on top of me popped me in the side of the face the way you hit a cat that was chewing something, not to hurt, just to startle. It made me look away from Domino. It was Rodrigo sitting across my waist, pinning me to the floor, but that wasn't right. He'd killed Domino, but he hadn't been the one that was pinning me down, trying to inject me with something so they could kidnap me.

"He'll hear you," Rodrigo said.

"Deimos," I said.

"I didn't make you remember your lover's death just now. You thought of him, not me; I would never have reminded you of why you hate me."

"You killed . . ."

"Your thoughts will bring it back, you will make yourself relive his death, your thoughts, not mine, yours."

"Rodrigo," I said, "where are we?"

"It is partially your dream, but the rest is . . . Control your thoughts or you will be trapped in the worst moments of your life. Trust me, you don't want that."

I forced my breathing to even out and did my best to empty my mind and just be in the moment, but I didn't like this moment, so I changed it. We were standing in the small forest of twisted trees again, but the sun was out, and the sea was shining out from the clifftop. I had never been any place that looked remotely like this.

"It's my memory," he said, and I turned back to him. His eyes were perfectly black, the iris so close in color to his pupil that it made him look blind with only the white of the eye to ruin the blackness. There was more white today, like a horse with wide, frightened eyes.

"Where are we?"

"In hell," he said, then grabbed my arm and started running through the trees again. There was enough light now to avoid the dead trees. They looked blackened, like fire had killed them years ago, but the grass was green with wildflowers growing up between the . . . vines. It was grapevines grown so tall they looked like trees to us. I realized that we were small, like children, but it was still us at the same time.

I used his grip on my arm to turn him around. "Stop running, you're not a child, this is a memory from when you were a child."

"I know, but I can't get out." He started dragging me toward the edge of the dead vines and the green grass that spilled out toward the edge of the cliff and the sea beyond. We were holding hands and running full out toward the edge of the cliff. I pulled and spun him around before we could get there.

"What's happening, Rodrigo?" I stared into his eyes and suddenly saw through his eyes. He was holding the hand of a little blond girl; it was Rodina. They were running as fast as they could in the dark toward the sea. He looked back and there was a figure dressed all in black with a white mask where the face should be; even her hands were covered in gloves. She was Harlequin before we'd freed them of the mask and hiding. She was running with a little blond boy in her arms; it was Ru.

There was a second Harlequin only a little taller than their mother running behind. Their father fought other figures dressed just like them. The Harlequin were fighting themselves. They moved in blurs of speed and grace that we couldn't follow with our eyes. Here were the Harlequin with the magic of the Mother of All Darkness running strong through them. They had to hide away, but they were gods as they moved over the battleground.

We stood at the edge of the cliff. Rodina was crying, her arm was bleeding, my arm was bleeding, our arm was bleeding. Our mother sat Ru down beside me; she took her glove off and touched my face with her bare hand. Rodrigo was startled; she never did that in public, couldn't show herself, not even a hand. She pressed Ru's hand into Rodina's, so that the three of them held hands on the clifftop.

She told them that she loved them, and that she was sorry that she couldn't save them, and then she turned and went to fight beside their father. They fought well, but there were only two of them against a small army. They died bravely, but they still died.

Rodina had dragged them all to the very edge of the cliff, crying and screaming for their parents. Ru was silent, face pale, but he didn't cry. Rodrigo would remember that years later, that the only one of them that didn't cry was Ru.

The masked and hooded figures cleaned their blades and turned to the three children. One held a gloved hand out to them and spoke in a man's voice. "Come along, it is over."

Rodina had looked at him, then at Ru, then back to him. A look came over her face that she still had today: fierce determination and a totally fuck-you attitude. She took a step backward. Rodrigo hesitated, then took it with her; only Ru held back, leaning on their clasped hands.

He said, "No, Dinnie."

The Harlequin that had spoken said, "Don't be foolish, we will not hurt you."

Another Harlequin stepped forward, and her voice was female. "You're safe."

"The Dark Queen wants you at her side; we would never harm you," another woman said.

"She can't have us!" Rodina yelled in that little-girl voice, and stepped backward into thin air.

Rodrigo used a gesture that he'd just learned, and his mother had told him was very rude, as he let his sister drag him over the edge of the cliff. Ru's face on the cliff terrified for a moment as he screamed, "No!" and tried to break his sister's grip on his hand. It was too late; they fell together while the Harlequin rushed to the edge, trying to save them.

Rodina and he fell in utter silence glaring up at the figures on the clifftop. Ru shrieked all the way down.

34

I JERKED AWAKE IN the back of the SUV, my heart pounding, pulse choking me. "You're safe, it was just a dream," Ru said.

I turned and found his face inches from mine, but he looked just like his brother, so that for a second I wasn't sure I'd really woken up or if the dream had just changed. I pushed away from him, but the seat belt kept me pinned. I started to panic, but Pierette said, "It's okay, Anita, you're awake."

I leaned against her and she put her arms around me.

"What's wrong, Anita? Why are you looking at me like you're afraid of me?" Ru asked.

"I dreamed about your brother and all of you, but mainly Rodrigo."

"I'm sorry, Rodina and I are still dreaming about him, too."

"This is the first time I've dreamed about him," I said.

"Why would you dream about him tonight?" Pierette asked, stroking my hair and laying a kiss against the side of my face.

"Rodrigo said it was because I was sleeping next to Ru."

"I did not cause your dream, Anita," Ru said.

"I know you didn't do it on purpose," I said.

"Anita, perhaps it is just a nightmare," Truth said.

"Maybe." I looked at Ru. "How about I tell you part of my dream and you tell me if it's a real memory from your childhood, or just dream garbage that got in my head."

"Whatever I can do to help," Ru said.

Then I realized something: The SUV wasn't moving. "Wait a minute, why aren't we moving?"

Ethan answered, "There's a multicar pileup. We're stuck until the police and ambulances get here."

"What caused the accident?" I asked.

"We weren't close enough to see," Ethan said.

"Tell Ru your dream," Nicky said.

I told him and the rest of the car the part that seemed to be Rodrigo's memory. It was hard to tell in the car's dimness, but I think he went pale. "One of my earliest memories is falling and screaming. The fact that I screamed was one of the reasons Roddy and Dina thought I was weak."

"You were a child," I said.

"We were all children," he said.

Hard to argue with that, so I didn't try.

"Are you saying that Anita dreamed a true memory from your childhood?" Truth asked.

"Yes," Ru said.

Wicked asked, "What else happened in the dream, Anita?"

I told them.

"If the memory was real, then we're going to take the warning seriously," Ethan said.

"We have get Anita to the Circus, where she'll be safe," Pierette said.

"We can't levitate over the wreck in front of us," Nicky said.

"There are fewer cars behind us," Pierette said.

"If you have an idea, share," Wicked said.

"We move the cars behind us, so that we can turn the SUV around, and then we drive over the median."

"That will take us farther way from the Circus," I said.

"Only until we find an exit and side roads to take us past the accident," Pierette said.

"If we were able-bodied, then it would be easy enough for just the four of us to pick up the cars and move them to the side of the road," Truth said.

"We don't have to pick them up, just move them out of our way," I said. "Maybe I can help with that?"

"How?" Pierette asked.

"I'll put on my badge and the U.S. Marshal windbreaker and tell them it's imperative we get to a crime scene."

"Let's start with that," Nicky said, "and if they still won't move their cars, then we push them out of the way."

My phone rang and I jumped like I'd been slapped. Nervous, who, me? "Marshal Blake."

"Anita, it's me."

"Edward, I don't recognize this number."

"I had to change numbers when I got the new phone," he said.

"Why did you need a new phone?"

"Monster ate the old one," he said, and before I could ask what kind of monster, he continued talking. "What the hell is happening in St. Louis?"

"You'll have to be more specific," I said.

"You may have hit a record for the number of hate-group attacks on vampires in a single night in one city."

"Oh, that," I said, like it didn't impress me.

"What else has happened?" he asked.

"Did you meet Queenie when you were here last time?"

"We saw her, she's one of the few that covers her face like old-school Harlequin," he said.

"She's used magic to damage the marks between Jean-Claude and me."

"What does that mean for your powers and his?"

I loved that he didn't argue, or ask stupid questions, but went right for the important parts. "Still figuring that out, but if I can get to Jean-Claude and redo the marks in person, then we should be all right."

"Why did you say it like that, if you can get to him?"

"Tell him that Deimos may have been fucking with your dream," Nicky said.

I told him.

"Didn't Deimos mess with people's emotions last time?"

"Some, yeah. He got in the audience's head."

"What if he got in the heads of the hate groups?"

I thought about it for a second or two, then said, "Jesus, Edward."

"I'm packed and heading to the airport. I'll be on the ground in two hours."

"Not from New Mexico you won't."

"I just finished up a monster hunt in Louisville, Kentucky. Lucky for you, that puts me a lot closer."

"I'll take the help."

"St. Louis put a call out for more marshals to come help with the overwhelming number of supernatural-related crimes, so it's not just me heading your way."

"Bernardo's welcome, but you mean Olaf, too."

"He's farther away than I am, so I'll be on the ground before he gets there."

"I do not need tall, pale, and scary here while we're dealing with this shit."

"If we have to fight Deimos in dragon form, we'll need all the help we can get."

"Olaf is a good man in a fight, Anita," Nicky said.

"Fine, though maybe the reason he keeps screwing with people's emotions is that he isn't able to do the whole dragon thing anymore."

"You know we can't count on that, Anita."

"Yeah, I know we have to plan for worst-case scenario, not best."

"Could your rogue Harlequin be working with your dragon?"

"I don't know."

"Kaazim was a good asset with us in Ireland, but isn't Queenie his master vamp?"

"Yes, he's under guard as a precaution."

"Good."

"Let me know when you get on the ground; I've got to move heaven and earth, or at least a few cars, so I can get to Jean-Claude before dawn."

"Move a few cars?"

"We're stuck in traffic behind a multicar pileup."

"It's three in the morning in St. Louis, not Los Angeles," he said.

"It's been that kind of night," I said.

"Everything that's made it that kind of night has been enemy action up to this point, right?"

"Yeah."

"Anita, what if this is more enemy action?"

"A sniper rifle could shoot out tires, or even take out a driver and cause an accident like this," Ru said.

"Even if someone caused the accident, it doesn't change the problem. We need to move cars out of our way so we can back up and get to the Circus," I said.

"Then go do that, I'll be there as soon as I can," Edward said, then hung up. If you wanted comforting he wasn't always your guy.

"Do you really think someone caused this pileup?" I asked everyone within earshot.

"It doesn't matter what caused it," Nicky said, "our goal doesn't change. We need to get Anita to the Circus of the Damned before dawn."

"Is trying to move the cars behind us the most efficient way to do that?" Pierette asked.

"If Truth and I were healed we could fly her to the Circus," Wicked said.

"She has flown with us before," Truth said.

"I have," I said.

"How about if I borrow Anita's windbreaker and badge and see if I can get people to move their cars, while Anita heals them?" Ethan said.

"Strangers in cars are more likely to believe you're the marshal than that I am," I said.

"Why do I feel like I should apologize for that?" he said.

"No apologies needed, just the sad sexist truth."

"I'll put my blank windbreaker on and follow Ethan around and play marshal with him," Nicky said.

"I can deputize you both; hell, that would be one way to get enough preternatural marshals to cover the craziness happening all over here."

"We'll be your special deputies any day, you know that," Ethan said, smiling.

I unbuckled my seat belt to take my windbreaker off and handed it to him. "You've both been with me on out-of-town marshal gigs. You know how it's played."

Nicky got out, settling his blank windbreaker more solidly in place, then put his head back inside, one hand touching the open door. "Back when I was a bad guy I went undercover as all sorts of lawmen."

"Just remember to tone down the menacing vibes," Ethan said as he got out of the SUV.

"I'm missing an eye; I can't be good cop." Nicky looked at me as Ethan closed the door on his side. "Just like they'll believe a man is the U.S. Marshal before they'll believe you are, I'm missing an eye, so with all these scars no one ever believes I'm the good cop."

"Sexist, ableist bastards," I said.

He smiled and it made me think I'd rather be having sex with him in the back of the SUV. He grinned then, fierce and happy. He'd read my mind, and that was enough to make him shut the door and go whistling down the road.

"Is he whistling?" Pierette asked.

"Yep," I said.

"He's happy," Ru said.

"Of all the men in your life I understand Nicky the least," Pierette said.

"That's okay, you're not sleeping with him, and I understand him just fine."

"That you truly love and enjoy such a variety of men with such varied tastes is intimidating. I do not know if I can keep up with you."

"It's not a contest," I said, studying her face in the bar of light from the streetlight above us. Hmm, I was hoping for more shadow in the back of the SUV.

"If you are going to heal us as a faster method of getting you back to Jean-Claude, then let us not delay," Wicked said.

I smiled at him, knowing it wasn't just the normal sexual eagerness. I didn't blame him for wanting to be healed if it was possible.

"In the back of the SUV?" Truth asked, sounding a little dubious.

"We have had sex in worse places," Wicked said.

"Not while injured this badly."

"We could try it on the verge under the trees, if you want more room." I was smiling while I offered it.

"I would rather stay in the back of the car until my arm is healed," Truth said.

"Sex on bare grass is overrated," Wicked said.

"Back of the car it is, then," I said.

"I'll guard from outside the car," Ru said, reaching for the door handle.

"I'm fine staying inside. Nathaniel's teaching me that sometimes I like to watch, too," Pierette said.

"Watching knowing you will enjoy later is one thing, but watching without that is quite another," Ru said. He got out before I could figure out what to say to that, and then Wicked reached over the seat to stroke his fingers down my face. It turned me to him with his handsome face cut by light and shadow so the bandage on his left side almost glowed.

"Do you mind if Pierette guards and watches us at the same time?"

"Will it excite you to know she's watching?"

I thought about that in the small confines of the SUV. "It might."

"Then she can watch." He stroked his hand up and down the side of my face.

"We are not at our best injured like this," Truth said.

"So don't judge us too harshly," Wicked said.

I finally realized they were talking to Pierette. I had a moment of almost jealousy, and then I thought about having a night where it was the four of us, where I could watch both men above us, entering us at the same time, pleasuring us at the same time, and the thought of it tightened things low in my body so hard and fast that it made me gasp.

"What is wrong?" Wicked asked, dropping his hand.

"Nothing," I said, "just thinking of a night that Pierette and I had that we might be able to duplicate when you're both feeling better."

She said, "You mean the night . . ."

I put a finger on her lips to stop her from saying *Micah and Nathaniel*, because even the most poly of men don't like being compared to someone else in the midst of things. "Yes, that night."

She kissed my fingertip, then slid her mouth over my finger until she took me in down to where the knuckle joined my hand. Her mouth was warm and wet as she drew it slowly back up. My pulse was up, my breathing already fast.

"That was most helpful," Truth said.

"Very helpful," Wicked said. Their voices let me know that I wasn't the only one enjoying myself.

She kissed the tip of my finger again, then said, "If I can be more helpful, just let me know."

"If I need a helping hand, I'll let you know," I said.

"Or mouth," she said.

One of the men made an eager sound, the endorphins already helping to dull the pain. Perfect.

35

PIERETTE WAS BEING a little too delightfully helpful while I took my body armor and weapons off, so she had to stand outside the SUV on guard duty instead of getting to watch. I told her she was a bad voyeur; they were only supposed to watch. She laughed and went to lean against the side of the SUV. Ru was standing straight and every inch on guard duty on the other side.

I took off the T-shirt that I'd just put on from the bag Pierette had given me, which left me in the push-up bra that Nathaniel had probably packed. My sports bras were finally even with my lace lingerie ones.

"Leave the bra and panties if they match," Wicked said.

I finished taking off the tactical pants to join the socks and boots on the floorboard, then went up on my knees so that the stark light could show that the lingerie matched. Wicked held out a hand, and then Truth offered his hand; I took the help, though it actually made climbing over the backseat harder, not easier, but the feel of their hands in mine was worth a little awkward scrambling.

I glanced through the back window and saw that Nicky and Ethan were actually making progress getting people moved out of our way. The problem was that new cars kept coming in behind the ones that were making a path for us. It was like doing a jigsaw puzzle where the picture expanded every time you got close to finishing it and more new pieces rained down on you.

Truth and Wicked pulled me down to them in my matching lingerie. "The two of you are wearing too many clothes," I said.

"My shirt, if you can call the hospital gown a shirt, will have to stay on, too many bandages," Truth said.

I reached for the waist of the scrub pants he was wearing, then leaned in and gave him a soft kiss. "It'll be easier for me to get you out of your pants if you lie down."

He smiled and used his one good arm to help him move lower until he was lying on the blankets that someone at the Circus had thought to put in the back for them. I lifted the hospital gown up and out of the way so I could reach the drawstring on his pants. I'd felt his body eager somewhere in all the climbing into the back, but as the heel of my hand brushed against the front of his body he was soft, which meant just scooting himself from sitting to lying down had hurt that much.

I tried to call the *ardeur*, but I was empty, there was nothing to call. I had been able to heal with sex before that, but it had required sexual interest from everyone participating. I wasn't sure anything I could do on my own would replace the instant lust of the *ardeur*.

I reached down the links to Jean-Claude, hoping for some help. He answered the call, his voice whispering through me. "*Ma petite*, what has delayed you?"

The fact that he didn't already know where I was and why I was delayed was a really bad sign. I reached for him down the marks between us, reached as hard as I'd ever reached outside of a life-or-death emergency.

I tried to think the next part out loud, but it was as if it crumbled before I could focus. I said it out loud, no longer certain he would hear me. "I don't know where you are, or what you're doing, Jean-Claude. I can't see you in my head."

"Nor I you, *ma petite*, whatever is wrong with the marks between us is growing worse."

"How can Queenie be doing this? I thought the brujas were there to keep her magic under control."

"They are keeping her from adding to her magic, *ma petite*. We all believed that would be enough."

"Obviously it's not."

"I am aware."

"How is she still damaging our connection like this if she can't keep fueling her spell?"

Truth grabbed my hand, and I got a glimpse of Jean-Claude's face lying against blue silk, and then the image flickered like an old TV set losing its station. I reached out to Wicked, and I didn't even have to ask for him to take my hand. The moment I could touch both of them, the image was back.

"*Ma petite*, I can see you, I know where you are and that you are holding the Wicked Truth's hands."

"Can you read my mind? Do you know why we're delayed?"

"Traffic, a wreck, a large collision."

"Yes!" Then I couldn't see him anymore, no matter how tightly I held on to Wicked and Truth.

His voice was all I had when he said, "*Ma petite*, I fear that if you do not come to me soon, the vampire marks between us will be broken irrevocably."

"No, I won't let that happen." Then even his voice was gone. I screamed his name. Wicked and Truth were asking me what was wrong. Ru and Pierette opened their doors and were looking for danger. They had their guns out pointing safely down, but there was no safety for us if I didn't get to Jean-Claude.

I heard shouting, and then Ru said, "Nicky's got a motorcycle."

The thought of riding on a motorcycle scared me—there's a reason they call them *donorcycles* in emergency rooms, but losing Jean-Claude terrified me more. I climbed back over the seat to find my clothes on the floorboard. I scrambled into them: socks, pants, boots, T-shirt. I almost left the body armor, but it would protect me from falling off a motorcycle just like it would from a bullet, not as well, but it beat a T-shirt and skin. I was still putting guns, knives, and ammo back in place when Nicky pulled up on a large motorcycle. It was black and chrome and big; the seat stretched long enough for two. Nicky held out a black helmet to me.

"Where's your helmet?" I asked.

"Put on the helmet, get on the bike. I felt Jean-Claude fading from your mind."

I took the helmet and put it on. It was a little big and I was struggling to adjust it when Ethan reached up and did it for me. He wasn't wearing my marshal windbreaker anymore. I had time to think it, and then Ru was holding the jacket for me to put on. He handed me my badge on its lanyard. I tried to put it over my head, but the helmet was too big. I had a choice of taking the lanyard off, putting it into one of the MOLLE straps on the vest, or . . . Nicky revved the engine on the motorcycle. "Now, Anita!"

I shoved my badge into the pocket on the windbreaker and got on the back of the motorcycle behind Nicky. I didn't know where to put my feet. Ru told me where to put my feet, and the moment my boots were in place, Nicky said, "Hold on."

I had time to slide my arms underneath his windbreaker, and the moment he felt me touch him, the motorcycle roared forward. I grabbed at Nicky and managed to wrap my hands more securely around his waist, pressing my body as tightly to the back of his as possible.

He must have felt me holding on more securely, because he hit the gas. I buried my face against his body as much as the helmet would let me, tightened my arms around his waist until my muscles ached with it.

He yelled over the sound of the engine, "We're going over the median here." He didn't bother to tell me to hold on tighter, I was holding on as hard as I could already. He slowed down, which made my pulse a little happier, then demonstrated that this kind of motorcycle wasn't made for off road. It felt like my teeth were going to rattle out of my head. Then we were over to the other side of the highway. There were some screeching brakes from other cars; I just closed my eyes and thought, *I trust Nicky. I trust Nicky.* I did trust him; it was the motorcycle and the other drivers on the road that I didn't trust. I held on to Nicky and prayed that we'd make it to Jean-Claude before it was too late.

36

I WAS SO LOST in my fear of speeding down the highway with nothing between us and the wind, and the constant thread of loss in my head and my heart for Jean-Claude, that I almost missed my necromancy whispering to me that there was something dead near us. I had two handguns on me: one on the front of my vest, and the second at my hip in a drop holster. I went for the holster, because to get to the one on the front of my vest I'd have to lean back from Nicky before I could even reach the gun, so I went for the holster.

They tried to grab me under my arms on both sides but only got one arm—the one with the gun. The vampire grabbing at the arm that was still holding on to Nicky missed. The vampire holding my right arm tried to pull me off the bike, but I tightened my hold with my other arm around Nicky, and that was my mistake. If you're riding a motorcycle with someone you need to move in the same direction to keep the bike balanced. The vampire had my arm so I couldn't move with Nicky. I felt the bike start to skid. The vampire holding my right arm grabbed the gun belt at the back of my waist and lifted me up as the motorcycle skidded faster and went over on its side with Nicky still on it. Brakes screeched behind us as the cars reacted to Nicky wrecking and the sight of someone being pulled off the back of the bike and into the night sky.

I didn't have time to see where Nicky and the motorcycle went, because the vampire tossed me in the air as if he meant to throw me into traffic. I screamed. He grabbed me in a bear hug, but instead of falling backward we went skyward fast, so much faster than any vampire I'd ever seen fly. I screamed again, and that cost me the seconds I could have used for trying to aim my gun into the meat of his body. I could have shot him, fallen a short distance, survived, but by the time I tried to turn the gun in against his body the world was black sky with the city lights spread below my dangling feet. His arms were around my waist and one of my arms was across his shoulders. My other hand was wrapped around my gun; all I had to do was pull. I was so scared I tasted metal on my tongue. I was holding my breath, or maybe it was the rush of cold air around us stealing it away.

"Shoot me and we both die," the vampire said, in a voice that sounded neutral, as if he didn't care which choice I made. He let go of my waist and I suddenly had to use both arms around his neck, or I'd have fallen. He pulled my gun out of my hand and let it fall. For a second I thought he meant to drop me, too, and then his arms went around my waist, and I admit that I breathed a sigh of relief. Yes, the bad vampire had me up in the air, but he wasn't going to drop me—yet. I'd thought that I was afraid of flying, but in that moment I realized I was afraid of really big, enormous heights and falling from them. Fuck.

I wrapped my legs around his body as close and tight as any lover. Now if he wanted to drop me he'd have to peel my body off one limb at a time. "I liked that gun," I said, trying for as neutral a voice as his; pretty sure I failed, but it's not about winning, it's about doing your best. And I was doing my damn level best not to panic. Phobias suck.

His face was kissing close as he said, "I would accuse you of trying to seduce me, but I can feel your fear."

"So now what?" I asked.

"We await your rescuer," he said.

"Great, we'll just hang out until they come kill you, and take me back to earth."

"But who can fly up here and save you now that the Wicked Truth are too injured? Who else is with you that flies as well as I do?"

I stared at him, and I knew my face showed all the fear as I said, "Jean-Claude."

He smiled, but it was the kind of smile serial killers use before things get even worse. "Yes, our would-be king will come rescue his fair maiden, or if he is too afraid to leave his castle then your knight in shining armor, Damian, might come to fight the dragon and save you. Whichever comes, we will kill him."

I said the thing that cops know not to, because bad guys don't need a reason. "Why?" I asked, like the *why* mattered when all that mattered was stopping him. I wasn't afraid for myself anymore.

"Because we do not want to be ruled by Belle Morte's catamite, no matter how powerful he has grown."

I locked my arms and legs tighter around the vampire holding me in his arms. I slid my hand to touch his neck, bare skin to bare skin. It had worked with our Wicked Truth. I prayed that me touching any vampire would gain me power enough for this.

"Are you seriously trying to seduce me? That is a fool's errand, Anita Blake. I am what in modern day is called an asexual. Nothing you can offer will tempt me." I opened my link to Jean-Claude first. I thought at him as hard as I could, *Flying is a trap, don't come.*

Jean-Claude breathed the barest touch of power through me. *I hear you,* ma petite. *I will warn the others.* Then the connection was gone again. It was like every time I touched a vampire I could use them like temporary batteries to reach Jean-Claude.

"I feel the power of your master, Anita Blake. Good, call out to him."

"I told him not to come."

"He will come anyway." The vampire pressed his cheek against mine and said, "Men in love will always come to rescue their ladies in distress. It is a law of the universe as real and dependable as the gravity that will take your king to his final resting place."

I buried the top of my head in the crook of his neck, so he couldn't tear my throat out as easily. I slid my hand down his back like I was being romantic, but I was searching for weapons. The cloth seemed smooth and my legs around his waist told me that he wasn't carrying anything there, so unless he had an ankle holster on he was unarmed. Of course, he was floating far enough up in the air that I guess weapons were superfluous, but how did he plan to kill Jean-Claude or Damian if they did show up? I resented that he was treating Damian like an afterthought. They'd kill him if he showed up, but he was collateral damage. They wanted Jean-Claude.

"I was told you had no gift for deceit, Anita, but you are quite subtle searching me just now."

I went back to a two-armed grip around his shoulders just in case he got tired of waiting for Jean-Claude. "Thanks, I guess."

"You are calm now, why?"

I shook my head, a snuggling motion under better circumstances. Now I just didn't want him to bite me. "What were you going to do if Nicky hadn't found the motorcycle?"

"You did make it easier for us, thank you, but our plan is still intact. My improvisation only put me ahead of schedule."

I fought not to tense up, but he felt it.

"You've thought of something, please share."

Since I didn't have a plan to get away, keeping in as much of my captor's goodwill as possible seemed like a good idea, so I told the truth. "The rest of your people aren't in place yet, that's why we're just hovering and not going anywhere."

"There are no other people," he said.

"If Jean-Claude comes up here to rescue me now, you'll try and take him out, but you're waiting for your reinforcements."

"I have no reinforcements; it is just I."

"Liar," I said.

"You are no lycanthrope to smell a lie upon my skin. You are guessing."

He was right, but I settled more comfortably into his arms, because I was right, too. We floated in the night sky, caught between the stars and the more brilliant lights from the ground. The setting was romantic if you weren't bothered by heights.

"Who are you?" I asked.

"I do not need to tell you that."

"I know, but tell me anyway," I said.

"Trappolino, now why did I tell you that?" It was one of the names from Italian comedy, the commedia dell'arte. It was where all the names for the Harlequin came from; most of them who had survived their dark queen's death worked for us now, but not all of them.

"You're one of the Harlequin who didn't come in from the cold," I said, and my heart was beating fast again, my breath tight in my throat.

"That I am one of the Harlequin that you and your master could not tame, that frightens you. Good, it is good that you are afraid of us. You should be afraid of us."

"How many of you are there?" I asked.

He shook his head, but his cheek rubbed against my hair like a cat marking someone as his. "I feel the draw of you, Anita, and it is not sexual. All the others who have come in contact with you thought with their loins, and it blinded them to the true attraction. You are the first true necromancer in a thousand years to be allowed to come into their full power. You should have been killed as soon as we heard that an American vampire master had a human servant that could raise zombies."

"You spied on us that early?"

"Yes, but it was the traitors among us that reported that you were

no danger to us. They said your powers were nothing to worry about."
He ran his hand over my hair until his fingers played at the back of
my neck. He kissed my forehead, then my temple, and stopped pulling his face away so he could look into my eyes. I didn't remind him
that he was asexual so what was with all the kissing, because honestly
asexuality was so far away from how I viewed my sexuality that I just
didn't understand the parameters.

He studied my face. "I hate you for slaying our queen, but somehow you hold an echo of her, a taste of her. How can that be?"

"Maybe all necromancers taste alike?" I said, staring into his eyes
from inches away.

"There is something in your eyes that reminds me of when I was
human and she came to me in the dark."

"The Mother of All Darkness brought you over as a vampire
personally?" I asked.

He nodded. "I was one of the last she made before she was betrayed the first time." His voice sounded thick and slow, like he was
having trouble thinking clearly. I wanted him to be ours, mine. I
wanted him to tell me everything he knew about the rogue Harlequin and the plot to kill Jean-Claude. I needed him to share everything with me.

"You must be much older than you feel," I said.

"I thought it was your gift to know the age of every vampire
you met?"

"You must have some power that I haven't seen before, because I
can't tell with you. That's very impressive," I said; flattery will get a
long way with most men, even the undead ones.

"Our dark queen gave power to me and the others she created.
You cannot be blamed for not understanding the difference between
modern vampires and what we once were."

"Tell me the difference, Trappolino."

"Let me show you, Anita." His eyes started to glow like fire behind dark glass, his face thinning down until it was flesh over bone.

I was wrapped so close to him that I could feel his entire body losing flesh so that it was like hugging a corpse that had decayed somewhere dry. His face was nothing but a skull with a thin layer of flesh hiding bone; his eyes were like staring into brown fire or burning water. I had the sense of hidden depths that were inviting me to dive into them and be lost.

I blinked and was back to hugging an animated corpse, while we floated in the star-filled sky defying gravity as if that apple had never hit Newton in the head.

"I should have known you could gaze into my eyes and not be caught," he said as his body started to fill back out. I'd never touched a vampire while they reversed the process and came back to "life." It was weirdly more unnerving in reverse. Then I realized that the vampire I was holding on to had changed skin tone. He'd started out the utter white of a Caucasian vampire; now he was Black. He didn't even have that slightly sickly pallor that all vampires had regardless of skin tone. If I had seen him on the street I'd have passed him by as human. But it was more than that, his features had changed to match the darker skin.

"Now that is interesting," I said.

"Have I truly impressed you at last?" he asked.

"Yes, and honestly the whole floating-as-if-it's-effortless-and-you-could-do-it-forever thing is impressive, too."

He smiled, then frowned. "Why am I so happy that I've impressed you?"

"I don't know," I said.

"Liar," he said.

"I've never met a shapeshifter that could change into different people before," I said.

"I am not a shapeshifter."

"Then how did you change yourself so completely?"

"Why are your king and your knight not coming?"

I didn't want to answer the question, so I asked one instead.

"Why did Deimos decide to kill Jean-Claude instead of taking over his power base?"

"He still wants that."

"Then why do you want to kill Jean-Claude?"

"Because Deimos does not share power. He consumes it, but he allows no one else at his feast."

"Jean-Claude shares. I share."

"I will gain nothing from a vampire kiss that exists on seduction alone for its power."

"Are you sure of that?"

He frowned at me with his new face. "It is the necromancy that attracts us like moths to a flame; I thought I was proof against your wiles."

"Why does Deimos not sharing power make you want to kill Jean-Claude?"

"If Deimos will not share power, then I want to take every bit of it away from him."

"Then let's do that," I said.

"Let us do what?" he asked.

"Let's take Deimos's power away from him."

"I am supposed to have delivered you to him by now. He will know something is wrong."

"Take me to Jean-Claude, let me reestablish our connection. That keeps all of our power out of Deimos's reach."

"You are too weak to offer me such bargains, Anita."

"Join us, Trappolino. Help us defeat Deimos and we'll help you find your own power."

"But, Anita, I already have my own power."

We weren't floating anymore. I was lying down on . . . grass. Trappolino was lying beside me on the grass, propped up on one elbow, staring down at me.

"Fuck," I said.

"I told you, Anita, I don't want to do that with anyone."

"So that much was true," I said.

"I have told you very few lies."

"I should have known that no vampire could hover that long in one place; it's just not possible."

"Deimos wanted me to test the waters; if you had been completely proof against my vampire wiles, then he would have had you killed."

"But you mind-fucked me and I don't even know at what point you did it."

He smiled and trailed one dark finger down the side of my face.

"Did you really change your appearance or was that illusion?"

His smile widened. "My secret to keep."

"My answer to discover," I said.

"Exactly."

"So now that you've mind-fucked me better and more thoroughly than any vampire in years, what's next?"

"I let them take you to Deimos as planned."

"Do you want him to be more powerful?"

"I have no choice, Anita."

"There are always choices," I said.

"I convinced you that we floated forever, when you as a vampire expert know that is impossible. All your weapons are gone, even your armor, and even saying that to you there is no panic, no frantic hand movements searching for them."

I tried to be upset, but I couldn't seem to manage it. I felt distant and peaceful almost. "You sneaky bastard, you drugged me."

"I did capture you with my gaze."

"But you didn't keep me under with your vampire wiles."

"I manipulated your mind while you were under the influence."

"Like manipulating a person's dreams," I said.

"Yes," he said, smiling like I'd said something smart. He stroked my hair like I was a child. "Now I can tell my new master, Deimos, that you fell into my eyes like taking candy from the proverbial baby.

He will see you as safe and try his own wiles." He looked up as if he'd heard something, then leaned over me and whispered, "Deimos chose me because I am asexual; he wanted only vampire mind powers to be tested on you. I will tell him how easily you fell and stayed under my control. It will make him bold, and hopefully careless. His mind powers are not his strong suit; add that he is tempted by flesh, and I think you should be able to distract him."

I whispered back, "Without Jean-Claude I'm not as into sexy."

Trappolino planted a gentle kiss on my cheek, then another one on my lips. He drew back for a second, then kissed me with more passion than he said he ever felt. "Sex does not move me, but power does, Anita Blake." His eyes seemed to grow larger until they filled my vision like dark water shimmering in the moonlight, covering the ocean, and then you drown.

37

I LAY IN THE big bed in Jean-Claude's room on the royal blue silk sheets with too many pillows, but there was no one else in the bed with me. I couldn't remember that ever happening. I never went to bed alone anymore. I tried to sit up and look around the room, but my hands were tangled in the sheets, I was tangled in the sheets and I couldn't sit up. The harder I tried to unwind myself from the sheets, the more they tightened until I called out for Jean-Claude to come help me, but he wasn't there. The room felt cold and empty, as if he'd never be there again.

I woke gasping, trying to move my hands, and still couldn't. I reached out to Jean-Claude down the marks that bound us together and there was nothing. It was like a huge echoing emptiness. I remembered then about Queenie damaging the vampire marks. I hadn't gotten to him in time to fix the damage, and now it just felt gone. The panic came first, then anger. Queenie was supposed to be part of our security. Some fucking security.

I tugged on my hands and knew before I rolled my head back to look that my wrists were chained to something behind me. I looked back to see a pair of handcuffs fastened over a chain. It was threaded around pipes set into a wall that was covered in white paint that was flaking off. The whole wall looked like it needed to be scraped and repainted. The ceiling was so high overhead that it was lost in a tracery of thick metal beams. There was enough light for me to see that, but the ceiling was lost to darkness. I pulled on my hands again, but it rattled the chains against the pipes, which wouldn't help me get free and might attract whoever had chained me up. I did appreciate the extra chain through the handcuffs because otherwise it would have pulled my shoulders up at a really uncomfortable angle while I'd been unconscious. That was a good way to get nerve damage.

I couldn't remember how I got here, or . . . what did I remember? I looked down at my clothes. Tactical pants, boots, and a black T-shirt that didn't help much because it was what I wore as a U.S. Marshal if I worked with the local police, or traveled out of state on a warrant of execution. My body armor was gone along with all my weapons. No big surprise there; if the bad guys captured me they weren't going to let me keep the dangerous stuff. I seemed to be lying on a pile of rolled-up carpets. Persian ones with bright colors like stained glass, glowing and vibrant even in the dim light. I raised my head and shoulders as much as the restraints would allow and finally found the light source.

A tall floor lamp stood against a partial wall to my left. There was a big overstuffed chair by it with a small table by the arm of the chair, a book sitting on the table with an empty glass beside it with a metal handle and framework around the glass part like something you'd drink a hot beverage out of if you wanted to be able to see what you were drinking. I couldn't read the book titles from here; that probably wasn't important. There were big industrial-looking stairs leading up to the second level above the reading nook. The top had metal safety rails that looked like they were meant to keep heavier things than just people from falling off the edge.

I didn't know where I was, or how I got here, but I did know that I couldn't see anybody guarding me. I looked back at the handcuffs. The last time I'd worn a pair had been with Nicky, though my hands had been behind my back for a very carefully negotiated bondage scene. I suddenly remembered my gun falling until it vanished out of sight toward the ground.

I got snatched off the motorcycle. I'd seen Nicky wiping out on the highway. He'd slid into a grassy area between the highways, so that was good. At least he hadn't gone into traffic; about the only thing that could have killed him would be to have been run over by a large enough truck. Even then, if it missed his head and didn't sever his spine, he'd heal. He'd gone into the grass, though; he was safe. I believed that logically, but the fluttering tightness in my gut wasn't entirely convinced. I said a prayer that Nicky would be okay. I got that sense of comfort that comes sometimes. It helped calm the panic.

I stopped trying to figure out what I did or didn't remember. It didn't matter right now; all that mattered was getting the hell out of here. I scooted back toward the pipes until I could sit up with my hands to one side. What I wouldn't have given for a handcuff key right now. If I'd been a regular cop who arrested people instead of executing them, I might have had one shoved in a pocket somewhere. They'd have probably found it and taken it along with all my other gear, but I had a moment of wishing. But wishing wouldn't save me.

I had to either get one hand out of the cuffs, break the chain, or tear the pipe out of the wall and slide the cuffs off. I stood up, finding solid footing in the pile of carpets. I started to wrap my hands around the chains to see if I could find the literal weak link, but then I felt one of the cuffs shift more than the other. I had small hands and small wrists. Regular cuffs didn't always fit petite women or juvenile offenders, just like you had to have extra-large boot cuffs for some men.

I tried to pull on just the one wrist, but I couldn't get the leverage to pull hard enough that way. I found that solid footing among the carpets again and backed up until the chains were taut, and then I leaned back as hard as I could, letting the cuffs slide up my wrists to the heel of my hand. It slid a little further down my left hand. I tried folding my fingers together to make my hand as small as possible and tried again. That helped a little more, but to get my hand out I was going to have to bleed myself. Totally worth it.

I grabbed the chain with my right hand so I wouldn't hurt that hand for no reason, then pulled as hard as I could on my left. I kept steady hard pressure. It started to hurt, but I didn't stop pulling. I wanted out of here.

"I should let you bleed yourself," said a voice.

I stopped pulling and whirled toward the voice. Rodrigo stepped out of the darkness at the far end of the room. It was a dream: another fucking nightmare like in the car.

"You're not dreaming, Anita," he said, stalking toward me, putting that sway in his walk like his sister did sometimes. A menacing, predatory catwalk strut.

"You're dead."

"No, I'm undead," he said.

"The shotgun blast took out your chest."

"Missed my heart, though," he said.

"Then you healed, you're still a wereleopard."

"No, Anita, I died and then I rose again."

"Shapeshifters can't be vampires."

He stopped just short of the pile of carpets. He looked identical to Ru, until you got to his eyes. They both had black eyes, but Ru made them shine with happiness, sympathy. There was nothing sympathetic in these, and anything that made Rodrigo happy would probably hurt someone else. He grinned, flashing dainty fangs.

"Now, Anita, you know that the Mother of All Darkness was a shapeshifter and a vampire. She sent you visions of it, hunted you with the spirit version of her great cat."

"That's her, she was the first vampire. You are so not her, Rodrigo."

"I would never dare dream of comparing myself to our delightfully evil queen, but I've been standing in this room hiding in the shadows since before you regained consciousness."

I shook my head as if that would make it not true, but unless there was a secret door that had the world's quietest hinges in the room, he hadn't walked in from anywhere else.

"You can't be a vampire. You can't be alive."

"Why didn't you behead me when I died?" He studied my face. "You didn't want to upset my siblings. How touching."

"If you'd been alive as a vampire all this time, you would have reached out to Rodina and Ru. You wouldn't have let them mourn you like this."

"If I had been my own master when I first rose, I would have contacted them, but Deimos found me and claimed me for his own."

"I'm dreaming like I was dreaming in the car."

He lowered his voice then. "Dream manipulation was one of the first vampire skills I acquired that weren't standard."

"If this is true and I'm not dreaming, then how did you become a vampire? I watched you bleed out, there were no vampire bites on you that I saw. You would have had to be bitten twice more before you died for a chance to rise from the grave."

"The Mother of All Darkness bit us all with her original body and its ancient strain of vampirism. It's very different from your modern watered-down strain."

"The Mother of All Darkness lost her original body longer ago than you've been alive."

"She put it into hiding like the Traveller has, and like the Lover of Death did, before you found it and destroyed it. As long as the body exists they can hop right back into it, which is what she did when she bit the three of us."

"I don't believe you."

"Perhaps I should use my vampire wiles on you and sink my new fangs into your tender flesh."

"You haven't been undead that long yet, Rodrigo, you don't have the juice to use vampire wiles on me."

"Trappolino says you fell easily to his vampire gaze. Your protection is much less now with your marks to Jean-Claude broken."

"He's almost as old as the Mother of All Darkness was, and you aren't him either."

"We shall see what I am, Anita, won't we?" He turned and looked farther down the wall that I was chained to. I heard a door open, but I couldn't see it. Apparently part of this wall was recessed and had a door in it. A man walked toward us. He was tall with thick black curly hair cut short and a neatly trimmed mustache and beard. The latter was a little too long to be fashionable, but the rest of him looked modern and well-groomed in a black suit, his charcoal-gray shirt buttoned up to a black-and-silver diagonally striped tie. His black dress shoes gleamed with polish.

"Anita Blake, meet Deimos, son of Ares, God of War, and the next king of all the vampires in the world."

38

I'D HAD A lot of vampires walk toward me over the years, and this one was supposed to turn into a real-life fire-breathing dragon, so it was something of a letdown that he looked so human. He was handsome in a very masculine way, but he was my first ever dragon vampire, come on. I expected a little pizzazz. He didn't even have a good sexy menacing walk like Rodrigo. He was dressed like a male model, but he walked in like a bull about to destroy a china shop. His fists were at his sides, chest out, shoulders back, letting everyone know that he was the biggest, baddest thing in the room. Sometimes the men who do that can back it up, but short of stepping into a professional fight, that much posturing usually meant just the opposite. He swaggered into the room, but it felt more like he was whistling in the dark past the graveyard.

I glanced at Rodrigo as if he could give me a clue, as if we were friends, which we weren't. He smiled at me, but it left his black eyes empty as a shark's. Sociopaths aren't great at picking up emotional social cues.

Deimos's English was great, but his accent was thick enough that I had to concentrate to understand him, though I appreciated him speaking English so I didn't have to learn ancient Greek or whatever his original language was. "Anita, it is good to finally see you face-to-face, though I do wish that you were wearing a dress instead of those mannish clothes." Okay, maybe I wasn't that happy about him speaking English. At least if he'd spoken his original language I wouldn't have understood that he'd started our conversation off by insulting my clothing.

"If you wanted me to dress for a formal kidnapping you should have said so in the invitation. Unless otherwise specified, most kidnappings in America are casual only."

He frowned. I hoped I hadn't exceeded his modern English, because I was kind of proud of the level of snark.

There was a sound in the room that made me turn toward Rodrigo. He seemed to be choking or trying not to choke. I started to ask him if he was all right, automatically, then I remembered I didn't like him, and then I realized that Rodrigo was trying not to laugh out loud.

"Are you making fun of me?" Deimos asked.

"You started it," I said, and I realized I wasn't afraid at all. I should have been, Rodrigo on his own was part of my nightmares, but it was like I just couldn't find any fear. I felt empty and light, as if Jean-Claude's marks being gone had taken more of me away than just him.

Rodrigo had turned away from us and moved a little farther into the shadowed room. He was breathing heavily, as if swallowing the laughter had cost him.

"You came to us dressed like a warrior; it is unbecoming in a woman," Deimos said.

I looked back at the vampire in his stylish suit, then at Rodrigo, who was wearing a nearly identical outfit to me—black and tactical as if he were one of our security people. "I'm a U.S. Marshal with the Preternatural Branch; I was dressed for work when you had me kidnapped."

"I will not want my wife to work in law enforcement," he said.

"Well, bully for you."

"I do not understand."

"Yeah, let me try for less slang and more clarity," I said.

"Clarity is good, we should be very clear with each other," he said.

"At least we agree on that," I said, moving a little to face more toward him, the chains rattling as I moved. I should probably play nice until I got unchained, but I didn't seem to have any nice left in me. Fuck it.

"We will agree on many things once we are married."

"Excuse me, what did you say?"

"My lord Deimos, we discussed that you would ease her into your grand plan," Rodrigo said.

"She asked for clarity between us; I am giving her what she asked for."

"I do not believe that is what she meant, my lord."

"Are you seriously telling me that the grand plan is to steal me away from the man I'm in love with and planning to marry, so you can force me to marry you?"

"It will not be force once you are my human servant, Anita. You will come to me willingly, joyfully, and see only me after it is done."

"I've been Jean-Claude's human servant for ten years, and trust me when I say it took him a couple of years to convince me that us dating was even an option."

"I did not follow all of your words, but of course you did not want to tie yourself to Jean-Claude. He is corrupt and has turned you into his whore. I will treat you as a queen should be treated."

I looked at Rodrigo. "Are we having a language barrier issue here, Rodrigo? Because I sure as hell hope so."

"Speak to me, not my slave."

"Slave, really?" I said, and looked harder at Rodrigo. "Did you trade being the trusted right hand of the Queen of All Darkness to become this guy's slave?"

He looked angry but made sure that only I saw the expression. "I was briefly the Bride of a necromancer before I sacrificed my life to save her and two of her lovers. Then I woke as a vampire and Deimos called to me; without the protection of a more powerful master I had no choice but to answer him."

Deimos was just suddenly in front of Rodrigo; I hadn't seen him move. He slapped the smaller man in the face hard enough that the sound echoed through the huge open space. Rodrigo crumbled to the floor. I thought for a second Rodrigo had been knocked out, and then he groaned and pushed himself slowly up on one elbow.

Deimos turned toward me with his hand still raised. I slid one foot back and found as much balance as I could in the folded carpets, though I wasn't sure what I was going to do with the fight stance with my hands still chained to the pipe.

"It's hardly a fair fight if she's chained up," Rodina said as she walked into the room.

I wanted to stare at her, but I didn't dare take my attention away from Deimos. If he hit me as hard as he'd hit Rodrigo he might snap my neck. Especially now that I didn't have Jean-Claude's vampire marks to protect me.

Deimos lowered his arm and turned toward Rodina. Good, now I could keep an eye on both of them at the same time. "She is only a woman, there is no fair fight between her and me."

Well, at least he and I agreed on one thing.

"She is your future queen, is she not?" Rodina asked, walking into the room with that predatory sway she had. Maybe she and Rodrigo could give Deimos lessons on how to enter a room with menacing flair.

"She will be my queen."

"Not if you hit her so hard you break her neck," Rodina said, keeping her distance from Deimos and circling around him to get closer to her brother, who was still on the ground.

"It is good that you admit how weak she is; that is better than these stories that paint her as such a fierce warrior that her fellow marshals have named her War. As if any woman could be mentioned in the same breath as my father."

I opened my mouth to say something, but Rodrigo made some motion that made me look toward him. The look on his face pleaded with me not to make things worse. It reminded me of Ru. Was he going to come walking through the door next? Were they all traitors? I didn't think Brides could even do that. Didn't they have to obey me? I wanted to blurt out an order to Rodina to take me home, but if I still had that kind of control over her I wanted to wait until Deimos wasn't standing there. I was pretty sure he'd kill her to keep her from helping me. I'd wait to try it when we were alone. If we got a chance to be alone.

I wanted to ask him about Athena, Goddess of Righteous War, but Rodrigo was right; I could debate mythology and misogyny with Mr. Crazy later. "Echo and Fortune are going to know you've abandoned your duty at the hospital, Rodina."

"I've got it covered," she said.

"Stop talking to them," Deimos yelled.

"She's supposed to be my Bride and one of our bodyguards. The fact that she betrayed us to you and helped make all this shit happen is important to me."

He seemed to think about that for a second, then said, "That I understand, but could you refrain from using vulgar language?"

"Who are you, my dad?"

"Are you trying to anger me, Anita?"

"You kidnapped me, didn't you think that would upset me?"

"You will be the wife of a god, why would that upset you?"

I stared at him and realized he meant it. I looked at Rodina and Rodrigo as the saner options in the room. Rodrigo dabbed at the blood on his mouth with the back of his hand. Rodina said, "Perhaps, my lord, you can tell Anita how you can free her of the *ardeur* and replace it with so many better things."

"Ah, yes, I can show you a new way to feed, Anita. One that does not whore you out for power."

"That's the second time you've used the word 'whore' in reference to me or Jean-Claude. Whores take money for sex, we don't."

"Jean-Claude is a whore for power, he always has been."

"You talk like you know him, but I know he doesn't know you."

"Um, that may be my fault," Rodrigo said.

"Brother, what did you do?"

"He told me the truth: that your master is an incubus and he has shared his curse with you, turning you into a succubus, but I have cured you of the taint of it. As my wife, I will show you more honorable food to feast upon."

I really wanted to argue with him, but technically everything he said was true, except for the whole being-his-wife thing. That was so not happening. I still wasn't afraid, or as afraid as I should have been. "There's nothing dishonorable about sex," I said.

"You already feed on anger, Anita, and that is your talent, not the false king's."

I frowned at Rodina. "Tattletale."

She shrugged. "I told you I wanted a ruler that would let me be evil, and you were never going to be that for me. He's already let me out of the moral cage you had me trapped in, Anita."

"What does that mean?" I asked.

"Our new king feeds on fear and pain," she said.

"He let you torture someone," I said.

She just smiled.

What I wanted to say was *I should have killed you*, but that seemed impolitic when I was still chained up with no vampire marks to help me contact anyone for help. "So, Deimos, you're a night hag feeding on fear."

"No, they feed only on fear. I feed on rage as you do, and sorrow. Oh, the feast when a village is burning around the people running and screaming. Holding their children so tight. Their despair perfuming the air. The pain as they burn alive. It is all food for us."

"Are you saying that you burn entire towns down just so you can feed on the pain and sorrow of the people that live there?" I asked.

"I did, but Rodrigo convinced me that to take over Jean-Claude's lands would require a softer hand upon the throne."

"Good for Rodrigo," I said; the sarcasm was lost on Deimos.

"I will teach you how to feed as I do, Anita."

"I don't want to feed like that."

"Would you rather feed on lust like a rutting goat?"

"The *ardeur* isn't just about lust. I can feed on friendship and love, not just sex."

"You are no devotee of Aphrodite, Anita. Though you may not be the warrior that the media has claimed, I believe that your true devotion is to Ares, my father. As a marshal you execute vampires and shapeshifters that had killed humans, so you bring vengeance like my mother, Tisiphone. You were made to be by my side, Anita." He came toward me, holding out his hand.

I tugged on the chains, because I really didn't want him to touch me.

"You complained about being forced to fuck everyone because of the *ardeur*. I thought you'd be happy with a different alternative," Rodina said.

"Is that what you told yourself to get around the whole being-my-Bride thing?"

"Partly," she said.

Deimos was suddenly standing right beside me. I stumbled backward trying to get away, but the chains limited how far I could run. Was he that fast, or was he rolling my mind that easily? That thought finally scared me.

I pulled back to the length of the chains, stumbling a little in the carpets. He reached out for me. I plastered myself against the wall. If he could roll my mind from across the room, him touching me would be bad.

"Don't touch me."

"You cannot stop me," he said, reaching his hand out toward my face.

"Consent matters, you son of a bitch."

His fingertips touched my face. "Look at me, Anita."

I closed my eyes.

His hand traced the side of my cheek until he cradled the entire side of my face. His fingers were buried in my hair past my forehead. God, he had big hands, and I didn't mean that in a good way. "Look at me, Anita." His voice was low and trying to be sexy, but I had years of Jean-Claude's amazing voice in my head. Deimos wasn't ballparking for sexy.

I could feel his breath warm on my face as he whispered, "Anita, my sweet, sweet queen, gaze into my eyes."

I didn't fight him, I didn't even struggle, I just leaned against the wall as far as the chains would let me and kept my eyes closed. It was simple and he was less likely to hit me. Before Jean-Claude's marks I hadn't been sturdy enough to trade blows with a vampire. I got hurt back then, and I had no way to know if I was back to being human frail. If I was, then I was going to try less-violent resistance until I was out of options.

He kissed me, softly; the beard and mustache felt weird. I'd never dated anyone with a full beard before. The thought was so ordinary that it helped me think. Him touching my cheek didn't make his powers stronger on me, and neither did his kiss.

Jean-Claude's bloodline touch made everything stronger; a kiss was like a supernatural powerhouse move, but Deimos left me cold. I reached out to Jean-Claude, my turn to whistle in the dark past the graveyard. There was a pulse in the dark, not a word or a sight of him, but I knew it was him. I knew the feel of his energy almost better than my own. Our marks weren't completely severed, just damaged. I'd felt it when Trappolino touched me. It was like my necromancy was helping me reach out to him. If more vampires touched me, would I be able to reach Jean-Claude and let him know where I was?

"Open your eyes and behold your husband," Deimos whispered against my face. He was actually gentler about it than I thought he would be. He leaned back and I could breathe a little easier. "Why is she not reacting to my touch?"

"She's been with Jean-Claude and his bloodline for ten years; touching her won't win her to you, my lord," Rodina said.

"You need for her to meet your gaze," Rodrigo said.

"Look at me, Anita." And there was nothing gentle in his voice now.

"Nope."

"What did you say to me?"

"I said 'nope,' as in 'no.'"

"If you hit her that hard, you might kill her." Rodrigo's voice was very close.

"She is supposed to be a worthy opponent of monsters," Deimos said.

"She was with a full set of Jean-Claude's marks on her." Rodina was closer, too.

"Until your own marks take the place of his, we have no idea how fragile she is," Rodrigo said.

I really wanted to see what was happening, like had they grabbed his arms, but I couldn't risk it.

"Fine," Deimos said, "then how hard can she be hit?"

"Perhaps we could just try to hold her eyes open for you, my lord?" Rodrigo said.

"Then do it!"

Vampire gaze was the strongest mind-fuck most vampires ever had. I'd already fallen into Trappolino's gaze. I did not want Deimos to capture me with his eyes. It was time to struggle.

39

THE TRICK TO really good struggling is to use every part of your body, and to remember what their goal is and not give it to them. They wanted to make me gaze into Deimos's eyes, so I turned my back on him and looked at the peeling paint on the wall. Turning around confused him; he even asked Rodina and Rodrigo why I'd done it. I enjoyed staring at the wall and not having to close my eyes. That was beginning to bug me. I wanted to see to fight, but I didn't have to see my target to hit it. My wrists were bound but my elbows weren't; I drove one back into Deimos's gut, hard and sharp. He made a nice *umph* sound, but it didn't bend him over; the next elbow did. He stumbled back from me, unable to make noise while his diaphragm seized up.

Someone's hand pinned my cheek against the wall. I had a second to see Rodrigo's dark eyes, and then I looked down at his mouth, his chin. I'd spent years dealing with vampires when I wasn't powerful enough to meet their eyes in a conversation. You pick a point to stare at that's below eye level; the chest was good, but Rodrigo's face was too close to mine for that. I memorized the thin delicate lines of his mouth as his hand trapped the side of my face against the brittle sharpness of the peeling paint as it crumbled under me.

I pushed my hands into the wall, trying to move my head, but

Rodrigo's hand was steady and with him standing to the side of me I couldn't reach him with my upper body. I tried to find a more stable place to stand in the pile of carpets.

"If you kick me, I will hit you in the face," Rodrigo said; he'd read my body language.

Rodina was reassuring Deimos behind me. I didn't catch everything, but he seemed puzzled that I didn't want to be his, why I preferred Jean-Claude, and other things that sounded delusional to me. "Any woman would prefer you to Jean-Claude," she said. The fact that Deimos didn't call her a liar on that meant he was lying to himself, or truly delusional. Vampires can tell if you're lying, but not if they believe the lie. He really believed that he was God's gift to women, no matter who the other man might be, but my man was Jean-Claude, he was my vampire. I reached for him again, and there was the pulse of his power. He was still out there, we were still connected, I just needed more vampires to touch me, and then maybe Jean-Claude could find me. We had a private army here in St. Louis if they could just get to me.

Rodrigo's lips got so close to mine that I thought he was going to kiss me; instead he breathed, the barest of whispers, "Reach for Nathaniel or Micah, quickly."

I didn't argue because Rodrigo was a wereleopard and a vampire. I was the one who had marked Nathaniel and Damian; I reached for them now with Rodrigo being both for me. I caught a glimpse of Nathaniel, wide startled eyes looking up. I heard other voices, high and urgent. "Where is she?" Then Damian was standing beside Nathaniel, hugging him from behind, and the picture was clearer. Them touching each other was fuel for our vampire marks, just like Rodrigo on my end. I let them read my mind. They knew everything I did.

I learned that it wasn't later the same night I'd been taken, it was the next night. It scared me that I'd been out that long, and the connection flickered.

"Fear," Deimos said behind us. "What did you do to make her afraid, Rodrigo?"

"She thought it was still the first night she was taken; I told her it was the night after that."

Deimos's power flowed over me, riding my fear, feeding it until terror tightened my throat, squeezed my chest, and I fought not to scream. Nathaniel and Damian tried to send me love and positive energy to balance it, but they were scared for my safety, and Deimos's magic fed on that, too. He overwhelmed the connection, and it broke until it was just me pressed against the wall with Rodrigo's lips set in a thin line, a slight tremor down his arm. Using him to jump-start me to Nathaniel and Damian meant the fear was filling him up, too. That calmed me. I'm not sure why, but if Rodrigo was still tied to me even that much, then maybe there was something left of his time as my Bride. Death should have freed him from me. Then I felt the warm rush of his leopard, spilling down his hand into me. My panther blinked awake, golden eyes and fur like ink starting to come closer to the surface.

Rodrigo lowered his head just enough so I could see that his eyes were the same yellow-and-gold mix of Ru's beast. They were identical in every way.

"Where did the delicious fear go?" Deimos said. He was walking back toward us.

I felt Rodrigo's leopard shut down like he'd turned a switch. I did my best to tell my leopard to go back asleep, because Rodrigo was right; we needed to hide the fact that he had helped me contact my people. If Deimos didn't already know.

"How did you contact Jean-Claude and an animal just now?" Deimos asked. He was still a little distance away, outside the tangle of carpets, I thought. They were uneven footing.

He could only sense vampire and wereanimal, but not the flavor, that was good. "I'm in a triumvirate of power with him." I said it like that explained anything.

"Triumvirates are rare and powerful, that is true. Vampire, human servant, and beast to call: Jean-Claude, you, and the local Ulfric Richard Zeeman."

"Yep," I said, relieved that he'd been so oblivious to exactly who I'd contacted.

"I felt their fear before the connection was broken."

"Only night hags can cause fear and then feed on it," I said.

"Yes, but can they cause sorrow?"

I was suddenly choking on tears. The sense of loss was overwhelming, like he'd carved out my body and I was empty, lost from everyone. I'd lost everyone. Rodrigo let go of me, and I saw a shine of tears in his black eyes before he stepped back. Apparently the sorrow traveled to him, too. Deimos had touched me, and his powers weren't more; maybe it was that my powers were still stronger through touch?

I felt the carpets shift under my feet as Deimos came up behind me. "Where did the sorrow go? I was feasting on it and now you are calm again. Why?"

"I don't know," I said, and that was partially true. I was beginning to think how to help my people find me; what were my resources? A vampire who was also a wereleopard, and another wereleopard. If I could get Rodina and Rodrigo to touch me at the same time, maybe I could give Nathaniel and Damian a louder way to find me?

He grabbed my shoulder and spun me around so hard and fast that I half fell in the carpets, gripping the chains to keep me from falling to my knees. I stared at Deimos's chest; I would memorize his tie instead of looking at his face.

"Look into my eyes, Anita, or I will drown you in terror and feed on it, until you beg for me to stop."

"Apparently I can't stop you from using that part of your power." My voice sounded remarkably calm even to me.

"Or did sorrow bother you more? I could drink your tears down like the blood I will take later."

I tried to hide the spurt of fear, but his power resonated with it. "Sorrow frightens you more, interesting."

I did not want to be interesting to him, not like that, because he was right; sorrow scared me a hell of a lot more than fear. He leaned over me, sniffing my hair like I was wearing his favorite perfume. "I prefer the way you smell when you're afraid, but if you do not look into my eyes I will find the key to despair inside you and turn it until you weep broken pieces of your grief onto the floor at my feet."

It's funny how you never know what will scare you until it does. My heart sped up, my pulse thudding so hard in my throat it was threatening to choke me. He laid his fingers against my arm and made a sound like a normal person would make over a meal that smelled divine.

"You are so afraid that your skin is cool to the touch."

I swallowed hard to get past my pulse, and to try and get control of my heart rate. If I could slow that down, the pulse would slow; once that happened my body would calm down and so would I.

"If you control your fear I will rouse it again."

"There is just no win with you, is there," I said, and I let my voice have that edge of shakiness that a racing pulse can give you.

"You cannot defeat me, Anita; I am a demigod and in this modern age I will be a god, for there are none left alive to dispute my claim to whatever throne I wish to occupy." He sniffed my hair again, drawing it in the way a wereanimal will do when it's scenting for prey. I felt his body react like he had heard something. I had a small spurt of hope. If it was the next night then Edward would be here, hell, Bernardo and Olaf might be here, too. There was no downside to having Edward and Bernardo here to lend their skills to our security guards, and in that moment Olaf coming into the room would have been fabulous, because he was really good at killing things and I wanted Deimos dead.

"He is awake," Deimos said.

"I'll get him," Rodina said.

"No, let them bring him to us."

I had no idea who *them* was, or who *he* would be, but the fear that had quieted down spiked right back up, because I had a long list of *him*s that I did not want to see dragged into this room. I was assuming that whoever it was had just woken up the same way I had, from either vampire interference or being drugged. Who else had they taken? Shit. It wasn't Jean-Claude, Nathaniel, or Damian, but that still left a lot of people I cared about.

"She's so afraid of who it will be, we must capture more of her lovers so I may drink her fear for them."

The *more of her lovers* put my heart rate and pulse higher still until my breathing came in a ragged gasp like I was on the verge of a full-blown panic attack. I didn't have those, damn it. Then I realized Deimos was using his power to spike my real fear, like feeding small sticks into a fire to keep it going. It was very subtle. Everything else he had done had been ham-fisted, but not this.

"You've been feeding everyone's fear like the guy who attacked Jean-Claude with holy water, and all the fires from the flame of God or whatever they call themselves."

"I have, and the more fires they start, the more attacks on vampires in your city, the more fear it causes in everyone."

"And you feed on it," I said.

"I could sleep for a hundred years here and feed through the small and large fears of the people here. I had no idea that city living offered so much more energy than the country."

"Don't get comfortable," I said, "you won't be here that long."

He laughed and looked down at me. I forgot and glared up at him. "Are you threatening me?" he said with an amused and condescending smile that men have been giving women since time began. Then I realized I was staring into his brown eyes and there was no draw to them. I watched the realization of it on his face. He snarled at me, flashing fangs. His eyes glowed, not like brown glass with light behind it as it should have for a brown-eyed vampire, but silver, like glass reflecting light except the black of the pupil was a slit, like the eye of a viper. I remembered Deimos's snake form that he sent to possess Jean-Claude months ago. Richard and I had thought the head looked like a viper, but the ghostlike snake had only had glowing, silver eyes with no pupil. There was nothing ghostly about these eyes; they were all too real as they stared into mine.

He hadn't been able to roll me because he hadn't been using his real eyes. These eyes swept over me like a silver ocean, but not to drown me, as if I was floating on the surface of it, gently rocking in the water that was far too still to be an ocean. A silver lake, maybe, but if it was water then where was the sky? A thick bank of fog rolled in and covered where the sky should have been, and then I was standing on solid ground, but the fog was so thick I couldn't see what ground I was standing on, even when I looked down at my feet. Then I realized that I was wearing flat sandals; I didn't own a pair. High-heeled, strappy ones, yes, but nothing like this. I was wearing a dress, but it was like no dress I'd ever owned—loose and lightweight, tied at the waist with rope or something softer and prettier than rope. The dress was pale lavender and the rope, or belt, was darker, almost purple. It made me think of Nathaniel's eyes.

Nathaniel was suddenly there in the fog with me. I almost cried out, but he put his hand over my mouth and put his finger against his own lips. I nodded, letting him know I understood. He took his hand away from my mouth and smiled. I wrapped my arms around his waist, smiling up at him, and then I realized he was wearing a shorter version of my dress, in the same lavender color. I traced my hands up his bare arms and realized it was a tunic; we were both wearing tunics à la ancient Greece. Jean-Claude used to dress me up in his dream visits, too. I guess everyone likes something familiar. Nathaniel's auburn hair was done up in some complicated hairdo with wildflowers starred throughout it. He touched my hair, and I realized that mine mirrored his, down to the flowers in my hair.

Deimos's voice somewhere in the fog: "Anita, come to me."

Nathaniel took my hand in his and started leading me through the fog away from the voice. I followed his lead, because I had no idea how to get out of the dragon's eyes.

"Anita, take my hand and I will lead you out of this fog to the safety of my arms."

The fog was beginning to thin ahead of us, and I thought I could see moonlight. There was a sound behind us like a click or a hiss, I didn't know what, and then a roaring sound echoed through everything. I glanced back to see an orange glow in the fog behind us.

Nathaniel started to run, pulling me along with our joined hands. The fog opened up to a clearing surrounded by small, stunted trees. It reminded me of the trees on the clifftop in the dream I'd had in the car. But this time there was no cliff, just three women standing together in the center of the clearing. They were dressed similarly to us except for the color, which was black. It matched their hair, and though it was hard to tell in the moonlight I knew that one had pale tan skin, one dark. Neva in the center was the oldest, still standing tall and straight, unbent by age, but her skin showed a lifetime of being out in the sun without care, her bones delicate the way some people look over seventy.

It was the three brujas of the rodere, the wererats' witches in the moonlight. No, not sunlight. No, they were inside in the fighting pit, the heart of the wererats' power. Nathaniel and I were running full out now with the roar of the dragon behind us. The fog glowed with fire, but there was no heat and the fog never lifted except in front of us.

Nathaniel's feet hit the sand of the fighting pit and then it was all gone. I was chained to the wall in the warehouse with Deimos holding me in his arms. He pushed me away from him, so that I stumbled in the pile of carpets. It was better than sleeping on the floor, but I was really beginning to wish for more even ground.

"Who has such magic that they could interfere between me and my prey?" he demanded, which meant he hadn't seen anyone else in the vision he'd created for me. "They are using your reluctance to join with me as a thread to find you, somehow. If you let me give you my marks without struggle, then it will be over, and no one will be able to take you from me."

"Why would I stop fighting now? I know that all our people are searching for me. It's our territory, we know it better than you do, and they will find me."

"It won't matter once you bear my marks. In fact, their magic will join with mine and Queenie's and make me even more powerful."

"Fuck you."

"When I have taken the last of Jean-Claude's whoredom from you, perhaps your language will not be so slatternly."

"I don't even know what that last word means."

"Basically he's calling you a low-class, dirty streetwalker," Rodina said.

"Damn, he is new in town if he thinks that anything about Jean-Claude is low-class."

She almost smiled, then fought it off. Then all trace of smiles were gone. "Why are they bringing our brother?"

"I'm told on occasion he sleeps with her."

"Sleeps, not fucks," she said.

"The language you young women use today." He damn near *tsk*ed at us.

"She smelled of leopard twice tonight. Once when you were near her, Phobos, and just now. From all reports leopard is her animal to call, not Jean-Claude's but hers alone. Is she gaining power through the two of you?"

"I have betrayed her in every way, and she has sworn to kill me; why would I help her, even if I knew how?" Rodrigo asked.

"That is the question, isn't it, Phobos?"

Two cloaked figures who were completely covered, including masks, entered the room carrying Ru by his arms, which seemed to be bound behind his back. I realized there was a rope around his ankles that went behind his back to connect to his arms. They'd hog-tied him. It was not a comfortable way to be tied up, and depending on how tight they did the knots it could be really uncomfortable. Ru's head was hanging down, so I couldn't see his face. He seemed to be out cold.

"Nice to know one of you didn't betray us," I said.

"He was happy to see me at first," Rodrigo said, "and then he defied me." The look on his face as he said the last part would have scared me once, but honestly I had bigger problems right now.

"I thought he'd join us once he realized Rodrigo was alive," Rodina said.

"Where do you want him?" one of the masked figures asked.

"Mischa, you took a blood oath to Jean-Claude; you shouldn't be able to betray him like this."

"Deimos offered stronger blood and I took it." I couldn't see anything but his bright blue eyes behind the mask. He was back in full Harlequin gear and all in black. Once black meant they had come to kill you. White meant they were still there to observe. Red had meant punishment or pain, drawing blood. They were dressed in black, but then all our security wore black. I hadn't thought about the color code and the fact that we didn't have one anymore. So many rules had gone away when the old vampire council had been destroyed.

"I expected better of you, Goran."

The other cloaked figure looked at me with reddish-brown eyes in his mask. "I go where my master goes; it is the way of things."

"He was physically abusing you."

"You forced us to go to therapy and we went," Mischa said.

"He is treating me with more respect," Goran said, "and we are both happier now that we are back to our true work."

"Which is?" I asked.

"Serving a vampire worthy of us," Mischa said.

Deimos said, "Lay him at his sister's feet, she's the one that tied him up."

I looked at Rodina then. She actually looked uncomfortable, like she was embarrassed at what she'd done. I wasn't sure it was possible for her to feel bad about anything she'd done. I guess she really did love both her brothers, she just had a weird way of showing it.

"My lord Deimos, once we told our brother of your glorious plan and he refused to join, I had no choice but to detain him."

"Why not kill him?" Deimos asked.

Rodina tried to be very still, face blank, but the very carefulness screamed how she felt about the idea of killing Ru.

"My lord," Rodrigo said, "we are not ordinary siblings, the three of us shared a womb. It is a connection beyond any other."

"No connection is beyond the one you owe to me, Phobos."

Rodrigo went to one knee. "I meant familial connection only, my lord."

Ru chose that moment to wake up, raising his head off the floor to look around. "What did you do to me, sister?"

"Hush, brother, we are in the middle of something," she said.

Ru turned his head as far as he could to either side, and when he saw me he said, "Anita, I am so sorry that they betrayed you."

"He is still loyal to Anita, he is of no use to me," Deimos said.

"He will come around," Rodina said.

"We have hunted together for our whole lives," Rodrigo said. "Ru will come back to us."

"And what use is that to me?" Deimos asked.

"The three of us are unstoppable, as you well know, my lord," Rodina said.

"I remember the three of you helped bury me in the earth for so long that I thought I would go mad."

I was pretty sure he had gone mad, but I kept that to myself, because the first rule in dealing with delusional people is never try to pop their crazy. Agree with it, or just stay quiet.

"We followed our queen's instructions as we now follow yours, my lord," Rodrigo said.

"You and your sister follow me, but your little brother does not."

"He will, my lord, I promise you that," Rodrigo said. He looked at his brother tied up on the floor and there was no pity in his face.

"Would you truly use your infamous skills as a torturer on your own brother?" Deimos asked.

"I prefer that to killing him."

"I've seen your skills," Mischa said, "and so has your brother. You might ask him if he prefers a quick death to being at your mercy, since you have none."

"I will not—" Ru started to say.

I interrupted him. "Don't finish the sentence."

Like a good vampire Bride, he had to stop. "What would you have of me?"

"Live to fight another night."

"If that is what you prefer, then I will endure what my brother has planned for me tonight."

"I have other uses for your sibling's sadistic skills tonight. They can torture you tomorrow," Deimos said.

Two more black-cloaked figures came in carrying another unconscious person between them, but this one was on his back and covered in chains. It was Nicky. I think my heart stopped for a second, and then two more cloaked Harlequin entered the room holding his legs and I could finally see what was wrong with him. I screamed.

40

THEY'D DRIVEN A huge stake through his heart, as if they hadn't wanted to miss. I fell to my knees holding on to the chains above my head because I had to hold on to something.

"He's alive," Rodina said; she was on her knees, too.

"What the fuck did you do to him?" I screamed.

"I didn't do this," she said, on all fours. She sounded like she was in pain. Good.

"The motorcycle wrecked, remember," Ru said; his voice sounded strained from being tied up on the floor, or maybe from feeling every emotion in me right that moment.

"I remember," I said.

"No one put a stake through your werelion," Rodina said.

"Then what's sticking out of his chest?"

"The great vampire hunter can't tell the difference between a stake and a tree," Mischa said.

"Tree," I said, and looked back at Nicky's . . . body, that's what I kept thinking when I looked at him.

I tried to see past all the horrible emotions that were stopping me from being able to think. I forced myself to look at Nicky, to really look at him instead of just reacting. I started with the thing that had scared me the most, the wood sticking out of him. No one made stakes that big. It had to be at least six inches around and over a foot long. The top was sharp and pointed like a huge spear, not like someone had done it on purpose, but like it had been broken off and just weathered into a nasty point. I could also now see that it wasn't in the middle of his chest, and it was lower than his heart, more through his side. The bottom of the tree was at least five inches below the back of his body. It looked like someone had cracked it free instead of cutting it. If he'd been human he'd have died. Hell, a lot of shapeshifters would have died, but Nicky's upper body was wider than most; his sheer physical size had given the tree extra room to go through him without killing him instantly. There was dried blood all over his clothes, but nothing that looked fresh. They'd wrapped him in heavy chain up and down his body; even as injured as he was, they'd still been afraid of him.

His head hung back loose and at an angle that looked so uncomfortable that I wanted to hold him, cradle his head in my hands. I wanted to check his pulse, feel if his skin was cool to the touch.

The two Harlequin holding his hips and legs started to lower him to the floor, but Goran from the front said, "We can't put him down."

"How long are we supposed to stand here and hold him?"

"Scaramouche, you traitorous bastard, I recognize your voice."

"Once our new king has his way with you, it won't matter if you know who we are."

The figure standing beside him sighed, which vampires don't have to do since breathing is optional. "Until that task is finished, it did matter," his vampire master, Capitano, said.

"You only need hide your identity from Anita if you doubt me; do you doubt me?" Deimos said.

"No, my lord, of course not" was the only answer he could give.

"We will torture him until you do what I want, Anita," Deimos said, as if it was just a pleasant suggestion.

Capitano said, "I fear, my lord, that the Rex is unconscious, and beyond pain."

"Then kill him."

"If you kill him, I will never give you what you want," I said.

"If we don't get him to a hospital soon, he's dead anyway," Rodina said, getting to her feet.

"We could take him to a hospital now, Anita," Deimos said.

"Why would you do that?"

"Let me mark you as my own, and then I will have Nicky taken to a hospital."

"Once you've marked me, then you'll just kill him."

"Give me your word that you will allow me to mark you without fighting me, and I will have him taken to the hospital now."

"You'll have them carry him away and pretend to take him to a hospital, but you won't do it for real. Even if you don't kill him, you'll just let him die."

"If he is useless to me as a pawn to persuade my queen to protect me, then I will kill him in front of you. I tasted the despair in you when you thought him dead. I think you would do anything to save him."

"I would, but that's not what you're offering."

"Do not kill him in front of her, my lord, I beg you; I did that once with another of her loves and it did not go well," Rodrigo said.

"Perhaps an act of kindness will win where threats will not," said Trappolino as he came into view unmasked but still cloaked. His skin was almost as dark as the cloth. We all pretend that white and black mean the same for skin tone as they do for anything else, but it's not true. Almost no one is actually white or black in color, but Trappolino was the closest I'd ever seen in real life. I had thought I dreamed this face, but apparently I'd dreamed the other, or he'd made an illusion of it. Better than any mask if you could put a false face into someone's mind.

"What are you suggesting?" Deimos asked.

"With help, I will transport her lover to the closest hospital."

"I can't trust you either," I said.

"I was not one of the Harlequin that came to St. Louis and took blood oath with Jean-Claude. I did not take oath with him and then break it as the others did."

I couldn't really argue with him. "You're telling me to trust that your word is good?"

"Have I ever broken an oath that I made to you?"

"No."

"Are you calling me an oath breaker?" Mischa said.

"Aren't you?" Trappolino said.

Mischa took a step toward the other vampire, but that rocked Nicky's body. He didn't moan, just moved far too bonelessly for comfort. I knew death when I saw it, and it was close. "If you want to move you have to tell the rest of us," Capitano said.

"You should be able to move with us as in battle, anticipating our moves," Mischa said.

"We have not been able to do that since our dark queen died," Capitano said.

Trappolino said, "Indecisiveness will kill Anita's lion."

I said, "You'll have to take him to one of the hospitals that treats supernatural injuries."

"Tell me, and I will go there," he said.

I told him the two hospitals and if it was close enough, the one with the best trauma center. Did I trust him? No, but what choice did I have? If Trappolino's word was no good, then Nicky was dead. If someone didn't take him to the hospital now, he would die. Trust or not, it was Nicky's only hope.

"I will not give my permission to lose the only prisoner I have that moves Anita's heart."

There was the sound of fighting just out of sight down the same damn hallway that everyone seemed to enter through. Trappolino looked toward the sounds, then said, "Others have returned with someone that may not move her heart as deeply, but for the purpose of possessing Jean-Claude's power and making it your own he is perfect."

The four Harlequin holding Nicky moved as a unit so they could all look toward the sound. "A prize indeed," said Capitano.

"Oh, shit," Scaramouche said.

My pulse sped up, and I had to swallow past the instant panic. Who did they have? Damn it. I knew how Nicky and I got captured, but the rest should have been protected better than this. How many of our Harlequin had turned on us? How compromised was our security? I said a prayer of safety for all of us, but I didn't get that usual peaceful wash of energy. Normally I just accepted that, because I knew that not every prayer is answered, but tonight I could have really used the reassurance.

41

DEIMOS YELLED, "DO not hurt him!" There was a roar in his words like the sound of a forest fire when it rolls toward you and there's nowhere left to run. I had to shake my head to clear the illusion, if that was what it was, before I heard another male voice that had no fire in it, but plenty of whine. "Then tell him not to hurt me."

"Demolition Man." I whispered his name, but sometimes I still forget how good supernatural hearing is.

"I'm coming, Anita, and I hope I get a chance to make you scream my name before we break you."

Normally I would have had something quippy to say, but I was still chained to the wall. Antagonizing a werewolf that had betrayed us all didn't seem smart, so I'd wait. When I got free he was going to jail or into the ground. The thought made me feel better. Looking at Nicky still hanging motionless between the four men sucked all the goodness right back out.

"If you keep delaying, Nicky will die," I said.

Trappolino glanced at me and nodded. He moved them forward into the hallway. I could hear some protests from the other group that I still couldn't see, but Deimos told them, "Let them through, then you can bring your more lively prize to me."

A few seconds or a minute passed, and then Demolition Man

stepped through. He was dragging someone with the help of another man on the other side of the prisoner, but Demolition Man was so big that I couldn't see past him from the floor. I stood up so I could get a better view, catching my foot in the carpets again. I might have kicked them in frustration, but I could see the man on the other side of Demolition. It was Kane.

"You son of a bitch!" I said, and pulled at the chains hard enough to make the pipe I was attached to give a metallic groan. Then I saw the long brown hair spilling forward to cover his face, but I didn't need to see his face to know who it was being dragged unconscious through the door. Nicky was safe, but Richard wasn't.

42

I WANTED TO SWEEP Richard's hair out of the way so I could see his face and judge how hurt he was, but no one cared what I wanted. They just dragged him into the room like he meant nothing, his hiking boots dragging on the floor. "If your lack of restraint has made the Ulfric useless for torture, I will take it out of your hide," Deimos said.

"He shouldn't have tried to fight back," Demo Man said. He dropped Richard's arm, only Kane holding him up keeping him from landing face-first on the concrete floor. I could see that Richard's hands were cuffed behind his back.

Rodrigo hurried to catch the arm that Demo had dropped. "If he hits his head on the floor it won't help him wake up sooner."

"Wise Phobos," Deimos said.

"Put him on the rugs so he doesn't get injured further," Rodina said, in that tone of voice that women use when they want the men to know how utterly stupid they've been. I was grateful to the traitorous bitch but didn't understand why she cared.

"I didn't know you cared so much for the wolf king," Demo said.

"I don't, but from this point on all injuries should be purposeful, so that we know how much harm is being done, how much pain he can take. If he's injured accidentally there's no way to monitor either the amount of damage or the pain you wish to inflict. Accidents can kill a subject before you have everything you want from them. In this case, our lord Deimos wants to use the Ulfric to elicit Anita's cooperation, and since he is the only one that Kane managed to bring back we must use him as a precious resource, not something to be thrown around the room without care," she said.

It would never have occurred to me to save someone so I could torture them better later, but then causing pain wasn't a hobby of mine.

"You did not tell me your sister was wise as well as beautiful, Phobos."

"She has always been both," Rodrigo said, as he started moving Richard toward the rugs.

Kane followed his lead, but said, "I wasn't the muscle sent to grab someone from Anita's family. I was just the lookout."

"What did you just say?" I asked.

He smiled at me, but it was the kind of smile that has nothing to do with humor and everything to do with causing someone else pain. "When Nicky turned out too hurt to use, our new king sent people out to find someone else that you'd be willing to cooperate to save."

"I just fucking woke up from whatever Trappolino did to me; for all you knew Deimos would roll me like dough, putty in his metaphysical hands."

"Deimos has been trying to enter your mind for hours. The drugs were supposed to soften your resistance to him, but they didn't."

"You're oversharing," Rodina said, "but you've always been a chatty bitch."

"She is right, beware that your tongue does not displease me enough to have it removed from your head," Deimos said.

Kane looked startled then; maybe he hadn't spent that much time with his new lord and master. That made me wonder, did Asher know what Kane had done? He wouldn't betray Jean-Claude and me like that, he wouldn't, but there was the tiniest bit of doubt that I couldn't shake. I decided to give Asher the benefit of the doubt, but if he wasn't a traitor, then it meant that he hadn't realized what Kane was doing. Asher was supposed to be Kane's master; the werehyena shouldn't have been able to do anything like this without Asher knowing. So either Asher had betrayed us, or he had no more control over Kane as his *moitié bête*, his beast half, than he did over Kane as his lover. I preferred incompetency to outright betrayal, but neither looked good for Asher.

"I apologize for any insult," Kane said, giving an awkward half bow while he was still holding Richard's arm. He looked unhappy, as if it had never occurred to him that his new boss might torture him as well as any victims he brought home.

"I'm not complaining, but what stopped you from getting my family? Richard is a lot harder target to take."

Kane opened his mouth, then looked sideways at Deimos and closed it, but Demolition Man either didn't see the danger or thought that it would only be aimed at Kane. Neither of them was great at reading a room for emotional context, and if I was lucky maybe it would get them hurt by their new king. I hoped so.

"The people you sent after Anita's family ran into Richard and his bodyguards. The fight attracted the police. Once the cops realized that someone had tried to grab a fellow officer's family member, they put their own guards on the hotel. Deimos ordered all of us not to engage with the police, so once they were on site the family was out of reach."

"Was my family hurt?" I asked. Suddenly all the problems I had with them didn't seem important.

Demolition Man ignored me. Deimos told him, "Answer her."

"They're fine," Kane said, and helped Rodrigo get Richard's upper body over the rugs, then let go, saying, "He won't bump his head now."

"Your brother recognized Richard from old pictures when you

were together, so he ran to him for safety, or they might have grabbed him and run before the police arrived," Demo Man said.

"The job is only half done," Rodrigo said.

"We don't need the kid anymore, we have Richard."

"I don't mean kidnapping her family, I mean putting Richard higher on the rugs."

Rodina made an exasperated sound and took the arm Kane had dropped. They pulled Richard up higher onto the rugs until he was lying right beside me. He was still on his stomach with all that wavy brown hair hiding his face. I knelt down beside him, but my hands were still chained too high on the pipe for me to touch him. "What if he suffocates facedown like that?" I asked.

They exchanged a look; Rodina eye-rolled, and made sure I knew how much a hardship it was for the two of them to grab Richard and turn him face up beside me. His hair finally spilled to either side of his face so I could see him. The left side of his face was already red and puffy where I was assuming Demo had hit him.

I walked on my knees until I could touch my leg to his shoulder. He didn't react at all. It made that leftover anxiety about Nicky flare so that I studied Richard's chest to watch it rise and fall. He was alive, and I had to believe that Nicky would stay alive, too. We would all be all right. I had to believe that as long as I could, because to think anything else would take the heart out of me, and I needed to hold my shit together so we could get out of here.

"We will start with harming the Ulfric, but we cannot kill him, for that risks Jean-Claude's life and hers."

I felt relieved, but I should have remembered that Deimos could feel emotions. "It is not your hope I feel, Anita, it is the lack of despair I miss, so I know that learning I dare not kill Richard for risk to Jean-Claude and you made you feel safer for the two of you."

What could I say, he was right. "Yeah, death being off the table is hopeful."

"If we cannot do the ultimate threat with you or Richard, then I will send different people after your little brother, or perhaps your sister, or stepmother. They look lovely in their photos."

My gut tightened up at the thought of any of them at the mercy of this thing. I wondered why my father and grandmother weren't on the list, but I didn't want to ask in case it was just an oversight. Three of my family in danger was plenty.

"The police won't leave her family unguarded," Rodina said.

"Perhaps we could take some of the Ulfric's family. I am told that Anita went to extraordinary lengths to rescue them years ago," Deimos said.

I stared up at him because that had been at least nine years ago. None of the people who had betrayed us had worked for us back then, or even been in town as far as I knew. Did that mean we had a traitor that had been with us with us for that long? Someone we'd trusted for nearly ten years? Shit, who could it be?

"Your pulse has sped up again, you are on the verge of fear again, almost panic, why?" Deimos asked.

"She's wondering which of her longtime people betrayed her," Rodina said.

"If you're still enough of my Bride to read my thoughts, then how the fuck were you able to betray me to him?"

"Rodrigo is no longer your Bride, but my ties to him still exist. I am pulled in more than one direction now."

"And what of me, sister?" Ru asked.

I admit that I'd almost forgotten about him. He had to know that, and that made me feel bad about it. "You aren't the one who should be apologizing to me, Anita."

"If you would only join us, Ru," she said.

He struggled against the rope; it had to be uncomfortable or worse by now. "Are you sure you're not cutting off his circulation?"

"I will adjust his bonds, if we're not torturing him tonight, but he should be fine for at least another hour," she said, sounding as matter-of-fact as if she were talking about needing to put away the groceries if they weren't going to cook tonight.

Richard woke up, blinking around as if he wasn't sure where he was, which meant that Demo Man had hit him harder than he should have, but no surprise there since the big werewolf had made it clear he thought Richard was too nice and not violent enough to rule the pack.

Richard turned his head and saw me; the moment our eyes met there was a spark of power that had been not missing but dulled, like taking the shine off a piece of silver. He tried to reach out to me automatically even though he had to feel his hands in handcuffs. I wanted to reach out to him, too, but I knew better than to try. He began pushing himself farther up the pile of rugs, with his feet and legs getting closer to the wall and to me.

"Awake? Very good, Ulfric," Deimos said. "Let us begin."

"Begin what?" Richard asked.

"Torturing you," Deimos said.

43

RICHARD GOT HIMSELF sitting up leaning shoulder to shoulder with me. Just the feel of his weight next to me helped calm all the negative emotions inside me. I leaned my head against his shoulder and so wanted him to put his arm around me. It was a craving to be closer to him. Once it had been just part of being in love with him. Now it was more than that, or less. We weren't in love with each other anymore, maybe that would come back, maybe it wouldn't, but the physical attraction was back in spades.

"The two of you are part of a true triumvirate of power now; you have me to thank for Jean-Claude giving you the fourth mark and sealing the three of you into one of the first true triumvirates of power that I've seen in two thousand years, give or take."

"We did the fourth mark to keep you from possessing Jean-Claude the last time you were in town," I said.

"As I said, you have me to thank for it," Deimos said, and he looked so self-satisfied, like he really had done us a favor.

Richard said, "Thank you," then kissed the top of my head; I turned and raised my face up toward him. He leaned down toward me and we kissed, soft lips, eager mouths, tongues exploring, and finally teeth. Richard took my lower lip between his teeth and it was just enough pain that it made me want more. He bit down just a little too much. I tasted blood, sweet copper pennies in my mouth, and then Jean-Claude was there in the kiss and the blood and the good pain. Whatever Queenie had done to the marks broke like chains unsnapping. Richard's hands were on my face, the edge of the cuffs brushing my cheek, and then the *ardeur* rose up inside me like a wave of warmth and desire that spilled from us and outward into the room.

I heard people scream, but I didn't care because I was in Richard's arms. I tried to touch him back, but my hands were still chained to the wall. Then there were other hands, other people, and the *ardeur* didn't differentiate or care. More just meant more energy to feed on, and that was all the *ardeur* wanted. Fangs sank into my neck and then there was a roaring sound and the *ardeur* scattered. It wasn't gone; I could feel it inside me like a piece of myself was home again. Jean-Claude was there in my head, our heads, Richard's and mine. I expected him to be in the big bed downstairs, but he was sitting in the big conference room with Dev standing at his back with his hands on Jean-Claude's shoulders. He'd stood like that with me in Ireland when he helped us fight off fairie glamour. I realized that of all the people I was magically connected to, he had been the one that had been most lost to me when the vampire marks weren't working. It hadn't even occurred to me to contact Dev as if he were just missing from me.

I stared at our Mephistopheles, our Devil, our Dev, with his yellow hair streaked with white, so it was among the palest of our blonds, his skin pale gold as if he was always sun-kissed. He was six feet three inches tall with broad shoulders to match the height. I stared into his blue-hazel eyes with their pale brown around the irises and even now the connection wasn't as strong as it should have been. Why would the links to our pure-blooded gold tiger be the hardest hit?

"Because he is a dragon, *ma petite*, and tiger energy threatens him." He had dirt on the side of his face, and his white shirt was covered in dust or grit. I started to think at him, *What happened?*, but something large smashed me into the wall; Richard's arm cushioned my head and held me as we blinked up at something in front of us.

What I thought at first was, *There's a wall in front of me, a wall that wasn't there before.* Then I realized that made no sense, no one would put a wall a few feet from the first wall. It wasn't wide enough to be a hallway, it was like a crawl space that you walked through. It was so narrow that Richard would have to put his back to one wall and go out sideways. Then the wall breathed. I watched the surface rise and fall and suddenly I could see it.

The belly scales were glistening and white like mother-of-pearl; the dim light caught pastel rainbows in it as he breathed. I looked up and up and all I could see was the shining white of the belly scales. The warehouse ceiling had to be at least thirty feet high, but it wasn't high enough for Deimos. His neck and head curled downward because there wasn't room for him to stretch upward. His head was bent downward toward us. The top of him was black, so that he mingled with the darkness near the top of the roof, but his silver eyes shone down at us like twin moons.

My first thought was not that we were in terrible danger, but that he was beautiful. I actually said it out loud: "Beautiful."

He leaned his head down toward us and spoke in a deeper, rumbling version of his human voice. "I appeared before you as the most handsome of humans, and you did not think I was beautiful, but you find this form beautiful." He had a mouthful of sharp teeth that detracted a little from the beauty, but not much.

"I do," I said, and it was the truth.

"She's right," Richard said, "you're amazing."

"People usually run screaming when they see me like this," he said, peering down at us with his twin moon eyes, shining and silver like moonlight on water. We forgot for a second that he was not just a dragon but a vampire. One second we were staring into those huge eyes, and the next we were falling into the silver shine of them like moonlight on water. The trouble is once you dive through the moonlight the water underneath is black and there is no light to lead you back.

44

I STOOD IN THE center of the village surrounded by flames, every building ablaze. The high-pitched screams of women filled the night. The men had run outside to try and fight; their bodies lay burned and twisted, the heat of our flame breaking bones as their bodies turned in upon themselves. A baby was crying somewhere nearby, high and pitiless. We stood in the center of the destruction and consumed their terror and grief. A woman crawled out onto the street with her baby in her arms and another baby old enough to walk. She was coughing, the small child crying, covered in soot and dirt. The baby in her arms wasn't crying. She stared down at it, trying to get it to cry, or move. She threw back her head and wailed to the night sky above. It was a sound beyond prayers, or words; it was a sound of such pain that anyone who heard it would know what it meant and would try to give aid. I stepped forward, but a man's hand was on my shoulder. His bearded face smiled so happily. How could he be happy in the face of such overwhelming loss? He told me that this was the moment of ultimate pain and to drink deep of it. I jerked free of his hand and ran toward the little family crying in the firelit dark. I felt something behind me and turned to see a dragon rising up and up above me until he blotted out the stars. "Now we feast on flesh and terror." He opened his mouth, but there was no fire to breathe, just huge, pointed teeth.

I woke with a gasp in the dark and for a second I thought I was home in the underground of the Circus of the Damned. I thought I had fallen asleep wrapped around Jean-Claude's nude body because he was cold to the touch as only the dead can be, but two things were wrong. I was still dressed, and the body didn't feel like Jean-Claude. This was too broad through the shoulders, more like Richard or Dev, or Nicky. The moment I thought his name I remembered him being hurt. I stopped for a second in the confusion and prayed that he was alive; there was a moment of peace, and then my hand touched beard. No one in my life had a full beard. I froze then like a rabbit in the long grass, hoping the fox won't find them. I forced myself to be still and not scream, because I didn't know if that would wake Deimos, because that was who it was, and him dead for the day was better than him awake.

I forced myself to begin slowly and calmly to explore where we were with one hand, because I was curled on my side against his body. Would me moving wake him like it can when you're sleeping beside someone? I didn't know how dragon vampires worked; it was my first one. I knew I desperately did not want him to wake up right now, so I reached carefully with one hand to explore. I knew what we were in, but part of me hoped, really hoped I was wrong. Maybe we were in a lightless dungeon where the darkness never ceased without flame or flashlight to pierce it.

The first wall was right up against his shoulder; my one foot was already resting against the other wall. I had to swallow hard against the rising panic and force myself to take even, shallow breaths; I wasn't up to deep breaths, but I tried to control my breathing, because you can't have a full-blown panic attack until you lose control of your breathing. I raised my hand upward, praying that I would reach far up into the dark, but I knew that wasn't the truth. I knew before my fingers touched the top less than a foot above me that I was in his coffin with Deimos. I'd originally gotten claustrophobia waking up just like this with a different vampire, but that had been a human vampire, and I'd known she wouldn't wake until dawn. I did not know that about this vampire. Some of the ancient ones weren't trapped until sunset; they just needed to stay in the dark, underground they could wake earlier even, and Deimos was ancient.

I lay there curled around his cooling body and tried to think logically about what my options were before I started moving around too much and chanced waking him up early. I had no idea how much time had passed, so for all I knew we were minutes from sundown, but that kind of thinking fed my panic and made it harder to think. What were my options? What resources did I have to get the fuck out of here? *None*, screamed the panic in my head, and maybe that had been true last time before the vampire marks, before my necromancy had come into its own. I had magic, damn it. They could take all my weapons, but they couldn't take my magic.

I lowered my shields and reached out to everyone and anyone that I was connected to psychically. It started as just a calm *I'm here*, and then it became the metaphysical equivalent of the panic. I screamed out into the blackness for someone to find me.

I heard a noise outside the coffin. I wasn't sure what it was at first, and then I heard soft skittering on the wood, then a soft squeak. Rats, there were rats on top of the coffin. There was a time in my life when I would have been more afraid, like, *Oh, great, it's not bad enough I'm trapped in a coffin with a vampire, but now rats are going to crawl inside and start nibbling on me*, but that was before I made Rafael, king of all the wererats, my animal to call. I hadn't tried to talk to regular rats before, only the very special kind they had in their inner sanctum, but I was willing to try.

I thought, *I'm here*. The rats stopped moving. Had they heard me? I thought, *I'm here, get help, tell Rafael*, and then I felt ridiculous. They were rats and I was trying to make them into Lassie: *Go get help, girl, Timmy's down the well again.* I'm locked in a coffin with an ancient vampire that turns into a fifty-foot-tall dragon, and can breathe fire, and apparently rolled me completely with his eyes, and he wants to replace the warmth and pleasure of the *ardeur* with feeding on terror, despair, and misery.

The rats squeaked high-pitched and scattered. I almost yelled *Don't leave me*, but caught myself in time. These were just regular rats, not the super-intelligent and sometimes mystical ones that lived inside the wererats' inner sanctum of power. Those understood way more human words than was comfortable sometimes. But I'd seen the three brujas in a vision with Nathaniel, hadn't I? Or had that been a dream, too? They were looking for me. They were helping Nathaniel look for me.

I reached out to Nathaniel, but it was like hitting a wall that dissolved around me, so there was nothing to touch, nothing to reach for; I was back to being alone in my head. Okay, falling into Deimos's eyes had damaged what Jean-Claude had repaired through kissing Richard. Where was he? Was he in a coffin with one of the other vampires? Did Rodrigo need a coffin since he was still a were-leopard? Did that kind of vampire do better in daylight? I had no idea. But Trappolino would need one, and Capitano, and Mischa, so if they would physically fit in a single coffin there were plenty to hold Richard and a vampy bunkmate.

I lay there in the dark and was starting to lose my battle with the claustrophobia. It makes small spaces feel smaller, like they're closing around you like a fist to cut off your air and . . . I couldn't lie here. Even if it woke Deimos early I had to try to get out.

The coffin was a bigger model because Deimos in human form was still a bigger guy. It wasn't as impressive now that I'd seen him in dragon form, but it still gave me enough room to turn and get my hands under me. The vampire never moved except where I accidentally moved his arm, or hand. He rolled like a real dead body; ancient or not, he was out for the day. Thank God. I made sure it was a hinged coffin on only one side, because with the older vamps some-times the lid was lift-off with no hinges, or with things on both sides that could lock down. How it's put together changes the balance point on the lid. I raised my hips slowly; I didn't want to bang myself on the lid. I'd hit my head on the first coffin I'd woken up in like this, given myself a mild concussion. I did not want to do that again, or hurt my back, or . . . I didn't know if I still had Jean-Claude's vampire marks to rely on, so I had to treat myself like I was just a regular easier-to-hurt-and-kill human.

I raised my hips and had room to sort of get up on my knees, but my back was pressed against the satin lining of the coffin. I pushed with my shoulders and back against the lid, slowly, cautiously, just to see if the lid would move at all. It did, in fact there was a thin line of light. The thrill of adrenaline-backed relief made me a little weak. I took a deep breath, and Deimos's scent was masculine, but not sweaty, or anything that human. Vampires don't really sweat all that much normally. I smelled modern aftershave and soap and all the scent modern humans have on their skin, but underneath that was some-thing that made the back of my neck creep. It was the scent of vam-pires, especially ones that were over a thousand years old. The closest I've ever described it is snakes; it smelled vaguely of snake cages. Jean-Claude never smelled that way; neither did Damian or Asher. I didn't know why some did and some didn't, but if you got enough of them in coffins in an underground hiding place it was stronger. I'd learned to know they were there just from that nose-wrinkling smell. Whatever it was, Deimos had it.

I had to put my arm over his body to get a better place for my hand and move all of me closer to him, pushing on his thighs and hips to get the balance point I needed to open the coffin lid enough to get my fingers through and lift that way. I lifted and there was the crack of light again. I balanced on my knees and one hand, lifting with the one hand and shoulders so I had enough room to get higher on my knees, getting both sets of fingers under the crack and lifting.

I heard footsteps but the lid was already open too far to pretend, so I just opened it, grabbed the lip of the coffin, and used it to help me roll out of the coffin to a crouch down behind it. With the lid up, I was hidden from view.

"I told them not to leave you in here without a guard," Goran said.

I lowered the lid on Deimos's coffin, and I could see the big were-bear standing at the top of a small flight of stairs that led up to the room's only door. Goran was completely hidden behind the traditional Harlequin outfit, even his hands were gloved, but in one gloved hand he held a water bottle. The second I saw it I was thirsty. Thirstier than I'd ever been; all I could think of was getting to that water. Goran had it opened by the time I got there. I started drinking. The water wasn't cold, but that didn't matter. I drank half the bottle before I stopped to look around or even think much. My neck hurt. I touched where it hurt and found two large puncture marks. The edges were ragged and hurt to touch.

"Rodrigo has a rough technique," I said.

"It is Deimos that is rough, Rodrigo did the other side." I found another set of fang marks on the other side of my neck, but these bites were much smaller, neat and sort of tidy. The edges didn't hurt to touch.

"That's the reason you're so thirsty, you fed two of them in one night," Goran said.

"I've fed Jean-Claude and Asher in one night and I wasn't this dehydrated."

"Did you feed the *ardeur* on them as they took blood?" The question seemed utterly neutral, not salacious like Scaramouche would have implied, or jealous like Kane. Goran was just gathering information.

"Yes," I said.

"Have you ever fed multiple vampires in one night without feeding the *ardeur*?"

I thought for a minute as I sipped the water. "I don't think so, no."

"Have you ever had a vampire take too much blood at one feeding?"

"Yes, enough to be nauseous and dizzy, a little faint."

"But not craving water?" Goran asked.

"No, food, especially protein, is good afterward, but I'm not craving it. I just know it's good for me, and bad if I go too long without feeding my own hungers."

"So, you've never woken craving water like this?"

"No, never."

"That is interesting," he said.

I finished the last of my water. He pulled out a second bottle from the small soft-sided cooler he had in his hand. This one seemed a little colder, or maybe seeing the cooler made me imagine it was colder; either way it was better, though I was less frantic drinking it.

"Come, let us take water to the Ulfric, he will need it."

I glanced at the room. There were five coffins scattered throughout the room, counting Deimos's. The light I'd seen from the coffin was electrical lights strung throughout the room. The windows high up on the far wall had been bricked up. The vampires could sleep snug and safe until night fell.

"Richard isn't in here?"

"Deimos would not allow either of you to share a coffin with anyone but himself." He motioned me ahead of him through the door. I didn't argue with the gentlemanly gesture, or question if he simply didn't want me at his back. He was taking me to Richard; that was all I cared about in the moment.

45

WE CAME OUT of the door into a wider-than-normal hallway, then turned left. There were other rooms on the left side of the hallway, but just a blank wall on the right, so probably an outer wall. The hallway was huge, as in big enough to drive a forklift or things a little bit bigger through. The hallway wasn't just tall and wide, but long, so that I wasn't a hundred percent sure the room at the far end was the big room.

I sipped my water and debated on asking something that could be used against me, but I wanted to know badly enough to look weak in front of Goran. "How was Nicky when you dropped him off at the hospital?" The weak part was admitting that anyone meant that much to me, enough that hurting them might make me do what the bad guys wanted.

Goran looked down at me with his reddish-brown bear eyes. I think I'd startled him with my question. "He was alive when we saw the doctors take him into the ER."

I nodded, my stomach tight. I'd have liked for him to be more reassuring, but he'd been honest and that was better, I guess. "I appreciate that you told me the truth and didn't try to soften it with things you don't actually know for certain."

"I smell that underneath your worry for Nicky you mean that."

"I thought you sort of liked Nicky."

"I do."

"Is it naïve to say, then why betray him, why betray all of us?"

"It is naïve, but you already know why I betrayed you and Nicky."

"Because Mischa decided to betray us, and you go wherever your vampire master goes," I said, sipping the water he'd given me, and for the first time I wondered if it could be drugged. It had been sealed and opened in front of me, and in the normal world that would make it safe, but when dealing with spies and assassins there are more options.

I must have done something to let him guess my thoughts, because he said, "The water is safe, Anita."

"Two days ago, I would have taken your word, because I knew it was good." I finished the water in the bottle because if there was something in it, too late now. "Now all I can do is hope that you're not lying to me."

"I am sorry that my word is no longer good enough to reassure you, truly I am."

"Me, too, Goran, we'll miss you at grappling practice next week."

"Deimos has replaced Jean-Claude's vampire marks with his own. I will continue to train with Nicky and the others on your security team as usual, though not next week. It will take longer than that to rebuild the stairs."

I stopped walking and looked at him. "What stairs? What are you talking about?"

Goran stopped and looked down at me. "I thought Jean-Claude would have told you when he contacted you mind-to-mind the last time."

"Well, he didn't, so you tell me."

"When Deimos could not possess your mind as quickly as we had planned, we had to find a way to keep your security and the other Harlequin from finding us before Deimos had possessed you, so we used carefully placed explosives to . . ."

"What did you blow up?" I actually took a step toward him, without thinking about it, as if I would attack him here and now, because all I could see in my head were images of the people I love blown up, hurt, and dying. My chest was tight, throat closing with the fear of what might have happened. I tried to feed the anger to chase back the dread, but for the first time I couldn't stay angry. I was so scared that I could taste metal on my tongue.

"They are not hurt, Anita, we used only enough explosives to bring down the stairs. No one can go in or out of the underground until emergency services clear the way. The explosion was designed to do as little damage as possible to the structure while trapping as many of your potential rescuers so that they could not interfere before Deimos possessed you."

"How do you know that no one was hurt?" I asked.

His eyes flinched like he wanted to look away from my face, but then went back to the serious eye contact we both liked. It was enough of a tell for me to say, "You have someone trapped down there pretending that they're still loyal to us."

"Deimos possessed you last night, and all who were tied to Jean-Claude are now tied to him. By the time they clear the debris and free your people, there will be no traitors because we will all be loyal to Deimos. It is done, Anita. You could not hold on to your anger just now because it lost to the sorrow and grief that is Deimos inside you. You will become more his creature every day, as we all are."

I shook my head. "No."

"I am sorry that it causes you distress, Anita, truly, but it is done."

"It's not done until I say it's done," I said, glaring up at him.

Rodina yelled at someone, "You're hurting him!"

"I thought that was the idea," Demolition Man said.

"I'll only hurt him as much as I need to hurt him, because I know what I'm doing. You're going to hurt him so badly it will take him days to heal."

"Who are they talking about?" I asked.

"I do not know, but I can smell Richard and Ru."

"Why torture them if you've won?" I asked, starting to run toward the open door.

"I have never shared a victory with Lord Deimos, but some men save their cruelest actions not for the battlefield, but for after they have won."

"Fuck that," I said, and ran faster.

46

A MAN SCREAMED, BUT it wasn't Richard's voice, so who was it? The fact that I didn't know who Rodina was torturing and trying to get Demo Man to stop torturing made me stop running and try to get closer to the door without them seeing me. I pressed myself against the wall to the right of the doorway trying to see into the room, but that half with the platform and guardrail was empty. Before I went to the other wall where they'd likely see me, body memory kicked in and I went for my gun, which wasn't there. Damn it.

I felt Goran coming up behind me; his energy was prickling along the back of my body, and then deep inside me where the beasts lived something stirred. It was black-furred, but I didn't mistake it for my panther. The fur was rougher, thicker, a different texture even at a glance. That huge black body turned toward me, almost lost in the darkness where all the beasts stayed, and then it turned and looked at me and the thrill of surprise went through me from my head to my fingers and toes, because it was totally unexpected. The face was as white as it was black, with narrow white lines encircling the black around the eyes. For a split second I thought *reverse panda*, but the white line above the eyes had a wide white stripe down between the eyes, around the black nose, and then spilled down its throat and onto the chest, where it was hidden from me because the animal was still on all fours. The bear went up on its hind legs, towering above me. I gazed upward in front of me as if the bear really was standing there with the white spreading down the throat to touch the edge of the chest. I tried to think—spectacled bear, Andean bear—and I knew I was wrong. They were small bears compared to grizzly, or Kodiak, or even polar bears, and this one was bigger than all of them.

I heard Goran sniffing the air loud and snuffling. He was scenting my bear. He moved closer, his breath warm on my hair, then hot against the side of my face. It made me close my eyes and relax into his energy for a second, and then the bear inside me roared and forced me to whirl around to face Goran. I started to swipe at him with a huge, clawed paw, but I remembered in time that I didn't have one of those in this form.

"Back up," I said, and there was a rumble in my chest like I'd swallowed a roll of thunder. I stared up at him; his human form seemed almost as big as the bear in my head.

"I would never hurt you, Anita," Goran said. He started taking off one of his gloves. "Please, skin-to-skin contact. It's been so long, longer than you can imagine."

"What the hell are you doing out here?" Demolition Man said in the doorway. He was rubbing one hand up and down his arm like there were goose bumps to get rid of. Apparently the energy of our bears had interrupted the torture. Great. I hadn't even had to step into the room, damn efficient.

Rodina yelled, still in the room, "Use your nose, I can smell the bears from here."

"This isn't like any bears I've ever smelled," Demo said.

"You are too young, your beast is too young to remember," Goran said. He had his glove off now. He held his hand out toward me.

"Just touch her," Demo said.

"Only if you want to die," Goran said.

"Mischa said you were cave bear, this isn't that," I said.

"Do you know what we are?"

"Older, a short-faced bear, a giant short-faced bear," I said.

"What the hell is a short-faced bear?" Demo asked.

"We are," Goran said, but neither of us did more than glance at him. The energy was building between us, but it wasn't like most of my other beasts. There was no danger of shapeshifting; my bear was standing upright to be as tall and intimidating as possible, but she wasn't ready to attack either. She was waiting, trying to judge the bear in front of us. The man in front of us.

"Why does she, my bear, think of you as a bear first and man second?"

"Don't all wereanimals think that way?" Goran asked.

Demo and I actually answered together: "No."

I glared at him, and it was like I felt my bear turn her head and give him a measuring look. It was the kind of look I gave someone when I was deciding if I could take them in a fight, or if I would have to kill them now, instead of later. The only extra calculation that she made that I didn't was—is it food?

I did not want to eat Demolition Man. Not as meat, like she was thinking, and definitely didn't want him to be food for the *ardeur*. Then I remembered that the *ardeur* was gone. Deimos had taken it and put despair and terror in its place like in the dream he'd given me. I did not want to feed on people's tragedies. I was already a cop; I saw people on their worst days. I did not want that to be part of my magic. My bear looked at me and the longer I stared at her face the more beautiful it became. Her eyes weren't brown of any shade, but a deep grayish blue. Bears didn't have eyes like that, but she did. She looked at Goran and approved.

"Has she decided if I may touch you?" Goran asked.

"Yes, she says yes," I said, and held my hand out to him. The moment his skin touched mine the energy was incredible. It chased over my skin in goose bumps, it blew my hair in a wild tangle around my face, it curled against the wall behind me and asked wordlessly what did we want to do with all of it.

I wanted to go home, but home wasn't a building, it was people, the people I loved. Deimos had taken them from me in a way that I didn't understand. The vampire marks intermingling me with Richard and Jean-Claude had terrified me once, made me run away from both of them. Now I had so many people running through my head and heart for so long that it was part of home now. I wanted that back.

Goran's heart was in my head, because I could feel his loneliness; it wasn't like just losing someone you loved. It was losing all your people, everything you'd ever known, your whole world lost until you were the last survivor. We have a word for it now: *endling*. Goran was the last of his kind on the planet. The Mother of All Darkness had destroyed his master by destroying all the bears that that ancient vampire could call to his aid. Then she had given Goran to Mischa, the only vampire she had in her employ that could call bear. She gave Goran away like he was a stray puppy that needed a new home. Mischa hadn't wanted him. He'd wanted a priestess, a bear priestess, a mother of animals, walker of the void, one of the dreamers that re-creates the world each winter and brings it out alive and growing again in the spring. But the Mother of All Darkness destroyed any magic she thought might rival hers, so she killed all the holy women of Goran's people to defeat a vampire that had created a territory here in America before that was even the dream of a name for this land. I drank down Goran's sorrow, his eons of grief, his fear of Mommy Darkest. If Deimos had only known what a feast he had right beside him; but he hadn't seen Goran's magic, because Mischa didn't see it.

Someone was crying and it was Goran, kneeling in front of me while we held each other. His arms held me so tight it was almost hard to breathe, but I didn't tell him to let me go, because I was feeding on him. It was awful and wondrous, and I realized there were tears running down my face. I could not contain all of his emotions without some of them spilling out. I held him and cried with him. I pushed back his hood so that I could kiss the top of his head, put my cheek against the disarray of his brown curls.

I fed and fed and still there was no end to his grief. I thought when I fed that I would take some of his emotions and heal him, but that wasn't how it worked. This new magic from Deimos found Goran's pain and fanned the flames of it. I couldn't take his pain away, but I could make him feel every drop of it while I fed. There was no healing to this way of feeding. Deimos was a night hag that could cause the fear he needed to feed on. I couldn't cause the emotion but as long as I fed on it, the bad memories kept coming and they would keep coming, until I let him go.

I tried to step away, but he wouldn't let go. He started to pray in a language so ancient that perhaps no one alive spoke it except him. He prayed to the bear goddess and her mischievous cubs; he thanked her for returning to him. He thanked her for the freedom to cry. I saw Mischa striking him again and again for showing any emotion. We hated Mischa but were afraid to die with him, so we could not kill him ourselves.

"If I free you from him, you can kill him," I said.

"Free me from my bond and I will kill him for both of us."

"I am the breaker of bonds," I whispered as I raised his face upward to look at me.

"The Mother of All Darkness called herself that," Goran said, and now he was afraid, and I fed on that, too.

"I drank her power down and I have become she, because Jean-Claude and Nathaniel, the tigers, and all the others are not here to keep me safe."

"I will keep you safe," Goran said.

"How?" I asked.

"Magic," he said, and like so often when things go mystical I didn't understand and I didn't have time to ask, before Goran tried to save me for himself.

47

GORAN WHISPERED A prayer and I felt something stir, and once I would have said something old stirred, but some things are ageless. They always were and always will be; so long as one person remembers, they remain. But she hadn't been waiting for someone to pray to her; she had been busy. She was there in the first cool morning in summer reminding us to eat and store and pack away food, because winter was coming. She was there in autumn reminding us to gather everything we could, to find our warm burrow, our snug house, our cave, our tree, our hole, our shelter. She was there when winter finally came in snow, ice, and cold, warning us to hide and find our safe space. Home is where you are safe, and if you are not safe then it is not home and you should seek it elsewhere, but first you must survive the winter. She was the warning to go deep into the cave dark with our stored food, our stored fat, with our bodies well-fed enough to last through the cold until warmth and new food returned, but there was wisdom in the quiet, healing in rest, dreams in the long sleep, power in the void that can only come from a solitary journey. No one can help you cross the great dark, but if you do, then you come back bearing magic. The kind that creates from the darkness and emptiness of space and time, where there is nothing but rest and quiet and nightmares and dreams that new ideas come, new inventions, new thoughts, new life. The great bear mother brings her cubs out of the winter dark, as we all should bring new things out of the silence and patience that is winter. It is not a time for rushing. Once, nature forced us to rest and think deep thoughts, but we have lost all that with lights that never go out, work that never ceases, stories and songs and art and fun that is never gone from us. No wonder you're tired, she said, no wonder you are sad, you have lost yourself to constant movement. No animal can eat enough to go without rest, or ease, it is not sustainable.

I felt her touch my face with a huge paw, the claws combing through my hair, and then it was a hand touching my face so gently. It was the memory of my mother tucking me in at night when I believed the world was safe and I would never lose her. It was Jean-Claude cupping my face, staring at me with that soft look as he marveled that we loved each other. It was me letting him hold me so that I could let go of all the bad things and believe for a second that his arms were shelter from all winter storms. It was me staying awake so that I could feel Micah and Nathaniel asleep on either side of me and let the sound of their breathing, the weight of their bodies pressed against me, be my shelter and my safety. It was Richard returned to us, his arm trailing across the bed over Jean-Claude's and Micah's bodies to touch mine. It was Dev's arm coming from the other side of Nathaniel, his hand scooping around me so that Micah snuggled closer to me in his sleep and Dev and Richard finally divided us all up, with Dev's hand going low and Richard's going high. It had taken months to finally be able to share the bed peacefully for all of us. It was adding Pierette to the bed and the laughter as we all tried to find a new spot. It was home.

The memories helped her start to rebuild what had been broken, but she needed more than thoughts. She was about reality, food and comfort, shelter, and warmth. Things that could be touched, tasted, smelled, enjoyed in that cozy we-have-enough-to-weather-the-storm way. Goran smiled up at me and it was a good smile, but it wasn't home. The bear thought it was a good beginning. A spring that would bring cubs and fresh greens to eat, berries, and I was suddenly craving pie. I was craving blackberry pie. I hated blackberries in or out of pie, but Jean-Claude loved blackberry pie. When he'd given me the first two vampire marks I hadn't realized it, didn't even know what vampire marks were, but that day at lunch I'd ordered blackberry pie and was halfway through enjoying it when I realized I hated that kind of pie. I'd had no idea why I ordered it. Jean-Claude would explain later that a vampire could taste food through his human servant. Me tasting it that first time by accident on my part had been his first chance to taste it in six hundred years, give or take. I'd hated that he could use me like that, and then two years later, give or take, one of our favorite date nights was going to a restaurant so he could sit across from me while I ate. Part of the fun was picking the menu together and trading things he loved for things I didn't so he could taste, and I could watch him enjoy the food. It was still one of our favorite date nights if it was just the two of us.

I could taste blackberries on my tongue and then I heard Jean-Claude's voice: *"Ma petite."* He was the first breath of spring when snow still lay on the ground and that day the wind touched your face and it was like a promise that winter would not stay forever.

I had been trapped in winter, freezing to death without any hope of spring. It seemed impossible that a vampire had taught me to open my heart up and believe that there was more than bloody crime scenes, executing vampires, raising the dead, and going home to cuddle my favorite toy penguin. Drink coffee and repeat. That had been it, my life was death, cold, and then I'd met Jean-Claude, and everything started to change.

Crocuses pushing their way up through the snow, that was the visual I had, but the bear goddess gave me one of the early spring ephemerals flowering beneath the trees before the leaves bring their shade. Spring beauties like white-pink stars across the ground, yellow trout lily, violets, pink lady slippers, three-petaled trillium, and the first green shoots through the leaves, and the tight curl of baby leaves on shrubs. The first beauty and green food of the year.

I thought Nathaniel, but it was Richard who came next. Early spring full of storms to knock the petals off all the flowers, to shake the forest with lightning and thunder until even a bear would find a cave to hide in, or the thickest part of the forest where the bare branches interweave and form shelter for all.

Then darkness fell and all the spring greenery vanished. It was the Mother of All Darkness, trying to bury the world. She didn't care if spring ever came. The Bear Goddess thought that was short-sighted if you wanted to eat. There must be life to feed upon. The Mother of All Darkness no longer cared about that, she just wanted to destroy it all and she would use me to do it. She liked this new me and offered me a chance to feast on the fear and despair of a world where vampires ruled over the humans and there was no one left to worship spring, or travel the void of winter and bring back new life.

"You are no goddess," Goran said, "and you never were."

"Goddess enough to destroy yours." I realized it was my mouth that her words were coming out of, and that scared me. It gave the darkness power for me to fear it.

"My Goddess was not destroyed, she cannot be killed, what you took from me made me forget that, but the Great Bear Mother was only waiting for me to notice that she was there in every leaf, every berry sweet on the bramble; the night cannot conquer us, only our fear of the dark can do that." Goran helped me to my feet and the touch of his hand, the sight of his maskless face helped remind me of spring and that the storm shall pass and there is shelter in each other's strength.

"Here is your fear made flesh." It was Mischa and he'd left his mask behind, too. He stood tall with his blond hair in disarray, bright blue eyes enraged. Anger was his first and favorite emotion.

"I do not fear you anymore," Goran said.

"Then I will teach you anew," Mischa said. I felt the shiver of his power flow through the hallway, as the blue of his eyes filled up and over his pupils so they glowed like solid blue pools. I started to stare at his chest, avoiding the eyes, but the bear told me not to fear him. The darkness had made him strong, but it was Goran's fear that had given him strength.

The Mother of All Darkness used my lips to say, "Tame your bear."

Goran looked at me with terror raw in his eyes; I touched his hand and that awful power that Deimos had put inside me fed on it, but that was not what I wanted to feed on, or do. I wanted to help Goran. We were bears, they do not fear anything. Nothing is bigger, nothing is stronger, not if it walks on the ground and is solid enough to feel claws and teeth.

I saw my face through someone else's gaze for a second and knew my eyes were black, but it was not the void of creation, it was the darkness at the end of the world when there is nothing left, not even despair.

I smelled the scent of his skin. Wolves running through the forest, the scent of pine, and blood. Richard was beside me, blood running down his face, but more of it on his hand so it was slick with blood. There was more blood on his bare chest, though I couldn't see a wound. He smiled down at me and said, "Not my blood."

I squeezed his hand, feeling the slickness of the blood, and I knew that wasn't his either. I didn't know what he'd been doing while I'd been having my spiritual awakening with the Bear Mother, but she and I approved. Blood meant food, blood meant survival, blood meant we had won against any that opposed us. We had protected what was ours.

"I've seen the Ulfric fight and I am not afraid of him," Mischa said.

"I've got two men with me, not just one."

"Goran is already mine, stupid girl."

I squeezed Goran's hand and I said a prayer, not to the Bear Goddess inside me, but to the God I knelt for in church, the one I prayed to every day. Mother Bear didn't mind that I prayed to him, she had no problem with my God, and I prayed that my eyes would be full of my own power, and the Mother of All Darkness would be banished from my eyes and every last bit of me.

I looked up at Goran and he smiled, the fear fading away as he stared into my shining brown eyes, cognac diamonds sparkling in the light—sunlight, moonlight, firelight. "You are light in the dark and nothing she can do will change that."

Mischa screamed, "There is no light for you, bear. I will keep you in the dark with me forever!"

"You wanted a bear priestess, not Goran. She forced you together," I said, and my voice was calm in the face of his anger, because the Mother of Bears was still with us. Her calm was my calm.

"I obeyed my queen."

"Why are you the only vampire up, Mischa?"

"My queen woke me with the sun still in the sky, that is how powerful she is, still."

"You felt Anita messing with your animal to call, that's what woke you," Richard said.

"Come to me, Goran," Mischa said, holding out his hand.

Goran went very still beside me as if waiting for Mischa's energy to pull at him, but I knew it wouldn't work, because I could feel Goran inside me. I could feel our bears curled around each other and two wolves circling around us, Richard's big cinnamon and my white with the black markings on her back and head.

"Call another bear, for this one no longer answers to you," Goran said.

"Did she fuck you, too?"

"She gave me back my goddess and my faith."

"I really must get in line for a taste; for you to turn Goran this easily you must be a goddess of love indeed," Mischa said.

"You'll never know," I said.

"Once Deimos wakes for the night, you will do anything he says. He has no interest in sex, so I shall ask for you."

"There is only one master in Deimos's kingdom, and he does not share anything." It was Ru, limping into the hallway to join us. He was shirtless, covered in blood, one eye already swelling shut. I was betting I knew who Rodina had been carefully torturing before Demolition Man interfered. I wondered where Rodina was, but not enough to leave this moment and check.

Then I heard a sound down the hallway in front of us. Mischa turned sideways so he could keep an eye on us and look for the source of the noise. "Is the blond vampire a good guy?" It was Edward. He was out of sight using some bit of cover in the hallway.

"Bad guy," I said, and relief filled me like its own kind of magic.

The gunshot was loud and echoing in the hallway, and Mischa's head exploded in a red mist. The body had started to fall when Edward stepped out of hiding dressed in full U.S. Marshal tactical gear. He gestured and the hallway was full of men in tactical gear. The cavalry had arrived.

48

SOME OF THE people riding to my rescue were St. Louis SWAT, but one of them was nearly seven feet tall and that had to be Marshal Otto Jeffries, aka Olaf. Normally seeing him scared the hell out of me, but today I was happy to see him.

Richard kissed me on the cheek and said, "Go, I don't have the training for this, I'll help Ru."

I loved him for acknowledging it and just telling me to go, that he'd help the wounded. It made me go up on tiptoe and kiss him on the mouth. It was sweet copper pennies and the taste of him. Then I led Goran forward, because he did have the training.

Then Deimos was inside my head whispering, "That was the master vampire . . ." and he kept talking in my head.

The words came out of my mouth before I could stop them, "You just got the master vamp. Great shooting, as always." I was even smiling.

"What about the others?" Edward asked, walking toward me with Olaf at his back like an oversized shadow.

"Dead, all dead," I said, smiling and looking like I meant it, while inside I was trying to stop myself from lying.

"You slew all the other vampires before we arrived?" Olaf asked in his deep voice that sounded sinister or sexy depending on if you were into voices and if you knew his idea of sex was only survivable by him.

I tried not to say it, but it came out anyway: "Yes." I turned to Goran, trying to tell him to say it was a lie, to help me, but he looked at me and shook his head. He was my bear to call and if I wasn't master enough to stand up against Deimos there was nothing he could do. Shit!

"What about the rogue shapeshifters?" Edward asked, which meant he'd spoken to someone in St. Louis who knew more details.

I shook my head.

Edward was staring at me from inches away now. His blue eyes had gone almost completely gray like they did when he killed, or he was in the head space for it. We were standing outside the closed door to the room with the vampires in it. I'd woken up in the fucking coffin with Deimos. Damn it, if he got away he'd be able to call me to him. I did not want to wake up in a coffin with him tomorrow. We had to kill him now.

"Who is this?" Olaf asked, and even behind the full tac gear with his face hidden I could feel the animosity at finding me holding hands with yet another man that wasn't him.

"This is Goran, he's with us now."

"Anita saved me from my master's death taking me to the grave with him." It seemed a strange thing to say, but I realized he was trying to tell me that if Deimos died then so did I.

"We found some body armor with *U.S. Marshal* on it," one of the SWAT guys said. The voice told me it was Hill, but in full gear that was the only hint I had besides height.

"Thanks, Hill, it would be good to get back into my gear."

"How did you kill them without your gear?" Edward asked.

"Luck, and unexpected help." I actually bobbled Goran's hand in mine as if making it clear he'd helped. Kane and Scaramouche were here somewhere. SWAT would kill Kane; we wouldn't even need Edward or Olaf to help. I prayed that Asher didn't die with him, but

I wasn't worried about Kane. Scaramouche on the other hand would be in full gear with all his weapons. If they believed my lie, then he'd help Rodina move all the coffins to a new location and I would still belong to Deimos. If I managed to tell them Deimos was in the room beside us, Scaramouche would attack and he was more than human fast, unlike the local SWAT guys. Of the group only Edward and Olaf were faster than human normal. Hell, Olaf was a werelion, but even they weren't Harlequin that had trained with us. He'd kill the humans before they could react. Damn it.

Deimos breathed through me, "Leave now, take them with you to safety. Scaramouche will hide and they will never know how close they came to his sword."

Hill was handing me my body armor. I tucked my T-shirt into my pants, refastening the belt, and put it on. It felt good to strap it into place, more like me again. He handed me the Springfield Range Master that he knew rode on the front of the vest when I was in full gear. I knew that if I had a gun, Deimos could make me shoot them.

"No one else need die, Anita. Leave and take them with you, and no more harm need come to anyone this day." It seemed so reasonable; in a way it *was* reasonable. If we all left right now, no one else would die today, but what about tonight?

Hill asked, "What's wrong? You got another gun you carry as your main now?" He was still holding out the Range Master. Deimos told me to take the gun.

"Are you okay?" Edward asked.

"Sure," I said, and even managed a smile. I reached for the gun and the moment it was in my hand it felt more like me. It was like the gun was a comfort object and I guess in a way it was. I fell into the rhythm of putting my weapons where they belonged, and it was as if with each piece of gear that went into place, I rebuilt a part of myself that Deimos had compromised. I knew I was more dangerous armed if Deimos owned me, but it was also a way of shielding myself. I had never realized before that I didn't just feel safer from bullets and criminals in full tactical gear, but it somehow strengthened my metaphysical protections, too. Weird what you learn in the middle of a crisis, because this was one and we weren't out of it yet.

"Let's get out of here; I need some fresh air and sunlight," I said. I tried to tell Edward with my eyes that it was safer to leave. Once we were outside, we could regroup; I could fight harder to not be Deimos's puppet, but if I broke free now some of the men would die. Hill's wife had just had their first baby. Hermes had two kids about the same age I was when my mother died. It wasn't just them dying, it was all the damage it would do to their families. I'd survived some of that kind of trauma, and I didn't want that for anyone else. And because I cared about the people in the hallway and was worried about what would happen to them, it gave Deimos more power over me. *Just leave*, he whispered, *just leave and they will all be safe*.

I felt another piece of me walking up behind us; my wolf woke, sniffing the air, but I already knew it was Richard. I could feel him like a warm wind at my back, with an edge of storm so I could smell rain, and lightning was so close it made the hair on my body stand up as if when it struck it would be close enough to hit us, injure us, kill us.

My bear turned her white-and-black face to me; it helped chase back some more of Deimos. Mama Bear had started with me to help me come back home, and she wasn't finished yet. I turned to see Richard carrying Rodina over one shoulder, unconscious, with Ru using his other arm as a crutch. His limp was bad enough that I wasn't sure he could have walked unaided. "Richard, Wyatt," Edward said, remembering a different identity that Ru had used in public on one trip. I'd have never remembered it, but I wasn't Edward.

"Is that your sister?"

"Yes." And there was strain in his voice, which meant he was in serious pain.

"Where's Demolition Man?" I asked.

"He's been demolished," Ru said, and he laughed, enjoying the joke, or maybe humor was how he dealt with the pain.

I smelled pie baking, the blackberry pie that Nathaniel had experimented with for years until Jean-Claude declared it perfect. He still preferred it with cream poured over it instead of ice cream. We'd won him over to homemade whipped cream flavored with vanilla, or even a little cinnamon. Vanilla was what Nathaniel always smelled like to me, his hair and skin, I was never sure why since he was one of the least vanilla people I'd ever met, and Micah, who was closer to it, reminded me of cinnamon. Sweet with a bite to it, a flavor that would dominate if you used too much, but used sparingly it was just right. By the time I finished thinking and tasting my thoughts, Richard had caught up with us. I grabbed Ru's other arm, and a second black shape moved inside me. This one slicker, sleeker, and smaller than my bear. My leopard guiding us out because we needed outside. Sunlight would be better, it would help. Mama Bear gave me the visual of coming out of the dark cave and that first kiss of warm sunlight on our faces, warming our fur and chasing the last edge of cold and darkness away. It was time for sunlight and to get the hell out of this dark place. This wasn't our cave, it was his cave, and we had no business here. It was a trap in so many ways.

Edward said, "I ask again, Anita, are you okay?"

"Yes, and no, get us out of here and into the sunlight. I've had enough dark, dim shit for a while."

Edward stared at me a little too long but finally said, "Let's go."

Everyone about-faced and started out, guns at the ready, double-checking their back track, because you never know when the monster might sneak up behind you. For the first time when following Edward in a vampire's lair, I left my guns holstered. Deimos wasn't in my head telling me to shoot them, but that could change, and even the fact that I could still smell blackberry pie like a promise of home couldn't take away the fear of what Deimos would order me to do next.

49

THE WAREHOUSE WAS set in the center of gravel and cement as if they'd started with gravel, then cemented over it, but they hadn't maintained it so that the parking area was a mixture of broken cement and gravel. It was a discouraging sort of place, but the sunshine felt amazing. Warmer than I remembered it, as if I'd been lost in the dark for weeks instead of only forty-eight hours.

One good thing about SWAT and the preternatural marshal service was that there were no ambulances in sight, nor the usual crowd of police of every flavor because a cop had been kidnapped. If it had been a regular police scene, everyone unconscious or covered in blood would have been forced into an ambulance and then a hospital, but in SWAT land there was no one nearby but us. They'd call up everyone else when they were sure the scene was secure. I had to stop them from calling because the scene was so not secure.

I didn't need to worry, Edward had it under control. "We need to debrief Blake and the rest before we call anyone else to the scene." No one argued; we were the preternatural experts and I'd worked with our SWAT enough that they believed the expert part.

"Does the woman need medical attention sooner?" Hermes asked, motioning at Rodina, still on Richard's shoulder.

"She's a shapeshifter," I said. "As long as her head and heart are intact she'll be fine." And they took my word for it because they trusted me. I was glad it wasn't a lie.

"Keep an eye on the exits in case we missed something," Edward said.

They actually looked at me. "I'm not at my best, guys, so do what he says." Again, they didn't argue but just scattered to watch the exits. I prayed that I wouldn't do anything that betrayed their trust.

Edward reached for my hair, pulling it aside so he could see Deimos's big messy bite. Then he moved to the other side and exposed Rodrigo's neater marks. "Did Jean-Claude do either of these?"

"You know he didn't, these bites are too fresh to be three days old."

Olaf said, "How much did the one vampire need to feed? Three of you are wearing his bites."

"Vampires don't bite three people in two days just to feed," Edward said.

"He's trying to take us away from Jean-Claude," Richard said.

I opened my mouth to add to that, but nothing came out. Deimos was in my head saying, *Say nothing.* Damn it.

"Edward killed him, you are safe now," Olaf said, but he was studying my face like he smelled a lie, or at least a half-truth.

I decided to see what Deimos would let me say out loud. "You got any holy water on you?" I asked.

"You know I do," Edward said.

"You know what you need to do with it," I said.

"Before dark?"

"Always."

He looked at Richard and Ru. "What about them?"

"He needs me connected to my wolves, so he didn't dare try to break me free the way he did to Anita," Richard said.

"And the wereleopards," Olaf asked.

I could taste blackberry pie again with that thick vanilla-flavored cream and that touch of cinnamon just like Nathaniel made it, and how Jean-Claude loved it. "I need them," I said.

"Put cuffs on Rodina before she wakes," Ru said, his voice sounding tired now.

"Is she under arrest?" Olaf asked.

"No, but I knocked her out and I'd rather have time to explain before she tries to kill anyone."

"Why did you knock your sister out?" Edward asked.

"She was torturing me."

"And why was your sister torturing you?" Olaf asked; he sounded interested.

"She wants me to become a traitor with her, but I am loyal to Anita and Jean-Claude."

"And who are you to Anita?" Olaf asked of Goran.

"I am Anita's bear."

"When did you get attacked by a werebear?" Edward asked.

"At the same time when I caught most of my strains of therianthropy."

"You've never reacted to bear shapeshifters before."

"They weren't the right kind of bear," I said.

"And he is," Olaf asked.

I turned to Goran with a smile, which he returned. If you didn't know better you might mistake it for that first blush of love.

Olaf's lion rose in a rush of heat and predatory energy that made my skin crawl. His cave-dark eyes turned lion orange.

My lioness rose up, sniffing the air. "We don't have time for this," I said.

"There is never time for this," Olaf said, emphasizing the last word a little too much.

Rodina made a small sound. "Cuffs, please?" Ru asked.

"Put her on the ground," Edward said.

Richard had to let go of Ru so he could lay Rodina as gently as he could on the rough surface of the broken parking area. Edward knelt to put cuffs on her, and Ru started to collapse. I caught him and the moment I touched skin-to-skin it steadied both of us.

I wrapped my arms around him, one arm around his waist to hold him tight to the front of my body so that he didn't fall. I remembered that I was wearing body armor and I didn't know how hurt he was, so I started to ease up on rubbing his nude upper body against the roughness of the vest, but he wrapped one arm around my neck and put the other around my waist as if he couldn't raise it high enough for anything else. He held me tight, and I held him back, burying my face in the bend of his neck. There was sweat on his skin, but underneath that was him, Ru, and under that was his leopard. The scent was exactly what I needed to open me up to Nathaniel and Micah. They weren't together. That seemed wrong. Bear was in my head telling me without words that I was overthinking this. I stopped thinking and just felt the man in my arms, my hands exploring his bare back and finding bruises, but no cuts. It made me trace my hand between the front of our bodies so I could see if he was cut there, but his flat stomach seemed whole, just slippery with cooling blood; it cools so fast if it's not still coming from you. I drew back enough to look into his eyes and watch the human black change to yellow leopard and felt my own eyes go. It felt like I fell into his eyes, or he fell into mine, and then I was staring into Micah's yellow-green leopard eyes in his human face, and then Nathaniel's lavender eyes spilling to leopard gray. It was like something inside me that had been blocked broke open and I could feel Nathaniel and that he was sitting up in a strange bed in a dark room with Damian lying on his stomach beside him. The vampire was out for the day, so they were closer to the surface than the underground of the Circus. I tried to follow the scent of leopard to Micah the way I could Nathaniel, but Micah was my Nimir-raj, my leopard king, not my animal to call. It was a different connection. I could get glimpses of him but not like the others. The goddess hovering close to me didn't like that. She wanted me to have them back, because leopard was my animal to call, not Jean-Claude's; that was why it was so strong even with Deimos in my head.

I felt her power follow my thoughts of Micah downward until she touched him, rolled her power over his skin until he gasped and called for security. I guess I didn't blame him for being worried. I tried to tell him it was me, but the bear didn't feel enough like me. I felt his panic, fear that I was the one being attacked, and I fed on his fear, which made his panic worse. I tried to break the connection, but I realized in a way Micah was right. I wasn't doing this, and though the Mother of Bears thought she was right to do it, if she'd been wrong to do it, I couldn't have stopped her.

She found the black tiger inside Micah, a second beast he could turn into just as solid as his leopard form. I held a rainbow of beasts, but I couldn't change shape; only Micah and Dev of our people had secondary cross-species shapes. It was incredibly rare. Dev had started as a gold tiger and acquired lion at the same time that Micah had gotten his secondary shape. Mama Bear found that interesting.

We had to leave Micah alone, because I couldn't figure out how to explain why he could smell bear. Nathaniel pushed toward me with his power as I reached toward him. He knew that Ru and I were holding each other, and that I'd used him as my doorway back to my leopards, back to him. I saw his mouth move, but there was no sound, and then Deimos closed his power around me, and Nathaniel was just gone again. It staggered both Ru and me. We started to fall, and I made sure that I landed on the bottom, so I didn't hurt him any more.

Olaf was there glaring down at us, maybe because Ru was on top of me, but I was past caring. I lay there and just wanted the loves of my life back in my head, and not just in my heart.

"Handcuffs," I said.

Olaf frowned at me. "What did you say?"

"Handcuffs, you need to handcuff me."

Olaf actually called Edward over. "You want us to handcuff you, so the vamp that bit your neck doesn't control you," he said.

I nodded, and even that movement hurt the big bite that Deimos had given me.

Edward lifted Ru off me and said, "Turn on your back."

I just did what he asked without thinking about it. Thinking gave Deimos more openings to fuck with me. My gun being on the vest made being on my stomach not the most comfortable, but Edward was right, I had to be cuffed behind my back, not in front. "Cuff her," Edward said, and it took me a second to realize he was talking to Olaf.

Olaf knelt over me, one knee on either side of me. That's not how they teach you to do it, but Olaf didn't have to worry about me fighting; I wanted the cuffs on. I needed them on to feel that I was safe to be around. Olaf put a hand on either of my upper arms; his hands were so big they encircled my arms like he could have held my arm plus another one. He lifted me easily and surprisingly gently to my feet. He kept his hands on my arms, but I didn't tell him to let go. If Deimos tried to get me to hurt someone now, I couldn't.

Edward came to stand in front of me. He asked, "The vampire I killed in there wasn't the dragon, was it?"

I shook my head. Deimos didn't seem to be policing body movements as much as words.

"He made you lie to me."

I nodded again.

"I'm going to take your weapons until we get the bite cleansed, okay?"

I gave him another nod.

"Will you trust Olaf to hold some of your gear?"

I hesitated, then nodded.

Edward started to take off the weapons that I'd just put back on, but it had to be done. I was too dangerous armed, and Deimos was too loud in my head. Olaf had so many more MOLLE straps on his vest and so much more body that my weapons disappeared among his with room for him to carry more. I don't usually mind being small, but in that moment I had some serious body real estate envy. Edward took my main gun and the knives he knew I carried most, but he was right; it was easier dividing them up between them.

"The dragon is in the room with the closed door that you stopped us from searching, isn't he?"

I nodded.

"Are there other vampires in the room?"

I nodded. Ru told him the number.

"Why can you talk, and she can't?" Olaf asked.

"Rodrigo bit me trying to persuade me to join them, but he is not as powerful as Deimos."

"Your brother died in Ireland," Edward said.

"It's a different kind of vampirism that lets a wereanimal rise as the undead," I said.

"Even with his chest blown open by a shotgun?"

"Rodrigo did the dainty bite on my right, so yeah, trust me, he's a vampire and still a wereleopard."

I watched Edward file that away for later. "Richard, can you tell me something about Deimos?"

"We've seen him in dragon form."

"How big was he?"

Richard tried to say it but couldn't. "I'm not free to speak."

"The wererats are waiting down with the ambulances, they're the ones that found your location. They could take you and the twins to a safe place until we kill this bastard," Edward said.

"I want to stay and help," Richard said.

"You said it earlier, Richard, you don't have the training for this." In my head I thought that if the worst happened Jean-Claude might survive losing one of us, but not both.

"I heard what you just thought," Richard said. He put his hand against my face, then looked at Olaf. "I'm going to kiss her, if you can give us a little room."

Olaf just let me go and stepped back without a word. Brownie point for him.

Richard cupped my face in his hands, so that the eye contact was intimate and inescapable. It made me want to pull away from that serious gaze, but with my hands cuffed behind my back my options were limited. I fought off the urge to tell him to let me go.

"If you really want me to let you go, I will," he said.

I thought about it, then realized I didn't, I was just wanting to lash out at someone. Richard and I had spent years lashing out at each other. It was like an old habit that all the stress was bringing out. I realized I was scared. I didn't want to die and leave Jean-Claude and everyone else behind. I didn't want to lose the life that we'd built together. I didn't want the last time I saw my family to be the disaster at the restaurant.

I looked up at Richard's perfectly brown eyes, paler than mine, more milk chocolate to my dark. "You won't die here, like this," he said.

"You don't know that," I said.

"I have faith that our story doesn't end here."

"I wish I was that confident."

"You usually are, what's different this time?"

"I haven't had a vampire really roll me like this with their eyes in so long. I thought it was my necromancy protecting me, but it turns out it was Jean-Claude's vampire marks, not me."

"All couples are stronger together than apart, that's the point of being a couple," he said.

"Deimos is in my head, Richard, he's controlling me in daylight."

"Oh, honey, you thought you were invincible when it came to vampires and now that you're not you're shook."

I thought about that for a minute, lowering my eyes so I wasn't staring into his. I couldn't think clearly staring into his face. It left me staring at his throat, strong and permanently tanned. If he ran outside like Micah did, I wondered how dark Richard would tan.

336 LAURELL K. HAMILTON

"If you want me darker I can do that, just tell me if you want tan lines or no tan lines," he said.

It made me smile and look back up at him. It was the face that almost launched me all the way to the altar once. "But I was an idiot, and ruined it," he said. He dropped one of his hands and slid the other so his fingers were laced through my hair.

"We both had our issues," I said.

"But I told you to quit working with the police, that I worried about you every time you went out the door."

"You know better now," I said.

"Yes, and I won't ask you to wear my mother's wedding dress just because it fit you."

I rolled my eyes at that but smiled. "All that lace and little buttons at the collar."

"You looked adorable, which I knew you hated, but after what had happened to my mom in Tennessee I wanted her to be happy."

"More than you wanted me to be happy, at the time."

"I'm so sorry, Anita."

"Hell, Richard, I wanted your mom happy after what happened." They had sent her finger and a lock of Richard's brother, Daniel's, hair in a box to us as a warning of what they were willing to do, and in two hours they'd do worse unless we did what they wanted us to do. Then they would let them go, but the henchmen they'd sent with the box and the message had confirmed my worst fears that they had already been raped, both of them. They weren't going to let them go covered in DNA of crimes we could prove. They'd killed all the other witnesses to their crimes. They had a sorcerer that could raise demons for real; human sacrifice lets you raise more powerful demons.

The look on his face let me know he'd relived all of it with me. "You saved them, Anita. You faced a demon to save my mom. She is so happy that we're dating again."

"I'd have probably worn the dress for her, after everything that happened."

"I know you would have," he said.

"But I couldn't quit my job."

"I know that now."

"Neither of us was ready to marry back then," I said.

"I thought it was just me you weren't ready to marry," he said.

"Now you know better."

He stared down at me and I suddenly flashed on his face above me during sex; it tightened things in my body so hard and fast that if he hadn't caught me I might have fallen. "I felt that." His voice had already gone a little hoarse from catching the edge of my reaction.

"Is it the *ardeur*?" Olaf asked.

"Maybe," I said, staring up at Richard.

"The *ardeur* could heal . . ." He stopped before he finished the sentence. I felt him fight not to even finish the thought in case someone was listening. I had to struggle not to finish the thought for him, or for myself. It was the closest I'd ever come to that empty Zen mind, because I couldn't afford to let Deimos sense that spurt of hopefulness. The struggle to keep from overthinking meant the flash of lust was gone, too.

Richard could feel that, so he didn't try to come on strong. He put his arm behind me and found my arms in the cuffs. He laughed and said, "We've never tried it with handcuffs behind the back before."

"I think it would just be awkward and super uncomfortable on bare ground," I said, laughing back.

"You like being tied up," he whispered.

"The big bed has so many fun attachment points," I said.

"It does," he said, and he slid his arm behind my back over my arms and bound hands. He pressed us together, asking, "Is that okay?"

"As good as we're going to get right now," I said.

"I want it better than that," he said, and moved to stand behind me.

"What do you have in mind?" I asked, because I hadn't caught up to his thinking yet. I was trying so hard not to overshare in my thoughts to whoever might be eavesdropping. I hadn't realized how much my thoughts anticipating sex helped get me in the mood until now.

He slid his arm around my waist and pressed our bodies close. The height difference put my bound hands at his groin. He leaned his head down to whisper, "Play with me while I kiss you."

"Too public," I said.

"Give us some privacy," Richard said.

"You're both compromised by the big bad vampire, we can't leave you alone," Edward said.

"Ru and I are used to watching a lot more than this," Rodina said; her voice made it clear that it was just a burden she had to deal with.

"I can turn my back if it will make you more comfortable," Goran said.

"We're out of sight of SWAT," Edward added.

"That much I knew," I said.

Richard leaned over, pressing his body against my hands. "If you don't want to do it at all, as in it doesn't appeal to you, don't do it, but if you want to touch me, then play with me, please."

"I do want to," I said.

"Then what's wrong?"

"It's like Jean-Claude and the *ardeur* took away all my embarrassed awkwardness and now it's back."

He used the arm around my waist to press us even closer together, so that I could feel him bumping my hands. "Only if you want to, but I'm going to kiss you now."

He used his free hand to stroke up the side of my face and bend me back toward him so that I was looking up at him over my shoulder. I opened my hands and the press of him through his jeans filled my hands. I played my hands over and around him, exploring him through the heavy cloth of the jeans, and wished the pants weren't in the way. His eyes fluttered shut, mouth half parting. I could see the blood in the corner of his mouth where someone had hit him.

I stopped moving my hands to ask, "Will a deep kiss hurt?"

"No, and if it does it will be a good hurt."

I could feel him growing harder inside his pants; my own body started to react, wet and starting to tighten at just the feel of him in my hands. But I couldn't keep looking back over my shoulder forever, so I couldn't watch his face, which I wanted to do. "Help me see your face," I said in a voice gone lower and a little husky.

"How?" he asked, voice breathy.

"Hand, gently around my throat, keeping me looking up at you."

He hesitated, but I squeezed a little harder on his body where it lay trapped in his jeans. That was enough; his hand slid around the front of my neck, and he found that point where his thumb and forefinger went just at the hinge of my jaw so he forced my head back so I could see his face. The hand wasn't tight, I could breathe just fine, but it took some of the strain off my neck and shoulder muscles looking up and behind. I played with him in my hands, squeezing and kneading him as he strained against the front of his jeans.

"Now, kiss me," I said.

He pressed his mouth to mine and he kissed me. It started almost gentle, then grew until it was like he was trying to come inside my mouth, but I wanted him inside me in so many ways. I opened my mouth wider for him and thought about having other things thrust down my mouth besides his tongue. He was so hard pressed against my hands; the pants that had been foreplay had become frustration. His hand tightened at my throat and at my waist as he held me in place. I made eager noises for him, my tongue finding the cut in the side of his mouth, so that the pain was sharp and fresh for him. He made an eager noise low in his throat. I tasted his blood in my mouth and wanted more, needed more, so much more.

Jean-Claude had woken for the day. His bloodlust was inside me, wanting to bite down on Richard's lip, to tear at him . . .

Richard drew back, eyes full of midnight fire, Jean-Claude's power riding him. I felt both their needs for blood and flesh. It was the moment if you were a new vampire or werewolf when you could accidentally tear your lover's throat out. We waited in that breathless moment where they fought for control, and I trusted them to find that control.

Then Deimos was in my head. "You cannot have her back, she is mine now!"

Jean-Claude lay there in his silk sheets that I could feel along our skin. I felt his power through Richard's body like hot and cold intermingled until I cried out from it. Deimos was chased back for a moment as Jean-Claude spoke urgently in my head. "He has given you no vampire marks, only dampened mine. He is powerful enough that his eyes and his bite have damaged our connection more, but he has not marked you. I can fill Richard with my power, and when you come to me again, *ma petite*, I will chase out his sorrow and fill you with passion once again."

Deimos screamed through me, "She is mine! I will take all that is Jean-Claude's and make it mine." The power left my head ringing, and the kiss was done, all the passion was gone like an instant cold shower. Deimos didn't have any heat to offer anyone. His fire was only for destruction.

50

RICHARD GOT A police car ride with lights and sirens to get him to the Circus of the Damned. If he and Jean-Claude could see each other in person, it would heal Richard of Deimos's taint, and help offset what he'd done to me. I sent Goran to guard Richard in case more traitors tried to recapture him. Goran didn't want to leave me, and Richard didn't want to take him, but I had Edward, Olaf, and SWAT close enough that if I yelled they'd come running. Richard would have only the cops in the patrol car; for his and their sake I wanted Goran there just in case. They finally agreed with me and left. Ru was hurt enough that he took an ambulance ride to the hospital. Once Edward realized I wasn't Deimos's human servant, but it was just one bite, he tried to send me with Richard.

"I can't risk getting near Jean-Claude while Deimos can control me."

"We can put you in the back of a police car until we kill the vampire," Edward said.

I shook my head. I tried to think of a flattering way to talk about Deimos so he wouldn't stop me from talking. "Deimos's power is amazing and horrible. He feeds on terror and sorrow. He can find your worst memories and force you to relive them or share his own memories where he destroyed entire towns and fed on the despair and pain of the people he was burning alive."

"Are you saying he's like a night hag vampire and can cause you to be afraid so he can feed on it?" Edward asked.

"Exactly," I said.

"Not my favorite type of vampire," Edward said.

"They have to touch you for it to work," Olaf said. "Kill them before they can close with you."

"Not all of them have to touch you to raise fear," Edward said.

"Deimos doesn't have to touch," Rodina said. We'd kept her up with us to pick her brain about Deimos, and then she'd get to sit in the back of a patrol car until we could decide what to do with her. Ru would never testify against her about the torture, so we didn't have anything to charge her with, and if we couldn't charge her I wasn't sure what to do with her.

"I noticed," I said.

"Can you stop him from using his magic on us?" Olaf asked.

"I've never tried to protect anyone that wasn't metaphysically connected to me, but night hags are rare in America. So, I haven't had a lot of experience trying," I said.

"Once the fighting starts, he could control your powers, not just your body," Rodina said.

It was weird that the only two women were both handcuffed, but I guess some days are weirder than others. "Which is why we need to cleanse my . . ." I couldn't finish the sentence; he wouldn't let me.

"Bite mark before we engage," Edward said.

I tried to say yes, but all Deimos would let me do was nod. He hadn't known that cleansing a bite with holy water could negate a vampire's control over someone. I'd only cleansed myself once of a bite like this. "He rolled me, Edward. Like the bad old days before I got my power up. I woke up in his coffin this morning."

"But you got out," Edward said.

I nodded. "He's fucked with the vampire marks and all my people. Queenie helped him do it, she betrayed us."

"I heard that Kaazim is under guard in case he knew."

"I hope he didn't know, I like him," I said.

"He was a good man to have at our backs in Ireland."

"He was."

"If you hurt Anita, I may be compromised," Rodina said, "because to cause her pain literally causes all her Brides pain."

"Is Nicky well enough to survive it?" I asked.

"Once they got the tree out of his side he started healing the damage," Edward said.

It must have shone on my face because he added, "He's going to be fine, but I can call the hospital and have him sedated while we cleanse your wound."

"Yes, please."

Rodina said, "I'd say sedate me, too, but I want to be here to save Rodrigo if possible."

"He betrayed me a second time, Rodina."

"Deimos is the first vampire to roll you like a human in how long?" she asked.

"Almost ten years, I think."

"He was standing there when Roddy rose from the grave for the first time. Some master vampires can feel when a lesser vamp is about to come out, and they'll wait for them like a collector. Anything powerful enough to do that means the new vampire has no choice but to follow the master vampire waiting for them. Roddy had hoped for a new evil ruler to follow, but . . . you saw it last night: Deimos is too unstable to be king. Rodrigo and I want an evil ruler to follow that will let us indulge ourselves, but first they need to be a strong leader. We hoped it was him, but powerful isn't the same as strong of will."

"Do you want Rodrigo to be on the save-if-possible list?" Edward asked.

"Maybe, I mean if he rolled me then maybe Rodrigo had no choice either."

"I thought he was a bad guy when you met him?" Edward said.

"He was, but he also reached out to me in dreams and helped me while Richard, Ru, and I were captured."

"We will do what we can, but if he attacks us as a vampire then we will have no choice," Olaf said.

"That's fair," I said.

"Are you willing for Kane to die even if it kills Asher?" Edward asked.

"Richard will tell Jean-Claude and Asher what Kane's done."

"Are you willing to pull the trigger on Kane?" Edward asked.

"I won't go out of my way to kill him today, but I won't risk anyone else's life to keep Kane alive either."

"Okay," Edward said.

"But first we put Rodina in the back of a police car, and you cleanse the bite."

"Let me stay and try to save Roddy."

"You betrayed me before your brother introduced you to Deimos. I can't trust you, so you go in the back of a patrol car until I decide what to do with you." She tried to argue, but in the end we had her walked down to the police cars to wait.

When we were alone in our little corner of the parking lot with a small stand of trees beside us and the warehouse, Edward said, "It will take Olaf and me both to cleanse your wound."

"It was just you last time," I said.

"Last time was Nikolaos, she was only a thousand years old. You couldn't hear her in your head in broad daylight. I've never seen any vampire control you like this one."

"How much will it hurt to cleanse the bite mark?" Olaf asked.

"Like pouring acid in a wound," Edward said.

"Like shoving a red-hot blade against the wound, except it's liquid so it's more like pouring molten metal on the skin," I said.

"That is a great deal of pain."

"Yeah, I'd hoped to never have to do it again."

"It's usually done over a series of days," Edward said.

"But just like last time I need this cleansed before dark, because he'll get more powerful once the sun sets."

"Last time you held still for me to do it; I think Deimos will force you to fight this time," Edward said.

"Agreed."

"One of us will have to hold you or pin you down while the other one pours the holy water."

"Even through a gag I'm going to scream, so better warn the other cops, or they'll come running."

"It made you scream last time?" Olaf said.

"Oh, yeah."

"I would like no gag, if possible," Olaf said.

"You say that now, but we did it in a small bathroom, my ears were ringing from her screams."

"I'm sorry, Edward, you never told me."

"If you could be that brave, then I wasn't going to complain about my ears ringing from the sound of abject pain." He smiled a little as he said it. It helped me smile back. We'd done this once; we could do it again.

"I'll pour the holy water, Olaf will hold," Edward said.

"Why can't you hold?"

"Because you're more than human strong, and he's a shapeshifter and I'm not."

"Shit," I said.

Olaf came up behind me and asked, "Are you ready?"

I looked at Edward.

"We're losing daylight."

I nodded. "Do it."

Olaf wrapped his arms around me from behind like Richard had, but luckily Olaf was nearly a foot taller than Richard, so my cuffed hands weren't as close to a certain area of his body as they had been with Richard. I was happy with that, but Olaf was still pressed as close as he'd ever been to me, and my hands were already tied behind my back and he preferred his women tied down. He wasn't really doing anything I could complain about yet, so why was my heart already beating faster?

"Guys, are we sure this is a good division of labor?" I asked.

"I have done nothing yet, but you are already afraid," Olaf said, stroking his free hand through my hair, exposing my neck and the bite marks.

"Tell him the truth, Anita," Edward said, pulling out a vial of holy water from the equipment bag he'd rucked in from his car.

"I already fit your victim profile of petite dark-haired women. Now I'm handcuffed, weaponless, and in your arms. Why shouldn't I be afraid?"

"I promised Edward and others that I would never hunt my victim of choice on American soil. I have never broken that promise."

"What about Dr. Patience Reed in Washington State?" I asked. She'd gone missing after we finished up a case that we'd worked with Olaf and others.

"I did not mean to kill her, but I was too new at being a werelion. My beast rose during sex and I only have scattered memories after that, until I woke hours later covered in her blood."

I looked up at him, not afraid anymore, but impressed he'd actually answered that truthfully. "Wow, I'm sorry that was your first experience as a werelion."

"I have gained control over my beast now."

"Your control has been impressive on the cases we've worked since then," I said, and it was such ordinary talk at least for the three of us that I stopped being afraid and relaxed into his arms.

"I'm glad you didn't kill the doctor on purpose," Edward said. "Now hold Anita's head so we can get this done."

Olaf moved so that my head was pressed into his chest as comfortably as it was going to get with the body armor on. He pressed his hand against the side of my head and held me in place while Edward poured the first dose of holy water on the bite.

51

SOME PAIN IS too bad to take silently; you have to struggle against it, you can't just give in without a fight, or I couldn't. We ended up on the ground because even Olaf couldn't hold me standing. He wrapped his legs around mine so I wouldn't keep pushing up with my heels trying to get away from the pain. He used his size to pin me to the ground, pin me against his body. He was so strong, too strong, I hated his strength because it kept me from escaping the pain. Deimos loved my pain and drank it down through the bite that was causing me to hurt so badly.

I heard voices. "I'm going to crush her face if I keep pushing."

"Hold her hair."

A hand grabbed my hair and jerked my head to the side. It reminded me of Nicky and made me open my eyes wider, but it was Edward looking down at me; his helmet was gone and his hair looked so yellow, like I was seeing things in bright colors, and then I saw the bottle of holy water in his hand and I begged him to stop, not to do it.

Deimos was in my head, telling me to get away, to come help him, at the same time that he ate my pain. He was conflicted because the pain made him stronger, but he needed me to pretend to be healed, pretend to no longer be in his control, so I could get my weapons back, so I could . . . He showed me what he wanted. Shooting Olaf between the eyes didn't bother me that much, but doing the same to Edward? No. He roared through my head, *YES!*

I screamed, "No!" Body bowing, hands straining, as I fought to be free to help my master and fought to be free of him. The handcuffs snapped and my hands-free state fed Deimos's commands in my head. I froze for a second, and then my hand brushed against Olaf's body and circled around that most intimate of parts and squeezed. I heard him yell, and then his hand was around my wrist. It would have been a race to see who crushed which body part sooner, but Edward poured holy water on my neck and the pain distracted me, helped Olaf move my hand. I was facedown on the ground with his knee grinding into my back.

"I have better cuffs in my bag," Olaf said; his voice sounded strained.

Deimos whispered, *Tell them what they want to hear and come to me.* That made so much more sense than him telling me to fight my way free. It stopped me from struggling, like I was thinking about what he was saying, like I could think again, almost. Something moved in the leaves near my face. I blinked, trying to see what I was hearing, or sensing, and there was a rat looking back at me. The rat turned its head to one side so I could stare into the round, black eye. It was like a mirror, a black mirror that I could fall into. Deimos screamed at me, which made me jerk away from the rat's gaze.

"Anita," Edward asked, "Anita, are you all right?"

"There's a rat." Olaf sounded unhappy, but not like he was surprised to see it. That seemed weird.

"Rafael's rats found Anita and this place."

"I didn't think wererats were this small," Olaf said.

"They aren't, but all the rats belong to Rafael," Edward said. I heard the clink of chains.

No, don't let them tie you up again, Deimos said.

"I'm okay, you don't need the chains," I said; my voice was rough from screaming but it sounded like me.

The rat looked at me again, that one shining black eye; tiny claws touched my hand, a different rat, and I could see Rafael standing by the emergency vehicles. He was the proverbial tall, dark, and handsome. His heritage carved into the high, slightly square cheekbones, the rich brown of his skin, those kissable lips. He held up a black mirror in his hand; it opened like a door and I fell through to find Neva and the other two brujas standing in the center of the sand of the fighting pit. Neva looked up at me and her black eyes were full of stars. "Remember who you are."

I was back on the concrete and gravel with the leaves blown up to the edge of the parking lot. I could see every piece of trash in among the leaves; there was a half-eaten beetle. It was freshly dead like something had just taken a bite out of it.

"Anita," Edward said.

I looked at him and I could see every weapon he was carrying, not just the obvious ones, but the hidden ones. I knew everything he had on him just like that. I could see what was hidden, and I wasn't surprised when Edward said, "Your eyes." I knew my eyes were black and full of stars just like Neva's because the power came from a kindred source.

"Why do her eyes look like Obsidian Butterfly's eyes?" Olaf asked.

I looked at him and could see all his weapons and everything else he was carrying on him, just like I could with Edward. Obsidian Butterfly was an Aztec goddess or thought she was Itzpapalotl; hell, maybe she was for all I knew. One thing I knew for sure was that she was a powerful vampire and the Master of the City of Albuquerque. She had placed a piece of her magic inside me without my permission and with an invitation for me to return with Jean-Claude for a visit. I never planned to visit again. The old vampire council had been afraid of her, too. They'd basically drawn a circle around Albuquerque, New Mexico, declaring *here be monsters* and leaving her the hell alone. What I hadn't known until recently was that the rodere, the wererats, had their own brand of magic and it was close kin to Obsidian Butterfly's power.

"The wererats," I said, and realized that wasn't enough explanation.

"We saw the rats," Edward said.

Something moved behind him. I looked back at the warehouse wall with its bricked-up windows. The wall was solid like Edward and Olaf's tactical pockets, but just like with what they were carrying I could see that there was something dangerous behind the bricks. I realized that Deimos wasn't screaming in my head anymore; had it been the wererats and Obsidian Butterfly's power? I didn't overthink it, I just said, "The dragon is right behind that wall." I pointed at it.

Edward didn't argue. He dropped the chains he'd gotten out of Olaf's gear bag and reached for a box, one of two, that I didn't even remember being there before.

Olaf got silver fireproof suits out of his bag and Edward's. "Why didn't you start with the suits?"

"Vampires don't rise until dark, dragons included," Olaf said.

"I didn't know either."

"Now we do," Edward said, and had the assembled LAW, light anti-tank weapon, in his hands.

"How do you keep getting those?"

Edward didn't answer me, he probably wouldn't have answered me anyway, but he was busy getting into his silver suit. I didn't have one of those, so what was I going to do? I sat up and looked around and spotted the SWAT guys watching the exits. I reached for the mic on my vest that was there when I worked with local police, but it wasn't there. I couldn't remember why it was missing.

"Tell SWAT to get away from the building," I said.

Edward hit his mic and did what I asked. SWAT drew back, or at least the ones I could see, and that was great, but that delay meant Edward wasn't ready when the wall burst outward and fifty feet of dragon rushed out. I had a moment to admire him glistening in the sunlight, all white belly scales and dark head and back. It was like something out of a fairy tale, and then fire poured out of his mouth and the mythical moment turned into a nightmare. Olaf was the only one in his suit. Edward was still putting the head part on, and I was shit out of luck.

52

OLAF THREW A silver cloth over me; then I felt his weight on top of me and then heat poured over us. I wanted to scream, but one factoid I remembered about fire was that breathing in superheated air was deadly, so I held my breath, which was stupid because before the heat left I had to take a gasping breath. If breathing had been the wrong thing to do, that would have been it. Olaf moved so that I wasn't pinned under his weight, but I wasn't sure if I could uncover myself and not fry. Fire-breathing dragons were a new category for me, and I admit to a second of hesitation inside my silver cocoon of safety.

I heard the *whoosh* and knew it was Edward deploying the LAW. I'd been with him once when he used one and it wasn't a sound you forgot. Would Deimos blow up when it hit him? I didn't know, so I stayed under the only protection I had. I heard an explosion, then a thunderous sound and heat, but it wasn't just heat, it felt like the fire was closer this time and the flames moved against the silver blanket. It was the weirdest sensation, like air and water and heat made into something that could touch you. It took all I had not to scream as it rushed over the top of the blanket. I thought I heard men screaming, but I couldn't be sure, and then it stopped again. The silence seemed louder this time.

"Shoot it again," Olaf said.

"It's too fast," Edward said.

I yelled, "Can I come out?"

"Yes, it's running," Edward said.

I threw back the silver blanket and found them both running across the parking lot toward the rapidly vanishing backside of the dragon. Gunfire let us know that he'd run into the SWAT officers or other local police. Olaf was almost out of sight even in the silver suit that made moving awkward, but Edward wasn't far behind. I was impressed that they could run at all, let alone that fast.

I stood there with no weapons, I didn't even know where my badge was, but as I watched them run out of sight I couldn't just stand here and do nothing. I looked down at the men's bags and decided that they'd be okay with me borrowing. I could see everything they had in their bags' layers from what I could possibly see with my physical eyes, which meant my eyes were still full of stars. It helped me see a handgun in Edward's bag that would fit in the front of my vest. It was his old Heckler & Koch USP 45 that he'd carried as his main gun until H&K made a tactical version you put a suppressor on, and there were grenades. Of course Edward would have grenades. I normally don't like them, but today I stuffed two of them into the big pockets of the tactical pants and was bending over to get a third when a bullet whizzed past me, and I threw myself behind the boxes and bags. I hit the ground flat, and I was small enough that it hid me. The second shot went through the bag near my head. I had cover but it wasn't hard cover. Fuck!

My hyena stirred to life, snarling and giving that gibbering sound that should make you run if you're alone in the dark. I knew who it was before he screamed, "Anita, you bitch! You spoil everything, everything!"

I had the gun out and ready as I belly-crawled forward trying to see around the bag without getting shot. Another bullet went through the bag, and I was glad it was Olaf's bag without the grenades. I started to peek around the bags to aim, but the moment I thought about it I could suddenly see not just the contents of the bag, but through the bag to what was on the other side. I could see Kane walking toward me with the gun in his hand, raising it for another shot. I trusted what I saw and sat up, aimed, and fired before I could think about it. Kane screamed and fell to the parking lot, holding his stomach where I'd shot him. I should have shot him in the chest, but I didn't want to risk Asher. Damn it.

I came out of cover cautiously, gun aimed at him while he writhed on the ground.

"Toss the gun away, Kane."

"Or what? You won't kill me. You love Asher too much to risk killing him when I die."

"Toss the gun, Kane, I mean it."

He tossed the gun. "Asher broke up with me, but you knew that."

"I didn't know that." I moved wide around him to get closer to the gun he'd thrown but kept my eyes on him. He'd attacked me before, but never with a gun.

"Don't worry, he can't wait to tell you and Jean-Claude what a good boy he's been, according to his therapist. The one you made him go to!"

"I thought you were going to therapy with him." I kept my gun aimed at him as I bent down to pick his up.

"I don't need therapy, there's nothing wrong with me!"

I started to reach for the fallen gun, and it was suddenly harder to "see" it. My eyes must have returned to normal. I had to glance down to touch the gun on the ground. The moment I touched the grips I knew the gun was an out-of-the-box Glock. I hated the grips they came with, and most cops I knew modified them, like tailoring clothes, so they fit better. Kane started to roll up on his side. "Don't move," I said, and pointed my gun more solidly at him. His Glock was in my hand, but I didn't want to look away long enough to find a place to put it in my vest.

He pressed his hand to his stomach wound. "If you kill me, Asher will die just like Scaramouche."

"What are you talking about? Scaramouche is dead?" I asked.

"When Deimos turned into a dragon he broke the wall and knocked the coffins over. Capitano burned up in the sun. Look if you don't believe me."

"Don't so much as twitch, Kane, I mean it." I backed up, angling for a closer look into the room that Deimos had destroyed. I glanced quick and saw coffins scattered around. I had a second to see two bodies charred into black sticks. I hadn't heard them scream; had they slept through it all, or had the dragon breathing fire on me distracted me? I guess it didn't matter.

"I just see the dead vampires," I said.

Kane pressed his hand to his stomach and groaned. "Scaramouche is near the door where he ran in to try and save his master, but it was too late."

I took a step back and looked toward the door, and there he was, Scaramouche. He lay on his side, one hand outstretched toward the burned bodies. I couldn't see anything wrong with Scaramouche except that his eyes were wide open and frozen in death.

I caught movement and put all my attention back on Kane. He tried to sit up and fell back to the ground, writhing with one hand pressed to his stomach. "This really hurts."

"Good," I said, and meant it.

I heard gunfire in the distance, and a sound like a roar that was between a lion, a bear, and an elk, or maybe my mind was just trying to find common ground with a sound I never thought I'd hear outside of dream, or nightmare.

"You're not going to run off and let me bleed to death, are you?"

I had no radio or even my phone. I had no way to call for medical, or anything. "Damn it."

He curled up on his side, clutching his stomach, moaning. I heard the dragon's roar and the sound of fire, something bigger on fire than the bodies in the house. I couldn't stand here and do nothing.

"You are always such a pain in the ass," I said.

"Asher dumped me for you and Jean-Claude, nothing I've ever done to you is as bad as that," he said, and rolled himself into a tighter ball, then shuddered in pain as if that hurt more. Stomach wounds were supposed to be a slow kill, plenty of time for the hospital, but I wasn't used to shooting to wound; maybe I was wrong.

"Shit, don't die, Kane." I went over toward him, gun still out, but I didn't want to shoot him again until I'd seen the hole I'd already put into him. "Uncurl yourself so I can see the wound."

"It hurts too much."

"You always were a whiner," I said.

"You shot me!"

"You shot at me first! Now show me your damn wound."

He held his hand up toward me; it was covered in blood, fuck. His other hand had something in it, and I shot him in the chest before I had time to think it through. His hands collapsed to either side and a second Glock fell to the ground beside him. It was one of their subcompacts, which is one reason I missed it, but that was no excuse. I should have patted him down, wounded or not. I walked wide around him with the gun in my right hand pointed at him solid. If he had so much as twitched again I'd have put one in his head. He was a shapeshifter and that meant harder to kill. I got to the other side and kicked the subcompact away from his hand. He was dead, I knew it when I saw it, but I wasn't bending down to take his pulse. That had horror movie surprise written all over it.

I said a prayer that Asher would survive Kane's death, and then I found a home for my borrowed Heckler & Koch USP 45 on my vest. It took time to change out holsters from the empty Springfield and put in the H&K so the gun rode secure. I checked the Glocks for ammo automatically. The full-size Glock was down to thirteen; the subcompact had all ten with one in the chamber. I pulled out an AR magazine from its pouch on my vest and put it in Edward's equipment bag. He had my AR-15 with him, so I didn't need extra ammo right now anyway. I put the subcompact in the empty pouch. I didn't like Glocks, but I liked having eleven extra bullets if I ran out. I was not searching Kane's body for his holster, so I put the full-size Glock in Edward's bag. I was going to rummage around in Olaf's bag to see if he had anything else I wanted to borrow, but the dragon roared again. Deimos was still alive; that meant everyone else was still in danger. I had two grenades, eleven rounds in the H&K, eleven in the little Glock. I had three extra magazines for my AR-15 when I got it back from Edward. It would be enough or it wouldn't, but either way I had to get in the fight. I grabbed the silver fire blanket off the ground and started running toward the sounds of fresh gunfire.

I glanced at Kane's body as I ran past, and I felt bad about killing him. It wasn't that he hadn't earned it, and it wasn't just about Asher. I killed people professionally, but they were usually strangers. It was always harder to kill someone you knew, even if they tried to kill you first. It slowed me down, as if all the heavy thoughts were physical weight. I let them go, had to; I'd feel guilty about Kane later, and I'd feel worse if Asher . . . I screamed out loud, "Run, damn you, run!" and I ran.

53

THEY HAD CORNERED Deimos at the cliff's edge over the river. He was on all fours with a long snaky tail twitching like an angry cat. He tried to go up on his back legs, but the moment that his front feet left the ground they poured so many bullets into him that I could actually see them like black rain going sideways into the dragon. He gave that unearthly scream again, his muzzle thrown upward like a howling dog.

There was a huge semicircle of armed people around Deimos. I spotted Edward and Olaf in the front, their silver fire suits flashing in the sunlight. The people on either side of them had no fire gear, but there were no crispy-crittered bodies anywhere that I could see either. How the hell were they keeping Deimos from flaming people?

He started to rear up again and they plastered him with bullets again. It was like the ultimate firing squad except that the target wouldn't die. I realized that silver bullets were expensive, and most police departments couldn't afford that many of them. Most of the cops on site had either never had silver ammo or had used up all they had rounds ago. How did we kill Deimos without enough silver to take out his head and heart? I'd never tried to kill anything this large.

I trained with blades, I was good with them, but I didn't train with anything big enough to chop through a neck that thick. Edward had shot him with two different antitank missiles; did that mean that Deimos was fireproof?

"It is hard to see from here, but the dragon is bleeding," Rafael said.

I whirled around and there he was in person. I ran to him like we weren't watching the biggest gun battle I'd ever seen off in the distance complete with fifty-plus feet of dragon. I jumped into his arms, wrapping my arms around his neck. He caught me and startled, laughing, because I'd never greeted him like this in all the time we'd been together.

He kissed me lightly, drawing back to study my face. "I love this greeting, *bebe*, but what have I done to deserve it?"

"You saved the day with your magic," I said.

"So this is a thank-you," he said, smiling.

"Yes, and I know you'll have some ideas about how to kill the dragon." I was beginning to feel a little silly with the sound of gunfire as our background music. I unwrapped my arms from his neck, and he put me down.

"I have never had to kill a dragon before, *mi amor*."

"They don't have enough silver ammo to shoot it to death," I said.

"But we did learn that it can only breathe fire if it rears up on its hind legs," he said.

"So that's why everyone is willing to get this close to it," I said.

"But you are right, the police do not seem to have enough silver bullets to finish this fight."

"Edward hit it with antitank missiles. Why didn't that damage it more?"

"I did not see that happen, so I do not know."

I squeezed his hand in mine and realized that I depended on Rafael to have ideas when I was out of them. I went to him when I needed advice and didn't know where else to go. "I'm used to you having an idea when I'm out of them. You and your brujas know more formal magic than I do. Do they have anything that will help us slay the dragon?"

"Perhaps we have come to your aid too many times, *mi amor*, slaying dragons is no small task."

"I'm sorry, you're right, but it's right there. It's on the cliff edge, we just have to push it over."

"Can it drown?" he asked.

"Not if it's like most vampires, no."

"Will the fall kill it?"

"No," I said.

"But if you used a missile or bomb on any other kind of vampire or wereanimal it would kill them, correct?" he asked, as he ran his fingers through mine.

"Correct."

"Then perhaps he is not like any other vampire," Rafael suggested.

I looked at him. "And if he's not, then what? How does that help us kill him?"

"I do not know."

Rafael drew me in against his body so he could put an arm across my shoulders. I let him do it, even put my arm around his waist, but I never stopped watching the dragon and the police at the cliff's edge. In dragon form he was proof against sunlight, and he seemed to be fireproof, both of which was unlike any vampire I knew. So maybe we were thinking about this all wrong.

"You've thought of something," Rafael said.

I nodded. "In almost all the legends about dragons being slain, the knight cuts off the head."

"Beheading kills almost everything," Rafael said.

"But what if decapitation is the only thing that kills dragons?"

"Then we must figure out a way to take its head," he said.

I leaned against him, resting my head on the side of his chest. I realized that he was wearing a suit not that unlike what Jean-Claude had worn to dinner with my family, so why had I hated Jean-Claude in a suit, but loved Rafael in his? Because Rafael always wore a suit. This was his style, just like Jean-Claude's was anything but. What was Deimos's style? What was a dragon's typical style? He'd stolen the princess, me, but how did that help us slay him?

Deimos roared and tried to stand up again, the bullets flew, and he closed his mouth and turned his head away from them. "Does he close his mouth every time they shoot at him?" I asked.

"I did not realize he closed it this time until you pointed it out," he said.

I waited and Rafael stood with me. Deimos tried to rise again, and the police fired, though fewer bullets, and I realized it was fewer bullets each time. God, they were running out of ammo and when they did, he'd burn them alive. Deimos closed his mouth and turned his great big dragon head away from the bullets again.

"He's protecting the inside of his mouth," I said.

"What do you think that means?" Rafael asked.

"I think he's only invulnerable on the outside; we need to get the missile down his throat, or maybe even a big enough bullet would do."

"How do you plan to shoot the dragon down its throat without getting incinerated?"

"I have no idea."

54

A VEHICLE ROLLED OUT from the crowd; it was the BearCat, one of SWAT's smallest armored vehicles. It looked like a tank had a bad night with an old-fashioned VW Bug with a bit of Terminator thrown into the mix. It looked like someone had an idea. "I need a radio to find out what they're thinking."

Rafael raised a hand and as if from nowhere his main bodyguard, Benito, came to stand at his side in a suit that I knew hid all sorts of weapons. "Bring the officer up, Anita needs his radio." There were two more suited bodyguards that came up to stand with us. They'd been staying back to give us privacy like they did when we were on a date. This was so not a date.

Two more of the wererats in full tactical gear came forward with a uniformed cop. He had his vest on, but other than that he looked woefully underdressed compared to them. "Hey, Officer"—I had to read his name tag—"Smitz, I'm Marshal Anita Blake, I need to use your radio." I realized I had no badge to show him, just the U.S. Marshal across my vest.

I didn't need to worry. "Of course, ma'am, whatever you need. Glad to have you back with us." He unhooked his vest mic so that the flexible cord stretched enough for me to take it. The dragon roared again, and I turned to see that the BearCat had reached the dragon.

I watched the dragon scrape claws down the armor as I spoke into the radio. "This is U.S. Marshal Anita Blake, the inside of the dragon's mouth is its vulnerable spot. Repeat. Aim inside the dragon's mouth."

The dragon was clawing at the BearCat but didn't seem to be able to pierce the armor, or at least from here it looked like the armor was holding up. Edward's voice: "Switch to channel twelve."

"I'm borrowing a uniform's radio," I said, basically asking if he was going to say anything he didn't want a regular cop to hear.

He repeated, "Channel twelve."

I let go of the mic button and asked, "Officer Smitz, I need to adjust your radio."

"I'll do it for you, ma'am," he said, reaching down and adjusting the buttons accordingly.

"Thanks," I said, then I hit the button. "Marshal Blake here."

"Anita, it's Ted."

"You're trying to push it off the cliff," I said.

"Yes, it's not just the throat that's the target, but it needs to flame when we shoot down the throat," he said.

"You're going to try and blow him up," I said.

"Yes."

"Blow him up down in the river with no loss of life except his," I said.

"Exactly," he said.

"We're running out of ammo," I said.

"Yes."

"Is there anything I can do to help?" I asked.

"A better delivery system for putting a missile or explosive charge down its throat, and more antitank weapons. We've reached out to the local National Guard, but that's going to take hours; we have minutes."

Rafael leaned over me to speak into the mic. I hit the button for him as he said, "There are drones up watching the action; some of them are already posting online."

"Civilian drones would need to be jerry-rigged," Edward said. "Again we're out of time. Once the BearCat pushes the dragon over, we need to hit it with everything we have."

"If there happened to be civilian drones that were already fitted with light payloads in place above us, what would you need them to do?" Rafael asked.

I looked at him. I forgot sometimes that Rafael's other business was sending his wererats around the world as mercenaries. I had nothing to do with that part of his life, other than that the wererats I knew came back worn out and world-weary, sometimes with a desert tan and almost always slimmed down as if they hadn't been able to eat enough to offset the physical activity.

"If?" I said, looking up at him.

"Hypothetically speaking," he said.

"Okay, hypothetically speaking, I would need to know how light the payloads are," Edward said.

"Hold up, Edward." I turned to Officer Smitz. "Give me your radio and you can walk away with plausible deniability."

"Are you kidding? I'd rather stay, please."

"Okay, but don't disappoint me later by oversharing," I said.

He crossed his heart and hoped to die. If he only knew how very likely that scenario would be if he betrayed the wererats and Edward. The dragon was struggling to push back the BearCat, but it looked like all those bullets and a couple of LAWs might have at least weakened it, because the BearCat was gaining ground.

"We're back on, Ted," I said.

Rafael leaned over the mic and said, "If they existed, very theoretically speaking, two antitank grenades."

"One drone with two grenades, that it?" Edward asked.

"Two drones with two grenades each," Rafael said.

I so wanted to ask why he happened to have the drones up there ready to go, but I could be curious later; the dragon was wrestling with the BearCat at the edge of the cliff. "Is the BearCat going over the side with it?"

"Not part of the plan," Edward said.

I wanted to protest that we needed to help them, but I'd worked with SWAT too long; they were going to work their part of the plan. They hoped not to go over the cliff with the dragon, but they knew it was a possibility when they decided to do it. I didn't have to like it, I just had to accept it, and since there wasn't a damn thing I could do to change it now, I focused on what I could do and did my best to let go of what I couldn't.

"Will it exploding in the dragon's breath be enough to kill it?" I asked.

"My people didn't want me coming this close to a dragon without theoretical backup, but none of them had information on fire-breathing dragons. It is a first even for us," Rafael said.

"So none of us know the optimal way to use the two chances we have," I said.

"He's not an animal, he's a person in dragon shape. If he blows the ordnance above his head and it doesn't kill him, he won't aim fire at the next drone," Edward said.

"So we need to shove it down his throat while he's flaming?" I asked.

"We need to force it into his mouth as he's in the process of flaming," Edward said.

"My theoretical pilots of my hypothetical drones will be very challenged to hit that small window of opportunity," Rafael said. He motioned at Benito, who got on his earpiece and started talking quietly and urgently to someone.

"I know some military drone pilots that are good enough to do it," Edward said.

"All my people are exceptional," Rafael said.

Benito stepped back closer to us. "Give the word and they are ready."

"Dragon is going over," Smitz yelled, not into the radio.

We turned to see the dragon falling backward, claws scrambling at the BearCat, which was reversing as fast as it could as the edge of the cliff started to crumble under both the dragon and the BearCat.

I prayed, "Dear God, don't let them go over, please don't let them go over."

The radio crackled to life in my hand. "The dragon will have to stand up on his hind legs to flame," Edward said.

Benito conveyed the information to his earpiece, then replied to us, "They have observed the dragon, they know what to do."

The BearCat backed up. The dragon fell. And now two people we'd never met using the skills they'd honed on video games were about to try and slay a dragon.

55

I RAN FOR THE edge of the cliff, but Rafael caught my hand. "Benito says that minimum safe distance is this way." Normally I would have listened to him, but . . .

"It's a dragon, a real live fire-breathing dragon . . ."

"Minimum safe distance with a view," Rafael said, "none of us have seen anything like this." I let him lead me to the spot his body-guards had chosen for him, because he was right, it would be really stupid to have survived Deimos kidnapping me only to die in the explosion when we killed him.

The dragon's back was almost camouflaged in the dark brown water, as if all the dragon had to do was lower its head and swim away, except here the Meramec River was only twenty feet deep and that wasn't enough water for the dragon to swim away in, if Deimos could swim. I had so many questions I wanted to ask about him as a dragon. He might be the last of his kind and we were going to kill him. I smelled wolf and then the scent of Richard's skin, as if I'd buried my face in the curve of his neck. My thoughts had drawn him to me; we were both biologists with degrees in preternatural biology and here was a real, fire-breathing dragon. They were supposed to be a myth, as in never existed. There was a small part of both of us that wanted him to swim away to safety, but the rest of us knew he was evil and if we let him escape he'd do more evil things to us, the people we loved. If he got loose on the freeway or a neighborhood he could kill hundreds, and if he gained control of Jean-Claude and his instability was in charge of every vampire in the country . . . *disaster* didn't begin to cover it.

I stood there gazing down at probably the last fire-breathing dragon on earth with Richard's thoughts and mine so intermingled I couldn't tell which belonged to who, but it didn't matter. We'd both come down to the same decision. Deimos had to die. If we could have saved the dragon we might have tried, but Deimos was the dragon. He'd been that first or maybe he'd been both. Son of Ares and one of the Furies, Drakon, Deimos, stood up, river water pouring off thirty feet of him, twenty feet and that long, serpentine tail hidden in the dark river.

He raised his head skyward, and flame roared upward in a huge plume. I could feel the heat even from this supposedly safe distance. Rafael put his arm around me and I think it was a protective gesture from the heat, but if the dragon had been closer and aimed that curling orange fountain at us, no amount of arms holding me would have kept either of us safe.

I was too busy looking at Deimos like he was wildlife, history, myth that I missed the drones. I almost forgot about them and why we were standing there until a fireball replaced Deimos's head, and then the shock wave hit us and I would have fallen except for Rafael's arms and Benito grabbing us both. Somewhere in there the sound registered, like the physics of the explosion was in separate pieces, or my mind divided it up so I could understand it.

The body fell backward into the river, sending the waves sloshing backward and outward. I expected the body to sink, but it was too wide and fell at an odd angle so that it lay half in the water and half on the bank. Distantly I heard shouting and realized it was the main group of police yelling their victory cries like at the end of a war. I knew that Richard had already contacted the university he taught at for the necropsy. He wanted to do one like they did on whales that washed up on the beach. I wondered: Would they need a bomb disposal unit for the necropsy? Or did bomb techs only do human-made explosives and leave the natural stuff to the scientists?

Rafael's phone rang; he glanced at the number, then said, "It's your fellow marshal Otto Jeffries." Officer Smitz was still with us, even though we'd let him have his radio equipment to himself, so we'd keep using everyone's legal names until we were alone, so Olaf was still Otto for now.

"Hello, Marshal Jeffries, she is right here," Rafael said, and handed me the phone.

"Otto, what's up?" I asked.

"The head is gone, and the stump burned, but we still must take the heart to be sure he does not rise again."

I stared down at the massive body in the river. "Richard has already contacted his university. They're putting together a scientific team to do a necropsy to learn what they can about dragon biology."

"It is a vampire," Olaf said.

"I know that, but it's also a fire-breathing dragon and I for one would like to know how the mechanism worked that let it breathe fire, wouldn't you?"

"It would be interesting, and help arm us better if we ever encounter another one, but until the heart is cut from the body is the vampire truly dead?"

I thought about that for a minute. "I've never had any vampire or shapeshifter that could heal itself after it was decapitated or heal a wound that was caused by fire. Have you?"

He thought about it, too. "No, I have not. Will we not hunt anything together this trip?"

"Deimos cracked the wall and let sunlight kill all the other vampires, and their deaths killed their animals to call."

"What of Kane?" he asked.

"Kane's dead." My stomach tightened. I hadn't thought about

Asher once I saw the dragon. I prayed again that Asher would be all right, but I needed to call and be sure.

"Who killed him?" Olaf asked.

"I did."

"Tell me."

"He tried to shoot me, and I was better."

"Of course you were better than him."

"Thanks, tell Ted that I have one of his handguns. The Heckler & Koch USP."

"I will tell him. So there is no one left to hunt together?"

I thought about it. "We have one more traitor at the Circus that was trapped with everyone in the underground, because they were reporting to Deimos and his people."

"Is it one of the old Harlequin?" he asked.

"My first thought is yes, but I'm not sure if that's true. Kane and Demolition Man weren't."

"I will stay in town to make sure the traitor is caught and the other imprisoned traitor executed."

"Thank you," I said, and for once I meant it. I remembered him throwing the fire blanket over me and the weight of his body shielding me. He'd saved my life at least twice and maybe three times over the years. I wasn't sure I'd ever really returned the favor. People tended to be afraid of Olaf and didn't put him in positions where he was a prisoner much. I guess when you're damn near seven feet tall and a trained fighter, most people either kill you or leave you alone. I was small and female; people kept thinking I was easier to handle no matter how many people I killed to prove otherwise.

"I hope we find someone to execute together before I leave town, Anita."

"I hope we get all the traitors in our house before you leave town, too." I really wasn't looking forward to sharing a kill with him; he tended to like killing people slowly and painfully. I just executed people, no muss, no fuss if I could manage it.

"We will find your traitors and execute them together," he said.

I agreed, then said, "I need to call Jean-Claude and make sure Asher woke up."

"It is not yet sunset."

"In the underground he wakes before dawn sometimes or has lately."

"Can you not contact Jean-Claude mind-to-mind now that Deimos is dead?"

"You're right, damn, you're right, the vamp that messed with me is dead. We killed him."

"Not personally," Olaf said.

"It was a group effort," I said.

"I do not find group efforts as satisfying."

"I know you don't." I made a good-bye noise at him and handed the phone back to Rafael. Then I closed my eyes and reached out to Jean-Claude and he was there. I could see him pacing the floor in his bedroom, dressed in black jeans and a black T-shirt; his boots were some of the lowest and most practical he owned. It scared me that he was dressed so normally.

"What's wrong?" I asked.

He looked up at me from all the miles apart and smiled so wide he flashed fangs. "How can you ask me that when I have been waiting for news of you?"

"Just open the marks between us, Deimos is dead."

He got a thoughtful look on his face, his eyes focused on things I couldn't see. I felt his power tugging down the metaphysical line that bound us. Once he touched me it was like flowers in a meadow opening up for the sun, all our people coming online in our heads and our hearts. The busy, happy hum of all of us inside me again, just the way it was meant to be.

56

RICHARD AS DR. Richard Zeeman reached out to local experts and put together a team to do the necropsy on Deimos's body. As U.S. Marshal Anita Blake I helped work the police angle so we could get them access to the body ASAP. First for science, but second, Olaf had a point about the heart needing to come out before sunset. I'd never, ever had a vampire rise after a beheading no matter how ancient or powerful, but Deimos was an exception to a lot of things. Did I really expect the body to sprout a new head like some lesser version of the Lernaean Hydra that Hercules fought? No, but Deimos was a creature out of Greek mythology that had turned out to be very real.

We had to add one extra series of experts that whale necropsies don't need: a bomb squad and demolition team. Listening to the bomb techs talk to the biologists about possible sources for the fire breathing inside Deimos was fascinating. Rafael had been right about videos from drones already posting online, so the entire world knew that fire-breathing dragons weren't a myth after all. There would be doctoral dissertations written about what they learned from his body, and probably some dissertations outside the sciences, maybe about mythology versus reality, or fire-breathing dragons in myth and reality. Richard and I would be giving interviews to various groups for a while, though it would have to wait until the police declared that it was no longer an ongoing investigation. Edward and Olaf, along with several officers across a wide variety of jurisdictions, stayed as guards for the scientists.

Rodrigo's coffin was the only one that didn't get tumbled into sunlight. When darkness fell, he rose again. I just couldn't get rid of this guy. He and Rodina had both betrayed us. Ru begged for their lives, but it was Rodrigo that had the bargaining chip. He knew who the last traitor was still inside the Circus of the Damned who had been reporting back to Deimos and company. That we needed to know. The name of the last traitor for his and Rodina's lives. We agreed on the condition that I used the *ardeur* to make them as strongly my Brides as Nicky is, but when I tried to raise the *ardeur* that night it wasn't there. I fed on their sorrows and grief, but I could not bind them to me with that. Rodina said, "I will bargain if you promise to never feed on me like that again." Ru agreed; even Rodrigo was shaken. Deimos is dead, but part of his legacy is still inside me.

Neither Richard nor I had been able to get to Jean-Claude in person inside the Circus of the Damned because the emergency crews will only evacuate people out of the underground, but they won't allow anyone inside. Most of the shapeshifters had been lifted out using a safety harness, except for those that stayed to guard Jean-Claude and the other vampires who were still dead for the day. The two traitors that Rodrigo gave us were two of the few to get lifted out during the day. Hortensio had put his master, Magnifico, in one of the big duffel bags the Harlequin *moitié bêtes* carry their vampire masters in if they have to travel during daylight. They are on the run for now, but the Harlequin loyal to us will find them. Olaf, Edward, and I may even go hunting with them. The front of the Circus was shut down because of the explosion, but the only damage had been to the stairs leading down to our home. Micah had put on a headset and communicated with emergency services to show them the debris on their side, so they could get advice on what pieces to move first to prevent another cave-in. They'd told Micah that he first needed heavy moving equipment or a block and tackle or . . . Micah explained that they had people on their side strong enough to move the stones. Then it was a matter of trial and error both below and above ground to get an opening big enough and stable enough to pull people to safety. If Nathaniel and Damian hadn't already been at the wererats' inner sanctum trying to work magic with the brujas, they'd have never gotten out in time to work the spell that helped the rats find me and report back. If Deimos's people had blown up the stairway just a bit earlier, then Edward and Olaf might not have found us in time. If one bite from Deimos did that much damage to me and Richard, and then a second night with a second bite especially for me, Deimos might have possessed me and used me to take over Jean-Claude just like they planned.

The wererats' brujas isolated Queenie mystically so when the Harlequin guards executed her, Kaazim survived her death. He still looks like he's thirty-something. If he's aging it doesn't show. Queenie did curse us all with her dying breath though. Something about an ancient evil that she awakened so that it would consume us, or maybe consume the city, or the world. So far nothing eldritch this way comes. She's dead, we're alive, time to party, once we've all healed.

Jean-Claude thinks that he has to fill me with his passion for life in person to chase out the last of Deimos's grief and terror. He's trapped below ground until nightfall, and even then he can only come out if the opening remains stable. It's why he's dressed in his oldest and most casual clothes. I hadn't seen him in those black jeans in a few years. I looked forward to getting him out of them at the Jefferson County house where Micah, Nathaniel, and the rest of us that need more sunlight to stay healthy and happy stay part of each week. Jean-Claude, Damian, and other vampires travel back and forth with us enough that we'd had metal storm shutters installed on the windows like you do for hurricanes near the ocean. The shutters were perfect for shutting out all daylight and sturdy enough that almost nothing was breaking them. Wrestling the shutters open and closed, on the other hand, sucked, so we'd recently converted the downstairs to push-button electric. So much easier.

Without the *ardeur* I wasn't recovering like normal, so I needed IV fluids for dehydration. Richard needed them, too, and he was a werewolf. I as a more normal human needed more fluids and finally more rest. They tried to keep me in the hospital, but I wanted to go to Nathaniel and Damian until our security vetoed having more of our primaries in a single location just in case there were more traitors that even Rodrigo didn't know about. Deimos hadn't liked sharing information much.

I got to kiss Nicky before I went home. He's going to be all right, but he won't be bodyguarding anyone for a while. The Wicked Truth are trapped in the underground waiting for me to regain my ability to heal them, if I ever do.

I finally got to do a quick shower and curl up in the main bedroom in Jefferson County by myself. There were guards on duty, but I was the only one who was supposed to rest. I got ready for bed, but it had been so long since I'd slept in the bed alone I couldn't sleep. I finally got up and found an oversized T-shirt, the kind I used to sleep in before I had anyone else in bed with me. There was a pile of stuffed toy penguins against the room's big picture window. I'd put bird feeders outside it so on the mornings that there wasn't a vampire in bed with me I could open the storm shutters and watch the birds. I got Sigmund, my favorite stuffed penguin, where he sat in pride of place on a little settee amid the pile of other toy penguins. I lay on the bed with Sigmund in my arms and still couldn't sleep. I realized I didn't know how to sleep on my own anymore. Damn.

Pierette finally knocked on the door and asked if I wanted some company, though one of the other guards yelled, "She's supposed to help you rest, nothing else for a few hours."

We promised to be good. I took off the sleep shirt, and she curled up nude and warm at my back. I kept Sigmund in my arms, though, so that he was our little spoon as we drifted off to sleep. Hours later Jean-Claude came home to find us asleep. I grabbed him around the neck and tried to drag him into bed with us, but he protested. "*Ma petite*, I am covered in dirt and debris. I must clean up first."

I finally blinked awake enough to truly look at him. His black hair was almost gray with dust, the same for the rest of his clothes. I let go of him and just stared. "How bad is the Circus?"

"Bad enough that they would like to evacuate everyone from the underground, but some of us have to stay to make sure there are no more traitors, or damage to parts of the cave system that aren't on any blueprint we ever filed when remodeling."

"Did Micah come with you?"

"No, he stayed on site to supervise. Dev stayed with Asher."

A piece of anxiety that I'd forgotten was sitting inside my chest loosened. "Thank God he woke up."

"Dev will monitor his energy, but I believe he will be fine metaphysically. Emotionally remains to be seen."

"Kane said Asher had broken up with him, did you know?"

"I did, but only after he had done it. His therapist thought it was important that he break up with Kane for his own sake rather than for mine or anyone else's."

"Agreed," I said.

Pierette held the sheets in front of her and started to slide out of bed. "I'll give you some privacy. I'm sure you have much to talk about."

"Do not leave on my account, I must clean up." He waved a finger in front of my lips. "Non, *ma petite*, it must be a quick shower, for dawn is fast upon my heels."

I had to concentrate to feel it, but he was right. "Okay, shower and come to bed. I can't promise I'll be able to sleep again, but I want to curl myself around you."

"That sounds lovely, *ma petite*. I will hurry so we do not get all of this on the clean sheets." He rushed off to go down the hallway to the bathroom with the biggest shower and the biggest bathtub, though there was no time for a bath. It was almost dawn.

"I must see that my master is tucked up safely in his temporary quarters," Pierette said.

"Thank Pierrot for letting you sleep your shift away with me today."

"He does not mind, my physical closeness to you and Jean-Claude gains him power, too." She got dressed, kissed me good-bye, and then hurried to her vampire half. They weren't romantic with each other, more like partners, but it was still her job to make sure he was safe for the day. Asher had survived losing Kane, Scaramouche hadn't survived losing his master, so it was better to be careful for every-one's sake.

I put Sigmund back in his place and was waiting in the bed with just me when Jean-Claude came back. He'd taken time to blow-dry his hair, which meant there was very little time left. He crawled into the warm pocket I'd made under the sheets. The cotton sheets might not be as sensuous as the silk he preferred, but the cotton held warmth better. We lay there facing each other, our arms intertwined, the front of our bodies touching as close as possible. "I feared I had lost you," he said.

"I was afraid of that, too."

"When I wake I will raise the *ardeur* in myself and feed upon you; I hope that will chase out this awful sorrow and fear."

"I used to bitch about having to feed the *ardeur*, but I'd rather feed on lust and love a thousand times over than people's grief and terror. As long as I'm feeding, they keep feeling these awful emo-tions. I think if I didn't stop, it would be like torture. You could break someone's mind with it."

He kissed me on the forehead, then on the mouth, his hand sliding along my neck under my hair. "We are not night hags to feed like vultures on other's pain. I will bring you back to me completely when I wake tomorrow night, I swear it."

"Don't give your word when we don't understand the magic," I said.

"You are mine and I am yours, *ma petite*, ever shall it be so, on this I give my word." We kissed again but this time with our hands exploring each other's bodies, legs entwining, and then he stopped abruptly. "We cannot sleep like this." He was right. We'd tried but my leg fell asleep, and he moved like he was dead and it was just not good. He turned over so that I was the spoon at his back. I held him close as dawn came. I felt his body tense and then relax, his last breath easing from between his lips. I'd heard enough people die to know what that last gasp sounds like, and it's just like this except that I knew Jean-Claude would live again come night. I kissed his neck, his shoulder, his back and settled down to hold him while he was still warm in our nest of sheets.

A soft knock at the door startled me awake. I woke in a panic like I expected to be back in the coffin with Deimos. It took me a few heart-pounding minutes to realize I was in the bedroom in Jefferson County, it was Jean-Claude beside me, and we were safe.

"What's wrong?" I asked, and my voice sounded like I'd slept too long and needed water, or something.

"Nothing's wrong, Anita"—it was Pierette—"but your family is here. They tried to call your phone, but you never answered."

"Shit," I said. I'd lost my phone, still didn't know where it was.

"Do you want me to send them away?"

"No, just give me time to brush my teeth and get some clothes on."

"I'll make coffee and see if Nathaniel left any of his biscuits in the freezer."

That made me smile; I missed him being here making breakfast and being all domestic. Pierette and I would have to muddle through on our own. Though there'd be other bodyguards around. There was no way that it was only Pierette and her now-dead-for-the-day master guarding both me and Jean-Claude.

The way the house was laid out, once I stepped out of the bedroom, I'd be looking into the living room. Hopefully Pierette would have herded my family into the kitchen so I could dash to the bathroom and get dressed. I got a pair of blue jeans, socks, and then debated on the T-shirt. Solid color would look dressier, but one of my penguin shirts would amuse me. The fact that I was more worried about dressing up for my family than for my girlfriend, or any other lover who might be part of the security detail, pissed me off. I thought about grabbing one of my older penguin ones in a color that looked terrible on me, but I realized that dressing so I'd look bad on purpose to thwart my family's expectations was still them controlling me. So what did *I* want to wear? Not for my family or against my family, but just me. What did I want? I looked back at Jean-Claude in the bed. His curls weren't as carefully styled as usual because he hadn't had time this morning. It made me smile to know that he trusted me not just with his perfection but with his imperfection and knew I'd love him either way.

I chose a black T-shirt and a black pair of Brooks running shoes, and to break up all the black I chose a necklace that he'd bought for me. It was a yellow gold, white gold, and black enamel king penguin with the markings done so well you could tell at a glance that it really was a king penguin. The original design had been silver and gold, but since most of our sweeties had a severe silver allergy, Jean-Claude had bought the original and had it remade, adding a cognac diamond eye. King penguins had brown eyes. He'd bought me more expensive penguin gifts over the years, but nothing had made me as happy, because nothing else had looked like the species. It made the biologist in me incredibly happy.

I put the clothes on the corner of the bed, then got one of the silk robes off the back of the bedroom door. Jean-Claude's was in black, of course; mine was red, Micah's was green, Nathaniel's was purple. Dev had felt left out, so we got him a blue one, which he almost never wore. Sometimes it's about the gesture, not the having. We were debating getting one for Richard but weren't sure what color to get. Angel had a gold robe, but it was on the back of the door to the upstairs bedroom that she considered hers. She liked more room when she slept, just like Nicky did. Maybe it was time for Pierette to have a robe, though I had no idea what color to choose.

I tucked the sheet up over Jean-Claude's shoulders, kissed him on the cheek, and went to get dressed.

57

ONCE I SAW myself in the mirror, I had a moment of wondering why any person in my life had loved on me yesterday. My eye makeup looked less heroin chic and more walk of shame. I had not taken the time to diffuse my hair with a blow dryer before bed like Jean-Claude had, so my hair had dried in interesting shapes. But the hair products that got the interesting shapes also meant that I could add a little water and style it into looking like I actually planned on my curls looking like this.

The hair and the T-shirt were so close to the same color that it was hard to tell where one began and the other ended. Moments like this made me understand why Jean-Claude usually put a contrasting color near his hair, but for today I liked the starkness of it. The gold chain with the king penguin pendant helped soften it a little, but maybe it wasn't soft I wanted today. I did decide to wear my Sig Sauer .380 in an inner pants holster, appendix carry, so that you only saw a slight imprint of the holster against the fabric of the blue jeans. If I'd worn black jeans even that wouldn't have shown. I debated on adding some blades but figured my family wouldn't get that out of hand and they'd want to hug me. It was family—they weren't going to grind their hips against mine, so they probably wouldn't notice the gun. There'd be no hiding the big blade down my spine, or the karambit under my shirt, or the straight blade, or . . . Girl jeans just weren't made for blade carry. Since most girl jeans didn't have pockets big enough for car keys or your whole hand, no big surprise that you couldn't carry concealed easily in them.

I stared into the mirror and debated on at least some eye makeup, when I realized I was procrastinating going out to meet my family. Okay, seeing my dad and my grandma. God, I hoped they hadn't brought her with them. Nicky had said it at the airport, I really was afraid of them. My grandmother hadn't hit me since I was fifteen and I hit her back, and I was a lot better at hand-to-hand combat than the boxing my dad had taught me back then. Logically I was safe, physically at least, but some fears aren't about logic.

"Fuck it," I told myself in the mirror, and went for the kitchen.

Pierette had found some of the frozen biscuits because I could smell them, rich and buttery. I was suddenly hungry, and then I smelled the coffee and it felt like my anxiety went down at least a couple of notches. I heard my dad say, "Momma, enjoy your coffee and biscuits." My stomach tightened and the anxiety came right back up.

"Keeping your guests waiting is rude, Fredrick. We raised her better."

"Grandma, you saw the videos from yesterday. Anita was part of the police force that killed a dragon, a real fire-breathing dragon," Josh said.

"All the police involved must be exhausted," Dad said.

"Anita was kidnapped by the dragon like a fairy-tale princess," Judith said.

I squared my shoulders back and walked through the big open doorway of my kitchen. Okay, Nathaniel's kitchen, but he wasn't here for today. I wondered if he'd found a kitchen to make his own with the wererats. I tried not to think too hard about him, because I needed to be present here and now for the next little bit. My family was seated around the big kitchen table with room to spare since it seated eight. The electric lights were on because the storm shutters were still closed.

"Well, she certainly doesn't dress like a princess," Grandma said from her seat at the kitchen table. She glared up at me as I came through the door.

"Mother Blake," Judith said.

"Mother, you promised," Dad said.

Andria said, "Grandma!"

Josh got up and hugged me, the height difference putting my face into his chest. I hugged him back but pushed away enough to look up at him and laugh. "When did my little brother get to be my big brother?"

"While you stopped visiting us," Grandma said.

"Don't you care that Anita could have died yesterday?" Josh asked.

"Of course, I am glad that she did not die, but if she would find a profession that was more ladylike she wouldn't have endangered herself."

"You thought being a lawyer wasn't ladylike enough," Andria said.

"It is better than being a police officer," Grandma said.

I patted Josh on the back and said, "Finish your biscuits. I need coffee."

"These are great, by the way," he said, sitting down with a big smile.

"I'll tell Nathaniel you said so."

"Are you telling me Nathaniel can cook, too?" Andria said, and smiled. She was doing her best to soften our grandmother's harshness. I smiled back, because I appreciated the effort.

"Do you have to live in the dark like this now that you're with the vampire?" Grandma asked.

"No, we just use the storm shutters to keep out the sunlight just in case," I said. I hit the first button on the wall near the door. The shutters that covered the big windows to the right side of the room opened with a smooth electric whine. The brilliant morning sunlight spilled across the table, dappled through the leaves of the trees outside. I hit the next button and the shutters over the sliding glass doors to the balcony opened.

"Is that the woods?" Josh asked.

"It is, it's a great view from the deck if you want to go out on it."

"Well, it certainly is blindingly bright," Grandma said. It was so her to bitch because it was too dark and now complain because it was too bright.

"Finish your breakfast before you go out and look at the woods," Dad said; Josh must have started to stand up.

Grandma was holding her hand up to shield her eyes. I hit the second button without being asked so that the brightest of the sunlight would be shielded. The room was now in brilliant light and deep shadow.

"Thank you," she said, sipping her coffee.

Pierette met me halfway with a cup of coffee. She was dressed for work, all black tactical though she wasn't wearing her vest, so she'd scaled down her weapons, too, though she still had two guns, at least two knives that I could see, and I knew there'd be a couple more hidden. I half wished I'd worn tactical pants just for the great pockets.

I took the coffee from her and leaned in to give her a kiss. She didn't fight it, or tell me she was on duty, she just kissed me back. I liked that about Pierette. If my family hadn't been our audience I'd have let her know just how much I liked her. Instead, I took the first sip of coffee and felt that anxiety slip away again.

"Fixed exactly the way I like it," I said.

"Nathaniel taught me," she said.

"Well, thanks for being a quick learner," I said, and kissed her again.

"Anita, please," Dad said.

"You do not have to rub your sinful ways in our faces," Grandma said.

"Grandma, Dad, obviously this is another member of Anita's poly group, just like Magda, who she introduced us to before dinner the other night," Andria said.

"Who is Magda?" Grandma asked; obviously no one had told her about the other woman I'd introduced them to.

"I'm Magda," the tall werelion said as she came into the kitchen. She was dressed in full tactical, complete with vest and more weapons, including her AR-15. I still needed to get some of my weapons back from Olaf and Edward. I'd been too busy going to the hospital to remember. Honestly, it wasn't like me to forget something like that. I'd call Edward after I finished with my family, though I'd have to borrow a phone to do it. Maybe they had my phone?

Magda stared down at me; her gray-blue eyes started to slide more to the gray side. It meant she wasn't happy. "Just came in for some coffee," she said, looking past me, taking her cue from my hesitation.

I switched my mug to one hand and touched her arm. "Hey, Magda, how about some sugar before the coffee."

She smiled as she bent down and I went up on tiptoe, so we met in the middle for a kiss. I put my hand on her vest to steady myself and my coffee off to one side, held sort of suspended out of the way. Magda put one arm around me, playing her strong fingers up my back like she was exploring, trying to figure out exactly what I was or wasn't wearing underneath my shirt. It made me press into the kiss, until if either of us had been wearing lipstick we'd have made a mess, but lucky for us we were au naturel today.

"The vampire has turned you into an abomination," Grandma Blake said.

"Grandma Blake!"

"Grandma!"

"That is an awful thing to say to Anita and her girlfriend," Andria said.

Magda and I drew back from the kiss. Pierette took the coffee cup from my hand as if I'd already spilled it or she was afraid I would spill it.

Grandma Blake stood up, clutching her napkin that had been in her lap. It was linen and matched the dishes that Nathaniel had picked out for the house. "I cannot sit here and watch my granddaughter with other women. It is unnatural; surely you agree that this is wrong, Fredrick."

"I am not comfortable with it, but it is Anita's life, Mother."

"The Pope says that it is a sin and that she will go to hell because of it. Don't you care about her immortal soul?"

"I'm already going to hell for marrying a vampire and raising the dead, might as well throw a little girl-on-girl love into the mix," I said.

Pierette coughed hard, like she was choking on something, maybe a laugh. Magda said, "If I am going to stay here for family matters, I need to let the other guards know to fill in my section."

"That won't be necessary," I said. "Go back out and I'll handle this."

"Are you sure?" she asked.

I nodded. "I'm sure, go. I've got this."

"We've got it," Pierette said.

Magda nodded at her, looked at me one more time, then turned around and left without the coffee she'd come for. Pierette offered me my coffee mug. I took it, though honestly even coffee didn't sound as good as it usually did.

"Sit down, Mother, I need to speak with Anita."

"I need to use the ladies' room," she said, "and I may stay there for a while so you may talk without me having to hear it."

"We gave you a choice of staying back at the hotel, Grandma," Andria said.

"The police said they tried to kidnap us once. I am afraid of being alone there now."

"I'm sorry that any of you were in danger because of my enemies," I said, and that I meant.

"Then let me go to the ladies' room and give your father time to have his talk with you." She threw the napkin on the table.

"I'll take her to the bathroom," Pierette said. "You talk to your dad."

I expected Grandma Blake to protest, but she just nodded and followed Pierette out the door toward the downstairs bathroom.

"We're so sorry, Anita," Judith said.

"I am sorry that your grandmother has been so . . . She is set in her ways."

"Dad, didn't you have something you wanted to say to Anita?" Josh said.

My dad nodded. "Please, Anita, sit down. I see that we can't stay here long with your grandmother like she is, so please sit."

I sat down but not in the chair my grandmother had just vacated. For some reason I didn't want to touch anything she'd touched. "Okay, I'm sitting, what now?"

"First, I will walk you down the aisle for your wedding."

Pierette came back into the room just as he said it. "Do you want me to leave again?"

"No, you are obviously part of Anita's life, so whether I approve or—"

"Fredrick," Judith said, touching his arm.

"Forgive me, Pierette, Anita."

"Did you actually say you'll walk me down the aisle to marry Jean-Claude?"

"I did."

"Wow, what changed?"

Andria sighed. "Can't you just take the good news for once? You always had to poke at things even when we children."

"Yeah, I haven't changed much." I turned back to our dad. "Honestly, after the dinner disaster I gave up on you agreeing."

"I can understand that; I behaved very badly at dinner, and I am so sorry for any part that my behavior played in what came after."

"If I hadn't stormed out, our security would have been in place. I let my temper get the better of me."

"So did I."

"You're both too much alike sometimes," Judith said.

I nodded. "Maybe we are."

"You asked what changed my mind. It was seeing Wicked and Truth injured like that. I didn't think they were vampires and it was holy water burning them as evil creatures. I just thought, there are two people hurting and maybe I can help them."

"You were great, Dad," Andria said.

He smiled at her and said, "Thank you, I appreciate you both backing me up." He held Judith's hand and then reached for Andria's. They had that moment of family solidarity that seemed to always be denied me.

Josh patted my shoulder. "I wasn't there either."

I smiled at him. "Thanks."

Dad turned to me. "If vampires were really evil, then I wouldn't have been moved by their pain and suffering. I would have hesitated to help them, but I didn't. Maybe there is more than one way to look at this, and I don't want to miss your wedding."

I stared into his blue eyes so like Grandma's and didn't believe it. It was too good to be true, and if being a cop had taught me anything, it was that if it's too good, then it's not real. "That's great, Dad."

Pierette pushed away from the cabinets where she'd been leaning. "Is that more of the shutters opening?"

I listened and there it was, distant. I didn't know why, but I ran for the bedroom and Jean-Claude. Maybe Grandma Blake was only opening the bathroom shutters so she had more light, but . . . she wouldn't do that, but even as I thought it I was running and praying.

There was light in the hallway, light coming under the door to the bedroom. I tried to open the door, but it was locked. I screamed, "Jean-Claude!"

"Stand back," Pierette said. She pushed me out of the way and kicked the door by the knob, by the lock trying to get that to break, but it was a good door and a good lock; we'd made sure of it.

"Grandma, don't do this! Don't do this!" I was leaning against the wall watching the sunlight under the door, knowing Jean-Claude was in there in a flood of early-morning light. It was too late. Oh God, it was too late.

Magda was there and together they burst through the door. That got me up and pushing my way through them. Sunlight spilled through the window and across the empty bed. My grandmother was dragging him by his arms to get him closer to the light. Pierette tackled her, and I rolled over the bed to get to Jean-Claude sooner. He lay on his stomach on the floor, with his hair spilled down his back, to the perfect spill of his hip and down his body, still perfect and whole.

Pierette had my grandmother pinned in the pile of stuffed toy penguins in the corner. "Why won't he burn? He's supposed to burn like the devil he is!" my grandmother shouted from the pile of stuffed penguins where Pierette had her trapped.

I collapsed beside Jean-Claude and the miracle of him lying there in sunlight unharmed. I touched his back and he was still cool to the touch, still dead to everything, but he wasn't burning.

"I wanted to show you that you will burn in hell with him if you marry him, but he won't burn!"

I didn't even look at her. I just kept staring at Jean-Claude. Magda threw the bedclothes over both of us. I pulled them down to see the shutter closing. Someone had hit the button to close them, but they didn't have to. Jean-Claude could be in daylight just like Damian could, like the Earthmover and Warrick had. I guess like Deimos's dragon form could stand in full sunlight and not burn. That was it, the list of vampires I'd seen in sunlight who didn't burn instantly, irrevocably to death from the slightest touch of sunlight.

When the room was dark again, I found Jean-Claude's hand and held it tight. "Call the police," I said.

"Anita, you wouldn't," Dad said.

I looked at him across the room where he stood in the doorway. "I want her charged with attempted homicide."

"She's not well," he said.

"Dad, she tried to kill Jean-Claude," Andria said.

He turned on her. "No, she wouldn't do that."

"She just did," I said.

Grandma Blake had gone quiet. Pierette got her to her feet. "He's already dead, it's not murder to burn a corpse," she said.

"Get her away from us, before I do something to her," I said.

Pierette led her out and when my dad tried to take his mother's arm, my girlfriend said, "Don't touch the prisoner."

"You're a lawyer, Andria, do something," Dad said.

"Dad, I saw her trying to kill him. I'm a witness, I can't be her lawyer."

"She's your grandmother," he said.

"If she poured gasoline over Judith and tried to light a match, would you feel the same way?" I asked.

"Anita, I am so sorry," Judith said.

Someone was crying and it wasn't me. Magda said, "The police have been called. We informed them that the victim was the fiancé of a U.S. Marshal, and a vampire."

"Thank you, Magda," I said; my voice sounded odd in my head, like it wasn't me at all.

"Is he hurt?" Dad finally asked.

"Not that I can find." I pulled back the sheets and moved his hair aside so I could see his face. It was still as beautiful as ever. I ran my hand over every part of him I could see; the only wounds on his back were the old whip scars from where he'd literally been a whipping boy for the noble son and heir he'd been raised with over six hundred years ago. I got my hands under his upper body and rolled him over. He still moved like the dead, boneless in a way that sleep never does.

I stared down at the pale perfection of him. I traced my fingers over the cross-shaped burn scar on his chest. He was unbelievably, magically unharmed.

There were sirens in the distance coming this way. I pulled the covers up over Jean-Claude's lower body and put his hand in my lap and held on. If it had been help it would have been too late, but sometimes prayers get answered, and sometimes the answer is yes.

58

I PRESSED CHARGES AGAINST my grandmother. She'll probably get off on diminished capacity, but it turns out that she was part of the hate group behind the Sunshine Murders and the group setting fire to our city. I guess I shouldn't be surprised. What did surprise us was someone who knew this house and where Jean-Claude slept had told her exactly what room he would be in, and they'd told my grandmother to open the window and let him burn. Outside of court I never want to see her again. Judith, Josh, and Andria are coming to the wedding, and Dad probably will still walk me down the aisle. Honestly, I'm not sure I care anymore. He kept saying *she's your grandmother, she's my mother*, as if that excused what she did and what she tried to do. It doesn't. Real family doesn't do shit like that to each other, and if they do they're just people you're related to, but they aren't your family. Jean-Claude used the *ardeur* to chase out the last dark taint of Deimos's power. I was able to heal the Wicked Truth until it was as if the injuries had never happened. It was miraculous even to me.

They say no matter how terrible, good things can still come out of it. Jean-Claude can go outside in daylight. He has seen his first blue sky in centuries; we went to the Missouri Botanical Gardens so he could see all the colors of the flowers in sunlight, smell the herb garden at noon when the sun has warmed everything until just brushing against it as you walk fills the air with scent. We're planning a group trip to the Florida Keys, because we can finally show Jean-Claude that those Caribbean waters have a shade of blue in them that matches his eyes.

Author's Note
and Bonus Deleted Scene

There are always scenes that have to be cut from a book. They can be great scenes like the one you're about to read, but they just don't fit into the present novel. Most of the time I put the scene into an outtakes folder and wait for another novel where it will fit, but for the first time I'm going to give you the cut scene here as an extra. Turn the page to see a very spicy scene between Anita and Nicky. (This scene originally took place while Anita was at the hospital trying to heal Wicked and Truth.)

NICKY WRAPPED HIS arms around me and lifted me so that I could wrap my legs around him. I'd forgotten we were wearing scrubs with nothing under them. He was already growing hard; it drew a small sound from me and made me grind myself against him. His fingers dug into my ass, pressing me tighter against him, which meant I couldn't move as well. He turned us so that I was toward the wall, switching his fingers from my ass to my thighs, so he spread my legs wider and could control the angle as he pinned me to the wall, rubbing the hard length of him back and forth between my legs. He changed the angle, drawing back so that if we'd been nude he couldn't have entered me, but he wasn't aiming for that, he was rubbing and rolling himself over that spot just there ahead of that place that so many men see as the only goal, but nobody in my life. That sweet pressure began to build between my legs, but it stayed just on that edge and didn't spill me over, even when he ground all that hardness against me in just the right spot.

"Just on the edge," I managed to gasp.

"Right where I want you," he said, his voice low with an edge of growl that made me shiver. He pinned me against the wall, holding me still. My lioness blinked amber eyes in the dark center of me. "No." Nicky growled the word, burying his face against the side of my neck. He set his teeth against my skin, biting me so fast and sudden that it froze my breath in my throat. I had a split second for my eyes to roll back in my head from the pain and the promise of disaster, and then the lioness was roaring for us to fight back. Nicky eased back enough to growl against my skin, one word, "No." I felt his lionlike heat pushing at my lioness. It was the soft version of him swatting me with claws. I didn't want to fight, I wanted to give in, I wanted Nicky to win.

My lioness faded back into the darkness. Nicky drew back, his voice so thick with growling it was hard to understand as he told me, "I am your Rex, never forget that."

"You are my Rex," I said, and I meant it.

"Unwrap your legs and stand against the wall."

I started to face the wall, but he told me to turn around and face him. I did what he asked. I wasn't sure what he had planned, but I didn't have to know, Nicky knew. He put my hands above my head, pinning my wrists against the wall. The moment I couldn't move my hands it hit that switch that flipped me so that I wasn't just wanting to bottom to Nicky, I was bottoming to him. It felt peaceful to know that I wasn't strong enough to free my hands. I knew I could have yelled for help and had it, but I didn't want to be saved.

Nicky raised the scrub top, baring my breasts to everyone, and there was no embarrassment about it now, instead it added to the thrill. He played with my breasts, running his hands back and forth over them, filling his hands with them, pressing and stroking until my nipples hardened. He rolled them between his thumb and forefinger, then pulled one nipple out until it hurt just a little, and then he pinched my nipple hard until I said, "Safeword." Yes, that was my real safeword.

"You like breast bondage," he said.

"I do."

He slapped the top of my one breast; it sent shock waves through me, like my body didn't know whether to say *ow* or *do it again*. I didn't safeword, so he slapped the top of the other breast. The impact thrilled through my body.

"Harder," I said.

Nicky didn't ask if I was sure; he trusted me to give him feedback, so he did what I asked. He slapped me harder, and my body jumped with the impact; if he hadn't had my hands pinned to the wall I would have stumbled. He studied my face waiting for me to safeword, and when I didn't he smiled. It was a smile that he only used when we were doing bondage. He enjoyed causing me pain because I enjoyed it, and I enjoyed that he enjoyed it.

"Harder," I said.

He smiled and slapped me so hard my entire body jerked, pulling against his hands where I was still pinned. "Safeword," I said.

He gave that low, masculine chuckle. "Look at those beautiful breasts all pink and red." He caressed them gently, tracing where he'd marked them. He was being so gentle, but the reddened skin hurt even from that.

"Safeword," I said.

"Oh, we will be doing more of this at home," he said.

"When you can tie me up and use both hands," I said.

"Yes," he said, and then he leaned down and kissed me. I felt his hand at the top of my pants, pulling them down. He whispered against my lips, "Now I'm going to make you come, and then I'm going to put my dick inside you until I'm done."

That sounded like a great plan to me, so I said, "Yes."

He slid his hand between my legs to find me already wet and eager. The preliminaries were done, so he found that one spot and began to stroke it with two fingers. It didn't take long for my breathing to get faster; the sweet weight between my legs grew and grew until one last stroke spilled me over the edge and brought me screaming.

He growled next to my face. "Quiet, or I'll stop."

I stopped screaming because I didn't want him to stop moving his fingers between my legs. I couldn't decide if it was one long orgasm or if I was falling from one to another to another. My knees went weak until his hand on my wrists was the only thing keeping me standing. My eyes had fluttered back into my head, so I was blind with pleasure. My body spasmed and jumped with it, so when he let go of my wrists I slid into his arms, helpless and liquid.

His voice was deep and still held that edge of growl when he said, "Now I'm going to shove my dick between your legs until I spill down your thighs. If once isn't enough I'll make you lick my dick clean, and I'll go again. Or maybe I'll invite someone else to fuck you bareback until we pour down your thighs." He knew that one of my favorite things was multiple partners, but nobody else in the room was on the short list of people allowed to fuck me without a condom, so it threw me out of the fantasy for a moment. Then he was forcing me to face the wall, bent over. Having to fight the afterglow of the orgasm to stand upright and brace helped clear my head a little more, and then Nicky was behind me, his hands on either side of my waist as he pressed himself against my ass; he put an arm around my waist and used his other hand to help find the angle he needed to press the head of himself against my opening. He started to push himself inside and it felt incredible because my body was still spasming from the orgasm.

"God, you're always so tight after you go, wet, but tight," he said. He pushed himself one delicious inch at a time inside me until he was as deep inside me as he could go, every part of him sheathed inside me. He curved his body over mine and held me for a moment with our bodies married together like that, and then he raised his body up and began to pull himself out of me. He had to work his way in and out until he had enough room to find his rhythm. It was gentle but deep, searching for that other spot inside the opening, and the last one deep inside. It was like he wasn't sure which one he wanted.

"I'm going to go soon," I said, because my body was choosing the spot closer to the opening.

"Go," he said, and as if it were permission the orgasm spilled through me and around him as he kept his rhythm. I started to scream his name, but he put his hand across my mouth to keep me from alerting the nurses, but I had this urge to bite his hand. He must have heard the thought because he said, "If you bite me I'll cover your mouth and nose until I'm finished."

I had one of those urges that you get in the moment. I said, "Do it."

"I won't be able to see your face from this angle, so I can't judge the color of your skin."

"Just for a few thrusts, please."

"Tap out when you're ready," he said, and then his hand slid over my nose and mouth. We'd never tried this kind of breath play. It didn't feel as immediate as other kinds, and then Nicky found the rhythm he liked at the end, which was hard and deep, slapping our bodies together. He tightened the arm around my waist, and his hand across my face, so that suddenly my body was aware it couldn't breathe. There was that moment of panic, but I knew he'd stop when I tapped his hand. It was ultimate trust on both our parts. I trusted that he'd stop, and he trusted that I'd tap before I passed out.

He fucked me as hard and as fast as he could, and I held my hands on the wall to keep myself in place for him; his hand was so tight on my face that I loved it, but I needed air. I was about to tap out when another orgasm caught me, and I forgot while my body writhed and bucked against his. His hand squeezed down tighter, and I started to see gray and white spots, and raised my hand to tap out, when I felt his body thrust deep inside mine and felt him shudder inside me, felt him go in a wash of warmth and pleasure. I managed to tap his arm and he let go, so I could take a gasping breath while he shuddered inside me again, his hands on my hips holding me in place while he orgasmed a second time.

He held me around the waist while we both caught our breath. His voice was breathy and hoarse as he said, "We need a mirror to do that again, so I can see your face."

"Or have someone spot for you like we are," Ethan said, his voice sounding strangely formal.

"For safety, yes," Nicky said, "but I want to see her eyes go frantic from lack of air while I fuck her."

I nodded. "Extra person for safety, mirror for safety and for your viewing pleasure." My voice sounded like I'd run miles. I could taste my pulse in my throat.

"The *ardeur* didn't rise," Truth said.

"Spectacular sex," Wicked said, "but no hint of the *ardeur*."

"Sorry," I said.

"I think she needs Jean-Claude for the *ardeur*," Ru said.

We all agreed, and then Nicky and I had to clean up once our legs were steady enough to use the restroom in Wicked and Truth's room. I didn't need privacy to call Micah now, so we had everything we needed in the room. Once we were clean and as presentable as we could get in the borrowed clothes, it was back to business. We had other disasters besides the *ardeur* being gone.

Bibliography

OWN WORKS

Guilty Pleasures
Beauty
Serpentine
Circus of the Damned
Burnt Offerings
Crimson Death
The Killing Dance
Kiss the Dead
Blue Moon
Danse Macabre
Narcissus in Chains
Dead Ice
Hit List
Rafael
Smolder

OTHER WORKS

Abadie, Marie-Jeanne. *Multicultural Baby Names: 5,000 African, Arabic, Asian, Hawaiian, Hispanic, Indian, and Native American Names.* Longmeadow Press, 1993.

Ann, Martha, and Dorothy Meyers Imel. *Goddesses in World Mythology*. Oxford University Press, 1995.

Duchartre, Pierre-Louis. *The Italian Comedy*. Dover Publications, 1966.

Fuller-Wright, Liz. "Dinosaur-Era Bird Tracks: Proof of 100-Million-Year-Old Flight?" *The Christian Science Monitor*, 28 Oct. 2013, https://www.csmonitor.com/Science/2013/1028/Dinosaur-era-bird-tracks-Proof-of-100-million-year-old-flight.

Gibbons, Ann. "The Greeks Really Do Have Near-Mythical Origins, Ancient DNA Reveals," Science.org, 2 Aug. 2017, https://www.science.org/content/article/greeks-really-do-have-near-mythical-origins-ancient-dna-reveals.

Hamilton, Edith. *Mythology*. Little, Brown and Co., 1942.

Köhler, Karl, et al. *A History of Costume*. David McKay, 1946.

Martin, Anthony J., et al. "Oldest Known Avian Footprints from Australia: Eumeralla Formation (Albian), Dinosaur Cove, Victoria." *Palaeontology*, vol. 57, no. 1, 2013, pp. 7–19, https://doi.org/10.1111/pala.12082.

Nicoll, Allardyce. *Masks, Mimes and Miracles*. Cooper Square Publishers, 1963.

Paré, Ambroise. *On Monsters and Marvels*. The University of Chicago Press, 1995.

Polyzoidou, Stella. "Women's Fashion: What Did Women Wear in Ancient Greece?" TheCollector, 16 May 2021, https://www.thecollector.com/womens-fashion-what-did-women-wear-in-ancient-greece/.

Rosenkrantz, Linda, and Pamela Redmond. *Beyond Jennifer & Jason*. St. Martin's Paperbacks, 1995.

Rule, Lareina. *Name Your Baby*. Bantam Books, 1988.

Slawson, Larry. "The Top 10 Deadliest Dinosaurs," *Owlcation*, 1 Jan. 2023, https://owlcation.com/stem/The-Top-10-Deadliest-Dinosaurs.